TIMES THREE

TIMES THREE

Robert Silverberg

SUBTERRANEAN PRESS 2011

Times Three Copyright © 2011 by Agberg, Ltd.
All rights reserved.

Dust jacket Copyright © 2011 by John Picacio. All rights reserved.

Interior design Copyright © 2011 by Desert Isle Design, LLC.
All rights reserved.

"Travelers in Time" Copyright © 2011 by Agberg, Ltd.
Hawksbill Station Copyright © 1968 by Robert Silverberg.
Up the Line Copyright © 1969 by Robert Silverberg.
Project Pendulum Copyright 1987 by Agberg, Ltd.

First Edition

Trade Hardcover ISBN
978-1-59606-319-8

Subterranean Press
PO Box 190106
Burton, MI 48519

www.subterraneanpress.com

Table of Contents

Introduction: Travelers in Time ||| 7

Hawksbill Station ||| 25

Up the Line ||| 169

Project Pendulum ||| 379

Travelers in TIME

Time travel has been a central idea to me, both as reader and writer, throughout my lifelong involvement in science fiction, ever since I encountered it in one of the first science-fiction stories I read: H.G. Wells' *The Time Machine*. I was ten or eleven years old then—this was more than sixty years ago—and I came away stunned by Wells' vision of the eons to come, which culminates in this unforgettable depiction of the very end of time:

"The darkness grew apace; a cold wind began to blow in freshening gusts from the east, and the showering white flakes in the air increased in number. From the edge of the sea came a ripple and whisper. Beyond these lifeless sounds the world was silent. Silent? It would be hard to convey the stillness of it. All the sounds of man, the bleating of sheep, the cries of birds, the hum of insects, the stir that makes the background of our lives—all that was over. As the darkness thickened, the eddying flakes grew more abundant, dancing before my eyes; and the cold of the air more intense. At last, one by one, swiftly, one after another, the white peaks of the distant hills vanished into blackness. The breeze rose to a moaning wind. I saw the black central shadow of the eclipse sweeping toward me. In another moment the pale stars alone were visible. All else was rayless obscurity. The sky was absolutely black....

"Then like a red-hot bow in the sky appeared the edge of the sun. I got off the machine to recover myself. I felt giddy and incapable of facing the return journey. As I stood sick and confused I saw again the moving thing upon the shoal—there was no mistake now that it was a moving thing—against the red water of the sea. It was a round thing, the size of a football perhaps, or, it may be, bigger, and tentacles trailed down from it; it seemed black against the weltering blood-red water, and it was hopping fitfully about...."

Soon after, I encountered John Taine's *Before the Dawn*, which provided a glimpse of that long-lost age when dinosaurs walked the earth, and H.P. Lovecraft's *The Shadow Out of Time*, which spoke of the grotesque intelligences that would inhabit the world millions of years hence. And then I found Robert A. Heinlein's dazzling story "By His Bootstraps," which introduced me to the perplexing paradoxes that time travel engenders, and, a couple of years later (this was 1950, now), Jack Vance's *The Dying Earth*, offering a very different picture of the end of days, haunting, poetic, mysterious, magical.

I was hooked—forever, as it turned out. I already knew, there in early adolescence, that my own time on earth was finite; but here was a kind of fiction that pierced the veil of the future and showed me things I could never hope to live to see with my own eyes. Out of an aching curiosity to know what lies ahead, not merely seven months or eleven years or even two centuries ahead, but millennia, thousands upon thousands of millennia, I searched out all the science fiction I could find, looking in particular for tales of voyages in

Introduction: Travelers in Time

time, wanting desperately to believe, at least for the nonce, in Wells' argument that "A civilized man...can go up against gravitation in a balloon, and why should he not hope that ultimately he may be able to stop or accelerate his drift along the Time-Dimension, or even turn about and travel the other way?"

I began writing science fiction myself almost immediately, and it was inevitable that I would turn my developing skills to time-travel stories almost from the first. The earliest I can recall was a piece called "Vanguard of Tomorrow," pretty much a straight imitation of "By His Bootstraps," with a little probability-altering thrown in. I wrote it when I was fifteen, and, I am relieved to say, it has never seen publication. A rather more skillful job was "Hopper," which I wrote when I was nineteen and expanded into the novel *The Time Hoppers* about a decade later, and then the time-paradox story "Absolutely Inflexible," a few months afterward. I sold both of these stories to magazines and they were published in 1956, "Hopper" appearing in the appropriately named *Infinity* and "Absolutely Inflexible" in *Fantastic Universe*.

Over the years I have returned again and again to the theme, eventually producing not simply imitations of classics by my betters but work that I could put forth as original contributions to the literature. Among these I would class "Hawksbill Station" of 1967 and the novel *Up the Line* of 1969, *Son of Man* of 1971, "When We Went to See the End of the World" of 1972, and "Many Mansions" of 1973, among others; and I have continued writing time-travel stories ever since, with the most successful of them, perhaps, being "Needle in a Timestack" (1983), "Sailing to Byzantium" (1985), and "Enter a Soldier. Later: Enter Another" (1989).

This present omnibus collection offers three examples of my fascination—obsession, I think it is fair to call it—with time travel. The earliest of them, *Hawksbill Station*, dates from a period when I was just beginning to find my mature voice as a writer. In some confusion I had given up the writing of science fiction in the winter of 1958-59, after four or five years of frenzied activity in which I had written enough of the stuff to fill three or four average careers. Still only in my mid-twenties, puzzled about my place in a genre that

I loved deeply but seemed unable to serve well, I turned away and wandered for a few years in a morass of *hackerei* that still gives me the creeps when I look at the titles of the things I was writing then— "I Was Eaten by Monster Crabs," "World of Living Corpses," "The Syndicate Moves In," and much godawful more.

And then Frederik Pohl, who had become editor of the important sf magazine *Galaxy*, teased me back into science fiction on a now-and-then basis by making me an offer I couldn't refuse, and I did a few short stories for him at a rate of about one every six months, and then a series of novelettes that became the book *To Open the Sky*, and by then—it was now 1965—I discovered that I was back into writing s-f in a major way. Only this time, because Pohl had given me the space to write the stories exactly as I felt they ought to be written, and so I was no longer (as I had been doing from 1955 to 1958) tailoring my product to some editor's notion of what was acceptable, I was far more satisfied with what I was writing: at last, stories which I as a critical reader would have been interested in reading. Thus began the second phase of my career, the so-called "new Silverberg" that elicited so much surprised comment in the mid-1960s. After the group of *To Open the Sky* stories came the expansion of "Hopper" into the Doubleday novel *The Time Hoppers*, which I finished in March of 1966, and in April I wrote to Pohl about another ambitious project that had grown out of my own deep interest in paleontology and my continued fascination with the idea of traveling in time. What I told him was: "I'm thinking in very science-fictional terms these days and I want to get these stories written while the fit is still on me. This one would be a novella—15,000 words, 20,000, somewhere within that range. I have it roughed out, though not solidly enough for me to want to talk much about the plot, except to say that the story takes place in a camp for political prisoners on Earth approximately two and a half billion years ago."

Fred gave me the go-ahead; I set to work immediately, and wrote the story in one white-hot week, 20,000 words, mailing it to him on May 5, 1966. By May 11 I had word of its acceptance. It was published in the August 1967 issue of *Galaxy* and brought me one of the

Introduction: Travelers in Time

most cherishable reader comments I have ever received: the famed science-writer Willy Ley, encountering me at a New York literary party, praised at great length the accuracy and richness of texture of my portrait of life in the early Paleozoic. I am not exactly indifferent to most people's praise of my work, but, although I absorb it with pleasure, I tend to forget it quickly; hearing Willy tell me in rumbling Teutonic tones how well I had brought the era of trilobites to life for him, though, is a memory that still glows brightly for me more than four decades later.

The story also brought me my first Hugo and Nebula nominations, though competition for both awards was stiff that year and I finished as a runner-up. At that point in my career, though, simply getting on the final ballot was exciting.

Despite Willy Ley's warm praise, there was at least one inaccuracy in the story—a deliberate one. The story takes place in the late Cambrian period, which according to modern geological theory was about 550 million years ago. Yet in my original proposal for Fred Pohl I placed the scene "approximately two and a half billion years ago," and even in the published story I set the Cambrian two billion years in the past. That was not a case of ignorance, but of a writer's outsmarting himself, for what I was doing was implying a revision, after the development of time travel, of our entire geological time scale. But I found no convenient way of working into the story a statement to the effect that scientists had once believed the Cambrian to be 550 million years ago but now knew it to be two billion plus, and in the end I just used the greater time scale without explaining what I was up to. This, of course, brought some critical comments from present-day geologists otherwise pleased with the work. So when the story was reprinted in the first of its many anthology appearances I cut the time span in half, putting the late Cambrian at *one* billion years ago—still a revisionist notion, but one less likely to draw attack. And I have kept it that way in all further printings of the story, as well as in the expansion to novel form that I carried out in the spring of 1967.

I expanded the 20,000-word story "Hawksbill Station" into the novel of the same name in the spring of 1967. Lawrence P.

Ashmead, the science fiction editor at Doubleday, had recently given me a two-book contract; the first book that I delivered was a short-story collection, *Parsecs and Parables*, and the second was a novel, *To Live Again*. Ashmead wanted some revisions on that book, which I was unwilling to do at that moment, and so, to replace it in his schedule, I suggested the expansion of "Hawksbill." He read the story in March 1967, approved the switch, and in late April I delivered the full manuscript. (Yes, I was that fast in those days.)

There are two basic ways of turning a novella into a novel. One is to pad the existing story by inserting a few new incidents, by extending brief conversations into lengthy ones, and by using three adjectives where one had served originally; this produces a story that is essentially identical to the original but two or three times as long. The other method is to provide entirely new narrative material, either by writing extensive prologues and epilogues or by interpolating some elaborate new subplot into the body of the story. I had employed the first method more than once, and had come to regard it not only as a bit of a fraud on the reader but also a considerable bore for the writer; so this time I opted for method two. I meant to expand the Paleozoic part of the story to some degree, yes, but my primary plan, as I had told Ashmead in my letter of March 3, 1967, was "to show much more of Barrett's career 'up front' in the 21st century, and develop a picture of him as a professional revolutionary who has been going through the motions in a total lack of conviction, and who now finds a new role to engage his energies at Hawksbill Station. I'll show the world that could exile men to the remote past this way; and I'll also open out the Hawksbill Station sequences to show more of the Paleozoic world than the immediate vicinity of the Station." All of which I did, and the book was duly accepted—Ashmead, who had a background in geology, made some cogent suggestions for improving the scientific detailwork—and was published in October 1968.

The two versions of the story, the short and the long, have very different textures. One provides a claustrophobic view of the Paleozoic and the other, while maintaining all that material, also takes the reader through the totalitarian and repressive world of the

Introduction: Travelers in Time

early 21st century. But the fact that the expanded version leaves the Cambrian from time to time to show the "present-day" background of the exiles brings us to the special problem that science-fiction novels, if they have a long enough publishing life, often encounter: sooner or later, as they march on through one reprint edition after another, many books are going to overlap the real dates of the period in which they are ostensibly set.

This is, after all, the 21st century right now. That century did indeed seem to be very far in the future when I set out to write the story that became *Hawksbill Station* in 1966, but the future has gobbled up the young man with the dark beard who wrote that story, and here we are, the aging author and his decades-old story, moving right along into the second decade of the once-distant 21st century. And the history of the late 20th century did not follow the path I described. I never seriously expected that it would; my concern was telling a tale of the early Paleozoic, not in doing a full-scale extrapolation of modern American politics. But, still....

In the fourth chapter I describe the meeting of Jim Barrett and Jack Bernstein in 1980, when they were twelve years old. 1980 in *our* time-line was the year of the Carter-Reagan presidential election. Not so in my story's, of course. Four years later, Bernstein, precociously political, invites Barrett to join his underground political group, which has a libertarian program, the goal being to dismantle as much of the American government's functions as possible. But in fact Ronald Reagan, himself something of a libertarian, was President of the United States in 1984, and *he* was working as hard as he could to dismantle the government's functions, doing it not as part of some small-time underground cabal but right out in the open, in the Oval Office itself. So we have already begun to leave real history behind, and my protagonist is still in his adolescence.

Indeed, the book began to diverge somewhat from the actual time track a lot earlier than that. Writing in 1966, when the Vietnam war was still heating up and American political discourse was starting to get unruly but had not approached the chaos level of 1968, I spoke of the breakup of the two political parties and their realignment into more clearly delineated conservative and liberal ones.

This did happen, more or less, but under the old party names, the Democrats moving left and the Republicans moving right. Then I predicted that the new American Conservative Party would win the election in 1972 (Nixon, a conservative Republican, *was* elected that year), then a boom and bust and a financial panic in '76 (we did have something approximating a financial crash, but no boom had preceded it), and the landslide victory of the new National Liberal Party in 1976. (Carter, a Democrat, was elected in 1976, but not by a landslide, and he wasn't much of a liberal, either.) After that I predicted vast disruptions in our political system, virtually of a revolutionary kind, leading to a repressive totalitarian government of the Orwellian sort, a secret political resistance, and the exiling of political prisoners to a concentration camp a billion years in the past.

Well, you'll have to forgive me. The crystal ball was a little cloudy. We didn't get the totalitarian takeover, we didn't get the underground resistance movement, and we didn't get time travel, either. What we did get is my book, *Hawksbill Station*, which not only provides a very detailed look at the landscape of the Paleozoic but which now can be understood as a parallel-world science-fiction novel set in an alternate 21st century different in many interesting ways from the one you happen to be inhabiting right now.

I hope you enjoy your visit there.

The two years between the writing of the magazine version of "Hawksbill Station" and the completion of the novel *Up the Line* were momentous ones for me. Everything was happening very fast in those days: the whole country was in turmoil over the war in Vietnam, not to mention the revolutions going on in the areas of sex, drugs, and rock & roll, and my own career was running at a highly accelerated pace, with books and short stories tumbling from my typewriter in implausible quantity. It all seems a bit of a blur to me, now, as I look back across four decades to it.

The year 1967, for example, brought the novels *To Live Again*, the expanded *Hawksbill Station, The Masks of Time*, and *The Man*

Introduction: Travelers in Time

in the Maze, along with the Nebula-winning short story "Passengers" and half a dozen others, and non-fiction books on such varied subjects as salvage archaeology, ghost towns of the American west, the quest for the Blue Nile, and the first six circumnavigations of the world. The following year—though disrupted by a catastrophic fire in February that wrecked my house and sent me into rented quarters for the rest of the year—produced *Nightwings*, *Across a Billion Years*, the much-anthologized short story "Sundance" and eight or nine others, and non-fiction books about ancient Chinese science, sequoia trees, the effect of climatic change on the pattern of world history, underwater archaeology, and the seven wonders of the ancient world. And in the autumn of 1968 I turned my overflowing energies to the task of writing what I hoped would be the time-travel novel to end all time-travel novels.

The scene would be ancient Constantinople, the capital of what we call the Byzantine Empire, though its own citizens never used that term. In December 1967 I had gone to Israel to do research on a big book on the history of Zionism—yes, I wrote that one in busy 1968 too—and on my way back I had stopped off in Istanbul for my first unforgettable immersion in the wonders of that extraordinary city, once the capital of the Eastern Roman Empire and then of its Ottoman successor, where Byzantine and Islamic architectural masterpieces jostle against each other in wondrous profusion. I came home with my mind reeling with startling images of that teeming, bewildering metropolis. So when I began looking around for a destination for my time travelers, ancient Constantinople was the immediate choice.

Heinlein had handled the time-paradox story to a fare-thee-well in the 1941 "By His Bootstraps," and then, as though not content with the job he had done there, he did it all over again, far more concisely and even more ingeniously, in 1959's "All You Zombies—". The perils that free-and-easy travel into the past might pose for the historical record had been dealt with by many writers, but never better, so I feel, than in the four "time patrol" novellas Poul Anderson wrote between 1955 and 1960 and brought together in a book called *Guardians of Time*. Despite the existence of the work of these two formidable predecessors and a vast body of other time-travel stories by Fritz Leiber, Jack Williamson, L. Sprague de Camp, Alfred Bester, and other such masters, I thought there was room for at least one more: a novel, somewhat comic in tone (though comic with a sharp edge, since I did not intend things to end well for my protagonist) that grappled head-on with the whole paradoxical concept of going back in time, examining all the problems that that could create (including a few new ones that I intended to invent) and, besides, allowing me to get down on paper some expression of the astonishment that my brief but memorable visit to Istanbul had engendered in me.

So, in September of 1968, I set out on my journey up the line.

As I've noted above, it had already been a productive year, but it had been a stressful one, too, because of the fire. The rented quarters I was living in were less than adequate, most of my reference books were in storage, and the expenses of rebuilding my damaged house were running well ahead of the insurance payments. I was still a young man, only in my early thirties, but as I began this complicated new book I wondered whether I would have the energy to do the job right.

Well, there was no choice, was there? I went down to the warehouse where my library had been stored since the fire and selected such books on Byzantine history as I could find in those hastily packed cartons, took a deep breath, and started to write. The tone and texture of the book became clear to me right away: first-person narrative, brief, elliptical chapters, a quick pace, lots of lively dialog. Glorious Constantinople itself would provide me with the descriptive richness that I want to achieve in all of my books. A new time paradox every two or three chapters would provide the science-fictional substance. It all began to come together very quickly, the chapters accumulating at a pace that left me a little breathless but eager to keep going, and I began to believe, tired though I was, that the whole project would be done in just a few weeks.

Wrong. Fatigue matters. There is a reason why airline pilots are required to rest between long-haul flights.

I had sketched an outline of my story before starting to write it. Trying to improvise anything so complex as a time-paradox novel

Introduction: Travelers in Time

is a risky game. So from the outset I knew my starting point and where I intended to finish, and I had a fairly good idea of what was going to happen in between. But as the pages piled up during those autumn days of 1968 (while all manner of craziness went on in the outside world, a bizarre presidential campaign in this country and the Soviet crushing of liberty in Czechoslovakia and French nuclear tests in the South Pacific and ever so much more) I paused two thirds of the way through the writing to re-read my manuscript, and discovered that about midway in the book I had built in a situation that would make it impossible for me to reach the ending that I had so carefully designed.

I don't remember now, more than forty years later, what the problem was. All I remember was that some quickly improvised plot twist that I had inserted in the middle of the book created an absolute barrier to my continuing the novel to its desired end. Everything I had written from that point onward had taken me in the wrong direction, and I was stranded with no way to move on. I threw myself groggily on the nearest couch and contemplated abandoning the book. No, I thought: not an acceptable response. Work it out, fellow. Work it out.

So after a long dismal weekend I began to create a new outline of the second half of the book, then and there, drawing charts and taping them to the wall of the dreary little room that was my office that year, and eventually I had something that seemed to make sense. I went back to the sticking point in the middle of the book, ripped out the situation, whatever it was, that I had belatedly discovered was a plot-killer, and worked onward again, this time straight to the ending that I had intended all along. I turned the book in to my publisher (Ballantine Books) around Halloween, and got a quick and delighted acceptance from Betty Ballantine in less than a week. Right after that I moved back into my house, which was not quite entirely rebuilt—the downstairs area was still a vast mess—but which did provide, once again, living quarters and my familiar work space.

And so I lived happily ever after, except for the day in the spring of 1969 when I got the galley proofs of *Up the Line* from Ballantine

Books. The novel ends, as you will shortly discover, in an unfinished sentence, and there is a good and proper reason why that sentence is like that. But Ballantine's copy editor evidently found an unfinished sentence esthetically displeasing, or something, and simply deleted it. The page looks much tidier without it, I agree, but that was not the ending I had had in mind. Of all the damage that copy editors have done to my carefully constructed prose over the ages, that ranks close to the top. But I wrote a nicely intemperate letter to Betty Ballantine ("Would you believe that your hired cretin had the audacity *to delete the final words of the book?*" is one of the milder sentences) and she had everything restored to the way I wrote it, which is the way you will read it here.

Looking back now at a novel I wrote more than half my lifetime ago, I remember, naturally, the difficulties of writing it in that exhausting year under those uncomfortable conditions and the dismay I felt at realizing that I had to reconstruct its plot two thirds of the way through. But by now those are only vague and hazy memories, and the book itself still seems full of life to me. I think it does add something original to the literature of time-paradox fiction, which was what I had set out to do. But there's more to it than that, though I may not have realized it at the time I was writing it. For that I call on the words of my friend Kim Stanley Robinson, who in an essay on *Up the Line* that he wrote in 2001 had this to say:

"The book...offers an image of, and discusses, the emergence of the postmodern view of the past as sheer spectacle and entertainment, with nothing substantial to teach us....But Silverberg's novel makes it clear that he himself does not agree with this postmodern attitude, that the past is there only to dazzle ignorant tourists and have some fun. The plot of the novel forms a strong critique of this view, as our protagonist, following his desires with little regard for history and what it could teach him, industriously replicates all his problems (including himself), until he is woven into a tangle more complicated than anything outside time-paradox fiction could easily be. By doing this the book makes it clear that the time-paradox genre can be used both to discuss attitudes toward history, and to

Introduction: Travelers in Time

express those moments in our life when we are most tied in knots by our desires and regrets."

Was it my conscious intention to deal with any such matters in *Up the Line*? After all this time, I can't say; but my guess is, probably not. On the conscious level the main thing hat I set out to do was to write a gaudy, intricate time-paradox novel and to provide a lively depiction of Byzantium in its prime, and I think I succeeded in doing that. But there's more to a novel than just its plot and its setting. Whatever else is in this one is there because novels are about people, and people are complicated entities who don't always act in their own best interests, and the character I call Jud Elliott behaves like a human being, which is to say that by following his own impulses he gets himself into a terrible tangle. The writer who invented Jud Elliott has done the same thing more than once in his own life. Because this is a science-fiction novel, the particular tangle Jud gets into is one that I have never found myself caught in, and you are not likely to experience it either. But Kim Stanley Robinson thinks that *Up the Line* is, among other things, a work of autobiographical fiction. He might just be right.

Hawksbill Station and *Up the Line* are works of the young Silverberg. *Project Pendulum*, the third book in this omnibus and one more attempt at wrestling with the concept of time travel, comes from a much later period in my career.

It was also the third novel I have written about twins. I am an only child who often wonders what it would have been like to have a sibling, and twinship is the most intimate form of siblingness there is, going back as it does to the womb itself. For nearly all my life I have had one member of a pair of twins as a close friend: first Saul Diskin, whom I met when we were in the fourth grade, and with whom I have maintained a warm friendship for more than sixty-five years, and later Jim Benford, by now a friend of forty years' standing. (I never managed to strike up much of a friendship with Saul's twin Marty, who died about fifteen years ago; I am on friendly terms with Jim Benford's twin Gregory, but Greg lives 400 miles away in Southern California, while Jim is my neighbor in the San Francisco Bay Area and we see each other all the time. But by watching both sets of twins in action over the years I did manage to form as good an idea of what it is to be a twin as an only child is likely to achieve.)

My first twin novel was *Starman's Quest*, which was the second novel I wrote, back in 1956. It's a time-paradox novel too, in a way, since it explores the effects of the Fitzgerald Contraction on a pair of spacegoing twins who are separated when one brother ends his spacegoing service aboard a hyperspace ship. The time-dilation phenomena inherent in faster-than-light travel see to it that the brother who remains in space gets to be nine years older than his twin, creating interesting problems for them when they are reunited. I revisited the theme in 1972 in my story "Ship-Sister, Star-Sister" (many years later expanded into the novel *Starborne*) in which another pair of twins, this time female, blind, and telepathic, maintains mental contact across a gulf of many light-years, one of them aboard a pioneering hyperspace ship and the other remaining behind on Earth.

In *Project Pendulum* (which I dedicated to the Benford twins) I dealt with twins once more. The book, written in 1986, was an outgrowth of my publishing relationship with Byron Preiss, who was my friend and publisher for many years until his death in an automobile accident in 2005. Byron was a book packager, someone who served as an intermediary between writers and publishers, setting up book projects and finding someone to write them. In the later years of his career, though, he began to publish books himself, and published a good many of mine. I first encountered him somewhere around 1975 and for the next thirty years we worked together on a great number of projects, in which I was involved sometimes as writer, sometimes as editor, sometimes as both. He was a charming, effervescent, brilliant guy who was also, unfortunately, more than a little disorganized in his business affairs; letters went unanswered, contracts got lost in his files, and his company was perpetually undercapitalized, so that he found himself constantly

Introduction: Travelers in Time

thinking up and selling new projects in order to pay the bills he had run up on his previous ones.

Despite the problems inherent in coping with Byron's tangled, labyrinthine business practices, I found Byron himself delightful and greatly admired his energy and ingenuity as a creative force, and I was always willing to listen to any publishing suggestion he wanted to put before me. In 1985 he told me that he was going to package a series of books intended for high-school-age readers for a small publishing house called Walker Books. Each book was to deal with one of the major themes of science fiction: alien beings, parallel worlds, supermen, and so forth. He wanted me to do the time-travel book.

The notion I came up with involved the physics of time travel: each journey in time, I postulated, had to be balanced by a journey of the same duration in the opposite direction. I imagined a two-pronged time machine whose passengers were of identical mass—identical twins, in fact. On the first swing of the time pendulum, one brother would go exactly five minutes into the past, the other five minutes into the future. Successive swings of the pendulum would be farther and farther apart—fifty minutes, five hundred minutes, five thousand minutes—until eventually one brother was touring the world of the dinosaurs and the other was looking at Earth of the far future.

I had two prototypes in mind. One was Wells' *The Time Machine*, which involves neither twins nor pendulums but does send a solitary time traveler on a tour of the future in a series of hops that brings him, ultimately, to the dying days of our planet. The other was A.E. van Vogt's 1941 story, "The Seesaw," in which the protagonist gets caught in an energy vortex that sends him wildly swinging back and forth in time, until, in the end, he arrives at the creation of the universe. Van Vogt provides only the briefest glimpses of the futures through which his hapless voyager passes. What I wanted to do was combine his pendulum concept with the sweep and grandeur of Wells' total vision of futurity. To do this I would be required to invent a series of futuristic worlds and couple them with a corresponding series of glimpses of the past, but both of these were old specialties of mine.

Very quickly, however, I realized that I had a tiger by the tail. The books in the series for which I had been asked to write *Project Pendulum* were supposed to be 30,000 words long at most—novellas, really, not much more than a hundred manuscript pages.

And I proposed to send my twin time-travelers through millions of years of past and future in the course of those hundred pages! I found myself faced with an enormous and dismaying task of compression, having assigned myself to cope with a structure that could have easily been employed in a novel ten times the length of the one I actually wrote. It was a struggle to hold it to the dimensions I had intended. In November 1986, when I had been working on the novel for six weeks or so, I wrote to Byron, "The thing has turned out to be a real horror—the plot I set up turned out to be so intricate, practically an interactive novel, that it's driven me around the bend. What with revisions and confusions I've managed only 90-odd pages, or 22,000 words, in a month and a half. But the job's so complicated that I don't see how I can finish it in less than 35,000 words, which may mean two more weeks."

And, of course, I did finish it, right at the end of the year. Originally I had planned to let the twins swing out until they were 190 million years apart, and then swing inward again until they had returned to Time Zero. But that would have made the book twice as long as the publisher wanted, and probably would have wiped the weary writer out, too. So when one brother had reached the incomprehensible world of 95 million years from now, where the human race had evolved to almost godlike form, and the other was back among the brontosaurs and the pterodactyls, I abruptly brought the curtain down. Given enough time and patience, I suppose I could have taken the reader on a complete tour of all that had ever happened and all that is yet to come, but that was not the book I had set out to write and it certainly not was the book I was going to make myself write just then. I held it to its proper length, and the pendulum swings are fast and furious, and I think that writing it that way increased the dizzying effect of the story. Surely very few science-fiction stories cover that much ground in so few words.

Introduction: Travelers in Time

And am I done now, after fifty-plus years, with writing time-paradox stories? Probably. It does seem to me that I have wrung all the variations on the theme that I can. But I can't really be sure of that. Only time will tell.

—Robert Silverberg
November 2009

Hawksbill STATION

1

Barrett was the uncrowned king of Hawksbill Station. No one disputed that. He had been there the longest; he had suffered the most; he had the deepest inner resources of strength. Before his accident, he had been able to whip any man in the place. Now, to be sure, he was a cripple; but he still retained that aura of power that gave him command. When there were problems at the Station, they were brought to Barrett, and he took care of them. That went without saying. He was the king.

He ruled over quite a kingdom, too. In effect it was the whole world, pole to pole, meridian to meridian, the entire blessed earth. For what it was worth. It wasn't worth very much.

Now it was raining again. Barrett shrugged himself to his feet in that quick, easy gesture that cost him such an infinite amount of carefully concealed agony, and shuffled to the door of his hut.

Rain made him tense and impatient, the sort of rain that fell here. The constant pounding of those great greasy drops against the corrugated tin roof was enough even to drive a Jim Barrett loony. The Chinese water torture wouldn't be invented for another billion years or so, but Barrett understood its effects all too well.

He nudged the door open. Standing in the doorway of his hut, Barrett looked out over his kingdom.

He saw barren rock, reaching nearly to the horizon. A shield of raw dolomite going on and on. Raindrops danced and bounced and splattered on that continental slab of glossy rock. No trees. No grass. Behind Barrett's sun lay the heavy sea, gray and vast. The sky was gray too, even when it didn't happen to be raining.

He hobbled out into the rain.

Manipulating his crutch was getting to be a simple matter for him now. At first the muscles of his armpit and side had rebelled at the thought that he needed help at all in walking, but they had fallen into line, and the crutch seemed merely to be an extension of his body. He leaned comfortably, letting his crushed left foot dangle unsupported.

A rockslide had pinned him last year, during a trip to the edge of the Inland Sea. Pinned him and ruined him. Back home, Barrett would have been hauled to the nearest state hospital, fitted with prosthetics, and that would have been the end of it: a new ankle, a new instep, refurbished ligaments and tendons, a swathe of homogeneous acrylic fibers where the damaged foot had been. But home was a billion years away from Hawksbill Station, and home there's no returning. The rain hit him hard, thudding against his skull, plastering the graying hair across his forehead. He scowled. He moved a little farther out of his hut, just taking stock.

Barrett was a big man, six and a half feet tall, with hooded dark eyes, a jutting nose, a chin that was a monarch among chins. He had weighed better than two hundred fifty pounds in his prime, in the good old agitating days Up Front when he had carried banners and shouted angry slogans and pounded out manifestoes. But now he was past sixty and beginning to shrink a little, the skin getting loose around the places where the mighty muscles once had been. It was hard to keep your weight up to par in Hawksbill Station. The food was nutritious, but it lacked...intensity. A man came to miss steak passionately, after a while. Eating brachiopod stew and trilobite hash wasn't the same thing at all.

Barrett was past all bitterness, though. That was another reason why the men regarded him as the Station's leader. He was solid. He didn't bellow. He didn't rant. He had become resigned to his fate, tolerant of eternal exile, and so he could help the others get over that difficult, heart-clawing period of transition, as they came to grips with the numbing fact that the world they knew was lost to them forever.

A figure arrived, jogging awkwardly through the rain: Charley Norton. The doctrinaire Khrushchevist with the Trotskyite leanings, a revisionist from way back. Norton was a small excitable man who frequently appointed himself messenger when there was news at the Station. He came sprinting toward Barrett's hut, slipping and sliding over the naked rocks, elbows lashing wildly at the air.

Barrett held up a meaty hand as he approached. "Whoa, Charley. Whoa! Take it easy or you'll break your neck!"

Norton halted with difficulty in front of the hut. The rain had pasted the widely spaced strands of his brown hair to his skull in an odd pattern of stripes. His eyes had the fixed, glossy look of fanaticism—or perhaps it was just astigmatism. He gasped for breath and staggered into the hut, standing in the open doorway and shaking himself like a wet puppy. Obviously he had run all the way from the main building of the Station, three hundred yards away. That was a long dash in this rain, and a dangerous one; the rock shield was slippery.

"Why are you standing around out there in the rain?" Norton asked.

"To get wet," Barrett said simply. He stepped into the hut and looked down at Norton. "What's the news?"

"The Hammer's glowing. We're going to get some company pretty soon."

"How do you know it's going to be a live shipment?"

"The Hammer's been glowing for fifteen minutes. That means they're taking precautions with what they're shipping. Obviously they're sending us a new prisoner. Anyway, no supplies shipment is due right now."

Barrett nodded. "Okay. I'll come over and see what's up. If we get a new man, we'll bunk him in with Latimer, I guess."

Norton managed a rasping laugh. "Maybe he's a materialist. If he is, Latimer will drive him crazy with all that mystic nonsense of his. We could put him with Altman instead."

"And he'll be raped in half an hour."

"Altman's off that kick now, didn't you hear?" said Norton. "He's trying to create a real woman, instead of looking for second-rate substitutes."

"Maybe our new man doesn't have any ribs to spare."

"Very funny, Jim." Norton did not look amused. There was sudden new intensity in his glittering little eyes. "Do you know what I want the new man to be?" he asked hoarsely. "A conservative, that's what. A black-souled reactionary straight out of Adam Smith. God, that's what I want those bastards to send us!"

"Wouldn't you be just as happy with a fellow Bolshevik, Charley?"

"This place is full of Bolsheviks," said Norton. "We've got them in all shades from pale pink to flagrant scarlet. Don't you think I'm sick of them? Sitting around all day fishing for trilobites and discussing the relative merits of Kerensky and Malenkov? I need somebody to *talk* to, Jim. Somebody I can really fight with."

"All right," Barrett said, slipping into his rain gear. "I'll see what I can do about hocusing a debating partner out of the Hammer for you. Maybe a rip-roaring Objectivist, okay?" Barrett laughed. Then he said quietly, "You know something, Charley, maybe there's been a revolution Up Front since we got out last news from there. Maybe the left is in and the right is out, now, and they'll start shipping us nothing *but* reactionaries. How would you like that? Say, fifty or a hundred storm troopers coming here for a start, Charley? You'd have plenty of material for your economics debates. And the place will go or filling up with them as the heads roll Up Front, more and more of them shipped back here, until we're outnumbered, and then maybe the newcomers will decide to have a putsch and get rid of all the stinking leftists that were sent here by the old regime, and—"

Barrett stopped. Norton was staring at him in blank amazement, his faded eyes wide, his hand compulsively smoothing his thinning hair to hide his distress and embarrassment.

Barrett realized that he had just committed one of the most heinous crimes possible at Hawksbill Station: he had started to run off at the mouth. There hadn't been any call for his little outburst just now. What made it all the more troublesome was the fact that he was the one who had permitted himself such a luxury. He was supposed to be the strong man of this place, the stabilizer, the man of absolute integrity and principle and sanity on whom the others could lean when they felt themselves losing control. And suddenly he had lost control. It was a bad sign. His dead foot was throbbing again; possibly that was the reason.

In a tight voice Barrett said, "Let's go. Maybe the new man is here already."

They stepped outside. The rain was beginning to let up now; the storm was moving out to sea. In the east, over what would one day be called the Atlantic, the sky was still clotted with swirling wisps of gray mist, but to the west a different grayness was emerging, the shade of normal gray that meant dry weather. Before he had been sent back here, Barrett had expected to find the sky practically black, because this far in the past there ought to be fewer dust particles to bounce the light around and turn things blue. But the sky had turned out to be a weary beige. So much for theories conceived in advance. He had never pretended to be a scientist, anyway.

Through the thinning rain the two men walked toward the main building of the Station. Norton accommodated himself subtly to Barrett's limping pace, and Barrett, wielding his crutch furiously, did his damnedest not to let his infirmity slow them up. Twice he nearly lost his footing, and each time he fought hard not to let Norton see what had happened.

Hawksbill Station spread out before them.

The Station covered about five hundred acres in a wide crescent. In the center of everything was the main building, an ample dome that contained most of the prisoners' equipment and supplies. Flanking it at widely spaced intervals, rising from the sleek rock shield like grotesque giant green mushrooms, were the plastic blisters that were the individual dwellings. Some huts, like Barrett's, were shielded by tin sheeting that had been salvaged from shipments arriving from Up Front. Others stood unprotected, naked plastic, just as they had come from the mouth of the extruder.

The huts numbered about eighty. At the moment, there were a hundred forty inmates at Hawksbill Station, which was pretty close to the all-time high, and indicated a rising temperature on the political scene Up Front. Up Front hadn't bothered to send back any hut-building materials for a long time, and so all the newer arrivals had to double up with bunkmates. Barrett and the others whose exiles had begun before 2014 had the privilege of occupying private dwellings, if they wanted them. Some men did not wish to live alone; Barrett, to preserve his own authority, felt that he was required to.

As new exiles arrived, they bunked in with those who currently lived alone. Private huts were surrendered in reverse order of seniority. Most of the exiles sent back in 2015 had been forced to take roommates by now. If another dozen deportees arrived, the 2014 group would have to start doubling up. Of course, there were deaths all up and down the line of seniority, which eased things a little, and there were plenty of men who didn't mind having company in their huts—who were eager for it, in fact.

Barrett felt, though, that a man who has been sentenced to life imprisonment without hope of parole ought to have the privilege of privacy, if he desires it. One of his biggest problems at Hawksbill Station was keeping people from cracking up because there was too little privacy. Propinquity could be intolerable in a place like this.

Norton pointed toward the big shiny-skinned green dome of the main building. "There's Altman going in now. And Rudiger. And Hutchett. Something must be happening!"

Barrett stepped up his pace, wincing a little. Some of the men entering the administration building saw his bulky figure coming over the rise in the humpbacked rod shield, and waved to him. Barrett lifted a massive arm in reply. He felt a mounting throb of excitement. It was a big event at the Station whenever a new man arrived—practically the only kind of event they ever had here. Without new men, they had no clue to what might be happening Up Front. Nobody had come to Hawksbill for six months, now, after a cascade of new arrivals late last year. They had been getting five or six a day, for a while—and then the flow stopped. And stayed stopped. Six months, and no one exiled: that was the longest gap Barrett could remember. It had started to seem as though no one would ever be sent to the Station again.

Which would be a catastrophe. New men were all that stood between the older inmates and insanity. New men brought news from the future, news from the world that had been left behind for all eternity. And they contributed the interplay of new personalities to a tight group that was always in danger of going stale.

Then, too, Barrett was aware, some of the men—he was not one—lived in the deluded hope that the next arrival might just be a woman.

That was why they flocked to the main building to see what was happening when the Hammer began to glow. Barrett hobbled down the path. The last trickle of rain died away just as he reached the entrance.

Within the building, sixty or seventy of the Station's residents crowded the chamber of the Hammer—just about every man in the place who was able in body and mind, and who was still alert enough to register curiosity about a newcomer. They shouted their greetings to Barrett as he moved toward the center of the group. He nodded, smiled, deflected their chattering questions with amiable gestures.

"Who's it going to be this time, Jim?"

"Maybe a girl, huh? Around nineteen years old, blonde, built like—"

"I hope he can play stochastic chess, anyway."

"Look at the glow! It's deepening!"

Barrett, like the others, stared at the Hammer, watching change come over the thick column that was the time-travel device. The complex, involuted collection of unfathomable instruments burned a bright cherry red now, betokening the surge of who knew how many kilowatts being pumped in by the generators at the far end of the line, Up Front. There was a hissing in the air; the floor rumbled faintly. The glow had spread to the Anvil, now, that broad aluminum bedplate on which all shipments from the future were dropped. In another moment—

"Condition Crimson!" somebody yelled. "Here he comes!"

A billion years up the time-line, a surge of power was flooding into the real Hammer of which this was only the partial replica. Potential was building up moment by moment in that huge grim room that everyone in Hawksbill Station remembered only too vividly. A man—or something else, perhaps just a shipment of supplies—stood in the center of the real Anvil in that room, engulfed by fate. Barrett knew what it was like to stand there, waiting for the Hawksbill Field to enfold you and kick you back to the early Paleozoic. Cold eyes watched you as you awaited your exile, and those eyes gleamed in triumph, telling you that they were glad to be rid of you. And then the Hammer did its work and off you went on your one-way journey. The effect of being sent through time was very much like being hit with a gigantic hammer and driven clear through the walls of the continuum: hence the governing metaphors for the functional parts of the machine.

Everything in Hawksbill Station had come via the Hammer. Setting up the Station had been a long, slow, expensive job, the work of methodical men who were willing to go to any lengths to get rid of their opponents in what was considered the humane, twenty-first-century way of doing it. The Hammer had knocked a pathway through time and had sent back the nucleus of a receiving station, first. Since there was no receiving station already on hand in the Paleozoic to receive the receiving station, a certain amount of unavoidable waste had occurred. It wasn't strictly necessary to have a Hammer and Anvil on the receiving end, except as a fine control to prevent temporal spread; without the receiving equipment, the field tended to wander a little, though. Shipments emanating from consecutive points along the time-line, sent back all in the same day or week, might easily get scattered over a span of twenty or thirty years of the past, without the receiving equipment to guide it in. There was plenty of such temporal garbage all around Hawksbill Station: stuff that had been intended for the original installation, but that because of tuning imprecisions in the pre-Hammer days had landed a couple of decades (and a couple of hundred miles) away from the intended site.

Despite such difficulties, the planning authorities had finally sent through enough components to the master temporal site to allow for the construction of a receiving station. It was very much like threading a needle by remote control using mile-long manipulators, but they succeeded. All this time, of course, the Station was uninhabited; the government hadn't cared to waste any of its own engineers by sending them back to set the place up, because they'd be unable to return. Finally, the first prisoners had gone through—political prisoners, naturally, but chosen for their technical backgrounds. Before they were shipped out, they were given instructions on how to put the parts of the Hammer and Anvil together.

Of course, it was their privilege to refuse to cooperate, once they reached the Station. They were beyond the reach of authority there. But it was to their own advantage to assemble the receiving station, thus making it possible for them to get further supplies from Up Front. They had done the job. After that, outfitting Hawksbill Station had been easy.

Now the Hammer glowed, meaning that they had activated the Hawksbill Field on the sending end, somewhere up around A.D. 2028 or 2030. All the sending was done from there. All the receiving was done here. Time travel didn't work the other way. Nobody really knew why, although there was a lot of superficially profound talk about the rules of entropy and the infinite temporal momentum that you were likely to attain if you tried to accelerate along the normal axis of time flow, which is to say from past to future.

The whining, hissing sound in the room began to grow painfully louder as the edges of the Hawksbill Field began to ionize the atmosphere. Then came the expected thunderclap of implosion, caused by an imperfect overlapping of the quantity of air that was being subtracted from this era and the quantity that was being thrust into it from the future.

And then, abruptly, a man dropped out of the Hammer and lay, stunned and limp, on the gleaming Anvil.

He looked very young, which surprised Barrett considerably. He seemed to be well under thirty years old. Generally, only middle-aged men were condemned to exile at Hawksbill Station. They sent only the incorrigibles, the men who had to be separated from humanity for the general good of the greatest number. The youngest man in the place now had been close to forty when he first arrived. The sight of this lean, clean-cut boy drew a hiss of anguish from a couple of the men in the room, and Barrett understood the constellation of emotions that pained them.

The new man sat up. He stirred like a child coming out of a long, deep sleep. He looked around.

He was wearing a simple gray tunic, with an underlying fabric of iridescent threads. His face was wedge-shaped, tapering to a sharp chin, and right now he was very pale. His thin lips seemed bloodless. His blue eyes blinked rapidly. He rubbed his eyebrows, which were blond and nearly invisible. His jaws worked as though he wanted to say something, but could not find the words.

The sensations incurred in time travel were not physiologically harmful, but they could deliver a rough jolt to the consciousness. The last moments before the Hammer descended were very much like the final moments beneath the guillotine, since exile to Hawksbill Station was tantamount to a sentence of death. The departing prisoner took his last look at the world of rocket transport and artificial organs and visiphones, at the world in which he had lived and loved and agitated for a sacred political cause, and then came the Hammer and he was rammed instantaneously into the inconceivably remote post on an irreversible trajectory. It was a gloomy business, and it was not very surprising that the newcomers arrived in a state of emotional shock.

Hawksbill Station

Barrett elbowed his way through the crowd toward the machine. Automatically, the others made way for him. He reached the lip of the Anvil and leaned over it, extending a hand to the new man. His broad smile was met by a look of glassy bewilderment.

"I'm Jim Barrett. Welcome to Hawksbill Station."

"I—it—"

"Here—get off that thing before a load of groceries lands on top of you. They may still be transmitting." Barrett, wincing a little as he shifted his weight, pulled the new man down from the Anvil. It was altogether likely that the idiots Up Front would shoot another shipment along a minute after sending a man, without worrying about whether the man had had time to get off the Anvil. When it came to prisoners, Up Front had no empathy at all.

Barrett beckoned to Mel Rudiger, a plump, freckled anarchist with a soft pink face. Rudiger handed the new man an alcohol capsule. He took it and pressed it to his arm without a word, and his eyes brightened.

"Here's a candy bar," Charley Norton said. "Get your glucose level up to par in a hurry."

The man shook it off, moving his head as though through a liquid atmosphere. He looked groggy—a real case of temporal shock, Barrett thought, possibly the worst he had ever seen. The newcomer hadn't even spoken yet. Could the effect really be that extreme? Maybe for a young man the shock of being ripped from his rightful time was stronger than for others.

Barrett said softly, "We'll take you to the infirmary and check you out, okay? Then I'll assign you your quarters. There'll be time later on for you to find your way around and meet everybody. What's your name?"

"Hahn. Lew Hahn."

His voice was just a raspy whisper.

"I can't hear you," Barrett said.

"Hahn," the man repeated, still only barely audible.

"When are you from, Lew?"

"2029."

"You feel pretty sick?"

35

"I feel awful. I don't even believe this is happening to me. There isn't really such a place as Hawksbill Station, is there?"

"I'm afraid there is," Barrett said. "At least, for most of us. A few of the boys think it's all an illusion induced by drugs, that we're really still up there in Century Twenty-one. But I have my doubts of that. If it's an illusion, it's damned good one. Look."

He put one arm around Hahn's shoulders and guided him through the press of Station men, out of the Hammer chamber, and down the corridor toward the nearby infirmary. Although Hahn looked thin, even fragile, Barrett was surprised to feel the rippling, steely muscles in those shoulders. He suspected that this man was a good deal less helpless and ineffectual than he seemed to be right now. He *had* to be, in order to merit banishment to Hawksbill Station. It was expensive to hurl a man this far back in time; they didn't send just anyone here.

Barrett and Hahn passed the open door of the building. "Look out there," Barrett commanded.

Hahn looked. He passed a hand across his eyes as though to clear away unseen cobwebs, and looked again.

"A Late Cambrian landscape," said Barrett quietly. "This view would be a geologist's dream, except that geologists don't tend to become political prisoners, it seems. Out in front of you is what they call Appalachia. It's a strip of rock a few hundred miles wide and a few thousand miles long, running from the Gulf of Mexico to Newfoundland. To the east we've got a thing called the Appalachian Geosyncline, which is a trough five hundred miles wide full of water. Somewhere about two thousand miles to the west there's another trough, what they call the Cordilleran Geosyncline. It's full of water too, and at this particular stage of geological history the path of land between the geosynclines is below sea level, so where Appalachia ends we've got the Inland Sea, currently, running way out to the west. On the far side of the Inland Sea is a narrow north-south land mass called Cascadia, that's going to be California and Oregon and Washington someday. Don't hold your breath till it happens. I hope you like seafood, Lew."

Hawksbill Station

Hahn stared, and Barrett, standing beside him at the doorway, stared also. Even now, he felt wonder at the sight of it. You never could get used to the sheer alienness of this place, not even after you had lived here twenty years, as Barrett had done. It was Earth, and yet it was not really Earth at all, because it was somber and unreal. Where were the swarming cities? Where were the electronic freeways? Where were the noise, the pollution, the garishness? None of it had been born yet. This was a silent, sterile place.

The gray oceans swarmed with life, of course. But at this stage of evolution there was nothing living on the land except the intrusive men of Hawksbill Station. The surface of the planet, where it jutted above the seas, was a raw shield of naked rock, bare and monotonous, broken only by occasional patches of moss in the occasional patches of soil that had managed to form. Even a few cockroaches would have been welcome; but insects, it seemed, were still a couple of geological periods in the future. To land dwellers, this was a dead world, a world unborn.

Shaking his head, Hahn moved away from the door. Barrett led him down the corridor and into the small, brightly lit room that served as the Station's infirmary. Doc Quesada was waiting for him there.

Quesada wasn't really a doctor, but he had been a medical technician once, and that was good enough. He was a compact, swarthy man with harsh cheekbones and a spreading wedge of a nose. In his infirmary he wore a look of complete self-assurance. He hadn't lost too many of his patients, all things considered. Barrett had watched him removing appendixes and suturing wounds and amputating limbs with total aplomb. In his slightly frayed white smock, Quesada looked sufficiently medical to carry off his role convincingly.

Barrett said, "Doc, this is Lew Hahn. He's in temporal shock. Fix him up."

Quesada nudged the new man onto a webfoam cradle and briskly unzipped his gray tunic. Then he reached for his medical kit. Hawksbill Station was well equipped for most medical emergencies, now. The people Up Front were not terribly concerned with what happened to the prisoners at the Station, but they had no wish to be inhumane to men who could no longer harm them, and they sent back from time to time all sorts of useful things, like anesthetics and surgical clamps and diagnostats and medicines and dermal probes. Barrett could remember a time at the beginning when there had been nothing much here but the empty huts, and a man who hurt himself was in real trouble.

"He's had a drink already," said Barrett. "I thought you ought to know."

"I see that," Quesada murmured. He scratched at his short-cropped, bristly reddish mustache. The little diagnostat in the cradle had gone rapidly to work, flashing information about Hahn's blood pressure, potassium count, dilation index, vascular flow, alveolar flexing, and much else. Quesada seemed to have no difficulty in comprehending the barrage of facts that flashed across the screen and landed on the confirmation tape. After a moment he turned to Hahn and said, "You aren't really sick, are you, fellow? Just shaken up a little. I don't blame you. Here—I'll give you a quick jolt to calm your nerves, and you'll be all right. As all right as any of us ever are, I guess."

He put a tube to Hahn's carotid and thumbed the snout. The subsonic whirred, and a tranquilizing compound slid into the man's bloodstream. Hahn shivered.

Quesada said to Barrett, "Let him rest for five minutes. Then he'll be over the hump."

They left Hahn slumped in the cradle and went out of the infirmary. In the hall, Quesada said, "This one's a lot younger than usual."

"I've noticed. And also the first in months."

"You think something funny's going on Up Front?"

"I couldn't really say. But I'll have a long talk with Hahn once he's got some energy back." Barrett looked down at the little medic and said, "I meant to ask you before. What's the report on Valdosto?"

Valdosto had gone into psychotic collapse several weeks before. Quesada was keeping him drugged and trying to bring him slowly back to an acceptance of the reality of Hawksbill Station. Shrugging, he replied, "The status is quo. I let him out from under the dream-juice this morning, and he was the same as he's been."

"You don't think he'll come out of it?"

"I doubt it. He's cracked for keeps. They could paste him together Up Front, but—"

"Yeah," Barrett said. "If he could get Up Front at all, Valdosto wouldn't have cracked. Keep him happy, then. If he can't be sane, he can at least be comfortable."

"What's happened to Valdosto really hurts you, doesn't it, Jim?"

"What do you think?" Barrett's eyes flickered a moment. "He and I were together almost from the start. When the party was getting organized, when we were all full of jism and ideals. I was the coordinator, he was the bomb-thrower. He was so steamed up about the rights of man that he was ready to mutilate any so-and-so who didn't toe a proper liberal line. I had to keep calming him down. You know, when Val and I were kids, we had an apartment together in New York—"

"You and Val weren't kids at the same time," Quesada reminded him.

"Well, no," Barrett said. "He was maybe eighteen and I was pushing thirty. But he always seemed older than his age. And we had this apartment, the two of us. And girls. Girls all the time, coming, going, sometimes living there for a few weeks. Val always said a true revolutionary needs lots of sex. Hawksbill would come there too, the bastard, only we didn't know then that he was working on something that would hang us all. And Bernstein. And we'd sit up all night drinking cheap filtered rum, and Valdosto would start planning terrorist raids, and we'd shut him up, and—" Barrett scowled. "To hell with it. The past is dead. Probably it would be better if Val was, too."

"Jim—"

"Let's change the subject," Barrett said. "What about Altman? Still got the shakes?"

"He's building a woman," Quesada said.

"That's what Charley Norton told me. What's he using? A rag, a bone—"

"I gave him some surplus chemicals to fool with. Chosen mainly for their color, matter of fact. He's got some foul green copper compounds and a little bit of ethyl alcohol and some zinc sulphate and six or seven other things, and he collected some soil and threw in a lot of dead shellfish, and he's sculpting it all into what he claims is female shape and waiting for lightning to strike it and bring it to life."

"In other words," Barrett said, "he's gone crazy."

"I think that's a safe assumption. But at least he's not molesting his friends any more, anyway. You didn't think Altman's homosexual phase would last much longer, as I recall."

"No, but I didn't think he'd go altogether off the deep end, Doc. If a man needs sex and he can find some consenting playmates here, that's quite all right with me, as long as they don't offend anybody out in the open. But when Altman starts putting a woman together out of some dirt and rotten brachiopod meat, it means we've lost him for keeps. It's too bad."

Quesada's dark eyes fell. "We're all going to go that way sooner or later, Jim."

"I haven't cracked up yet. You haven't."

"Give us time. I've only been here eleven years."

"Altman's been here only eight," said Barrett. "Valdosto even less."

"Some shells crack faster than others," said Quesada. "Well, here's our new friend."

Hahn had come out of the infirmary to join them. He still looked pale and shaken, but the fright was gone from his eyes. He was beginning, thought Barrett, to adjust to the unthinkable.

He said, "I couldn't help overhearing part of your conversation. Is there a lot of mental illness here?"

"Some of the men haven't been able to find anything meaningful to do at the Station," Barrett said. "The boredom eats them away."

"What's meaningful to do here?"

"Quesada has his medical work. I've got administrative duties. A couple of the fellows are studying the sea life, making a real scientific survey. We've got a newspaper that comes out every now and then and keeps some of the boys busy. There's fishing, and cross-continental hiking. But there are always those who just let themselves slide into despair, and they crack up. I'd say we have thirty or forty certifiable maniacs here at the moment, out of a hundred forty residents."

"That's not so bad," Hahn said. "Considering the inherent instability of the men who get sent here, and the unusual conditions of life here."

"Inherent instability?" Barrett repeated. "I don't know about that. Most of us thought we were pretty sane, and fighting on the right side. Do you think that because a man's a revolutionary, he's *ipso facto* nuts? And if you do think so, Hahn, what the hell are you doing here?"

"You're misinterpreting me, Mr. Barrett. I'm not drawing any parallel between antigovernmental activity and mental disturbance, God knows. But you have to admit that a lot of the people any revolutionary movement attracts are—well, a little unhinged somewhere."

"Valdosto," Quesada murmured. "Throwing bombs."

"All right," Barrett said. He laughed. "Hey, Hahn, you're suddenly pretty articulate, aren't you, for a man who couldn't even mumble a few minutes back? What was in the stuff Doc Quesada jolted you with?"

"I didn't mean to sound superior," Hahn said quickly. "Maybe that came out a little too smug and condescending. I mean—"

"Forget it. What did you do Up Front, anyway?"

"I was an economist."

"Just what we need," said Quesada. "He can help us solve our balance-of-payments problem."

Barrett said, "If you were an economist back there, you'll have plenty to talk about here. This place is full of nutty economic theorists who'll want to bounce their ideas off you. Some of them are almost sane, too. The ideas, that is. Come with me and I'll show you where you're going to stay."

The path from the main building to the hut where Donald Latimer lived was mainly downhill, for which Barrett was grateful even though he knew that he'd have to negotiate the uphill return in a little while, anyway. Latimer's hut was on the eastern side of the Station, looking out over it. Hahn and Barrett walked slowly toward it. Hahn was solicitous of Barrett's game leg, and Barrett was irritated by the exaggerated care the younger man took to keep pace with him.

He was puzzled by this Hahn. The man was full of seeming contradictions. Such as showing up here with the worst case of temporal shock on arrival Barrett had ever seen, then snapping out of it with remarkable quickness. Or looking frail and shy, but hiding solid muscles inside his tunic. Giving an outer appearance of general incompetence, but speaking with calm control. Barrett wondered what it was this sleek young man had done to earn him the trip to Hawksbill Station. But there was time for such inquiries later. All the time in the world.

Hahn swept his hand across the horizon and said, "Is everything like this? Just rock and ocean?"

"That's all. Land life hasn't evolved yet. Won't for quite a while. Everything's wonderfully simple here, isn't it? No clutter. No urban sprawl. No traffic jams. There's some moss moving up onto the land, but not much."

"And in the sea? Dinosaurs swimming around?"

Barrett shook his head. "There won't be any vertebrates for thirty, forty million years. They'll be arriving in the Ordovician, and we're in the Cambrian. We don't even have fish yet, let alone reptiles out there. All we can offer is that which creepeth. Some shellfish, some big ugly fellows that look like squids, and trilobites. We've got seven hundred billion different species of trilobites, more or less. And we've got a man named Mel Rudiger—he's the one who gave you the drink when you got here—who's making a collection of them. Rudiger's writing the world's definitive text on trilobites. His masterpiece."

"But nobody will ever have a chance to read it in—in the future."

"Up Front, we say."

"Up Front."

"That's the pity of it," said Barrett. "All that brilliant work, and it's wasted, because nobody else here gives a damn about the life and hard times of the trilobite, and nobody Up Front will ever know about it. We told Rudiger to inscribe his book on imperishable plates of gold and hope that it's found by paleontologists later on. But he says the odds are against it. A billion years of geology will chew his plates to hell before they can be found. And if they ever did turn up, they'd probably be used to start a new religion, or something."

Hahn sniffed. "Why does the air smell so strange?"

"It's a different mix," Barrett said. "We've analyzed it. More nitrogen, a little less oxygen, hardly any carbon dioxide at all. But that isn't really why it smells odd to you. The thing is, it's pure air, unpolluted by the exhalations of life. Nobody's been respiring into it except us lads, and there aren't enough of us to matter."

Smiling, Hahn said, "I feel a little cheated that it's so empty. I expected lush jungles of weird plants, and pterodactyls swooping through the air, and maybe a tyrannosaur crashing into a fence around the Station."

"No jungles. No pterodactyls. No tyrannosaurs. No fences. You didn't do your homework."

"Sorry."

"This is the Late Cambrian. Sea life exclusively."

"It was very kind of them to pick such a peaceful era for their dumping ground for political prisoners," Hahn said. "I was afraid it would be all teeth and claws."

Barrett spat. "Kind, hell! They were looking for an era where we couldn't do any harm to their environment. That meant they had to toss us back before the evolution of mammals, just in case we'd accidentally get hold of the ancestor of all humanity and snuff him out. And while they were at it, they decided to stash us so far in the past that we'd be beyond all land life, on the theory that maybe even if we slaughtered a baby dinosaur it might affect the entire course of the future. *Their* world."

"They don't mind if we catch a few trilobites?"

"Evidently they think it's safe," Barrett said. "It looks as though they were right. Hawksbill Station has been here for twenty-five years, and it doesn't seem as though we've tampered with future history in any measurable way. There's still a continuity, despite our presence here. Of course, they're careful not to send us any women."

"Why is that?"

"So we don't start reproducing and perpetuating ourselves. Wouldn't that mess up the time-lines! Say, a successful human outpost planted here in One Billion B.C., that's had all that time to evolve and mutate and grow?"

"A separate evolutionary line."

"You bet," Barrett said. "By the time the twenty-first century came around, our descendants would be in charge, whatever kind of creatures they'd be by then, and the other kind of human being would probably be in penal servitude, and there'd be more paradoxes created than you could shake a trilobite at. So they don't send the women here."

"But they send women back in time."

"Oh, yes," Barrett said. "There's a prison camp for women, too, but it's a few hundred million years up the time-line in the Late Silurian, and never the twain shall meet. That's why Ned Altman is trying to build a woman for himself out of dust and garbage."

"God made Adam out of less."

"Ned Altman isn't God," Barrett pointed out. "That's the root of his whole problem. Look, here's the hut where you're going to stay, Hahn. I'm rooming you with Don Latimer. He's a very sensitive, interesting, pleasant person. He used to be a physicist before he got into politics, and he's been here about a dozen years, and I might as well warn you that he's developed a strong and somewhat cockeyed mystic streak lately. The fellow he was rooming with killed himself last year, and since then Don's been trying to find some way out of the Station through the application of extrasensory powers."

"Is he serious?"

"I'm afraid he is. And we try to take him seriously, too. We all humor each other's quirks at Hawksbill Station; it's the only way we avoid an epidemic of mass psychosis. Latimer will probably try to get you to collaborate with him on his psi project. If you don't like living with him, I can arrange a transfer for you. But I want to see how he reacts to someone who's new at the Station. I'd like you to give bunking with him a chance."

"Maybe I'll even help him find that psionic gateway he's looking for."

"If you do, take me along," said Barrett. They both laughed. Then Barrett rapped at Latimer's door. There was no answer, and after a moment he pushed the door open. Hawksbill Station got along without locks.

Latimer sat in the middle of the bare rock floor, cross-legged, meditating. He was a slender, gentle-faced man with parchment-like skin and a somber, downturned mouth, and he was just beginning to look old. Right now he seemed at least a million miles away, ignoring them completely. Hahn shrugged. Barrett put a finger to his lips. They waited in silence for a few minutes, and then Latimer showed signs of coming up from his trance.

He got to his feet in a single flowing motion, without using his hands. In a low, courteous voice he said to Hahn, "Have you just arrived?"

"Within the last hour. I'm Lew Hahn."

"Donald Latimer." He did not offer to shake hands. "I regret that I have to make your acquaintance in these surroundings. But perhaps we won't have to tolerate this illegal condition of imprisonment much longer."

Barrett said, "Don, Lew is going to bunk with you. I think you'll get along well. He was an economist in 2029 until they gave him the Hammer."

Animation came into Latimer's eyes. "Where did you live?" he asked.

"San Francisco."

The glow faded as if doused. Latimer said, "Were you ever in Toronto?"

"Toronto? No," Hahn said.

"I'm from there. I had a daughter—she'd be twenty-three years old now, Nella Latimer—I wondered if you knew her—perhaps you knew her—"

"No. I'm sorry."

Latimer sighed. "It wasn't very likely that you did. But I'd love to know what kind of a woman she became. She was a little girl when I last saw her. She was—let's see— she was ten, going on eleven. Now I suppose she's married. I might have grandchildren. Or perhaps they've sent her to the other Station. She might have come to be politically active, and—" Latimer paused. "Nella Latimer—you're sure that you didn't know her?"

Barrett left them together, Hahn looking concerned and sympathetic, Latimer trusting, open, hopeful. It seemed as though they'd get along pretty well. Barrett told Latimer to bring the new man up to the main building at dinnertime to be introduced around, and went out. A chilly drizzle had begun to fall again. Barrett made his way slowly, painfully up the hill, grunting faintly every time he put his weight on the crutch.

It had been sad to see the light flicker from Latimer's eyes when Hahn said he didn't know his daughter. Most of the time, men at Hawksbill Station tried not to speak about their families. They preferred—wisely—to keep those tormenting memories well repressed. To think about loved ones was to feel the ache of amputation, desperate and incurable. But the arrival of newcomers generally stirred old ties. There was never any news of relatives, and no way ever to obtain any, because it was impossible for the men of the Station to communicate with anyone Up Front. Nothing could be sent forward in time so much as a thousandth of a second.

No way to ask for the photo of a loved one, no way to request specific medicines or equipment, no way to obtain a certain book or a coveted tape. In a mindless, impersonal way, the authorities Up Front sent periodic shipments to the Station of things that might be useful to the inmates—reading matter, medical supplies, technical equipment, food. But always it was a random scoop, unpredictable, bizarre. Occasionally they were startling in their generosity, as when they sent a case of Burgundy, or a box of sensory spools, or a recharger for the power pack. Such gifts usually meant that they were having a brief thaw in the world situation. A relaxation of tension customarily produced a short-lived desire to be kind to the boys in Hawksbill Station.

But they had a strict policy about sending information about relatives. Or about sending contemporary newspapers and magazines. Fine wine, yes; a tridim of a daughter who would never be embraced again, no.

Hawksbill Station

For all Up Front knew, there was no one alive in Hawksbill Station. A plague could have killed everyone in the place off ten years ago—but *they* had no way of telling that. They couldn't even be sure that any of the exiles had survived the trip to the past. All they had determined from Hawksbill's experiments was that a past-ward trip of less than three years was not likely to be fatal; it had been impractical to extend the duration of experiments past that point. What would a billion years across time do? Not even Edmond Hawksbill had known that for certain.

So they went on sending shipments back to the prisoners in the blind assumption that there were prisoners alive to receive them. The government whirred and clicked with predictable continuity, looking after those whom it had condemned to eternal separation from the State. The government, whatever else it might be, was not malicious. Barrett had learned long ago that there were other kinds of totalitarianism besides bloody repressive tyranny.

Barrett paused at the top of the hill to catch his breath. Naturally, the alien air no longer smelled strange to him. He filled his lungs with it until he was a little dizzied by it. Once again the rain ceased. Through the grayness came thin shafts of sunshine, making the naked rocks sparkle and glow. Barrett closed his eyes a moment and leaned on his crutch, and saw as though on an inner screen in his mind the creatures with many legs climbing up out of the sea, and the broad mossy carpets spreading, and the flowerless plants uncoiling and extending their scaly grayish branches, and the dull hides of eerie flat-snouted amphibians glistening on the shores, and the tropic heat of the coal-forming epoch descending like a glove to smother the world.

All that lay far in the future: Dinosaurs.

Little chittering mammals.

Pithecanthropus hunting with hand-axes in the forests of Java.

Sargon and Hannibal and Attila, and Orville Wright, and Thomas Edison, and Edmond Hawksbill. And finally a benign government that would find the thoughts of certain men so intolerable that the only safe place to which those men could be banished was deemed to be a rock at the beginning of time.

The government was too civilized to put men to death for subversive activities, and too cowardly to let them remain alive and at large. The compromise was the living death of Hawksbill Station. A billion years of impassable time was suitable insulation even for the most nihilistic ideas.

Grimacing a little, Barrett struggled the rest of the way back to his hut. He had long since come to accept the fact of his exile, but accepting his ruined foot was another matter entirely. He had always been strong physically. He had feared old age because it might mean a withering of his strength; but now the age of sixty had come upon him, and the years had not sapped him as much as he feared they might, although they had certainly sapped him; but he would still have had most of his strength, except for this absurd accident that might have happened to him at any age. The idle wish to find a way to regain the freedom of his own time no longer possessed him; but Barrett wished with all his soul that the blank-faced authorities Up Front would send back a kit that would allow him to rebuild his foot.

He entered his hut and flung his crutch aside, sinking down instantly on his cot. There had been no cots when Barrett had come to Hawksbill Station. You slept on the floor, then, and the floor was solid rock. If you felt ambitious, you went out and scrabbled together some soil, looking in the crevices and creases of the rock shield, collecting the fledgling earth a handful at a time, and you made yourself an inch-deep bed of soil to lie on. Things were a little better here now.

Barrett had been sent to the Station in its fourth year of operation, when there had been only a dozen buildings, and little in the way of creature comforts. That had been A.D. 2008, Up Front time. The Station had been a raw, miserable place, then, but the steady accretion of shipments from Up Front had made it a relatively tolerable place to live.

Of the fifty or so exiles who had preceded Barrett to Hawksbill, none remained alive. He had held highest seniority in the camp for almost ten years, since the death of white-bearded old Pleyel, whom Barrett had regarded as a saint. Time here moved at a one-to-one correlation with time Up Front; the Hammer was locked on this single point of time, forever moving forward in perfect step, so that Lew Hahn, arriving here today more than twenty years after Barrett had come, had departed from Up Front at a spot on the calendar exactly twenty years and some months along from the date of Barrett's expulsion. Hahn came from 2029—a whole generation past the world Barrett had left. Barrett had not had the heart to begin pumping Hahn for news of that generation so soon. He would learn all he needed to know in time, and small cheer it would be, anyway.

Barrett reached for a book. But the fatigue of hobbling around the Station had taken more out of him than he realized. He looked at the page for a moment. Then he put it away and closed his eyes.

Faces swam behind his lids. Bernstein. Pleyel. Hawksbill. Janet. Bernstein. Bernstein. Bernstein.

He dozed.

Jimmy Barrett was sixteen years old, and Jack Bernstein was saying to him, "How can you be so big and ugly and not care a damn about what's happening to the weak people of this world?"

"Who says I don't care a damn?"

"It doesn't even need saying. It's obvious. Where's your commitment? What are you doing to keep civilization from falling apart?"

"It isn't—"

"It is," Bernstein said scornfully. "You big lummox, you don't even read the papers, do you? Do you realize that there's a constitutional crisis in this country, and that unless people like you and me start taking action, there's going to be a dictatorship here in the United States before this time next year?"

"You're exaggerating," Barrett said. "As usual."

"See? You don't give a damn!"

Barrett was exasperated, but that was nothing new. Jack Bernstein had been exasperating him ever since they had met, four years back in 1980. They had both been twelve years old then. Barrett was already close to six feet tall, husky and powerful; Jack was skinny and waxen-looking, undersized for his age, even smaller when he stood beside Barrett. Something had drawn the two of them together: the attraction of opposites, perhaps. Barrett valued and respected the smaller boy's quick, nimble mind, and he suspected that Jack had sought him out as a protector. Jack needed protection. He was the sort of fellow you wanted to hit for no particular reason at all, even when he hadn't said anything, and when he finally did open his mouth you wanted to hit him even harder.

Now they were sixteen, and Barrett had reached what he hoped was his full growth, six feet five, well over two hundred pounds, and he had to shave every day and his voice was deep and black. Jack Bernstein still looked as though he were on the wrong side of puberty. He was five feet five, five seven at best, with no shoulders at all, arms and legs so thin Barrett thought he could snap them with one hand, a high reedy voice, a sharp, aggressive nose. His face was scarred by some skin disease, and his thick, tangled eyebrows made a solid line across his forehead, visible half a block away. Jack had grown more waspish, more excitable in adolescence. There were times when Barrett could hardly stand him at all. This was one of them.

"What do you want from me?" Barrett asked.

"Will you come to one of our meetings?"

"I don't want to get into anything subversive."

"*Subversive!*" Bernstein shot back at him. "A label. A stinking semantic tag. Anyone who wants to patch the world up a little, he's a subversive in your book, right, Jimmy?"

"Well—"

"Take Christ. Would you call him a subversive?"

"I think I would," Barrett said cautiously. "Besides, you know what happened to Christ."

"He wasn't the first martyr to ideas, and he won't be the last. Do you want to play it safe all your life? Do you want to sit there wrapped in muscles and fat and let the wolves eat the world? What's it going to be like when you're sixty years old, Jimmy, and the world is one big slave camp, and there you sit in chains saying, Well, I'm alive, so everything turned out pretty fair?"

Barrett said coolly, "Better a live slave than a dead subversive."

"If you believe that, you're more of a moron than I think you are."

"I ought to swat you. You buzz, Jack. Like a mosquito."

"Do you believe that thing you just said to me about a live slave? Do you? Do you?"

Barrett shrugged. "What do you think?"

"Then come to a meeting. Get out of your cocoon and *do* something, Jimmy. We need men like you." Jack's voice had shifted pitch and timbre. It had lost its reedy, querulous tone, and suddenly was lower, more assured, more commanding. "Someone of your size, Jimmy—of your natural authority. You'd be terrific. If I could only get you to see that what we're doing is important—"

"How can a bunch of high school kids save the world?"

Jack's thin lips quirked and clamped; but he seemed to choke back whatever quick burst of reply had offered itself. After a pause he said, still in that same strange new voice of his, "Not all of us are high school kids, Jimmy. Most kids our age are like you—they lack commitment. We have older people, in their twenties, thirties, some even older than that. If you'd meet them, you'd see what I mean. Talk to Pleyel, if you want to know what true dedication is like. Talk to Hawksbill." Mischief flared in Jack's eyes. "You might even want to come just to meet the girls. We've got some girls in the group. They're pretty liberated girls, I might as well tell you. Just in case you care about such things, and maybe you do."

"Is this a Communist group, Jack?"

"No. Definitely not. We've got our Marxists, sure, but we run right through the political spectrum. As a matter of fact, our basic orientation is anti-Communist, because we believe in a minimum of State interference with individual life and thought, and you know that Marxists are planners. In that sense we're virtually anarchists. We might even be termed Radical Rightists, since we'd like to dismantle a lot of the government apparatus. You see how meaningless these political tags are? We're so far to the left that we're right-wingers, and we're so far to the right that we're left-wingers. But we do have a program. Will you come to a meeting?"

"Tell me about the girls."

"They're attractive and intelligent and sociable. Some of them might even be interested in an apolitical boor like you, simply because you're such a big hunk of meat."

Barrett nodded. "The next time there's a meeting, maybe I'll go."

He was tired of Bernstein's nagging, more than anything else. Large issues of politics had never interested him in a really passionate way. But it pained him to be told that he had no conscience, or that he was sitting idly by while the world went to hell, and in his whining, persistent way, Jack had goaded him into making a move. He would go to a meeting of this underground group. He would get a firsthand look. He expected that he would find it full of embittered nuts and futile dreamers, and he'd never go to a second meeting, but at least Jack would never be able to throw in his face again the accusation that he had rejected the movement out of hand.

A week later, Jack Bernstein told him that a meeting had been called for the following night. Barrett went. The date was April 11, 1984.

It was a cold, windy, rainy night, with more than a hint of snow in the air. Typical 1984 weather. There was a hex on the year, people said. That man had written a book about 1984, long ago, predicting all sorts of terrible things, and though none of those particular terrible things had come to pass in the United States, there were other troubles in the land, and everything seemed typified by the weather. Spring was not going to come this year: that looked certain. Mounds of dull gray snow lay heaped everywhere in New York, here in mid-April, except on those streets that had the heating filaments embedded in the pavement, downtown. The trees were still bare, and not even the buds were stirring. A bad year for people, tense and stormy. Not such a bad year for revolution, perhaps.

Jimmy Barrett met Jack Bernstein at the subway station near the edge of Prospect Park, and they rode into Manhattan, getting off at Times Square. The train they rode on had a shabby, tattered look to it, but that was nothing unusual. Everything was tattered and shabby, here in the ninth year of what was being called the Permanent Depression.

They walked down Forty-second Street to Ninth Avenue and entered the lobby of a golden tower eighty stories high, one of the last skyscrapers to go up before the Panic. An elevator door creaked open for them. Jack pressed the button for the basement, and down they went.

"What am I supposed to say when they ask me who I am?" Barrett wondered.

"Leave everything to me," Jack said. His pale, blotchy face was transfigured with importance. He was in his element now. Jack the conspirator. Jack the subversive. Jack the plotter in basement corridors. Barrett felt uncomfortable, awkwardly big and naïve.

They emerged from the elevator, passed through a low-vaulted passageway, and appeared before a closed green door with a chair propped against it. A girl stood in the hallway beside the chair. She was nineteen or twenty years old, Barrett guessed: short and fat, with thick legs visible beneath her short skirt. She wore her hair short too, in the current fashion, but that was the only fashionable thing about her. Heavy breasts sagged unsupported within a red woolen sweater. Her only makeup was a smear of luminescent blue across her lips, unevenly applied. A cigarette dangled loosely from one corner of her mouth. She looked deliberately slovenly, coarse, cheap, as though she saw some virtue in hunching her shoulders in and pretending she was a peasant. She seemed a caricature of all the left-wing girls who marched in protest demonstrations and waved petitions. Was this sleazy tramp the sort of girl typical of the group? "Attractive, intelligent, and sociable," Jack had said, cunningly baiting his trap with the promise of passion. But of course Jack's idea of an attractive girl didn't necessarily match his. To Jack—unpopular, scrawny, sharp-tongued—any girl who would let him paw her a little would seem like Aphrodite. Grubby boys found virtues in grubby girls that Barrett, not so limited by nature, tended not to see.

"Evening, Janet," Jack said. His voice was edgy again.

The girl surveyed him coolly, then made a show of staring up at Barrett's full height.

"Who's that?"

"Jimmy Barrett. Classmate of mine. He's all right. Politically naïve, but he'll learn."

"You tell Pleyel you were asking him here?"

"No. But I'll vouch for him." Jack moved closer to her. In a possessive way he put his hand across her wrist. "Stop acting like a commissar and let us in, will you, lover?"

Janet disengaged herself. "You wait here. I'll see if it's okay."

She slipped within the green door. Jack turned to Barrett and said, "That's a marvelous girl. Sometimes she plays tough, but she's got real spirit. And sensuality. She's a very sensual girl."

"How would you know?" Barrett asked.

Jack colored and his lips compressed into a flat, angry line. "Believe me. I know."

"You mean you're not a virgin, Bernstein?"

"Knock it off, will you?"

The door opened again. Janet was back, and with her was a slim, reserved-looking man whose stubby hair was wholly gray, but whose face was unlined, so that he could have been fifty or thirty, and there was no telling. His eyes were gray too, and managed to be gentle and penetrating at the same time. Barrett saw Jack Bernstein stiffen to attention. "It's Pleyel," Bernstein whispered.

The girl said, "His name's Jim Barrett. Bernstein says he vouches for him."

Pleyel nodded amiably. The gray eyes moved quickly across Barrett's face, and it was a struggle not to flinch as those eyes excavated him. "Hello, Jim," Pleyel said. "My name's Norman Pleyel."

Barrett nodded. It sounded strange, hearing Janet and Pleyel calling him *Jim*. All his life, he had been *Jimmy* to everyone.

Jack blurted, "He's in my class. I've been working on him, getting to see his responsibilities to humanity. He finally decided to come down and attend a meeting. He—"

"Yes," Pleyel said. "We're glad to have you here, Jim. But you must understand one thing before you step inside. You're running risks by attending this meeting, even as an observer. This organization has met with official opposition. Your presence here may be held against you at some future time. Is that quite clear?"

"—yes."

"And also, since the rest of us live under constant risk, I'll have to remind you that everything that takes place here tonight is confidential. If we learn that you've taken advantage of your privilege as a guest to divulge anything you've heard, we'll be forced to take action against you. So if you step inside, you're exposing yourself to danger both from the presently constituted government and from ourselves. This is your chance to leave without stigma, if you wish."

Barrett hesitated. He glanced at Jack, whose face clearly registered distress; obviously Bernstein expected him to sidestep the risks and go home, undoing all the proselytizing work. Barrett considered the idea seriously. They were asking him to make an advance commitment before he knew anything about them; the moment he stepped through that door, he was placing himself in a matrix of responsibilities. To hell with the risks. "I'd still like to go inside, sir," he murmured.

Pleyel looked pleased. He opened the door. As Barrett stepped past the short, sullen-looking girl, he was surprised to see her staring at him with warm approval and even, perhaps, desire. She remained outside, guarding the door. Pleyel led the way within. Entering, Jack murmured to him, "That man is one of the most remarkable human beings of all time." He might have been speaking of Goethe or Leonardo.

The room was large and cavernous and cold, and had not been painted for at least eight years. Rows of bare wooden benches were lined up facing an empty stage. About a dozen people had pushed some of the benches into a rough circle. They included two or three girls, a balding man, and a group of what looked like college students. One of them was reading aloud from a long yellow slip of paper, and the others were punctuating his words with comments every few seconds.

"—in this present moment of crisis, we feel that—"

"No, it ought to be *all men must feel that—*"

"I don't think so. You make it sound stiff and—"

"Can we go back to the previous sentence, where you talk of the threat to liberty posed by—"

Barrett watched the wrangling without pleasure. It all seemed impossibly dull and dreary to him, this quibbling over the phraseology of a manifesto. That was essentially what he had expected to find here; a bunch of futilitarian hairsplitters in a drafty basement room, battling furiously over minute semantic differences. Were these the revolutionaries who would hold back the world from chaos? Hardly. Hardly.

In a moment, the discussion had turned into a scramble, with five people shouting suggestions for revision of the leaflet all at once. Pleyel stood by, looking pained but making no effort to salvage the meeting. There was a wounded and apologetic look on Jack Bernstein's face. The door opened again, and as a man in his twenties entered the meeting room, Bernstein nudged Barrett and said, "That's Hawksbill!"

The famous mathematician was an unimpressive sight. He was plump, frowzily dressed, and needed a shave. He wore thick glasses, no necktie, and a bulky blue pullover; his brown hair was curly but thinning, baring the crown of his scalp, but despite this he had the look of a college sophomore. There had to be more to the man than this, Barrett thought. Last year the newspapers had been full of the doings of Hawksbill; he had been a momentary hero of science, a nine-days' wonder when he stood up before that scientific congress in Zurich or Basel or wherever and read the text of his paper on the time equations. The newspapers had compared the work of twenty-five-year-old Edmond Hawksbill with the work of twenty-six-year-old Albert Einstein, and not to Hawksbill's disadvantage. So here he was, a member of this seedy revolutionary cell; and all his brilliance was on the inside. How could a man with such piggish little eyes be a genius?

Hawksbill put down his briefcase and said without preamble, "I ran the distribution vectors through the NYU computer while no one was looking. The indicated outcome is a breakup of *both* political parties, an inconclusive Presidential election, and the formation of a wholly different and nonrepresentative political system."

Hawksbill Station

"When?" Pleyel asked.

"Within three months after the election, plus or minus fourteen days," said Hawksbill. The voice that came out of the stocky body was entirely lacking in resonance and inflection; it was a pale stream of flaccid sound. "We can expect persecution to begin by next February as the new administration attempts to stifle dissent in the name of restoring order."

"Show us the parameters!" snapped the man who had been reading the draft of the yellow-paper manifesto. "Step by step, lay it out for us, Hawksbill!"

Pleyel said, "Surely that isn't necessary. If we—"

"No, I'll explain," the mathematician said, looking unruffled. He started to haul papers from his briefcase. "Item one. The election of President Delafield on the new American Conservative Party ticket in '72, resulting in fundamental changes in the economic role of the government, leading to the Boom of '73. Item two, the Panic of '76, ushering in the Permanent Depression. The victory of the National Liberal Party in '76, with the American Conservatives carrying only two states, that's item three. Now, if we cross-index the 1980 election, with its extremely subtle currents of disruption—"

"We know all that," came a bored voice.

Hawksbill shrugged. "It becomes possible to demonstrate mathematically, taking analog blocks of voter power, that neither major party is likely to achieve an electoral-vote majority this November, forcing the election into the House of Representatives, where, as a result of the situation that developed in the Congressional election of 1982, it will become impossible even to elect a President by that method. Whereupon—"

"The country will be in a mess."

"Precisely," said Hawksbill.

Barrett was aware that that last comment had come from a point not far from his left elbow. He looked down and saw Janet standing there. Absorbed in Hawksbill's droning words, he had not even noticed her enter the room, but there she was beside him, quite close, in fact.

Jack Bernstein seemed annoyed by that, judging by the glare on his face.

The girl said, "Don't you find what they're saying terrifying?"

Barrett realized that she was speaking to him. He said tensely, "I knew things were bad, but I hadn't realized they were *that* bad. If it really happens—"

"It will. If Ed Hawksbill's computer says it'll happen, it'll happen. The Second American Revolution, we're calling it. Norm Pleyel is in contact with important men all over the country, trying to head it off."

It seemed unreal to Barrett. Oh, he knew there were strikes, protest parades, sabotage incidents. He knew there were millions of people out of work, that the dollar had been devalued four times since 1976, that the Communist countries were keeping up the pressure even though their economies weren't in such good shape themselves. And that the nation's political structure was all snarled up, with the old parties extinct and the new ones split into minority blocs. Yet it had always seemed to him and to everyone he knew that things would settle down after a while. These people seemed to be taking a deliberately pessimistic view. A revolution? An end to the present constitution?

Janet offered him a cigarette. He took it, nodding his thanks, and flipped the ignition cap. They sat down on the bench together. Her warm thigh pressed against his. Jack was on the far side of her, looking more and more annoyed. Barrett found himself thinking that this Janet wouldn't be so bad-looking if she lost twenty pounds, got herself a decent brassiere, washed her face more often, put some makeup on…and then he smiled at his own easy acceptance. At first glance she had seemed to be a pig, but he had begun to edit that opinion already.

Sitting quietly in a corner of the room, he tried to follow the sense of the meeting.

The focal points were Hawksbill and his hecklers.

Pleyel, supposedly the leader of the group, remained to the side. Yet Barrett noticed that whenever the talk got too seriously astray, Pleyel cut in and rescued things. The man had the art of leading without seeming to lead, and Barrett was impressed.

Hawksbill Station

He was not impressed at all with the rest of what was going on, though.

Everyone here seemed fundamentally sure that the country was in a bad way, and fundamentally agreed that Something Ought To Be Done About It. But beyond that point all was in haze and chaos. They couldn't even agree on the text of a manifesto to be distributed outside the White House, let alone on a program for rescuing the constitution. These people seemed as fragmented as a high school chess club, and about as capable of exerting political force. Did Bernstein expect him to take this group seriously? What was their goal? What were their methods? Politically naïve he might be, but he was at least able to assess this committee of dedicated revolutionaries and find them wanting.

The talk droned on for nearly two hours.

Sometimes it grew passionate; mostly it was dull, all dialectics and hollow theory. Barrett noticed that Jack Bernstein, who surely was the youngest in the group, talked longest and loudest, shooting off cascades of verbal fireworks. Jack seemed in his element here. But all the talk came to very little. Barrett was taken by Pleyel's obvious dedication to his cause, by Hawksbill's obvious penetration of mind, and by Jack's obvious love for fiery rhetoric, but he was convinced that he had wasted his time by coming here.

Toward eleven, Janet said, "Where do you live?"

"Brooklyn. You know where Prospect Park is?"

"I'm from the Bronx. You work?"

"School."

"Oh. Yes. Right. You're in Jack's class." She seemed be measuring him. "Does that mean you're the same age he is?"

"Sixteen, yes."

"You look a lot older, Jim."

"You're not the first to say that."

"Maybe we could get together sometime," she said. "I mean, for nonrevolutionary purposes. I'd like to know you better."

"Sure," he said. "Fine idea."

Very quickly, he found himself arranging a date. He rationalized it by telling himself that it was the decent thing to do, letting this fat, homely girl enjoy a little glamour once in her life. No doubt she'd be an easy make. It did not occur to him then that he was casually disemboweling Jack Bernstein by picking up Janet this way, but later, when he thought about it, he decided that he had done nothing wrong. Jack had nagged him into coming here, promising him that he'd meet girls, and was it his fault that the promise had been fulfilled?

On the train back to Brooklyn that night Jack was taut and cheerless. "It was a dull meeting," he said. "They aren't all that bad."

"Perhaps not."

"Sometimes a few of them get carried away with dialectics. But the cause is a good one."

"Yes," Barrett agreed. "I suppose."

He did not then plan ever to attend another meeting. But he was wrong about that, as he would prove to be wrong about so many other things in those years. Barrett did not realize then that the pattern of his adult life had been fixed in that drafty basement room, or that he had involved himself in a binding commitment, or that he had begun a lasting love affair, or that he had been face to face with his nemesis that evening. Nor did he imagine that he had transformed a friend into a savage, vindictive enemy who would one day hurl him to a strange fate.

On the evening of Lew Hahn's arrival, as on every evening, the men of Hawksbill Station gathered in the main building for dinner and recreation. It was not mandatory—very little was, here—and some men usually chose to eat alone. But tonight nearly everyone who was in full possession of his faculties showed up, because this was one of the infrequent occasions when a newcomer was on hand, available to be questioned about events Up Front in the world of mankind.

Hahn looked uneasy about his sudden notoriety. He seemed to be basically a shy man, unwilling to accept all the attention now being thrust upon him. There he sat in the middle of the group of exiles, while men who were twenty and thirty years his senior crowded in on him with their questions. It was obvious that he wasn't enjoying the session.

Sitting to one side, Barrett took little part in the talk. His curiosity about the ideological shifts of the world Up Front had ebbed a long time ago. It was an effort for him to recall that he had once been furiously concerned about concepts like syndicalism and the dictatorship of the proletariat and the guaranteed annual wage. When he was sixteen, and Jack Bernstein was dragging him to cell meetings, he had hardly cared about such things. But the virus of revolution had infected him, and when he was twenty-six and even when he was thirty-six he had still been so deeply involved in burning issues that he had been willing to risk imprisonment and exile over them. Now he had come full circle again, back to the political apathy of his adolescence.

It was not that his concern for the sufferings of humanity had waned—merely the degree of his involvement in the political difficulties of the twenty-first century. After two decades at Hawksbill Station, Up Front had become misty and faint to Jim Barrett, and his energies centered around the crises and challenges of what he had come to think of as "his own" time—the Late Cambrian.

So he listened, but more with an ear for what the talk revealed about Lew Hahn than for what it might reveal about current events Up Front. And what it revealed about Lew Hahn was mainly a matter of what was not revealed.

Hahn didn't say much at all. He seemed to be feinting and evading.

Charley Norton wanted to know, "Is there any sign of a weakening of the phony conservatism yet? I mean, they've been promising the end of big government for thirty years, and it gets bigger all the time. When does the dismantling process begin, anyway?"

Hahn moved restlessly in his chair. "They still promise. As soon as conditions become stabilized—"

"Which happens when?"

"I don't know. I suppose they're just making fancy words."

"What about the Martian Commune?" demanded Sid Hutchett. "Have they been infiltrating agents onto Earth?"

"I couldn't really say," Hahn murmured. "We don't hear much news about Mars."

"How about the Gross Global Product?" Mel Rudiger wanted to know. "What's its curve? Still holding level, or has it started to drop?"

Hahn tugged thoughtfully at his ear. "I think it's slowly edging down. Yes, down."

"But where does the index stand?" Rudiger asked. "The last figures we had, for '25, it was at 909. But in four years' time—"

"It might be something like 875 now," said Hahn. "I'm not really sure."

It struck Barrett as a little odd that an economist would be so hazy about the basic economic statistic. Of course, he didn't know how long Hahn had been imprisoned before getting the Hammer. Maybe he simply wasn't up on the recent figures. Barrett held his peace.

Charley Norton jabbed a stubby forefinger forward and said, "Tell me about the basic legal rights of citizens nowadays. Is habeas corpus back? Search warrants? Where do they stand on gathering evidence through data channels without the knowledge of the accused?"

Hahn couldn't tell him.

Rudiger asked about the impact of weather control—whether the supposedly conservative government of liberators, dedicated to upholding the rights of the governed against the abuses of the rulers, was still ramming programmed weather down the mouths of the citizens.

Hahn wasn't sure.

Hahn couldn't rightly say much about the functions of the judiciary, whether it had recovered any of the power stripped from it by the Enabling Act of '18. He didn't have any comments to offer on the tricky subject of population control. He didn't know much about tax rates. In fact, his performance was striking for its lack of hard information.

Charley Norton came over to the silent Barrett and grumbled, "He isn't saying a damned thing that's worth anything. First man we've had here in six months, and he's a clam. He's putting up a good smokescreen. Either he's not telling what he knows, or he doesn't know."

"Maybe he's just not very bright," Barrett suggested.

"What did he do to get sent here, then? He must have had some kind of deep commitment. But it doesn't show, Jim! He's an intelligent kid, but he doesn't seem plugged in to anything that ever mattered to any of us."

Doc Quesada offered a thought. "Suppose this boy isn't a political at all! Suppose they're sending a different kind of prisoner back here now. Ax murderers, or something. A quiet kid who very quietly hauled out a laser and chopped up sixteen people on Sunday morning. Naturally he isn't interested in politics."

"And he's pretending to be an economist," Norton said, "because he doesn't want us to know why he really got sent here. Eh?"

Barrett shook his head. "I doubt that. I think he's just clamming up on us because he's shy or ill at ease. This is his first night here, remember. He's just been kicked out of his own world, and there's no going back, and it hurts. He may have left a wife and baby behind, you know. Or he may simply not give a damn tonight about sitting up there in the midst of you characters and spouting the latest word on abstract philosophical theory, when all he wants to do is go off and cry his eyes out. I say we ought to leave him alone. He'll talk when he feels like talking."

Quesada looked convinced. After a moment, Norton furrowed his forehead and said, "All right. Maybe."

Barrett didn't spread his thoughts about Hahn any further. He let the quizzing of Hahn continue until it petered out of its own accord as the new man proved an unsatisfactory subject. The men began to drift away. A couple of them went into the back room to convert Hahn's vague generalities and evasive comments into the lead story for the next handwritten editions of the Hawksbill Station *Times*. Mel Rudiger stood on a table and shouted out that he was going night-fishing, and four men stepped forward to join him. Charley Norton sought out his customary debating partner, the nihilist Ken Belardi, and reopened, like a festering wound, their discussion of planning versus *laissez faire*, a discussion which by now bored them both to the point of screaming, but which they could not end. The nightly games of stochastic chess began. The loners who had broken their routine by making visits to the main building this evening, simply to see the new man and hear what he had to say, went back to their huts to do whatever it was they did in them alone each night.

Hahn stood apart, fidgeting and uncertain.

Barrett went up to him and drew a quick, uneasy smile. "I guess you didn't really want to be quizzed tonight, eh?" he said.

Hahn looked unhappy. "I'm sorry I couldn't have been more informative. I've been out of circulation awhile, you see."

"Of course. I understand." Barrett had been out of circulation too, for quite a while, before they had decided to send him to Hawksbill Station. Sixteen months in a maximum-security interrogation chamber, and only one visitor during those sixteen months. Jack Bernstein had come to see him quite frequently. Good old Jack. After more than twenty years, Barrett hadn't forgotten a syllable of those conversations. Good. Old. Jack. Or Jacob, as he had liked to be called then. Barrett said, "You were politically active, I take it?"

"Oh, yes," Hahn said. "Of course." He flicked his tongue over his lips. "What's supposed to happen now?"

"Nothing in particular. We don't have organized activities here. It's every man for himself, essentially: the compleat anarchist community. In theory."

"Does the theory hold up?"

"Not very well," Barrett admitted. "But we try to pretend it does, and lean on each other when we need support, all the same. Doc Quesada and I are going out on sick call now. Care to join us?"

"What does it involve?" Hahn asked.

"Visiting some of the worst cases. Aid and comfort for hopeless causes, mostly. It can be grim, but you'll get a panoramic view of Hawksbill Station in a hurry. But if you prefer, you can—"

"I'd like to go."

"Good." Barrett gestured to Quesada, who came across the room to meet them. The three of them left the building. It was a mild, humid night. Thunder sounded in the distance, somewhere out over the Atlantic, and the dark ocean slapped at the obstinate ridge of rock that separated it from the waters of the Inland Sea.

Sick call was a nightly ritual for Barrett, difficult as it was for him since he had hurt his foot. He hadn't missed his rounds in years. Before turning in he stomped through the Station, visiting the goofy ones and the psycho ones and the catatonic ones, tucking them in, wishing them a good night's sleep and a healed mind in the morning. Someone had to show them that someone cared. Barrett did.

Outside, Hahn peered up at the moon. It was nearly full tonight, shining like a burnished coin, its face a pale salmon color and hardly pockmarked at all.

"It looks so different here," Hahn said. "The craters—where are the craters?"

"Most of them haven't been formed yet," Barrett told him. "A billion years is a long time even for the moon. Most of its upheavals are still ahead. We think it may still have an atmosphere, too. That's why it looks pink to us. And if it's got an atmosphere, why, it'll vaporize most of the meteors smashing into it, so there won't be so many craters gouged out. Of course, Up Front hasn't bothered send us much in the way of astronomical equipment. We can only guess." Hahn started to say something. He cut himself off after one blurted syllable. Quesada said, "Don't hold it back. What were you about to suggest?"

Hahn laughed, a self-mocking snort. "That you ought to fly up there and take a look. It struck me as odd that you'd spend all these years theorizing about whether the moon's got an atmosphere, and wouldn't ever once go up there to look. But I forgot."

"It would be useful if we got a commute ship from Up Front," Barrett agreed. "But it hasn't occurred to them to send us one. All we can do is to look and guess. The moon's a popular place in '29, is it?"

"The biggest resort in the System."

"They were just starting to develop it when I came here," Barrett said. "Government personnel only. A rest camp for bureaucrats in the middle of the big military complex up there."

Quesada said, "They opened it to selected nongovernmental elite before my trial. That was in '17, '18."

"Now it's a commercial resort," said Hahn. "I was there on my honeymoon. Leah and I—" He stopped again.

Barrett said hurriedly, "This is Bruce Valdosto's hut. Val's a revolutionary from way back, grew up with me, more or less. He stayed undercover longer. They didn't send him here till '22." As he opened the door, Barrett went on, "He cracked up a few weeks ago, and he's in bad shape. When we go in, Hahn, stand behind us so he doesn't see you. He might be violent with a stranger. Val's unpredictable."

Valdosto was a husky man in his late forties, with swarthy skin, coarse curling black hair, and the broadest shoulders any man had ever had. Sitting down, he looked even burlier than Jim Barrett, which was saying a great deal. But Valdosto had short, stumpy legs, the legs of a man of ordinary stature tacked wantonly to the trunk of a giant, which spoiled the effect completely when he stood up. It would have been possible, while he was still living Up Front, for Valdosto to have a different pair of legs fitted to his body. But in his years Up Front he had totally refused to go in for prosthetics. He wanted his own true legs, gnarled and malproportioned though they were. He believed in living with deformities and adjusting to them.

Right now he was strapped tightly into a webfoam cradle. His domed forehead was flecked with beads of sweat, and his eyes were glittering like mica in the darkness. Valdosto was a very sick man. Once he had been clear-minded enough to throw a sleet-bomb into a meeting of the Council of Syndics, giving a dozen of them a bad case of gamma poisoning, but now he scarcely knew up from down, right from left. It chilled Barrett to see Valdosto come apart this way. Barrett had known him more than thirty years, and hoped that he was not seeing in Valdosto's collapse a prefiguring of his own eventual decay.

The air in the hut was moist, as if a cloud of perspiration hovered below the roof. Barrett leaned over the sick man and said, "How are you, Val?"

"Who's that?"

"Jim. It's a beautiful night tonight, Val. We had some rain, but it's over, and the moon is out. How'd you like to come outside and get some fresh air? It's almost a full moon."

"I've got to rest. The committee meeting tomorrow—"

"It's been postponed."

"But how can it? The Revolution—"

"That's been postponed too. Indefinitely."

The muscles of Valdosto's cheeks writhed. "Are they disbanding the cells?" he asked harshly.

"We don't know yet. We're waiting for orders, and until they come we've just got to sit tight. Come outside, Val. The air will do you good."

"Kill all those bastards, that's the only way," Valdosto muttered. "Who told them they could run the world? A bomb right in their faces—a good little sleet-bomb, a fragmentation job loaded with hard radiation—"

"Easy, Val. There'll be time for throwing bombs later. Let's get you out of the cradle."

Still muttering, Valdosto allowed himself to be unlaced. Quesada and Barrett pulled him to his feet and let him get his balance. He was terribly unsteady, shifting his weight again and again, flexing his massive twisted calves. After a moment Barrett took him by the arm and propelled him through the door of the hut. He caught sight of Hahn standing in the shadows, his face somber with distress.

They all stood together just outside the hut. Barrett pointed to the moon. "There it is. It's got such a lovely color here, eh? Not like the dead thing that shines Up Front. And look, look down there, Val. The sea breaking on the rocky shore. Rudiger's out fishing. I can see his boat by the moonlight."

"Striped bass," said Valdosto. "Sunnies. Maybe he'll catch some sunnies."

"There aren't any sunnies here. They haven't evolved yet." Barrett reached into his pocket and drew out something ridged and hard and glossy, about two inches long. It was the exoskeleton of a small trilobite. He offered it to Valdosto, who shook his head brusquely.

"Don't give me that cockeyed crab."

"It's a trilobite, Val. It's extinct, but so are we. We're living a billion years in our own past."

"You must be crazy," Valdosto said in a calm, low voice that belied his wild-eyed appearance. He took the trilobite from Barrett and hurled it against the rocks. "Cockeyed crab," he muttered. Then he said, "Look, why are we here? Why do we have to keep on waiting? Tomorrow, let's get some stuff and go get them. First we get Bernstein, right? He's the dangerous one. And then the others. One by one, we pick them off, get all the goddam murderers out of the world so it's a safe place again. I'm sick of waiting. I hate it here, Jim. Jim? That's who you are, yeah? Jim—Barrett—"

Quesada shook his head sadly as Valdosto let a trickle of saliva run down his chin. The terrorist folded into a tight crouch, keening softly to himself, pressing his swollen knees against the rock. His hands clutched at the barrenness, searching for and not finding even enough dirt to make a decent handful. Quesada lifted him to his feet, and he and Barrett led the sick man into the hut again. Valdosto did not protest as the medic pressed the snout of the sedative capsule against his arm and activated it. His weary mind, rebelling entirely against the monstrous concept that he had been exiled forever to the inconceivably remote past, welcomed sleep.

When they went outside again, Barrett saw Hahn holding the trilobite on his palm and staring at the strange thing in wonder. Hahn offered it back to him, but Barrett brushed it away.

"Keep it if you like," he said. "There are more where I got that one. Plenty."

They went on.

They found Ned Altman beside his hut, crouching on his knees and patting his hands over the crude, lopsided form of what, from the exaggerated mounds where breasts and hips might be, appeared to be the image of a woman. He stood up smartly when they appeared. Altman was a neat little man with yellow hair and transparent-looking light blue eyes. Unlike anyone else in the Station, he had actually been a government man once, fifteen years ago, before seeing through the myth of syndicalist capitalism and joining one of the underground factions. With his insider's perspective on governmental operations, Altman had been invaluable to the underground, and the government had worked hard to find him and send him here. Eight years at Hawksbill Station had done things to him.

Altman pointed to his earthen golem and said, "I hoped there'd be lightning in the rain today. That'll do it, you know. The breath of life. But there isn't much lightning this time of year, I guess, even when it rains."

"There'll be electrical storms soon," said Barrett.

Altman nodded eagerly. "And lightning will strike her, and she'll get up alive and walk, and then I'll need your help, Doc. I'll need you to give her her shots and trim away some of the rough places."

Quesada forced a smile. "I'll be glad to do it, Ned. But you know the terms."

"Sure. When I'm through with her, you get her. You think I'm a goddam monopolist? Fair is fair. I'll share her. There'll be a waiting list, everything in order of application. Just so you guys don't forget who made her, though. She'll remain mine, whenever I need her." He noticed Hahn for the first time. "Who are you?"

"He's new," Barrett explained. "Lew Hahn. He came this afternoon."

"My name's Ned Altman," said Altman with a courtly, mincing bow. "Formerly in the government service. Hey, you're pretty young, aren't you? Still got the bloom on the cheeks. How's your sex orientation, Lew? Hetero?"

Hahn winced. "I'm afraid so."

"It's okay. You can relax. I wouldn't touch you. I've got a project going, here, and I'm off that kind of stuff. But I just want you to know, if you're hetero, I'll put you on my list. You're young and you've probably got stronger needs than some of us. I won't forget about you, even though you're new here, Lew."

"That's—kind of you," Hahn said.

Altman knelt. He ran his hands delicately over the curves of the clumsy figure, lingering at the tapering conical breasts, shaping them, trying to make them smooth. He might have been caressing a real woman's quivering flesh.

Quesada coughed. "I think you ought to get some rest now, Ned. Maybe there'll be lightning tomorrow."

"Let's hope so."

"Up, now. Up."

Altman did not resist. The doctor took him inside and put him to bed. Barrett and Hahn, remaining outside, surveyed the man's handiwork. Hahn pointed toward the figure's middle.

"He's left out something essential, hasn't he?" he asked. "If he's planning to make love to this girl after he's finished creating her, he'd better—"

"It was there yesterday," said Barrett. "He must be changing orientation again."

Quesada emerged from Altman's hut, looking gloomy. The three of them went on, down the rocky path.

Barrett did not make the complete circuit that night. Ordinarily, he would have gone all the way down to Don Latimer's hut overlooking the sea, for Latimer, with his obsession for finding a psionic gateway through which he could flee Hawksbill Station, was on his list of sick ones who needed special attention. But Barrett had visited Latimer once that day, to introduce him to Hahn, and he didn't think his aching good leg was up to another hike that far so soon.

So after he and Quesada and Hahn had been to all of the easily accessible huts, he called it a night. They visited Gaillard, the man who prayed for alien beings to come from another solar system and rescue him from the loneliness and misery of Hawksbill Station. They had visited Schultz, the man who was trying to break into a parallel universe where everything was as it ought to be in the world, a true Utopia. They had visited McDermott, who had not elaborated any imaginative and fanciful psychosis, but simply lay on his cot sobbing for all his wakeful hours, day after day. Then Barrett said good night to his companions and allowed Quesada to escort Hahn back to his hut without him.

"You're sure you don't want us to walk up with you?" Hahn asked, eying Barrett's crutch.

"No. No, I'm fine. I'll make it."

Hawksbill Station

They walked away. Barrett set out up the rocky slope. He had observed Hahn for half a day, now. And, Barrett realized, he did not know much more about him than when the man had first dropped onto the Anvil. That was odd. But maybe Hahn would open up a little more, after he'd been here awhile and came to realize that these were the only companions he was ever going to have.

Barrett stared up at the salmon moon, and reached into his pocket by habit to finger the little trilobite, before he remembered that he had given it to Hahn. He shuffled into his hut. He wondered how long ago Hahn had taken that lunar honeymoon.

It was a couple of years of pretty hard work before Jim Barrett had succeeded in remaking Janet to the proper image. He was unwilling to push her to change, because he knew right away that that would guarantee failure. He was more subtle about it, borrowing some of Norm Pleyel's tactics of indirect persuasion. They worked. Janet never actually became beautiful, but at least she stopped making a cult out of slovenliness. And the change was considerable. Barrett left home and started living with her when he was nineteen. She was twenty-four, but that didn't really matter.

By then the revolution had come, and the counterrevolution was getting under way.

The upheaval took place right on schedule in late 1984, fulfilling the prediction of Edmond Hawksbill's computer, and putting to rest a political system that had celebrated a very grim bicentennial only eight years earlier. The system had simply ceased to work, and into the vacuum had moved, as expected, those who had long mistrusted the democratic process anyway. The Constitution of 1985 was ostensibly intended as a stopgap document, creating a caretaker government that would supervise the restoration of civil liberties in the United States, then wither away. But stopgap constitutions and caretaker governments sometimes fail to wither when the time for withering comes.

Under the new setup, a sixteen-man Council of Syndics led by a Chancellor performed most of the governmental functions. The names were strange ones to a country long accustomed to Presidents, Senators, Secretaries of State, and the like. It had seemed that those posts were eternal and immutable, and suddenly they were not, for an entire new rhetoric of command had been inserted where the familiar words had been. The change was most emphatic at the highest levels; the bureaucracy and civil service continued much as before as it had to do if the nation were to avoid total disruption. The new rulers were oddly assorted. They could not be called either conservatives or liberals, as those abused terms had been understood throughout most of the twentieth century. They believed in an activist government philosophy, strong on public works and central planning, which might qualify them as Marxists or least as New Deal liberals. But they also believed in the suppression of dissent for the sake of harmonious endeavor, which had never been a New Deal policy, though it was inherent in the Leninist-Stalinist-Maoist perversions of Marxism. On the other hand, they were unreconstructed capitalists, most of them, who insisted on the supremacy of the business sector of the economy and devoted much energy to restoring the business climate of, say, 1885. In foreign affairs they were stark reactionary, isolationist, and anti-Communist to the point of xenophobia. It was, to put it mildly, a highly mixed governmental philosophy.

"It isn't a philosophy at all," Jack Bernstein maintained, hammering fist against palm. "It's just a gang of strong-arm men who happened to find a power vacuum and moved right in. They've got no overriding program of government. They simply do what they think is necessary to perpetuate their own rule and keep things from blowing up again. They grabbed power, and now they improvise from day to day."

"Then they're bound to fall," Janet said mildly. "Without a central vision of government, a power bloc is certain to collapse, in time. They'll make critical mistakes and find that there's no drawing back from the gulf."

"They've been in power for three years, now," Barrett said.

Hawksbill Station

"They don't show any sign of falling. I'd say they're stronger than ever. They're settling in for a thousand years."

"No," Janet insisted. "They're launched on a self-destructive course. It may be another three years, it may be ten, it may be just a matter of months, but they'll fall apart. They don't know what they're doing. You can't paste together McKinley capitalism and Roosevelt socialism and call it syndicalist capitalism and hope to rule a country this size with it. It's inevitable—"

"Who says Roosevelt was a socialist?" someone in the back of the room demanded.

"Side issue," Norman Pleyel warned. "Let's not get into side issues."

"I disagree with Janet," Jack Bernstein said. "I don't think the present government is inherently unstable. As Barrett says, they're stronger than ever. And here we sit talking. We talked right along while they took over, and we've been talking for three more years—"

"We've done more than talk," Barrett cut in.

Bernstein paced the room, hunched, tense, throbbing with inner energy. "Handbills! Petitions! Manifestoes! Calls for a general strike! What good, what good, what good?" At nineteen, Bernstein was no taller than he had been in the year of the great upheaval, but the baby fat was gone from his face. He was gaunt, fleshless, with savage cheekbones and sallow skin against which the pockmarks and scars of his skin malady gleamed like beacons. He affected a straggly mustache now. Under the pressure of events, they were all transforming themselves. Janet had dieted away her blubber, Barrett had let his hair grow long, even the imperturbable Pleyel had grown a wispy beard that he stroked as though it were a talisman. Bernstein glowered at the little group assembled in the apartment that Barrett and Janet shared. "Do you know why this illegal government has been able to sustain itself in power? Two reasons. First, it maintains an immoral secret police network through which it stifles opposition. Second, it maintains firm control over all the media of communication, and thereby perpetuates itself by persuading the citizens that they've got no alternative except three cheers for syndicalism. Do you know what's going to happen in another generation? This nation will be so firmly wedded to syndicalism that it'll settle down with it for the next few centuries!"

"Impossible, Jack," Janet said. "A system of government needs more to sustain itself than a secret police. It—"

"Shut up and let me finish," Bernstein said. There was a snarl in his tone. He rarely troubled to conceal his intense hatred for her any longer. Sparks flew when he was in the same room with her, which in the nature of things was quite often.

"Go ahead, then. Finish."

He drew a deep breath. "This is basically a conservative country," he said. "Always has been. Always will be, The Revolution of 1776 was a conservative revolution in defense of property rights. For the next two hundred years there were no fundamental changes in the political structure here. France had a revolution and six, seven constitutions, Russia had a revolution, Germany and Italy and Austria turned into entirely different countries, even England quietly transformed its whole arrangement, but the United States didn't budge. Oh, I know, there were changes in the electoral law, little touch-up jobs, and the franchise was extended to women and Negroes, and the powers of the President gradually expanded, but all that was within the original framework. And in the schools the kids were taught that there was something sacred about that framework. It was a built-in stability factor: the citizens wanted the system to remain as it was, because it had always been that way, and so on, round and round and round in an eternal circle. This nation *couldn't* change because it didn't have the capacity to change. It had been schooled to hate change. That's why incumbent Presidents always got reelected unless they were absolute dogs. That's why the constitution was amended maybe twenty times in two centuries, tops. That's why whenever a man came along who wanted to change things in a big way, like Henry Wallace, like Goldwater, he got stepped on by the power structure. Did you study the Goldwater election? He was supposed to be a conservative, yes? But he lost, and who fought him the hardest but the conservatives, because they knew he was a radical, and they feared letting a radical in."

"Jack, I think you're exaggerating the—"

"Damn you, *let me finish*." Bernstein's face was red. Sweat rolled down his haggard cheeks. "It was a country conditioned from birth against fundamental change. But eventually the existing government overextended itself and lost control, and the radicals finally did get in, and they changed things so much that everything fell apart and we got the constitutional crisis of 1982–84, followed by the syndicalist takeover. Okay. The takeover was such a trauma that millions of people are still in shock over it. They open up their newspapers and they see that there's no President any more, there's something called a Chancellor, and instead of Congress passing laws there's a Council of Syndics, and they say, what are these crazy names, what country is this, it can't be the good old U.S. of A., can it? But it is. And they're so stunned that they go into retrogression and start thinking they're hedgehogs. Okay. Okay. But the discontinuity has occurred. The old system's been replaced with something new. Kids are still being born. The schools are open, and the teachers are teaching syndicalism, because they'd goddam better well teach syndicalism if they want to keep their jobs. The fifth graders today think of Presidents as dangerous dictators. They smile at the big tridims of Chancellor Arnold every morning. The third-graders don't even know what Presidents were. In ten more years, those kids will be adults. In twenty more years, they'll be running society. They'll have a vested interest in the status quo, the way American adults always have, and to them *the status quo will be the syndicalists.* Don't you see? Don't you see? We're going to lose unless we grab the kids growing up! The syndicalists are getting to them, and educating them to think that syndicalism is true and good and beautiful, and the longer that goes on, the longer it's *going* to go on. It's self-perpetuating. Anybody who wants the old constitution back, or who wants the new constitution amended, is going to look like a dangerous fire-breathing radical, and the syndicalists will be the nice, safe, conservative boys we've always had and always want. At which point everything is over and done with." Bernstein subsided. "Give me a drink, somebody. Fast!"

Pleyel's soft voice cut across the hubbub. "That's well reasoned, Jack. But I'd like to hear some suggestions from you, some plan of positive action."

"I've got plenty of suggestions," Bernstein said. "And they all start by scrapping the existing counterrevolutionary structure we've established. We're using methods appropriate to 1917, or maybe to 1848, and the syndicalists are using 1987 methods and they're killing us. We're still passing out handbills and asking people to sign petitions. And they've got the television stations, the whole damned nexus of communications, all turned into a big propaganda network. And the schools." He held out a hand and ticked off programs on his fingers. "One. Establish electronic means for tying into computer channels and other media to scramble government propaganda. Two. Insert our own counterrevolutionary propaganda wherever possible, not in printed form but on the media. Three. Assemble a cadre of clever ten-year-olds to spread discontent in the fifth grade. And stop snickering! Four. A program of selected assassinations to remove—"

"Hold it," Barrett said. "No assassinations."

"Jim's right," said Pleyel. "Assassination isn't a valid method of political discourse. It's also futile and self-defeating, since it brings new and hungrier leaders to the fore, and makes martyrs out of villains."

"Have it your own way, then. You asked me for suggestions. Kill off ten syndics and we'd be that much closer to freedom, but all right. Five. Formulate a coherent schematic plan for a takeover of the government, at least as clear-cut and well organized as the syndicalist bunch used in '84-'85. That is, find out how many men are needed at the key points, what kind of job it would be to take over the communications media, how we can immobilize the existing leadership, how we can induce the strategic defections among the general staff of the armed forces. The syndicalists used computers to do it. The least we can do is imitate them. Where's our master plan? Suppose Chancellor Arnold resigned tomorrow and said he was turning the country over to the underground, would we be able to form a government, or would we just be a bunch of fragmented cells spouting stale theories?"

Pleyel said, "There is a master plan, Jack. I'm in contact with many groups."

"A computer-programmed plan?" Bernstein pressed.

Pleyel spread his long hands out eloquently in the gesture that meant he would rather not reply.

"It ought to be," Bernstein said. "We've got a man right in our group who's the greatest mathematical genius since Descartes, for God's sake. Hawksbill ought to be plotting templates for us. Where the hell is he, anyway?"

"He doesn't come around much any more," Barrett said.

"I know that. But why not?"

"He's busy, Jack. He's trying to build a time machine, or some such thing."

Bernstein gaped. A burst of bitter laughter, harsh and grinding, erupted from his throat. "A *time machine*? You mean, a literal and actual thing for traveling in time?"

"I think that's what he said," Barrett murmured. "He didn't exactly call it that. I'm no mathematician, and I couldn't follow too much of what he was saying, but—"

"There's a genius for you." Bernstein cracked his knuckles furiously. "A dictatorship in control, the secret police making arrests daily, the situation deteriorating all the time, and he sits around inventing time machines. Where's his common sense? If he wants to be an inventor, why doesn't he invent some way of tossing out the government?"

"Perhaps," Pleyel said gently, "this machine of his can be of some use to us. If, say, we could go back in time to 1980 or 1982, and take corrective action to forestall the causes of the constitutional crisis—"

"You're really serious, aren't you?" Bernstein asked. "While the crisis was going on, we sat on our cans and deplored the sad state of the cosmos, and eventually the thing we all predicted was going to happen happened, and we hadn't done a damned thing to prevent it. And now you talk about taking a crazy machine and going back and changing the past. I'll be damned. I'll be absolutely damned."

"We know much more about the vectors of the revolution, Jack," Pleyel said. "It might just work."

"With judicious assassinations, maybe. But you've already ruled out assassination as a means of political discourse. So what will you do with Hawksbill's machine? Send Barrett back to 1980 to wave banners at rallies? Oh, this is crazy. Pardon me, but you all make me sick. I'm going to go over to Union Square and puke, I think." He stormed out of the room.

"He's unstable," Barrett said to Pleyel. "He was practically frothing at the mouth. I wish he'd quit the movement, you know? One of these days he'll get so disgusted with our stick-in-the-mud ways that he'll denounce us all to the secret police."

"I doubt that, Jim. He's excitable, yes. But he's tremendously brilliant. He spouts ideas of all sorts, some of them worthless, some of them not. We've got to see him through the rough moments, because we need him. You should know that better than any of us, Jim. He's your childhood friend, isn't he?"

Barrett shook his head. "Whatever there was between Jack and me, I don't think it could have been called friendship. And it's been over for years, anyway. He hates my guts. He'd love to see me trampled in the gutter."

The meeting broke up soon afterward. There were the usual motions to investigate the recommendations put forth, and there were the customary assignments to prepare special reports on the findings. And that was that. The members of the counterrevolutionary cell drifted out. At last only Janet and Barrett were left, emptying ashtrays, straightening chairs.

She said, "It was frightening to watch Jack tonight. He seemed to be possessed by demons. He could have talked for hours without running out of words."

"What he said made some sense."

"Some of it, yes, Jim. He's right that we ought to be planning in greater detail, and that we ought to be putting Ed Hawksbill to more use. But it's the way he spoke, not what he said, that scared me. He was like a little demagogue, standing up there, pacing back and forth, spitting out words. I imagine Hitler must have been like that when he was starting out. Napoleon, maybe."

"Well, then, we're lucky Jack's on our side," Barrett said.

"Are you sure he is?"

"Did he sound like a syndicalist tonight?"

Janet gathered a bundle of discarded papers and stuffed them in the disposall. "No, but I could imagine him going over to the other side very easily. As you yourself said, he's unstable. Brilliant but unstable. Given the right sort of motivation, he could very well switch sides. He's restless here. He wants to challenge Pleyel for the leadership of the group, but he's afraid to hurt Norm's feelings, so he's stymied, and someone like Jack doesn't take well to being stymied."

"Besides which, he hates us."

"He only hates you and me," Janet said. "I don't think he's got anything personal against the others."

"Yet."

"He might transfer his hatred of us to the whole group," Janet conceded.

Barrett scowled. "I haven't been able to talk rationally with him in two years. I keep getting this tremendous surge of jealousy from him. Loathing. All because I happened to move in on his girlfriend, without knowing what I was doing. There are other women in the world."

"And I was never his girlfriend," Janet said. "Haven't you realized that by now? I dated him three, four times before you joined the group. But there was nothing serious going between him and me. Nothing."

"You slept with him, didn't you?"

Her cool dark eyes rose and leveled with his. "Once. Because he begged me. It was like sleeping with a dentist's drill. I never let him touch me again. He had no claim on me. Even if he thinks he did, it's his own fault for what happened. He introduced you to me."

"Yes," Barrett said. "He begged me to join the group, he harangued me. He accused me of having no commitment to humanity, and I suppose he was right. I was just a big naïve sixteen-year-old clod who liked sex and beer and bowling, and now and then looked at a newspaper and wondered what the hell all the headlines meant. Well, he set out to awaken my conscience, and he did, and in the course of events I found a girl, and now—"

"Now you're a big naïve nineteen-year-old clod who likes sex and beer and bowling and counterrevolutionary activities."

"Right."

"So to hell with Jack Bernstein," Janet said. "One of these days he'll grow up and stop envying you, and we can start working together to fix up the mess that the world's gotten itself into. Meanwhile we just go along from day to day and do our best. What else is there?"

"I suppose," Barrett said.

He walked to the window and nudged the control. The opaquing faded, and he looked out through the darkness at the street fifteen stories below. Two bottle-green police cars were angle-parked across the street; they had stopped a small blue-and-gold electric runabout, and the police were questioning its driver. From this far up, Barrett couldn't see much, but the man's high-pitched protests of innocence rose to window level. After a moment a third police car arrived. Still protesting, the man was shoved into it and taken away. Barrett opaqued the window again. As it turned gray and clouded, it showed him the reflection of Janet, standing nude behind him, the full globes of her breasts rising and falling expectantly. He turned. She looked immensely better, now that she had taken off that weight, but he couldn't find any delicate way of telling her that without implying that she had been a slob before.

"Come to bed," she said. "Stop staring out windows."

He moved toward her. He was more than two feet taller than she was, and when he stood beside her he felt like a tree above a shrub. His arms enclosed her, and he felt the soft warmth of her against him, and as they sank into the mattress he imagined he could hear Jack Bernstein's reedy, angry voice howling through the night, and he reached for her and pulled her fiercely into a tight embrace.

Rudiger's catch was spread out in front of the main building the next morning when Barrett came up for breakfast. Rudiger had had a good night's fishing, obviously. He usually did. Rudiger went out into the Atlantic three or four nights a week when the weather was good, using the little dinghy that he had cobbled together a few years ago from salvaged packing crates and other miscellaneous materials, and he took with him a team of friends whom he had trained in the deft use of the trawling nets. They generally returned with a good haul of seafood.

It was an irony that Rudiger, the anarchist, the man who profoundly believed in individualism and the abolition of all political institutions, should be so good at leading a team of fishermen. Rudiger didn't care for the concept of teamwork in the abstract. But it was hard to manipulate the nets alone, he had quickly discovered, and he had begun to assemble his little microcosm of a society. Hawksbill Station had many small ironies of that sort. Political theorists, Barrett knew well, tend to swallow their theories when forced back on pragmatic matters of survival.

The prize of the catch was a cephalopod about a dozen feet long—a rigid greenish conical tube out of which some limp orange squid-like tentacles dangled, throbbing fitfully. There was plenty of meat on that one, Barrett thought. Rubbery but good, if you cultivated a taste for it. Dozens of trilobites were arrayed around the cephalopod. They ranged in size from the inch-long kind that went into trilobite cocktails to the three-footers with baroquely involuted exoskeletons. Rudiger fished both for food and for knowledge; evidently these trilobites were discards, representatives of species that he had already studied, or he wouldn't have left them here to go into the food hoppers. His hut was stacked ceiling-high with trilobites, classified and sorted according to genus and species. It kept Rudiger sane to collect and analyze and write about them, and no one here begrudged him his hobby.

Near the heap of trilobites were some clusters of hinged brachiopods, looking like scallops that had gone awry, and a pile of snails. The warm, shallow waters just off the coastal shelf teemed with invertebrate life, in striking contrast to the barren land. Rudiger had also brought in a mound of shiny black seaweed for salads. Barrett hoped that someone would gather all this stuff up and get it into the Station's heat-sink cooler before it spoiled. The bacteria of decay worked a lot slower here than they did Up Front, but a few hours in the mild air would do Rudiger's haul no good. Barrett hobbled into the kitchen and found three men on morning mess duty. They nodded respectfully to him.

"There's food lying by the door," Barrett said. "Rudiger's back, and he dumped a load."

"He could have told somebody, huh?"

"Perhaps there was nobody here to tell when he came by. Will you collect it and get it under refrigeration?"

"Sure, Jim. Sure."

Today Barrett planned to recruit some men for the annual Inland Sea expedition. Traditionally, it was a trek that he always had led himself, but the injury to his foot made it impossible for him even to consider going on the trip this year, or ever again.

Each year, a dozen or so able-bodied men went out on a wide-ranging reconnaissance that took them in a big circular arc, looping northwestward until they reached the Inland Sea, then coming around to the south and back up the strip of land to the Station. One purpose of the trip was to gather any temporal garbage that might have materialized in the vicinity of the Station during the past year. There was no way of knowing how wide a margin of error had been allowed during the early attempts to set the Station up, and the scattershot technique of hurling material into the past had been pretty unreliable.

New stuff was turning up all the time. It had been aimed for Minus One Billion, Two Thousand Oh Five A.D., but didn't arrive until a few decades later. Now, in A.D. Minus One Billion, Two Thousand Twenty-Nine, things were still appearing that had been intended to arrive in the Station's first year of operation. Hawksbill Station needed all the spare equipment it could get, and Barrett didn't miss a chance to round up any of the debris from the future.

There was another and subtler reason for making the Inland Sea expeditions, though. They served as a focus for the year, an annual ritual, something to peg a custom to. The expedition was the local rite of spring. The dozen strongest men, going on foot to the distant rock-rimmed shores of the tepid sea that drowned the heart of North America, were performing the closest thing Hawksbill Station had to a religious function, although they did nothing more mystical when they reached the Inland Sea than to net a few trilobites and eat them.

The trip meant more to Barrett himself than he had ever suspected, also. He realized that now, when he was unable to go. He had led every such expedition for twenty years. Across the changeless, monotonous scenery, beyond the slippery slopes, down to the sea, eyes ranging the horizon at all times for the tell-tale signs of temporal garbage. Trilobite stew cooked over midnight fires far from the dreary huts of Hawksbill Station. A rainbow lancing into the sea somewhere over what was to be Ohio. The stunning crackle of distant lightning, the tang of ozone in the nostrils, the rewarding sensation of aching muscles at the end of a day's march. The pilgrimage was the pivot on which the year turned, for Barrett. And to see the grayish-green waters of the Inland Sea come into view was strangely like coming home to him.

But last year at the edge of the sea Barrett had gone scrabbling over boulders loosened by the tireless action of the waves, venturing into risky territory for no rational reason that he could name, and his aging muscles had betrayed him. Often at night he woke sweating and trembling to escape from the dream in which he relived that ugly moment: slipping and sliding, clawing at the rocks, a mass of stone dislodged from somewhere and crashing down with improbably agonizing impact against his foot, pinning him, crushing him.

He could not forget that sound of grinding bones.

Nor was he likely to lose the memory of the homeward march, across hundreds of miles of bare rock under a huge sun, his bulky body slung between the bowed forms of his companions. He had never been a burden to anyone before. "Leave me behind," he had said, not really meaning it, and they knew he was making only a formalized gesture of apology for troubling them, and they said, "Don't be a fool," and hauled him onward. But they worked hard to carry him along and in the moments when the pain allowed him to think clearly, he felt guilty about troubling them in this way. He was so big. If any of the others had suffered such an accident, it would not have been such a chore to transport him. But he was the biggest one.

Barrett thought he would have to lose the foot. But Quesada had spared him from the amputation. The foot would stay, though Barrett would not be able to touch it to the ground and put weight on it, not now or ever again. It might have been simpler to have the dead appendage sliced off; Quesada had vetoed that, though.

"Who knows," he had said, "someday they might send us a transplant kit. I can't rebuild a leg that's been amputated. Once we cut it off, all I can do is give you a prosthetic, and I don't have any prosthetics here."

So Barrett had kept his crushed foot. But he had never been quite the same since the accident. More than blood had leaked from him as he lay on the glistening rocks beside the Inland Sea. And now someone else would have to lead this year's march.

Who would it be, he wondered?

Quesada was the likeliest choice. Next to Barrett, he was the strongest man here, in all the ways that it was important to be strong. But Quesada couldn't be spared from his responsibilities at the Station. It might be handy to have a medic along on the trip, but it was vital to have one here.

After some reflection Barrett put down Charley Norton as the leader of the expedition. Norton was bouncy and talkative and got worked up too easily, but he was basically a sensible man capable of commanding respect. Barrett added Ken Belardi to the list—someone trekking from nowhere to nowhere. Let them go on debating—an endless ballet of fixed postures.

Rudiger? Rudiger had been a tower of strength on the journey last year after Barrett had been injured. He had taken charge beautifully while the others dithered around and gaped at the sight of their fallen, battered leader. Barrett didn't particularly want to let Rudiger leave the Station so long, though. He needed able men for the expedition, true, but he didn't care to strip the home base down to a population of invalids, crackpots, and psychotics.

So Rudiger stayed behind. Barrett put two members of his fishing team on the list, Dave Burch and Mort Kasten. Then he added the names of Sid Hutchett and Arny Jean-Claude.

Barrett thought about putting Don Latimer in the group. Latimer was coming to be something of a borderline mental case, but he was rational enough except when he lapsed into his psionic meditations, and he'd pull his own weight on the expedition. On the other hand, Latimer was Lew Hahn's bunkmate, and Barrett wanted Latimer around to observe Hahn at close range. He toyed with the idea of sending both of them out, but nixed it. Hahn was still an unknown quantity. It was too risky to let him go with the Inland Sea party this year. Probably he'd be in next year's group, though. It would be foolish not to take advantage of Hahn's youthful vigor. Let him get to know the ropes, and he'd be an ideal expedition leader for years to come.

Finally Barrett had chosen a dozen men. A dozen would be enough. He chalked their names on the slate in front of the mess hall, and went inside to find Charley Norton.

Norton was sitting alone, breakfasting. Barrett eased himself into the bench opposite him, going through the complex series of motions that constituted his way of sitting down without letting go of his crutch.

"You pick the men?" Norton asked.

Barrett nodded. "The list's posted outside."

"Am I going?"

"You're in command."

Norton looked flattered. "That sounds strange, Jim. I mean, for anyone else but you to be in command—"

"I'm not making the trip this year, Charley."

"It takes some getting used to. Who's going?"

"Hutchett. Belardi. Burch. Kasten. Jean-Claude. And some others."

"Rudiger?"

"No, not Rudiger. Not Quesada either, Charley. I need them here."

"All right, Jim. You have any special instructions for us?"

"Just come back in one piece, is all I ask." Barrett picked up a water flask and cupped it in his huge hands. "Maybe we should call it off, this time. We don't have all that many able-bodied men."

Norton's eyes flashed. "What are you saying, Jim? Call off the trip?"

"Why not? We know what's between here and the sea: nothing."

"But the salvage—"

"It can wait. We're not running short of material right the moment."

"Jim, I've never heard you talk this way before. You've always been big on the trip. The highlight of the year, you said. And now—"

"I'm not going on this one, Charley."

Norton was silent a moment, but his eyes did not leave Barrett's. Then he said, "All right, you're not going. I know how that must hurt you. But there are other men. They *need* the trip. Just because you can't go, you've no right to say we ought to call it off as pointless. It isn't pointless."

"I'm sorry, Charley," Barrett said heavily. "I didn't mean any of that. Of course there'll be a trip. I was just running off at the mouth again."

"It must be tough for you, Jim."

"It is. But not *that* tough. You have any ideas of the route you'll take?"

"Northwest route out, I guess. That's the usual distribution line for the odd-year garbage, isn't it? And then down to the Inland Sea. We'll follow the shoreline for, oh, a hundred miles, I guess. And come home via the lower path."

"Good enough," Barrett said. In the eye of his mind he saw the rippling surface of the shallow sea, stretching off to the distant western land zone. Year after year he had come to the edge of that sea and peered off toward the place where the Midwest would someday rise above the water. Each year, he had dreamed of a voyage across the continental heart to the other side. But he had never found the time to organize such a voyage. And now it was too late...too late....

We would never have found anything much over there, anyway, Barrett told himself. Just more of the same. Rock, seaweed, trilobites. But it might have been worth it...to see the sun drop into the Pacific one last time....

Norton said, "I'll get the men together after breakfast. We'll be on our way fast."

"Right. Good luck, Charley."

"We'll make out."

Barrett clapped Norton on the shoulder, a gesture that struck him instantly as stagy and false, and went out. It was odd and more than odd to know that he'd have to stay home while the others went. It was an admission that he was beginning to abdicate after running this place so long. He was still king of Hawksbill Station, but the throne was getting rickety beneath him. A crippled old man was what he was now, hobbling around snooping here and there. Whether he liked to admit it to himself or not, that was the story. It was something he'd have to come to terms with soon.

After breakfast, the men chosen for the Inland Sea expedition gathered to select their gear and plan the logistics of their route. Barrett carefully kept away from the meeting. This was Charley Norton's show, now. He'd made eight or ten trips, and he would know what to do without getting any hints from the previous management. Barrett didn't want to interfere, to seem to be vicariously running things even now.

But some masochistic compulsion in him drove him to make a trek of his own. If he couldn't see the western waters this year, the least he could do was pay a visit to the Atlantic, in his own backyard. Barrett stopped off in the infirmary. Hansen, one of the orderlies, came out—a bald, cheerful man of about seventy who had been part of the California anarchist bunch. The only training Hansen had ever had was as a low-grade computer technician for a freight railroad, but he had shown some knack for medicine, and these days he was Quesada's chief helper. He flashed his usual dazzling smile.

"Is Quesada around?" Barrett asked.

"No, sorry. Doc's gone over to talk about the trip. He's giving them some medical pointers. But if it's important, I could get him for you—"

"Don't," Barrett said. "I just wanted to check with him on our drug inventory. It can wait. You mind if I take a quick look at the supplies?"

"Whatever you'd like." Hansen stepped back, ushering Barrett into the supply room. The barricade was down for the morning. Since there was no way of locking the drugstore, Barrett and Quesada had devised an intricate barricade that was guaranteed to set off a ton of noise if anyone meddled with it. Whenever the infirmary was left unattended, the barricade had to be put in place. An intruder would inevitably upset the whole thing, creating enough loud bangs and crashes to summon a warder. That was the only way they had been able to guard against unauthorized raiding of their drug supplies by moody residents. They couldn't afford wasting their precious and irreplaceable drugs on would-be suicides, Barrett reasoned. If a man wanted to kill himself, let him jump into the sea; at least that didn't impose a hardship on the other residents of the Station.

Barrett looked down the rows of drugs. It was an unbalanced assortment, dependent as they were on the random largesse from Up Front. Right now they were heavy on tranquilizers and digestive aids, low on painkillers and anti-infectants. Which made Barrett feel even guiltier about what he was going to do. The man who had imposed the rules on drug-stealing was now going to take advantage of his privileged position and help himself to a drug. So much for morality, he thought. But he had known men to betray much more sacred trusts, in his time. And he needed the drug, and he didn't want to get into a lengthy fuss with Quesada over his use of it. This was simplest. Wrong, but simplest. He waited until Hansen's back was turned. Then he slipped one hand into the cabinet and palmed a slim gray tube of neural depressant, pocketing it quickly.

"Everything seems in order," he said to Hansen, as he left the infirmary. "Tell Quesada I'll stop by and talk to him later."

He was using the neural depressant more and more often nowadays to soothe his legs. Quesada didn't like it. He said, not quite in those words, that Barrett was developing an addiction. Well, to hell with Quesada. Let Doc try to walk around these paths on a foot like this, and he'll start reaching for the drugs too, Barrett told himself.

Scrambling along the eastern trail, Barrett halted when he was a few hundred yards from the main building. He stepped behind a low hump of rock, dropped his trousers, and quickly gave each

Hawksbill Station

thigh a jolt of the drug, first the good leg, then the gimpy one. That would numb the muscles just enough so that he'd be able to take an extended hike without feeling the fire of fatigue in his protesting joints. He'd pay for it, he knew, eight hours from now, when the depressant wore off and the full impact of his exertion hit him like a million daggers. But he was willing to accept that price.

The road to the sea was a long, lonely one. Hawksbill Station was perched on the eastern rim of Appalachia, more than eight hundred feet above sea level. During the first half dozen years here, the men of the Station had reached the ocean by a suicidal route across sheer rock faces. Barrett had incited a project to carve a path. It had taken ten years to do the job, but now wide, safe steps descended to the Atlantic. Chopping those steps out of the living rock had kept a lot of men busy for a long time—too busy to worry about loved ones Up Front, or to slip into the insanity that was so easily entered here. Barrett regretted that he couldn't conceive some comparable works project to occupy the idle men nowadays.

The steps formed a succession of shallow platforms that switch-backed to the edge of the water. Even for a healthy man it was a strenuous walk. For Barrett in his present condition it was an ordeal. It took him close to two hours to descend a distance that normally could be traversed in less than a quarter of that time.

When he reached the bottom of the path, he sank down exhausted on a flat rock licked by the waves, and dropped his crutch. The fingers of his left hand were cramped and gnarled from gripping the crutch, and his entire body was bathed in sweat.

The water of the ocean looked gray and somehow oily. Barrett could not explain the prevailing colorlessness of the Late Cambrian world, with its somber sky and somber land and somber sea, but his heart quietly ached for a glimpse of green vegetation again. He missed chlorophyll. The dark wavelets lapped against his rock, pushing a mass of floating black seaweed back and forth.

The sea stretched to infinity. He didn't have the faintest idea how much of Europe, if any, might be above water in this particular epoch. At the best of times most of the planet was submerged; here, only a few hundred million years after the white-hot rocks of the first land had pushed into view, it was likely that not much was above water on Earth except a strip of territory here and there.

Had the Himalayas been born yet? The Rockies? The Andes? Barrett knew the approximate outlines of Late Cambrian North America, but the rest was a mystery. Blanks in knowledge were not easy to fill when the only link with Up Front was by one-way transport; Hawksbill Station had to rely on the unpredictable assortment of reading matter that came back in time, and it was furiously frustrating to lack information that any college geology text could supply.

As he watched, a big trilobite unexpectedly came scuttering up out of the water. It was the spike-tailed kind, about a yard long, with a glossy eggplant-purple shell and a bristling arrangement of slender yellow spines along the margins. There seemed to be a lot of legs underneath. The trilobite crawled up on the shore—no sand, no beach, just a shelf of rock—and advanced landward until it was eight or ten feet from the waves.

Good for you, Barrett thought. Maybe you're the first one who ever came out on land to see what it was like. The pioneer. The trail blazer.

It occurred to him that this adventurous trilobite might very well be the ancestor of all the land-dwelling creatures of the eons to come. The thought was biological nonsense, and Barrett knew it. But his weary mind conjured a picture of a long evolutionary procession, with fish and amphibians and reptiles and mammals and man all stemming in unbroken sequence from this grotesque armored thing that moved in uncertain circles near his feet.

And if I were to step on you, he thought?

A quick motion—the sound of crunching chitin—the wild scrabbling of a host of little legs—

—and the whole chain of life snapped right in its first link.

Evolution undone. No land creatures ever to emerge. With the brutal descent of that heavy foot all the future would instantly change, and there would never have been a human race, no Hawksbill Station, no James Edward Barrett (1968–?). In a single instant he would have both revenge on those who had condemned him to live out his days in this barren place, and release from his sentence.

He did nothing. The trilobite completed its slow perambulation of the shoreline rocks and scuttered back into the sea unharmed.

Then the soft voice of Don Latimer said, "I saw you sitting alone down here, Jim. Do you mind if I join you?"

The intrusion jolted Barrett. He swung around rapidly, sucking in his stomach in surprise. Latimer had come down from his hilltop hut so quietly that Barrett hadn't heard him approaching. But he recovered and grinned and beckoned Latimer to an adjoining rock.

"You fishing?" Latimer asked.

"Just sitting. An old man sunning himself."

"You took a hike way the devil down here just to sun yourself?" Latimer laughed. "Come off it. You're trying to get away from it all, and you probably wish I hadn't disturbed you, but you were too polite to tell me to go away. I'm sorry. I'll leave if—"

"That's not so. Stay here. Talk to me, Don."

"You can give it to me straight if you'd prefer to be left in peace."

"I don't prefer to be left in peace," said Barrett. "And I wanted to see you, anyway. How are you getting along with your new bunkmate Hahn?"

Latimer's high forehead corrugated into a complex frown. "It's been strange," he said. "That's one reason I came down here to talk to you, when I saw you." He leaned forward and peered searchingly into Barrett's eyes. "Jim, tell me straight: do you think I'm a madman?"

"Why should I think that?"

"The esping business. My attempt to break through to another realm of consciousness. I know you're tough-minded and skeptical of anything you can't grab hold of and measure and squeeze. You probably think it's all a lot of nonsense, this extrasensory stuff."

Barrett shrugged and said, "If you want the blunt truth, I do. I don't have the remotest belief that you're going to get us anywhere, Don. Call me a materialist if you like, and I admit that I haven't done much homework on the subject, but it all seems like pure black magic to me, and I've never known magic to work worth a damn. I think it's a complete waste of time and energy for you to sit there for hours trying to harness your psionic powers, or whatever it is you think you're doing. But no, I don't think you're crazy. I think you're entitled to your obsession and that you're going about a basically futile thing in a reasonably levelheaded way. Fair enough?"

"More than fair. I don't ask you to put any credence at all in the assumptions of my research—but I don't want you to write me off as a total lunatic because I'm trying to find a psionic escape hatch from this place. It's important that you regard me as a sane man, or else what I want to tell you about Hahn won't be valid to you."

"I don't see the connection."

"It's this," said Latimer. "On the basis of one evening's acquaintance, I've formed an opinion about Hahn. It's the kind of an opinion that might be formed by any garden-variety paranoid, and if you think I'm nuts you're likely to discount my ideas about Hahn. So I want to establish that you think I'm sane before I try to communicate my feelings about him."

"I don't think you're nuts. What's your idea?"

"That he's spying on us."

Barrett had to work hard to keep from emitting the savage guffaw that he knew would shatter Latimer's fragile self-esteem. "Spying?" he said casually. "Don, you can't mean that. How can anyone spy here? I mean, even if we had a spy, how could he report his findings to anyone?"

"I don't know," Latimer said. "But he asked me a trillion questions last night. About you, about Quesada, about some of the sick men like Valdosto. He wanted to know everything."

"So? It's the normal curiosity of a new man trying to relate to his environment."

"Jim, he was taking notes. I saw him after he thought I was asleep. He sat up for two hours writing all my answers down in a little book."

Barrett frowned. "Maybe Hahn's going to write a novel about us."

"I'm serious," Latimer said. His hand traveled tensely to his ear. "Questions—notes. And he's shifty. Just try to get him to talk about himself!"

"I did. I didn't learn much."

"Do you know why he's been sent here?"

"No."

"Neither do I," said Latimer. "Political crimes, he told me, but he was vague as hell about them. He hardly seemed to know what the present government was up to, let alone what his own opinions were toward it. I don't detect any passionate philosophical convictions in Mr. Hahn. And you know as well as I do that Hawksbill Station is the refuse heap for revolutionaries and agitators and subversives and all sorts of similar trash, but that we've never had any other kind of prisoner here."

Barrett said coolly, "I agree that Hahn's a puzzle. But who could he possibly be spying for? He's got no way to file a report, if he's a government agent. He's stranded here for keeps, same as the rest of us."

"Maybe he was sent to keep an eye on us—to make sure we aren't cooking up some way to escape. Maybe he's a volunteer who willingly gave up his life in the twenty-first century so he could come among us and thwart anything we might be hatching. The dedicated sort, a willing martyr to society. You know the type, I think."

"Yes, but—"

"Perhaps they're afraid we've invented forward time travel. Or that we've become a threat to the ordained sequence of the timelines. Anything. So Hahn comes among us to scout around and block any dangerous activity before it turns into something really troublesome. For example, like my own psionic research, Jim."

Barrett felt a cold twinge of alarm. He saw how close to paranoia Latimer was hewing, now: in half a dozen quiet sentences, Latimer had journeyed from the rational expression of some justifiable suspicions to the fretful fear that the men from Up Front were going to take steps to choke off the escape route that he was so close to perfecting.

He kept his voice level as he told Latimer, "I don't think you need to worry, Don. Hahn seems like an odd one, but he's not here to make trouble for us. The fellows Up Front have already made all the trouble for us they ever will. Unless they've repealed the

Hawksbill Equations, there's no chance that we can bother anybody ever again, so why would they waste a man spying on us?"

"Would you keep an eye on him, anyway?" Latimer asked.

"You know I will. And don't hesitate to let me know if Hahn does anything else out of the ordinary. You're in a better spot to notice than anyone else."

"I'll be watching, Jim. We can't tolerate any spies from Up Front among us." Latimer got to his feet and gave Barrett a pleasant smile that almost seemed to cancel the paranoia. "I'll let you get back to your sunning now," he said.

Latimer went up the path. Barrett eyed him until he was close to the top, only a faint dot against the stony backdrop. After a long while Barrett seized his crutch and levered himself to a standing position. He stood staring down at the surf, dipping the tip of the crutch into the water to send a couple of little crawling things scurrying away. At length he turned and began the long, slow climb back to the Station.

Barrett wasn't sure of the exact point in time when it happened, but somewhere along the way they had all stopped thinking of themselves as counterrevolutionaries, and now regarded themselves as revolutionaries in their own right. The semantic shift had occurred early in the 1990s, happening in a gradual, processless manner. For the first few years after the upheavals of 1984–85, the syndicalists had been the revolutionaries, and rightly so, since they had overthrown an establishment more than two centuries old. Thus the conspirators of the antisyndicalist underground were of necessity counterrevolutionaries. But after a while the syndicalist revolution had institutionalized itself. It had ceased to be a revolution and had become an establishment itself.

So Barrett was a revolutionary, now. And the goal of the underground had subtly capitalized itself into The Revolution. The Revolution was coming any day now, any month, any year.... All it took was further planning, and then The Word would be given, and all over the nation the revolutionaries would rise....

He did not question the truth of those propositions. Not yet. He did his work, and went through the round of days, and waited hopefully for the downfall of the entrenched and ever more confident syndicalists.

The Revolution had become Barrett's whole career. He had slipped easily and without regret out of college without finishing: the college had been syndicalist-dominated, anyway, and the daily dollop of propaganda offended him. Then he had come to Pleyel, and Pleyel had given him a job. Officially, Pleyel ran an employment agency; at least, that was the cover story. In a small office far downtown in Manhattan he screened applicants for the underground while managing also to operate legitimately part of the time. Janet was his secretary; Hawksbill dropped in now and then to program the agency's computer; Barrett was taken on as assistant manager. His salary was small, but it allowed him to keep eating regularly and to pay the rent on the cramped apartment he shared with Janet. Thirty hours a week he dealt with innocent seeming activities of the employment agency, freeing Pleyel for more delicate work in other quarters.

Barrett actually enjoyed the cover job. It gave him a chance to deal with people, and he liked that. All sorts of unemployed New Yorkers drifted through the office, some of them radicals in search of an underground, others merely hunting for jobs, and Barrett did what he could for them. They didn't realize that he was barely out of his teens, and some of them came to look upon him as a source of all their guidance and direction. That made him a little uncomfortable, but he helped them where he could.

The work of the underground went on steadily during those years.

That phrase, Barrett knew, was a high-order abstraction nearly empty of content: "the work of the underground." What did it amount to, this work? Endless planning for an often-postponed day of uprising. Transcontinental telephone calls conducted entirely in oblique jargon that decoded out into subversive scheming. The surreptitious publication of anti-syndicalist propaganda. The daring distribution of undoctored history books. The organization of protest meetings. An infinite series of small actions, amounting in the long run to very little indeed. But Barrett, in the full flush of his youthful enthusiasm, was willing to be patient. One day all the scattered threads would come together, he told himself. One day The Revolution would arrive.

On behalf of the movement he traveled all over the country. The economy had revived under the syndicalists, and the airports once again were busy places; Barrett got to know them well. He spent most of the summer of 1991 in Albuquerque, New Mexico, working with a group of revolutionaries who in the old order of things would have been called extremist right-wingers. Barrett found most of their philosophy unpalatable, but they hated the syndicalists as much as he did, and in their separate ways he and the New Mexico group shared a love for the Revolution of 1776 and all the symbolism that went with it. He came close to being arrested a few times that summer.

In the winter of 1991–92 he commuted weekly to Oregon to coordinate an outfit in Portland that was setting up a northwest propaganda office. The two-hour trip became wearily familiar after a while, but Barrett kept to his routine, dutifully huddling with the Portland people on Wednesday nights, then hustling back to New York. The following spring he worked mostly in New Orleans, and that summer he was in St. Louis. Pleyel kept moving the pawns about. The theory was that you had to stay at least three jumps ahead of the police agents.

Actually, there were few arrests of any importance. The syndicalists had ceased to take the underground seriously, and they picked up a leader every now and then purely to maintain form. Generally, the revolutionaries were regarded as harmless cranks and were allowed to go through the motions of conspiracy, so long as they didn't venture into sabotage or assassination. Who could object to syndicalist rule, after all? The country was thriving. Most people were working regularly again. Taxes were low. The interrupted flow of technological wonders was no longer interrupted, and each year produced its new marvel: weather conditioning, color telephone picture transmission, tridim video, organ transplants, instafax newspapers, and more. Why gripe? Had things ever been any better under the old system? There was even talk of the restoration of the two-party system by the year 2000. Free elections had come back into vogue in 1990, though of course the Council of Syndics exercised a right of veto over the choice of candidates. No one talked anymore of the "stopgap" nature of the Constitution of 1985, because that constitution looked like it was on its way to becoming a permanent feature, but in small ways the government was amending the constitution to bring it more in line with past national traditions.

Thus the revolutionaries were thwarted at the root. Jack Bernstein's gloomy prediction was coming true: syndicalists were turning into the familiar, beloved traditional incumbent government, and the vast center of the nation had come to accept them as though they'd always been there. There were fewer and fewer malcontents. Who wanted to join an underground movement when, if everybody was patient, the present governor would transform itself into an even more benevolent institution? Only the embittered, the incurably angry, dedicated destroyers, cared to involve themselves in revolutionary activities. By late 1993, it looked as though the underground and not the syndicalist government would wither away as America's basic conservatism reasserted itself even in these transformed conditions.

But the last month of 1993 brought a transfer of power within the government. Chancellor Arnold, who had ruled the country for all eight years under the new constitution, died of a sudden aortal aneurysm. He had been only forty-nine years old, and there was talk that he had been murdered; but in any event Arnold was gone, and after a brief internal crisis the Syndics thrust forward one of their number as the new Chancellor. Thomas Dantell of Ohio took command, and there was a general tightening of security up and down the line. Dantell's responsibility as a Syndic had been to run the national police: and now, with the top cop in office, the genial tolerance of the underground movements abruptly ended. There were arrests.

"We may have to disband for a while," Pleyel said dismally in the snowy spring of '94. "They're coming too close. We've had seven critical arrests so far, and they're moving toward our leadership cadre now."

"If we disband," said Barrett, "we'll never get the movement organized again."

"Better to lay low now and come out of hiding in six months or a year," Pleyel argued, "than to have everyone go to jail on twenty-year sedition terms."

They fought the matter out in a formal session of the underground. Pleyel lost. He took his defeat mildly, and pledged to keep working until the police dragged him away. But the episode demonstrated how Barrett was moving toward an ever more important position in the group. Pleyel was still the leader, but he seemed too remote, too unworldly. In matters of real crisis everyone turned to Barrett.

Barrett was twenty-six years old, now, and he towered over the others literally and figuratively. Enormous, powerful, tireless, he drew on hidden reserves of strength in the most direct way: he had broken up one nasty street incident singlehanded, when a dozen young toughs attacked three girls distributing revolutionary leaflets. Barrett had happened along to find the leaflets fluttering through the air and the girls on the verge of suffering a nonideological rape, and he had scattered live bodies in all directions, like Samson among the Philistines. But under ordinary circumstances he tried to restrain himself.

His relationship with Janet lasted nearly a decade; he had lived with her for seven years. Neither of them had ever considered legalizing the arrangement, but in most ways it amounted to a marriage. They reserved the right to have separate adventures, and occasionally they did. Janet had set the trend in that, but Barrett had taken advantage of his freedom when the opportunity presented itself. Yet generally they felt themselves bound by a tie deeper than the government's marriage certificate alone could create. So it hurt him deeply when she was arrested one scorching day in the summer of '94.

He was in Boston that day, checking into reports that a Cambridge cell had been infiltrated by government informers. Late in the afternoon he headed for the tube station to return to New

York. The telephone he carried behind his left ear bleeped its signal, and Jack Bernstein's thin voice said, "Where are you now, Jim?"

"On my way home. I'm about to take a tube. What's wrong?"

"Don't take the Forty-second Street tube. Make sure you get off in White Plains. I'll meet you there."

"What's wrong, Jack? What happened?"

"I'll tell you about it when I see you."

"Tell me now."

"It's best if I don't," Bernstein said. "I'll see you in an hour or two."

The contact broke. As he boarded the tube, Barrett tried to reach Bernstein in New York, but got no answer. He called Pleyel, and the line was silent. He dialed his home number, and Janet did not answer. Frightened now, Barrett gave up. He might be making trouble for himself or the others by putting through this call. He tried to wait for the time to elapse, as the tube rammed him at two hundred miles an hour down the Boston-New York corridor. It was very much like Bernstein to call him and bait him this way, sadistically hinting at a dire emergency and then clamming up on the details. Jack always seemed to take a peculiar pleasure in inflicting little tortures of that sort. And he did not grow mellower as he grew older. Barrett left the tube as instructed at the suburban station. He stood at the exit lip for a long moment, staring warily in all directions and reflecting, not for the first time, that a man his size was really too conspicuous to be a successful revolutionary. Then Bernstein appeared and tapped his elbow and said, "Follow me. I've got a car in the lot out back. Don't say anything until we get there."

They walked grimly to the car. Bernstein thumbed the door panel and opened it on the driver's side, letting Barrett wait a moment before his door was opened too. The car was a rental job, green and black, low-slung, somehow sinister. Barrett got in and turned toward the pale, slight figure beside him, feeling as always a kind of revulsion for Bernstein's scarred cheeks, his bushy united eyebrows, his cold, mocking expression. But for Jack Bernstein, Barrett might never had joined the underground in the first place, yet it seemed incomprehensible to him that he could have chosen such a person as his most intimate boyhood friend. Now their relationship was purely business: they were professional revolutionaries, working together for the common cause, but they were not friends at all. "Well?" Barrett blurted.

Bernstein smiled a death's-head smile. "They got Janet this afternoon."

"Who got her? What are you talking about?"

"The *polizei*. Your apartment was raided at three o'clock. Janet was there, and Nick Morris. They were planning the Canada operation. Suddenly the door opens and four of the boys in green rush in. They accuse Janet and Nick of subversive activities and start searching the place."

Barrett closed his eyes. "There's nothing in the place that could upset anyone. We've been very careful that way."

"Nevertheless, the police didn't know that until they had searched the place." Bernstein steered the car on onto the highway bound for Manhattan and locked it into the electronic control system. As the master computer took over, Bernstein released the steering knobs, took a pack of cigarettes from his breast pocket, and lit one without offering any to Barrett. He crossed his legs and turned cozily to Barrett, saying, "They also searched Janet and Nick very thoroughly while on the premises. Nick told me about it. They made Janet strip completely, and then they went over her from top to bottom. You know that business out in Chicago last month, the girl with the suicide bomb in her vagina? Well, they made sure Janet wasn't about to blow herself up. The way they do it, they put her ankles into interrogation loops and spread-eagle her on the floor, and then—"

"I know how they do it," Barrett said tightly. "You don't need to draw a picture for me." He struggled to stay cool. It was a powerful temptation to seize Bernstein and bat his head against the windshield a few times. *The little louse is telling me this deliberately to torture me,* Barrett thought. He said, "Skip the atrocities and tell me what else happened."

"They finished with Janet and stripped Nick and examined him too. That was Nick's thrill for the year, I guess, watching them work

Janet over, and then putting on a display himself." Barrett's scowl deepened; Nick Morris was a maidenly little fellow of doubtful heterosexuality for whom this had surely been a scarifying ordeal and Bernstein's pleasure was all too close to the surface. "Then they took Janet and Nick down to Foley Square for close interrogation. About four-thirty they let Nick go. He called me and I called you."

"And Janet?"

"They kept her."

"They've got no more evidence on her than they had on Nick. So why didn't they let her go too?"

"I can't tell you that," said Bernstein. "Nevertheless, they kept her."

Barrett knotted his hands together to keep them from shaking. "Where's Pleyel?"

"He's in Baltimore. I called him and told him to stay there until the heat was off."

"But you invited me to come back."

"Someone's got to be in charge," Bernstein said. "It isn't going to be me, so it's got to be you. Don't worry, you aren't in any real danger. I've got a contact in an important place, and he checked the data sheets and said that the only pickup order was for Janet. Just to make sure, I staked Bill Klein out at your apartment, and he says they haven't come back looking for you in the past two hours. So the coast is clear."

"But Janet's in jail!"

"It happens," Bernstein said. "It's the risk we run."

The little man's dry silent laughter was all too audible. For months, now, Bernstein had seemed to be withdrawing from the movement, skipping meetings, regretfully declining out-of-town assignments. He had seemed aloof, alienated, scarcely interested in the underground. Barrett hadn't spoken to him in three weeks. But suddenly he was back in circulation, hooked into the movement's communication nexus. Why? So he could cackle with glee at Janet's arrest?

The car plunged into Manhattan at a hundred twenty miles an hour. Bernstein resumed manual control once they were past 125th Street, and took the car down the East River Tunnel, emerging at the vehicular overpass on Fourteenth Street. A few minutes later they were at the building where Barrett and Janet had lived. Bernstein called upstairs to the man he had left on watch there.

"The coast is clear," he told Barrett after a moment.

They went upstairs. The apartment had been left just as it had been after the police visit, and it was a somber sight. They had been very thorough. Every drawer had been opened, every book taken down from the shelves, every tape given a quick scan. Of course, they had found nothing, since Barrett was inflexible about keeping revolutionary propaganda out of his apartment, but in the course of the ransacking they had managed to get their grimy hands on every piece of property in the place. Janet's underclothes lay fanned out in pathetic array; Barrett glowered when he saw Bernstein staring wolfishly at the flimsy garments. The visitors had been neither gentle nor careful with the contents of the apartment. Barrett wondered how much was missing, but he did not have the stomach to take an inventory now. He felt as though the interior of his body had been laid open by a surgeon's knife, and all his organs removed, examined, and left scattered about.

Stooping, Barrett picked up a book whose backbone had been split, carefully closed it, and set it on a shelf. Then he clamped his hand against the shelf and leaned forward, closing his eyes, waiting for the anger and fear to subside.

In a moment he said, "Get hold of your contact in an important place, Jack. We've got to have her released."

"I can't do a thing for you."

Barrett whirled. He seized Bernstein by the shoulders. His fingers dug in, and he felt the sharp bones beneath the scanty flesh. The blood drained from Bernstein's face, and the stigmata of his acne glowed like beacons. Barrett shook him furiously; Bernstein's head lolled on the thin neck.

"What do you mean, you can't do a thing? You can find her! You can get her out!"

"Jim—Jim, stop—"

"You and your contacts! Damn you, they've arrested Janet! Doesn't that mean anything to you?"

Hawksbill Station

Bernstein clawed feebly at Barrett's wrists, trying to pull them from his shoulders. Shortly Barrett grew calm and released him. Gasping, red-faced, Bernstein stepped back and adjusted his clothing. He dabbed at his forehead with a handkerchief. He looked badly frightened; but yet his eyes glowed with sullen resentment.

In a low voice he said, "You ape, don't ever grab me like that again."

"I'm sorry, Jack. I'm under stress. Right now they might be torturing Janet—beating her—lining up for a mass rape, even—"

"There's nothing we can do. She's in their hands. We have no official channel of legal protest, and no unofficial one, either. They'll interrogate her and maybe then they'll release her, and it's out of our control."

"No. We'll find her and we'll spring her somehow."

"You're not thinking this through, Jim. Each individual member of this group is expendable. We can't risk personnel in the hope of getting Janet free. Unless you want to think of yourself as someone privileged, who can risk the lives or freedom of your comrades simply to recover someone you're emotionally involved with, even if her usefulness to the organization has ended—"

"You make me sick," Barrett snapped.

But he knew that Bernstein was speaking sense. No one in their immediate group had ever been arrested before, yet Barrett was aware of the general pattern of events that followed such an arrest. It was hopeless to think of forcing the government to disgorge a prisoner unless it wanted to. There were a dozen interrogation camps scattered about the country, and at this moment Janet might be in Kentucky or North Dakota or Nevada, no telling where, facing an uncertain prison sentence on an undefined charge. On the other hand, she might already be free and on her way home. Capriciousness is of the essence of things, in running a totalitarian government; this government was nothing if not capricious. Janet was gone, and no action of his could undo that, only the mysterious mercies of the government.

"Maybe you ought to have a drink," Bernstein suggested. "Get yourself settled down a little. You aren't even remotely thinking straight, Jim."

Barrett nodded. He went to the liquor cabinet. They kept a meager supply there, a couple of bottles of scotch, some gin, light rum for the daiquiris Janet liked so much. But the cabinet was empty. The visitors had cleaned it out. Barrett peered at the bare shelves for a long while, idly following the dance of dust motes within.

"The liquor's gone," he said at length. "It figures. Come on, let's get out of here. I can't stand the sight of this place any more."

"Where are you going?"

"Pleyel's office."

"They may have guards posted there waiting to arrest anyone who shows up," Bernstein said.

"So they'll arrest me. Why fool ourselves? They can arrest any of us, whenever the mood takes them. Will you come with me?"

Bernstein shook his head. "I don't think so. You're in charge, Jim. You do what you think is proper. I'll keep in touch, okay."

"Yeah."

"And I'd advise you to be less emotional, if you want to stay free much longer."

They went out. Barrett crossed town to the employment agency, checked the building cautiously from the street, saw nothing amiss, and entered it. The office was undisturbed. He locked himself in and began making calls to cell chiefs in other districts: Jersey City, Greenwich, Nyack, Suffern. The reports he got showed a distinct pattern of sudden simultaneous arrests, not necessarily of top leaders at all. Two or three members of each cell had been picked up in midafternoon. Some had been questioned and released unharmed; others remained in custody. No one had any clear idea of where anybody was, although Valkenburg of the Greenwich group had learned from an unidentified source that the prisoners were being distributed among four interrogation camps in the South and Southwest. He had no specific news of Janet. None of them did. They all sounded badly shaken.

Barrett spent the night on a couch in Pleyel's office. In the morning he went back to the apartment and started the dreary job of cleaning it up, hoping that Janet would appear. He kept picturing her in custody, a plump, dark-eyed girl with strands of white prematurely streaking her black hair, twisting and writhing in agony as the interrogators went to work on her, demanding names, dates, goals. He knew how they questioned women. There was always a component of sexual indignity in their approach; their theory, and it was a sound one, was that a naked woman being questioned by six or seven men wasn't likely to put up much resistance. Janet was tough, but how much pinching and prodding and leering could she take? Interrogators didn't have to use red-hot pokers, thumbscrews, or the rack to extract information. Simply transform a person into so much metabolizing meat, handle her flesh until she loses sight of her soul, and the will crumbles.

Not that Janet could tell them anything they didn't already know. The underground was scarcely a secret organization, despite the passwords and pretense. The police already knew names, dates, goals. These arrests were made purely to shatter morale, the government's sly way of letting its opponents know that they weren't fooling anybody. Capriciousness: it was the essence. Keep the enemy off balance. Arrest, interrogate, imprison, possibly even execute—but always in an amiable, impersonal way, with no aspect of vindictiveness. No doubt a government computer had suggested picking up X members of the underground today, as a strategic move in the continuing subterranean struggle. And so it had been done. And so Janet was gone.

She was not released that day. Nor the next.

Pleyel came back from Baltimore, grim, bleak-faced. He had been working on the problem from down there. He had learned that Janet had been taken to the Louisville interrogation camp the first day, transferred to Bismarck on the second, to Santa Fe on the third. After that the trail fizzled out. This, too, was part of the government's campaign of psychological warfare: move the prisoners about, shuttle them here, shuttle them there, baffle the rubes with the old shell game. Where was she? No one knew. Somehow life went on. A long-planned protest meeting was held in Detroit; government police stood benignly by, smugly tolerating the event but ready to suppress it if it grew violent. New leaflets were distributed in Los Angeles, Evansville, Atlanta, and Boise. Ten days after Janet's disappearance, Barrett cleared out of the apartment and took another one a block away.

It was as though the sea had closed over her and swallowed her up.

For a while, he continued to hope that she would be released, or that at the very least his information network would be able to tell him where she was being kept. But no news of her was forthcoming. In its impersonally arbitrary way, the government had chosen a small group of victims that day. Perhaps they were dead, perhaps they were merely hidden in the lowest level of some maximum-security dungeon. It did not matter. They were gone.

Barrett never saw her again. He never found out what they had done to her.

The pain became an ache, and in time, to his surprise, even the ache went away, and the work of the underground went on steadily, a ceaseless striving toward an always more distant goal.

A couple of days passed before Barrett had the chance to draw Lew Hahn aside for a spot of political discussion. The Inland Sea party had set out by then, and in a way that was too bad, for Barrett could have used Charley Norton's services in penetrating Hahn's armor. Norton was the most gifted theorist at the Station, a man who could weave a tissue of dialectic from the least promising material. If anyone could find out the depth of Hahn's revolutionary commitment, it was Norton. But Norton was away leading the expedition, and so Barrett had to do the interrogating himself. His Marxism was a trifle rusty, and he couldn't thread a path through the Leninist, Stalinist, Trotskyite, Khrushchevist, Maoist, Berenkovskyite and Mgumbweist schools with Charley Norton's skills. Yet he knew what questions to ask. He had served his time on the ideological battlefront, though it had been a long while past.

He picked a rainy evening when Hahn seemed to be in a fairly outgoing mood. There had been an hour's entertainment at the

Hawksbill Station

Station that night, an ingenious computer-composed film that Sid Hutchett had programmed the week before. Up Front had been kind enough to ship back a modest computer, and Hutchett had rigged it to do animations by specifying line widths, shades of gray, and progressions of raster units. It was a simple but remarkably clever business, and it brightened the dull nights. He was able to produce cartoons, satiric lampoons, erotic amusements, anything at all.

Afterward, sensing that Hahn was relaxed enough tonight to lower his guard a bit, Barrett sat down beside him and said, "Good show tonight?"

"Very entertaining."

"It's Sid Hutchett's work. He's a rare one, that Hutchett. Did you get a chance to meet him before he went off on the Inland Sea trip?"

"Tall fellow with a sharp nose and no chin?"

"That's the one," Barrett said. "A clever boy. He was the top computer man for the Continental Liberation Front until they caught him back in '19. He programmed that fake broadcast in which Chancellor Dantell denounced his own regime. God, I wish I had been there to hear that one! Remember it?"

"I'm not sure I do." Hahn frowned. "How long ago was this?"

"The broadcast was in 2018. Would that be before your time? Only eleven years ago—"

"I was nineteen, then. I guess I wasn't very politically oriented. I was an unsophisticated kid, you might say. Slow to awaken."

"A lot of us were. Still, you were nineteen, that's pretty grown up. Too busy studying economics, I suppose."

Hahn grinned. "That's right. I was deep in the dismal science."

"And you never heard the broadcast? Or even heard of it?"

"I must have forgotten."

"The biggest hoax of the century," Barrett said, "and you forgot it. The greatest achievement of the Continental Liberation Front. You're familiar with the Continental Liberation Front, of course."

"Of course." Hahn looked uneasy.

"Which group did you say you were with?"

"The People's Crusade for Liberty."

"I don't know it, I'm afraid. One of the newer groups?"

"Less than five years old. It started in California in the summer of '25."

"What's its program?"

"Oh, the usual revolutionary line," Hahn said. "Free elections, representative government, an opening of the security files, an end to preventive detention, restoration of the habeas corpus and other civil liberties."

"And the economic orientation? Pure Marxist or one of the offshoots?"

"Not really any, I guess. We believed in a kind of—well, capitalism with some government restraints."

"A little to the right of state socialism, and a little to the left of pure *laissez faire*?" Barrett suggested.

"Something like that."

"But they tried that system and it failed, didn't it, in the middle of the twentieth century? It had its day. It led inevitably to total socialism, which produced the compensating backlash of total capitalism, followed by collapse and the birth of syndicalist capitalism. Which gave us a government that pretended to be libertarian while actually stifling all individual liberties in the name of freedom. So if your group simply wanted to turn the economic clock back to 1955, say, there couldn't be much substance to its ideas."

Hahn looked bored at the string of dry abstractions. "You've got to understand that I wasn't in the top ideological councils," he said.

"Just an economist?"

"That's it."

"What were your particular party responsibilities?"

"I drew up plans for the ultimate conversion to our system."

"Basing your procedures on the modified liberalism of Ricardo?"

"Well, in a sense."

"And avoiding, I hope, the tendency to fascism that was found in the thinking of Keynes?"

"You could say so," Hahn said. He stood up, flashing a quick, vague smile. "Look, Jim, I'd love to argue this further with you some other time, but I've really got to go now. Ned Altman talked me into coming around and helping him do a lightning-dance in the hopes of bringing that pile of dirt of his to life. So if you don't mind—"

Hahn beat a hasty retreat.

Barrett was more perplexed than ever. Hahn hadn't been "arguing" anything. What he had been doing was carrying on a lame and feeble and evasive conversation, letting himself be pushed hither and thither by Barrett's questions. And he had spouted a lot of nonsense. He didn't seem to know Keynes from Ricardo, nor to care about the difference between them, which was an odd attitude for a self-professed economist to have. He didn't appear to have a shred of an idea what his own political party stood for. He hadn't protested while Barrett had uttered a lot of deliberately inane doctrinaire talk. He had so little revolutionary background that he was unaware even of Hutchett's astonishing hoax of eleven years ago.

He seemed phony from top to bottom.

How was it possible that this thirtyish kid had been deemed worthy of exile to Hawksbill Station, anyhow? Only the top firebrands and most effective opponents of the government were sent to the Station. Sentencing a man to Hawksbill was very much like sentencing him to death, and it wasn't a step that was taken lightly by a government that was now so very concerned with appearing benevolent, respectable, and tolerant.

Barrett couldn't imagine why Hahn was here at all. He seemed genuinely distressed at having been exiled, and evidently he had left a beloved young wife behind, but nothing else rang true about the man.

Was he—as Don Latimer had suggested—some kind of spy?

Barrett rejected the idea out of hand. He didn't want Latimer's paranoia infecting him. The government wasn't likely to send anyone on a one-way trip to the Late Cambrian just to spy on a bunch of aging revolutionaries who could never possibly make trouble again. But what *was* Hahn doing here, then?

He would bear further watching, Barrett decided.

Barrett took care of some of the watching himself. But he saw to it that he had plenty of assistance. If nothing else, the Hahn-watching project could serve as a kind of therapy for the ambulatory psycho cases, the ones who were superficially functional but were full of all kinds of fears and credulities. They could harness those fears and credulities and play detective, which would give them an enhanced sense of their own value, and also perhaps help Barrett come to understand the meaning of Hahn's presence at the station.

The next day, at lunch, Barrett called Don Latimer aside.

"I had a little talk with your friend Hahn last night," Barrett said. "The things he said sounded mighty peculiar to me, you know?"

Latimer brightened. "Peculiar? How?"

"I checked him out on economics and political theory. Either he doesn't know a thing about either, or else he thinks I'm such a damned fool that he doesn't need to bother making sense when he talks to me. Either way it's strange."

"I told you he was a fishy one!"

"Well, now I believe you," Barrett said.

"What are you going to do about him?"

"Nothing yet. Just keep tabs on him and try to find out why he's here."

"And if he's a spy from the government?"

Barrett shook his head. "We'll take whatever action is necessary to protect ourselves, Don. But the important thing is not to act hastily. It may very well be that we're misjudging Hahn, and I don't want to do anything that would make it awkward to go on living with him here. In a group like this we've got to avoid tensions in advance, or else we're likely to split apart altogether. So we'll go easy on Hahn. But we won't lay off him. I want you to report to me regularly, Don. Watch him carefully. Pretend to be asleep and see what he does. If possible, sneak a look at those notes he's been taking, but if you do, do it subtly and without arousing his suspicion."

Latimer glowed with pride. "You can count on me, Jim."

"Another thing. Get help. Organize a little team of Hahn-watchers. Ned Altman seems to be getting along well with Hahn; put him to work too. Get a few of the other boys—some of the sicker ones, who need responsibilities. You know the ones. I'm putting you in charge of this project. Recruit your men and give them their assignments. Gather your information and transmit it to me. All right?"

"Will do," Latimer said.

And so they kept an eye on the new man.

The day after that was the fifth day after Hahn's arrival. Mel Rudiger needed two new men for his fishing crew, to make up for the pair who had gone on the Inland Sea trek. "Take Hahn," Barrett suggested. Rudiger spoke to Hahn, who seemed delighted by the offer. "I don't know much about fishing with nets," he said, "but I'd love to go."

"I'll teach you what you need to know," Rudiger said. "In half an hour you'll be a master fisherman. You've got to remember, we're not actually dealing with *fish* out here. What we're netting are a bunch of dumb invertebrates, and it doesn't take much to fool them. Come along and I'll show you."

Barrett stood for a long time on the edge of the world, watching the little boat bobbing in the surging Atlantic. For the next couple of hours Hahn would be away from Hawksbill Station, with no chance of getting back until Rudiger was ready to come back. Which gave Latimer a perfect chance to scout through Hahn's notebook. Barrett didn't precisely suggest to Latimer that he ought to infringe on his bunkmate's privacy in this way, but he did let Latimer know that Hahn would be out at sea for a while. He could count on Latimer to draw the right conclusion.

Rudiger never went far from shore—eight hundred, a thousand yards out—but the water was rough enough there. The waves came rolling in with X thousand miles of gathered impact behind them, and they hit hard even where outlying fangs of rock served as breakwaters. A continental shelf sloped off at a wide angle from the land, so that even at a substantial distance offshore the water wasn't exceptionally deep. Rudiger had taken soundings up to a mile out, and had reported depths no greater than a hundred sixty feet. Nobody had gone past a mile out to sea.

It wasn't that they were afraid of falling off the side of the world if they should go too far east. What motivated their caution was simply that a mile was a long distance for aging men to row in an open boat, using stubby oars made from old packing cases. Up Front hadn't thought to spare an outboard motor for them.

Looking toward the horizon, Barrett had an odd thought. He had been told that the women's equivalent of Hawksbill Station was safely segregated out of reach, a couple of hundred million years up the time-line. But how could he be sure that was true? The government Up Front didn't issue press releases on its time-line prison camps, and, anyway, it was foolhardy to believe anything that came, however indirectly, from a government source. In Barrett's day, the public had not even known of the existence of Hawksbill Station. He had found out about it only during the course of his own interrogation, when as part of the process of breaking his will they had let him know where he was likely to be sent. Later, some details had leaked—probably not by chance. The nation discovered that incorrigible politicals were sent off to the beginning of time, yes, and subsequently it was made clear that the men went to one era and the women to another, but Barrett had no real reason to believe it was true.

For all he knew, there could be another Hawksbill Station somewhere else in this very year, and no one living here would have any way of knowing about it. A camp of women living on the far side of the Atlantic, say, or perhaps just across the Inland Sea.

It wasn't very likely, Barrett realized. With the entire past to dump the exiles into, the edgy men Up Front wouldn't take any chance that the two groups of deportees might somehow get together and spawn a tribe of little subversives. They'd take every precaution to put an impenetrable barrier of epochs between the men and the women.

Yet it was a tempting thing to consider. From time to time Barrett wondered if Janet might not be at that other Hawksbill Station.

When he examined the idea rationally, he knew it was impossible. Janet had been arrested in the summer of 1994, and had never been traced thereafter. The first deportations to Hawksbill Station had not begun until 2005. Hawksbill himself hadn't perfected the time-transfer process when Barrett had discussed it with him as late as 1998. Which meant that a minimum of four years, and more probably eleven, had elapsed between the time of Janet's arrest and the beginning of the shipments to the Late Cambrian era.

Hawksbill Station

If Janet had been in a government prison that long, the underground would surely have found out about it, one way or another. But there hadn't been any news of her at all. And therefore it was logical to conclude that the government had disposed of her, in all likelihood within a few days after her arrest. It was folly to think that Janet had lived to see 1995, let alone that she had been kept incommunicado by the government until Hawksbill had finished his research, then had been shot back into this segment of the past.

No, Janet was dead. But Barrett allowed himself the luxury of a few illusions, like anyone else. So he permitted himself sometimes to enjoy the fantasy that she had been sent back, which led him to the even more gargantuan fantasy that he might find her right here in this very epoch. She would be nearly seventy now, he thought. He had not seen her for thirty-five years. He tried and failed to picture her as a fat little old lady. The Janet who had lived in his memory all these decades was quite different, he knew, from any conceivable Janet who might possibly have survived. Better to be realistic and admit she's dead, he thought. Better not to hope to find her again, because the wish might just come true, and a dream would die a terrible death if it did.

But the idea of a female Hawksbill Station on this time-level raised interesting possibilities of a more useful sort. Barrett wondered if he could make the concept sound convincing to the other men. Perhaps. Perhaps with a little effort he could get them to believe in the existence of two simultaneous Hawksbill Stations on this level of time, separated not by epochs but merely by geography.

If they'd believe that, he thought, it could be our salvation.

The instances of degenerative psychosis were beginning to snowball, now. Too many men had been here too long, and one crackup was starting to feed the next. The strain of dwelling in this blank lifeless world where humans were never meant to live was eroding one after another of the Station's inmates. What had happened to Valdosto and Altman and the other psychos would ultimately overtake the rest. The men needed sustained projects to keep them going, to hold back the deadly boredom. As it was, they were starting to slip off into schizophrenia, like Valdosto, or else they were beginning to involve themselves in harebrained enterprises like Altman's Frankenstein girlfriend and Latimer's pursuit of a psionic gateway.

Suppose, Barrett thought, I could get them steamed up about reaching the other continents?

A round-the-world expedition. Maybe they could construct some kind of big ship. That would keep a lot of men busy for a long time. And they'd need to work up some navigational equipment—compasses, sextants, chronometers, whatnot. Somebody would have to design an improvised radio, too. Of course, the Phoenicians had got along pretty well without radios and chronometers, but they hadn't done open-sea voyaging, had they? They had kept close to the coast. But in this world there was hardly any coast, and the Station inmates weren't Phoenicians, either. They'd need navigational aids.

It was the kind of project that might take thirty or forty years, designing and building the ship and its equipment. A long-term focus for our energies, Barrett thought. Of course, I won't live to see the ship set sail, but that's all right. Even so, it's a way of staving off collapse. I don't really care what's across the sea, but I care very much about what's happening to my people here. We've built our staircase to the sea, but it's finished. Now we need something bigger to do. Idle hands make for idle minds...sick minds.

He liked the idea he had hatched. He had been worrying for weeks, now, about the deteriorating state of affairs at the Station, and looking for some fresh way to cope with it. Now he thought he had his way. A voyage! Barrett's ark!

Turning, he saw Don Latimer and Ned Altman standing behind him. "How long have you been there?" he asked.

"Two minutes," said Latimer. "We didn't want to interrupt you. You seemed to be thinking so hard."

"Just dreaming," Barrett said.

"We brought you something to look at," Latimer told him. Barrett saw the papers now, clutched in his hand.

Altman nodded vigorously. "You ought to read it. We brought it for you to read."

Hawksbill Station

"What is it?" Barrett asked.
"Hahn's notes," said Latimer.

Barrett hesitated for a moment, saying nothing, making no attempt to take the papers from Latimer's hand. He was pleased that Latimer had done this, but yet he had to be delicate about it. Private property was sacred at Hawksbill Station. It was very much a breach of ethics to meddle with something another man had written. That was why Barrett had not specifically ordered Latimer to search Hahn's bunk. He could not afford to implicate himself in so flagrant a misdeed.

But of course he had to know what Hahn thought he was doing here. His responsibilities as leader of the Station transcended the moral code, he told himself. So he had asked Latimer to keep an eye on Hahn. And he had asked Rudiger to take Hahn out on a fishing trip. Latimer had taken the next step without needing to be prodded.

Barrett said finally, "I'm not sure I like this, Don. To disturb his belongings—"

"We have to know about this man, Jim."

"Yes, but a society has to obey its own morality, even when it's defending itself against possible enemies. That was our gripe against the syndicalists, remember? They didn't play fair."

Latimer said, "Are we a society?"

"We sure as hell are. We're the whole population of the world. A microcosm. And I represent the State, which has to keep its rules. I don't know if I want to look at those papers you've got there, Don."

"I think you ought to. When important evidence falls into the State's hands, the State has an obligation to examine it. I mean, you aren't just watching out for Hahn's welfare. You've got the rest of us to look after too."

"Is there anything significant in Hahn's papers?"

"You bet there is," Altman put in. "He's guilty as hell!"

Barrett said calmly, "Remember, I never requested you to bring these documents to my attention. The fact that you went snooping is a matter between you and Hahn, at least until I see if there's cause to take action against him. Do we have that much clear?"

Latimer looked a little hurt. "I suppose. I found the papers tucked away in Hahn's bunk after he went out in Rudiger's boat. I know I'm not supposed to be invading his privacy, but I had to have a look at what he's been writing. There it is. He's a spy, all right."

He offered the folded sheaf of papers to Barrett. Barrett took them, glanced quickly at them without reading them, and tucked the sheaf into his hand. I'll look them over a little later," he said. "What's Hahn been writing, anyway? In a few words."

"It's a description of the Station, and a profile of most of the men in it that he's met," said Latimer. He smiled frostily. "The profiles are very detailed and not very complimentary. Hahn's private opinion of me is that I've gone mad and won't admit it. His private opinion of you is a little more flattering, Jim, but not much."

"The man's opinions aren't all that important," said Barrett. "He's entitled to think that we're nothing but a bunch of cockeyed old crackpots. Very likely we are. All right, so he's been having a bit of literary exercise at our expense, but I don't see that that's any cause for alarm. We—"

Altman said flatly, "He's also been hanging around the Hammer."

"*What?*"

"I saw him going there late last night. He went into the building. I followed him, and he didn't notice me. He was looking at the Hammer for a long time. Walking around it, studying it. He didn't touch it."

"Why the devil didn't you tell me that right away?" Barrett snapped.

Altman looked confused and terrified. He blinked his eyes five or six times and backed nervously away from Barrett, running his hands through his yellow hair. "I wasn't sure it was important," he said finally. "Maybe he was just curious about it, I mean. I had to talk things over with Don first. And I couldn't do that until Hahn had gone out fishing."

Sweat burst out on Barrett's face. He reminded himself that he was dealing with a mildly psychotic individual, and he kept his voice as steady as he could, masking the sudden alarm that gripped him.

Hawksbill Station

"Listen, Ned, if you ever catch Hahn going near the time-travel equipment again, you let me know in a hurry. You come right to me, whether I'm awake or asleep, eating, resting. Without consulting Don or anyone else. Clear?"

"Clear," said Altman.

"You knew about this?" Barrett asked Latimer.

Latimer nodded. "Ned told me just before we came down here. But I figured it was more urgent to give you the papers, first. That is, Hahn couldn't damage the Hammer while he's out in the boat, anyway, and whatever he might have done last night is already done."

Barrett had to admit that that made sense. But he could not easily shake off his distress. The Hammer was their only contact point, unsatisfactory though it was, with the world that had cast them out. They were dependent on it for their supplies, for their fresh personnel, for such shards of news about the world Up Front as the new men brought. Let some disturbed individual wreck the Hammer, and the choking silence of total isolation would descend on them. Cut off from everything, living in a world without vegetation, without raw materials, without machines, they'd be back to savagery within months.

But why would Hahn be fooling with the Hammer, Barrett wondered?

Altman giggled. "You know what I think? They've decided to exterminate us, Up Front. They want to get rid of us. Hahn's been sent here as a suicide volunteer. He's checking us out, getting everything ready. Then they're going to send a cobalt bomb through the Hammer and blow the Station up. We ought to wreck the Hammer and Anvil before they get a chance."

"But why would they send a suicide volunteer?" Latimer asked reasonably. "If their aim was to wipe us out, they could simply transmit a bomb, without wasting an agent. Unless they've got some way to rescue their spy—"

"In any case, we shouldn't take chances," Altman argued. "Wreck the Hammer, first thing. Make it impossible for them to bomb us from Up Front."

"That might be a good idea. Jim, what do you think?"

Barrett thought that Altman was crazy and that Latimer was far down the same road. But he said simply, "I'm inclined not to worry much about this bomb theory of yours, Ned. Up Front's got no reason to want to wipe us out. And if they did, Don's right—they wouldn't send an agent to us. Just a bomb."

"Even so, perhaps we should disable the Hammer on the possibility that—"

"No," Barrett said. He made it emphatic. "If we do anything to the Hammer, we're chopping off our own heads. That's why it's so serious that Hahn's been messing with it. And don't you get any ideas about the Hammer either, Ned. The Hammer sends us food and clothing. Not bombs."

"But—"

"And yet—"

"Shut up, both of you," Barrett growled. "Let me look at these papers."

The Hammer, he thought, would have to be protected. He and Quesada would have to rig some kind of guardian system for it, the way they had done for the drug supplies. But a more effective one, he added.

He walked a few steps away from Altman and Latimer and sat down on a shelf of rock. He unfolded the sheaf of papers.

He began to read.

Hahn had a cramped, crabbed handwriting that enabled him to pack a maximum of information into a minimum of space, as though he regarded it as a mortal sin to waste paper. Fair enough; paper was a scarce commodity here. Evidently Hahn had brought these sheets with him from Up Front, though. They were thin and had a metallic texture. When one piece slid against another, a soft whispering sound was produced.

Small though the writing was, Barrett had no difficulty in deciphering it. Hahn's script was clear. So were his opinions.

Painfully so.

He had written a detailed analysis of conditions at Hawksbill Station, and it was an impressive job. In about five thousand well-organized words Hahn had set forth everything that Barrett knew

Hawksbill Station

was going sour here. His objectivity was merciless. He had neatly ticked off the men as aging revolutionaries in whom the old fervor had turned rancid; he listed the ones who were certifiably psychotic, and the ones who were on the edge, and in a separate category he noted the ones who were hanging on, like Quesada and Norton and Rudiger. Barrett was interested to see that Hahn rated even those three as suffering from severe strain and likely to fly apart at any moment. To him, Quesada and Norton and Rudiger seemed to be just about as stable as when they had first dropped onto the Anvil of Hawksbill Station; but that was possibly the distorting effect of his own blurred perceptions. To an outsider like Hahn, the view was different and perhaps more accurate.

Barrett forced himself not to skip ahead to Hahn's evaluation of him.

He read doggedly on through Hahn's assessment of the likely future of Hawksbill's population: not bright. Hahn thought that the process of deterioration was cumulative and self-generating, and that any man who had been in the place more than a year or two would shortly be brought to his knees by the pressures of loneliness and rootlessness. Barrett thought so too, although he believed it would take a little longer for the younger men to cave in. But Hahn's reasoning was inexorable and his evaluation of the possibilities sounded convincing. How has he learned so much about us so fast, Barrett wondered? Is he that sharp? Or are we so totally transparent?

On the fifth page, Barrett found Hahn's description of him. He wasn't pleased when he came to it.

"The Station," Hahn had written, "is nominally under the authority of Jim Barrett, an old-line revolutionary who's been here about twenty years. Barrett is the ranking prisoner in terms of seniority. He makes the administrative decisions and seems to act as a stabilizing force. Some of the men worship him, but I am not convinced that he would be able to exert any real influence in the event of a serious challenge to his rule, such as a blood feud in the Station or an attempt to depose him. In the loose-knit anarchy of Hawksbill Station society, Barrett rules very much by the consent of the governed, and since the Station is lacking in weapons he would have no actual recourse if that consent were to be withdrawn. However, I see no likelihood of that, since the men here are generally devitalized and demoralized, and an anti-Barrett insurrection would be beyond their capabilities even if they had any need to mount one.

"By and large Barrett has been a positive force within the Station. Though some of the other men here have qualities of leadership, doubtless the place would have fragmented into disastrous confusion long ago without him. However, Barrett is like a mighty beam that's been gnawed from within by termites. He looks solid, but one good push would break him apart. A recent injury to his foot has evidently had a bad effect on him. The other men say he used to be physically vigorous and derived much of his authority from his size and strength. Now Barrett can hardly walk. But I feel that the trouble with Barrett is inherent in the life of Hawksbill Station, and does not have much to do with his lameness. He's been cut off from normal human drives for too many years. The exercise of power here has provided the illusion of stability for him and allowed him to keep functioning, but it's power in a vacuum, and things have happened within him of which he's totally unaware. He's in bad need of therapy. He may be beyond help."

Stunned, Barrett read that passage several times. Words stuck to him like clinging burrs.

Gnawed from within by termites...

...one good push...

...things have happened within him...

...bad need of therapy...

...beyond help...

Barrett was less angered by Hahn's words than he thought he should have been. Hahn was entitled to his views. He might even be right. Barrett had lived too long as a man apart from the others here; no one dared to speak bluntly to him. Had he decayed? Were the others being too kind to him?

Finally Barrett stopped going over and over Hahn's profile of him, and pushed his way to the last page of the notes. The essay ended with the words, "Therefore I recommend prompt termination of the Hawksbill Station penal colony and, where possible, the therapeutic rehabilitation of its inmates."

What the hell was this?

It sounded like the report of a parole commissioner! But there was no parole from Hawksbill Station. That final insane sentence let all the viability of what had gone before bleed away. No matter that Hahn's insight into the Station was keen and deeply penetrating. A man who could write, "I recommend prompt termination of the Hawksbill Station penal colony," was a man who was insane.

Hahn was pretending to be composing a report to the government Up Front, obviously. In brisk and capable prose he had dissected the Station and provided a full analysis. But a wall a billion years thick made the filing of that report an impossibility. So Hahn was suffering from delusions, just like Altman and Valdosto and the others. In his fevered mind he believed he could send messages to those Up Front, pompous documents delineating the flaws and foibles of his fellow prisoners.

That raised a chilling prospect. Hahn might be crazy, but he hadn't been in the Station long enough to have gone crazy there. He must have brought his insanity with him from Up Front.

What if they had stopped using Hawksbill Station as a camp for political prisoners, Barrett asked himself, and were starting to use it as an insane asylum?

It was a somber thing to consider: a cascade of psychos descending on them. Human debris of all sorts would rain from the Hammer. Men who had gone honorably buggy under the stress of long confinement would have to make room at the Station for ordinary Bedlamites.

Barrett shivered. He folded up Hahn's papers and handed them back to Latimer, who was sitting a few yards away, watching him intently.

"What did you think of that?" Latimer asked.

"I think it's hard to evaluate at one reading." He rubbed his hand over his face, pressing heavily against it. "But possibly friend

Hahn is emotionally disturbed in some way. I don't think this is the work of a healthy man."

"You think he's a spy from Up Front?"

"No," said Barrett. "I don't. But I think he thinks he's a spy from Up Front. That's what I find so disturbing about this stuff."

"What are you going to do to him?" Altman wanted to know.

Gently Barrett said, "For the moment, just watch and wait." He folded the thin, crinkling sheaf of papers and pressed it into Latimer's hands. "Put this stuff back exactly where you got it, Don. And don't give Hahn the faintest inkling that you've read it or removed it."

"Right."

"And come to me the moment you think there's something I ought to know about him," Barrett said. "He may be a very sick boy. He may need all the help we can give."

11

Barrett didn't have any steady women after Janet was arrested. He lived alone, although there was plenty of transient company in his bed. Somehow he regarded himself as guilty for Janet's disappearance, and he didn't want to bring the same fate on some other girl.

It was phony guilt, he knew. Janet had been in the underground before he'd ever heard of it, and doubtless the police had been watching her for a long time. When they had picked her up, it had probably been because they regarded her as dangerous in her own right, not because they were trying to reach through to Barrett. But he couldn't help that feeling of responsibility, that sense that he'd jeopardize the freedom of any other girl who moved in with him.

He had no difficulty finding companions, though. He was the virtual leader of the New York group, now, and that invested him with a kind of charismatic appeal that seemed irresistible to girls. Pleyel, ever more ascetic and saintly, had retired to the role of a pure theoretician. Barrett handled the day-by-day routine of the organization. Barrett dispatched the couriers, coordinated the activities of the adjoining areas, and planned the coups. And, like a lightning rod drawing energy, he became the focus for the yearnings of a bunch of kids of all sexes. To them, he was a famed hero of revolt, an Old Revolutionary. He was becoming a legend. He was almost thirty years old.

So the girls trooped through the little apartment. Sometimes he'd let one live with him for as much as two weeks at a time. Then he'd suggest that it was time for her to move on.

"Why are you throwing me out?" she'd ask, in effect. "Don't you like me? Don't I make you happy, Jim?"

And he would reply, essentially, "You're wonderful, doll. But one of these days the police are going to come for you, if you stay here. It's happened before. They'll take you away and you'll never be seen again."

"I'm small fry. Why should they want me?"

"To harass me," Barrett would explain. "So you'd better go. Please. For your own safety."

Eventually he would get them to leave. And then would come a week or two of monastic solitude, which was good for his soul, but as the laundry began to pile up and the linens started to need changing he'd realize that the monastic life has its disadvantages, and some other thrilled young revolutionary in her late teens would move into his apartment and dedicate herself to his earthly needs for a while. Barrett had trouble keeping his memories of them distinct from one another. Generally they were leggy kids, dressed in whatever was the current nonconformist fashion, and most of them had plain faces and good bodies. The Revolution tended to attract the sort of girl who couldn't wait to get her clothes off, so that she could prove that her breasts and thighs and buttocks made up for the deficiencies of her face.

There was always plenty of new young blood coming along, now. The police-state psychology introduced by Chancellor Dantell had seen to that. He ran a tight ship of state, but every time his minions came around to knock on a door at midnight, new revolutionaries were created. Jack Bernstein's fears that the underground would shrivel into impotence as a result of the government's wise benevolence had not quite come to pass. The government was not altogether infallible, and could not entirely resist being totalitarian; and so the resistance movement survived in a straggling way, and grew slightly from year to year. Chancellor Arnold's government had been shrewder. But Chancellor Arnold was dead.

Among the new people who came into the movement during those tougher years in the late 1990s was Bruce Valdosto. He showed up in New York City one day in the early part of 1997, knowing no one, full of unfocused hatreds and seething angers. He was from Los Angeles. His father had run a tavern there, and, when goaded too far by a government tax collector, had spit in the collector's face and hurled him out into the street. (The syndicalist government, notoriously puritan, was almost as tough with the makers and vendors of alcoholic drinks as it was with artists and writers.) Later that day, the tax collector had returned with six of his colleagues, and they had methodically beaten the elder Valdosto to death. His son, unable to halt the slaughter, had been arrested for interference with the functions of government officers, and was released only after a month of high-grade interrogation, the translation of which was torture. Then Valdosto set out on the confused transcontinental hegira that brought him to Jim Barrett's apartment in lower Manhattan.

He was little more than seventeen years old. Barrett didn't know that. To him, Valdosto was a short, swarthy man of about his own age, with immense shoulders and a powerful torso and strangely malproportioned little legs. He had thick tangled hair and the burning, ferocious eyes of a born terrorist, but nothing about his looks or his words or his actions betrayed his youthfulness. Barrett never did find out whether Valdosto had simply been born that way or had undergone accelerated aging in the crucible of the Los Angeles interrogation tank.

"When does The Revolution start?" Valdosto wanted to know. "When does the killing begin?"

"There won't be any killing," Barrett told him. "The coup will be bloodless when it comes."

"Impossible! We've got to remove the head of the enemy. Whack, like killing a snake."

Hawksbill Station

Barrett showed him the flow charts of The Revolution: the scheme whereby the Chancellor and the Council of Syndics would be taken into custody, the junior officers of the army would proclaim martial law, and a reconstituted Supreme Court would announce the restoration of the overthrown 1789 Constitution. Valdosto peered at the charts, picked his nose, scratched his hairy chest, clenched his fists, and grunted, "Nah. It'll never come off. You can't hope to take over a country by arresting maybe two dozen key men."

"It happened in 1984," Barrett pointed out.

"That was different. The government was in ruins anyway. Christ, there wasn't even any President that year, huh? But now we got a government of real pros. The head of the snake is bigger than you think, Barrett. You've got to reach behind the Syndics. Down to the bureaucrats. The little Fuhrers, the two-bit tyrants who love their jobs so much they'll do anything to keep them. The sort of guys who killed my father. They've got to go."

"There are thousands of them," Barrett said, alarmed. "Are you saying we should execute the entire civil service?"

"Not all. But most. Clean out the tainted ones. Start with a fresh slate."

The most frightening thing about Valdosto, Barrett thought, was not that he was fond of spouting bombastic, vehemently violent ideas, but that he sincerely believed in them and was fully ready to carry them out. Within an hour after meeting Valdosto for the first time, Barrett was convinced that he must have committed at least a dozen murders already. Later, Barrett found out that Valdosto was only a kid dreaming of avenging his father, but he never lost the uncomfortable feeling that Val was wholly lacking in the usual scruples. He could remember nineteen-year-old Jack Bernstein insisting, nearly a decade earlier, that the best way to overthrow the government was through a judicious campaign of assassination. And Pleyel, mild as ever, remarking, "Assassination isn't a valid method of political discourse." So far as Barrett knew, Bernstein's bloodlust had never passed the theoretical stage; but here was young Valdosto, offering himself as the Angel of Death to fulfill Jack's dreams of revolution. A good thing that Bernstein wasn't very deeply involved in underground activities any more, Barrett told himself. With the right encouragement, Valdosto could become a one-man terror squad.

Instead he became Barrett's roommate. The arrangement was an accidental one. Valdosto needed a place to stay on his first night in the city, and Barrett offered him a couch. Since Val had no money, he was in no position to find himself an apartment, and even after he had gone onto the payroll of what they now were calling the Continental Liberation Front, he continued to live with Barrett. Barrett didn't mind. After the third week he said, "Forget about looking for a place of your own. You might as well just go on living here."

They got along beautifully, despite the gulf in age and temperament. Barrett found that Valdosto had a rejuvenating effect on him. Though he was just coming up on thirty himself, Barrett felt older than that—ancient, sometimes. He had been active in the underground for nearly half his life, so that The Revolution had become a pure abstraction to him, a matter of unending meetings and secret messages and leaflets. A doctor healing one runny nose after another does not find it easy to think of himself as working step by step toward a world in which disease is extinct; and Barrett, immersed in the trifling rituals of the revolutionary bureaucracy, all too often lost sight of the main goal, or forgot that there was any such goal. He was beginning to slide into the rarefied realm inhabited by Pleyel and the other original agitators—a realm in which all fervor is dead and idealism is transmuted into ideology. Valdosto rescued him from that.

To Val there was nothing abstract about The Revolution. For him The Revolution was a matter of splitting skulls and twisting necks and bombing offices. He regarded the faceless officials of the government as his special enemies, knew their names, dreamed of the punishments he would inflict on each one of them. His intensity was contagious. Barrett, while drawing back from Valdosto's lust for destructiveness, began to remember that there was a central purpose fundamental to his network of daily routines. Valdosto revived in him the revolutionary dreams that were so difficult to sustain, week in and week out, across years and decades.

Hawksbill Station

And when he was not brooding of bloodshed, Valdosto was a lively, uproarious companion. He took some getting accustomed to, of course. He lacked almost all inhibitions, and liked to wander about the apartment naked, even when there were visitors; the first time he emerged that way he seemed like an impossibly grotesque anthropoid apparition, his barrel-thick body densely matted with coarse black hair, his legs so dwarfed that it could not have been too difficult for him to press his knuckles against the floor. And a few days later, when he had a girl in his room, the two of them emerged in a helter-skelter scramble, both of them bare, Val chasing her about the living-room while Barrett, Pleyel, and two others looked on in astonishment. The panicky girl, all white thighs and jiggling breasts, finally found herself trapped in a corner, and Val hauled her off in triumph for the consummation.

"He's the primordial kind," Barrett explained in embarrassment.

Soon Valdosto abandoned his more flagrantly bizarre antics, but there was never any predicting what he might do next. He appeared to be sublimating his terrorist urges in erotic gymnastics, and sometimes took his women on two and three at a time, tossing the cast-offs to Barrett. It was a wild few months at the outset for Barrett, but in time he adjusted to the fact that the place was likely to be stacked with sprawling exhausted naked females at any given time, and he joined the fun with unfeigned enthusiasm, telling himself that a revolutionary's life didn't necessarily have to be a dour one.

Barrett's apartment once again became a social center for the underground group, as it had been in the days when Janet had been living with him. The climate of fear had been eased again, and there was no need for exaggerated caution; although Barrett knew he was under surveillance, he did not hesitate to allow others to visit him.

Hawksbill came a few times. Barrett met him quite incidentally, on one of his rare ventures into nonrevolutionary social circles. Columbia University had been reopened after a three-year forced suspension of classes, and Barrett found himself journeying to Morningside Heights on a frosty spring evening in '98 to attend a party given by a man he knew vaguely, a professor of applied information technology named Golkin. Through the thick haze of smoke he spied Edmond Hawksbill across the room, and their eyes met, and they exchanged remote nods, and Barrett debated going over to say hello to him, and Hawksbill seemed to be debating the same thing, and after a moment Barrett thought, what the hell, I will, and he started to shoulder his way through the crowd.

They met in the middle. Barrett had not seen the mathematician for nearly two years, and he was startled by the change in his appearance. Hawksbill had never been a handsome man, but now it looked as though he had undergone some kind of glandular collapse, and the effects were unsettling to behold. He was completely bald. His cheeks, which had always had a grubby, unshaven look, were strangely pink. His lips and nose had thickened; his eyes were lost in orbits of flesh; his belly was enormous, and his entire frame seemed to have been embedded in new layers of fat. They shook hands briefly; his touch was moist, his fingers were soft and limp. Hawksbill, Barrett remembered, was only nine years his senior, and so not yet forty years old. He looked like a man at the edge of the grave.

"What are you doing here?" they both said at once.

Barrett laughed and outlined his tenuous friendship with Golkin, their host. Hawksbill explained that he had recently been co-opted for Columbia's faculty of advanced mathematics.

"I thought you hated teaching," Barrett said.

"I do. I'm not. I've been given a research appointment. Government work."

"Classified?"

"Is there any other kind?" Hawksbill asked, smiling faintly.

The sight of him made Barrett's flesh crawl. Behind the thick glasses, Hawksbill's eyes looked cold and alien; some effect of myopia robbed his gaze of all humanity, and staring into those eyes was like trading glances with a being from another world. Chilled, Barrett said, "I didn't realize you were taking the governmental shilling. Perhaps I shouldn't be talking to you, then. I might be compromising you."

"You mean, you're still plugging away at The Revolution?" Hawksbill asked.

"Still plugging away, yes."

Hawksbill Station

The mathematician favored him with a fluid smile. "I would think a man of your intelligence would have seen through that bunch of bores and misfits by now."

"I'm not as bright as you think I am, Ed," Barrett said quietly. "I don't even have a college degree, remember? I'm stupid enough to think that there's a meaning in what we're working toward. You once thought so yourself."

"I still do."

"You oppose the government and yet you work for the government?" Barrett asked.

Hawksbill jiggled the ice cubes in his drink. "Is that so hard for you to accept? The government and I have arranged a marriage of convenience. They know that I'm polluted with a revolutionary background, of course. And I know that they're a bunch of fascist bastards. However, I'm conducting certain research which is simply impossible for me to perform without financial assistance amounting to millions of dollars a year, and that obliges me to seek government grants. And the government is interested enough in my project, and aware enough of my special gifts, so that they're willing to back me without worrying about my ideology. I loathe them, they mistrust me, and we come to an arm's-length working agreement."

"Orwell called that doublethink."

"Oh, no," Hawksbill said. "It's *Realpolitik*, it's cynicism, but it isn't doublethink. Neither part is operating under any kind of illusion about the other. We're using each other, my friend. I need their money, they need my brains. But I continue to abominate the philosophy of this government, and they know it."

"In that case," said Barrett, "you could still be working with us, without jeopardizing your research grant."

"I suppose."

"Then why have you stayed away? We need your gift, Ed. We have no one whose mind can juggle fifty factors at once, as you do so easily. We've missed you. Can I lure you back to our group?"

"No," Hawksbill said. "Let's sweeten our drinks and I'll explain why."

"Good enough."

They went through the ritual of refilling. Hawksbill took a long, deep gulp. Some driblets of liquor appeared at the edge of his mouth and trickled down his fleshy chin, disappearing into the stained folds of his collar. Barrett looked away, taking a deep pull of his own drink.

Then Hawksbill said, "I haven't withdrawn from your group out of fear of arrest. Nor is it that I've lost disdain for the syndicalists, or that I've sold out to them. No. I left, if you must know, out of boredom and contempt. I decided that the Continental Liberation Front wasn't worthy of my energy."

"That's blunt enough," Barrett agreed.

"Do you know why? It's because the leadership of the movement fell into the hands of genial delayers like yourself. Where is The Revolution? It's 1998, Jim. syndicalists have been in power fourteen years, nearly. There's been not one visible attempt to push them aside."

"Revolutions aren't planned in a week, Ed."

"But fourteen years? Fourteen years? Perhaps if Jack Bernstein had been running things, we'd have had some action. But Jack got bitter and drifted away. Very well. Edmond Hawksbill has but one life to live, and he wants to spend it validly: I got tired of serious economic debates and procedural parliamentarianism. I became more involved in my own research. I withdrew."

"I'm sorry we bored you so, Ed."

"I'm sorry too. For a while, I thought the country stood a chance of getting its freedom back. Then I realized it was hopeless."

"Would you come to visit me anyway? Maybe you can help us get moving again," Barrett said. "We've got young people joining us all the time. There's a chap named Valdosto out of California with enough fervor for ten of us. And others. If you came, and lent your prestige—"

Hawksbill was skeptical. He could barely conceal his total scorn for the Continental Liberation Front. But yet he could not deny that he still supported the ideals for which the Front stood, and so Barrett maneuvered him into coming around. Hawksbill came to the apartment the next week. There were a dozen people there, most of them girls. They sat at Hawksbill's feet, eyeing him adoringly while he gripped his glass and exuded perspiration and weary sarcasm. He was, Barrett thought, like a great white slug in the armchair, damp, epicene, repulsive. But his appeal to these girls was frankly sexual. Barrett noticed that Hawksbill took good care to fend off their advances before they went too far. Hawksbill enjoyed being the focus of their desires—that was, Barrett suspected, why he came around so frequently—but he showed no interest in capitalizing on his opportunities.

Hawksbill consumed a good deal of Barrett's filtered rum, and offered a great many opinions on why the Continental Liberation Front was doomed to fail. Tact had never been Hawksbill's strong point, and he was often savagely incisive in his analysis of the underground's shortcomings. For a while Barrett thought it might be a mistake to expose the neophyte revolutionaries to him, since his raw pessimism might tend to dismay or permanently discourage them. But Barrett discovered that none of Hawksbill's young admirers took his dire accusations seriously. They worshiped the mathematician for his brilliance as a mathematician, but they assumed that his pessimism was simply part of his general eccentricity, along with his sloppiness and his fat and his flaccidity. So it was worth the risk of keeping Hawksbill around, spinning out his long streams of unresonant declamations, in the hope of seducing him somehow back into the movement.

In an unguarded moment when he was brimming with filtered rum, Hawksbill allowed Barrett to question him about the secret research he was doing on behalf of the government.

"I'm building a time transport," Hawksbill said.

"Still? I thought you'd given that up a long time ago."

"Why should I? The initial equations of 1983 are valid, Jim. My work's been assailed for a whole generation and no weak spot has developed. So it's merely a matter of translating theory into practice."

"You always used to look down your nose on experimental work. You were the pure theoretician."

"I change," Hawksbill said. "I've carried the theory as far as it needs to go." He leaned forward and ponderously clasped his interlaced fingers, pudgy and pink, across his gut. "Time reversal is an accomplished fact on the subatomic level, Jim. The Russians showed the way toward that at least forty years ago. My equations confirmed their wild guesses. In laboratory work it's been possible to reverse the time-path of an electron and send it back close to a full second."

"Are you serious?"

"It's old stuff. When we flip the electron around, it alters its charge and becomes a positron. That would be all right, except that it tends to seek out an electron moving forward up its track, and they annihilate each other."

"Causing an atomic explosion?" Barrett asked.

"Hardly." Hawksbill smiled. "There's a release of energy, but it's only a gamma ray. Well, at least we've succeeded in prolonging the lifetime of our backward-traveling positron by a factor of about a billion, but that still comes only to something short of one second. However, if we can send a single electron back in time for a single second, we know that there are no theoretical objections to sending an elephant back a trillion years. There are merely technical difficulties. We must learn to increase the transmission mass. We must get around the reversal of charge, or we'll simply be shipping antimatter bombs into our own past and wrecking our laboratories. We must find out, too, what it does to a living thing to have its charge reversed. But these are trivialities. Five, ten, twenty years and we'll solve them. The theory is what counts. And the theory is sound." Hawksbill burped grandly. "My glass is empty again, Jim."

Barrett filled it. "Why does the government want to sponsor your time-machine research?"

"Who knows? What concerns me is the mere fact that they authorize my expenditures. Mine not to reason why. I do my work and hope for the best."

"Incredible," Barrett said softly.

"A time machine? Not really. Not if you've studied my equations."

"I don't mean the time machine is incredible, Ed. Not if you say you can build it. What's incredible to me is that you're willing to let the government get hold of it. Don't you see what power this gives them? To go back and forth through time as they please, snuffing out the grandparents of people who trouble them? To edit the past, to—"

"Oh," said Hawksbill, "no one will be able to go back and forth through time. The equations deal only with going back in time. I haven't considered forward movement at all. I don't believe it would be possible, anyway. Entropy is entropy, and it can't be reversed, not in the sense I employ. The journey through time will be one way only, just as it is for all us poor mortals today. A different direction, is all."

To Barrett, much of what Hawksbill said about the time machine was incomprehensible, and the rest was infuriating in its smugness. But he emerged with the uncomfortable feeling that the mathematician was close to succeeding, and that, in another few years, a process for reversing the flow of time would be perfected and in the hands of the government. Well, he thought, the world had survived Albert Einstein. It had survived J. Robert Oppenheimer. It would survive Edmond Hawksbill, too, somehow.

He wanted to know more about Hawksbill's research. But just then Jack Bernstein arrived, and Hawksbill, belatedly remembering that he was under a security blanket, abruptly changed the subject.

Bernstein, like Hawksbill, had wandered far from the underground movement in recent years. To all intents and purposes, he had dropped out after the wave of arrests in the summer of '94. During the four years that followed, Barrett had seen him perhaps a dozen times. Their meetings were cold and remote. It had come to seem to Barrett that he had dreamed those afternoons when he and Jack had been fifteen, and had furiously debated every topic of any intellectual interest in Jack's small, book-crammed bedroom. Their long walks together in the snow—their collaborations on class assignments— their early days together in the underground—had any of that really happened? The past, for Barrett, was breaking off and sloughing away like dead skin, and his boyhood friendship with Jack Bernstein had been the first to go.

Bernstein was hard and cold, now, a compact, spare little man who might well have been carved from stone. He had never married. Since leaving the underground, he had gone into the practice of law; he had an apartment somewhere far uptown, and spent much of his time traveling on business. Barrett did not understand why Bernstein had begun dropping in on him again. Not out of sentiment, surely. Nor did he show any interest in the Continental Liberation Front's spasmodic activities. Perhaps it was the figure of Hawksbill that drew him, Barrett thought. It was hard to view anyone as frosty and self-contained as Jack as a hero worshiper, but maybe he had never shaken off his adolescent admiration for Hawksbill.

He came, he sat, he drank, occasionally he talked. He spoke as if every word cost him a pound of flesh. His lips seemed to close like clippers between each syllable. His eyes, small and red-rimmed, flickered with what might have been suppressed pain. Bernstein made Barrett acutely uncomfortable. He had always thought of Jack as a man ridden by demons, but now the demons appeared too close to the surface, too capable of bursting forth to seize innocent bystanders.

And Barrett felt the tingle of Jack's unvoiced mockery. As an ex-revolutionary, Bernstein seemed to share Hawksbill's idea that the Front was futile and its members self-deceivers. Without doing more than smiling secretively, Bernstein seemed to be passing judgment on the group to which he had devoted so many years of his own life. Only once did he let his contempt show, though. Pleyel entered the room, a dreamy figure in a flowing white beard, lost in calculations of the coming millennium. He nodded to Bernstein as if he had forgotten who he was. "Good evening, Comrade," Bernstein said. "How goes The Revolution?"

"Our plans are maturing," said Pleyel mildly.

"Yes. Yes. It's a fine strategy, Comrade. Wait patiently until the syndicalists die out unto the tenth generation. Then strike, strike like hawks!"

Pleyel looked puzzled. He smiled and turned away to confer with Valdosto, obviously unwounded by Bernstein's bitter sarcasm. Barrett was annoyed. "If you're looking for a target, Jack, aim at me instead."

Bernstein laughed harshly. "You're too big, Jim. couldn't possibly miss, so where's the sport? Besides, it's cruel to shoot at sitting ducks."

That night—late in November 1998—was the last time Bernstein came to Barrett's apartment. Hawksbill paid only one more visit himself, three months later. Barrett asked him, "Have you heard anything from Jack?"

"Jacob, he calls himself now. Jacob Bernstein."

"He always used to hate that name. He kept it a secret."

Hawksbill blinked amiably. "That's his problem. When I met him and called him Jack, he instructed me that his name was Jacob. He was quite sharp about it."

"I haven't seen him since that night in November. What's he been up to?"

"You mean you haven't heard?"

"No," Barrett said. "Something I should know?"

"I suppose," Hawksbill said, and snickered. "Jacob has a new job, and he's not likely to be paying social calls on leaders of the Front any more. Professional calls, maybe. But not social ones."

"What kind of new job?" said Barrett tightly.

Hawksbill seemed to enjoy saying it. "He's an interrogator, now. For the government police. It's a job that fits his personality quite well, wouldn't you say? He should make an outstanding success of it."

12

The fishing expedition returned to the Station early in the afternoon. Barrett saw that Rudiger's dinghy was overflowing with the haul, and Hahn, coming ashore with his arms full of gaffed trilobites, looked sunburned and pleased with his outing.

Barrett went over to inspect the catch. Rudiger was in an effusive mood, and held up a bright red crustacean that might have been the great-great-grandfather of all boiled lobsters, except that it had no front claws, and sprouted a wicked-looking triple spike where a tail should have been. It was about two feet long, and ugly.

"A new species!" Rudiger crowed. "There's nothing like it in any museum. God, I wish I could put it where it would be found. Some mountaintop, maybe."

"If it could be found, it would have been found," Barrett reminded him. "The odds are a twentieth-century paleontologist would have dug it out and put it on display, and you'd have known all about it. So forget it, Mel."

Hahn said, "I've been wondering about that point. Just how is it that nobody Up Front ever dug up the fossil remains of Hawksbill Station? Aren't they worried that one of the early fossil-hunters will find it in the Cambrian strata and raise a fuss? Say, one of the nineteenth-century dinosaur diggers? That would be something, if he turned up huts and human bones and tools in a stratum older than dinosaurs."

Barrett shook his head. "For one thing, no paleontologist from the beginning of the science to the founding of the Station in 2005 ever did dig up Hawksbill. That's a matter of record—it hadn't happened, so there was nothing to worry about. And if the Station came to light after 2005, why, everyone would know what it was. No paradox there."

"Besides," said Rudiger sadly, "In another billion years this whole strip of rock will be on the floor of the Atlantic, with a couple of miles of sediment sitting on top of it. There's not a chance we'll be found. Or that anyone Up Front will ever see this guy I caught today. Not that I give a damn. I've seen him. I'll dissect him. Their loss."

"But you regret the fact that science will never know of this species," Hahn said. "Twenty-first century science."

"Sure I do. But is it my fault? Science does know of this species. Me. I'm science. I'm the leading paleontologist of this epoch. Can I help it if I can't publish my discoveries in the professional journals?" He scowled and walked away, carrying the big red crustacean.

Hahn and Barrett looked at each other. They smiled, in a natural mutual response to Rudiger's grumbled outburst. Then Barrett's smile faded.

...termites...one good push...therapy...

"Something wrong?" Hahn asked.

"Why?"

"You looked so bleak, all of a sudden."

"My foot gave me a twinge," Barrett said. "It does that, you know. Here. I'll lend you a hand carrying those things. We'll have fresh trilobite cocktail tonight."

They started up the steps toward the Station itself. Suddenly there came a wild shout from up above, Quesada's voice: "Catch him! He's heading for you! Catch him!"

Jerking his head upward in alarm, Barrett saw Bruce Valdosto plunging down the steps along the face of the cliff, stark naked and trailing the shreds of the webfoam cradle in which he had been gently imprisoned. Perhaps a hundred feet farther up the cliff stood Quesada, blood streaming from his nose, looking dazed and battered.

Valdosto was a shattering sight as he stormed toward them. He had never been an agile man, because of his legs, but now, after weeks under sedation, he could scarcely stand upright at all. He lurched along, stumbling and dropping, scrambling to his feet and hurtling another few steps before he fell again. His hairy body glistened with sweat, and his eyes were wild; his lips were drawn back in a rigid grin. He seemed like some animal that had thrown its leash and was rushing pell-mell toward freedom and destruction together.

Barrett and Hahn had barely enough time to set down their load of trilobites when Valdosto was upon them. Hahn said, "Put your shoulder against mine and we'll block him." Barrett nodded; but he could not move fast enough, and Hahn seized him by the arm and pulled him into position. Barrett braced himself against his crutch.

Valdosto hit them like a plummeting stone.

Half running, half falling, he rushed down the steps and threw himself into the air when he was still ten feet above them. "Val!" Barrett gasped, and reached for him, but then Valdosto struck him, between chest and waist. Barrett absorbed the full momentum. His crutch was driven deep into his armpit, and he pivoted on his knees, twisting his good leg and sending a blazing message of pain the full length of his body. To avoid a dislocated shoulder he let go of the crutch, and as it fell backward he felt himself falling, and caught it again before he toppled. The net effect of his change of position was to slew him around sideways, creating a gap between Hahn and himself. Valdosto shot through that gap like a bounding ball. He eluded Hahn's clutching grasp and sped down the steps.

"Val, come back!" Barrett boomed. "Val!"

But he could do no more than shout. He watched helplessly as Valdosto reached the edge of the sea and, now slipping, now diving, launched himself into the water. His arms beat wildly in a madman's crawl. His dark head bobbed for a moment; then a towering wave fell on him and swept him under. When Barrett saw him again, he was fifty yards out to sea.

By then Hahn had reached Rudiger's beached dinghy and was pulling it free of its moorings. He waded out and began to row desperately. But the tide was in, and the tide was merciless; the waves flipped the boat about like a twig. For every yard Hahn rowed away from shore, he was hurled half a yard back. All the while Valdosto grew more distant, lashing the waves with his splayed hands, rising briefly above the surface, then vanishing again to reappear long moments later.

Barrett, stunned, stood frozen and aching at the place on the steps where Valdosto had burst past him. Quesada had joined him, now.

"What happened?" Barrett asked.

"I was giving him sedation and he went berserk. The cradle was open and he ripped his way out of it and knocked me down. And started to run. Toward the sea...he kept yelling that he was going to swim home...."

"He will," Barrett said.

They watched the struggle. Hahn, exhausted, was furiously trying to row a boat too heavy for a solitary oarsman in waves too rough to conquer. Valdosto, unleashing his last energies, was beyond the inner breakers and swimming steadily for the open sea. But the sloping shelf of rock turned upward in the area just ahead of him, and white water splashed against jutting stony teeth. At high tide there were whirlpools there. Valdosto headed unerringly for the roughest stretch of water. The waves took him, tossed him high, pulled him down again. Soon he was only a line against the horizon.

Hawksbill Station

The others were coming, now, attracted by the shouts. One by one they arrayed themselves along the shore or down the stone steps. Altman, Rudiger, Latimer, Schultz, the sane and the sick, the dreamers, the old, the weary, they stood motionless as Hahn lashed the sea with his oars and Valdosto leaped through the waves. Hahn was coming in, now. He fought his way through the surf, and Rudiger and two or three of the others broke from their stasis, seizing the boat, hauling it ashore, mooring it. Hahn stumbled out, white-faced with fatigue. He dropped to his knees and retched against the rocks while the waves licked at his boots. When he was through, he got shakily to his feet and walked over to Barrett.

"I tried," he said. "The boat wouldn't move. But I tried to get to him."

"It's all right," Barrett told him gently. "No one could have made it. The water was too rough."

"Maybe if I had tried to swim after him instead—"

"No," said Doc Quesada. "Valdosto was insane. And terribly strong. He'd have pulled you under if the waves didn't get you first."

"Where is he?" Barrett asked. "Can anybody see him?"

"Out by the rocks," said Latimer. "Isn't that him?"

Rudiger said, "He's gone under. He's been under three, four minutes now. It's better this way. For him, for us, for everybody."

Barrett turned away from the sea. No one approached him. They knew his relationship with Valdosto, the thirty years of it, the apartment shared, the wild nights and stormy days. Some of them had been here on the day, not so many years ago, when Valdosto had dropped onto the Anvil and Barrett, who had not seen him in more than a decade, let out a whoop of delight and pleasure. One of the last ties to a distant past had just been severed; but, Barrett told himself, Valdosto had been gone for a long time before today.

It was growing dark. Slowly Barrett began to climb the cliff to the Station. Half an hour later Rudiger came to him.

"The sea's calmer now. Val's been washed ashore."

"Where is he?"

"A couple of the boys are bringing him up here for the services. Then we'll take him out in the boat and give him the burial."

"All right," Barrett said. There was only one form of burial at Hawksbill Station, and that was burial at sea. They could hardly dig graves into the living rock for their dead. So Valdosto would be interred twice. Cast up by the waves, he would have to be taken out again, properly weighted, and sent to his resting place. Ordinarily they would have held the funeral by the shore, but now, as a tacit concession to Barrett's handicap, they were bringing Valdosto all the way up here rather than subject Barrett to another strenuous climb along the cliff steps. It seemed pointless, somehow, this dragging back and forth of lifeless flesh. It would have been better, Barrett thought, if Val had simply been swept out to sea the first time.

Hahn and several others appeared soon afterward, carrying the body wrapped in a sheet of blue plastic.

They laid it out on the ground in front of Barrett's hut. It was one of his self-imposed tasks here to deliver the valedictories; it seemed to him that he had delivered fifty such speeches in the last year alone. About thirty of the men were present. The rest were beyond caring about the dead, or else cared so much that they could not attend.

Barrett kept it simple. He spoke briefly of his friendship with Valdosto, of their days together at the turn of the century, of Valdosto's revolutionary activities. He outlined some of Valdosto's heroic acts. Most of them Barrett had learned about at second hand, for he himself had been a prisoner at Hawksbill during Valdosto's years of fame. Between 2006 and 2015, Val had almost singlehandedly reduced the government to a condition of battle fatigue, bombing and mining and killing.

"They knew who he was," Barrett said, "but they couldn't find him. They chased him for years, and one day they caught him, and they put him on trial—you know what sort of trial—and they sent him to us in Hawksbill Station. And for many years Val was a leader here. But he wasn't meant to be a prisoner. He couldn't adapt to a world where he was unable to fight against the government. And so he came apart. We had to watch it, and it was not easy for us. Or for him. May he rest in peace."

Barrett gestured. The pallbearers lifted the body and walked toward the east. Most of the mourners followed. Barrett did not. He stood watching until the funeral procession had begun to wind down the steps that led to the sea; then he turned and went into his hut. After a while he slept.

A little before midnight, Barrett was awakened by the sound of hasty footsteps outside his hut. As he sat up, groping for the luminescence switch, Ned Altman came blundering through the door.

Barrett blinked at him. "What's the matter, Ned?"

"It's Hahn!" Altman rasped. "He's fooling around with the Hammer again. We just saw him go into the building."

Barrett shed his drowsiness like a seal bursting out of water. Ignoring the insistent throb in his left leg, he pulled himself from his bed and grabbed some clothing. He was more apprehensive than he wanted Altman to see, and he kept his face frozen, masklike. If Hahn, fooling around with the temporal mechanism, smashed the Hammer accidentally or deliberately, they might never receive replacement equipment from Up Front. Which would mean that all future shipments—if there were to be any—would come as random shoots that might land in any old year and at great distances from the Station. What business did Hahn have with the machine, anyway?

As Barrett pulled on his trousers, Altman said, "Latimer's up there keeping an eye on him. He got suspicious when Hahn didn't come back to the hut at bedtime, and he got me, and we went looking for him. And there he was, sniffing around the Hammer."

"Doing what?"

"I don't know. As soon as we saw him go into the building, I came right down here to get you. That's what I was supposed to do, wasn't it?"

"Yes," Barrett said. "Come on!"

He stumped his way out of the hut and did his best to trot toward the main building. Pain shot like trails of hot acid up the whole lower half of his body. The crutch dug mercilessly into his left armpit as he leaned all his weight into it. His crippled foot, swinging freely, burned with a cold glow. His right leg, which had to bear most of the burden, creaked and popped. Altman ran breathlessly alongside him. The Station looked dreamlike in the salmon moonlight. It was terribly silent at this hour.

They jogged past Quesada's hut. Barrett considered waking the medic and taking him along. He decided against it. Whatever trouble Hahn might be up to, Barrett felt that he could handle it himself. There was some strength left in the old gnawed beam, after all.

Latimer stood waiting for them at the entrance to the main dome. He was right at the edge of panic, or perhaps he was over the edge. He seemed to be gibbering with fear and shock. Barrett had never seen a man gibber before.

He clamped a big paw on Latimer's thin shoulder and said harshly, "Well, where is he? Where's Hahn?"

"He—disappeared."

"What the hell do you mean? Which way did he go?"

Latimer moaned. His angular face was fishbelly white. His lips trembled and flickered before words would emerge. "He got onto the Anvil," Latimer blurted at length. "The light came on—the glow. And then Hahn disappeared!"

Altman giggled. "Can you beat that! He disappeared! Powie, right into the machine, eh?"

"No," Barrett said. "It isn't possible. The machine's only equipped for receiving, not for transmitting. You must be mistaken, Don."

"I saw him go!"

"He's hiding somewhere in the building," Barrett insisted doggedly. "He's got to be. Close that door! Search the place until you find him!"

Altman said mildly, "He probably did disappear, Jim. If Don says he disappeared—"

"Yes," said Latimer, equally mildly. "That's true, you know. He climbed right on top of the Anvil. Then everything turned red in the room and he was gone."

Barrett clenched his fists and pressed his knuckles against his aching temples. There was a white-hot blaze just behind his forehead that almost made him forget about the pain in his foot. He saw his mistake clearly, now. He had depended for his espionage on two men who were patently and unmistakably insane, and that had been itself a not very sane thing to do. A man is known by his choice of lieutenants. Well, he had relied on Altman and Latimer, and now they were giving him precisely the sort of information that such spies could be counted on to supply.

"You're hallucinating," Barrett told Latimer curtly. "Ned, go wake up Quesada and get him over here right away. You, Don, you stand here by the entrance, and if Hahn shows up I want you to sing out at the top of your lungs. I'm going to search the building for him."

"Wait," Latimer said, catching Barrett's wrist. He seemed to be making an effort to gain control of himself again. "Jim, do you remember when I asked you if you thought I was crazy? You said you didn't. You said you trusted me."

"So?"

"Well, don't stop trusting me now. I tell you I'm not hallucinating. I saw Hahn disappear. I can't explain it, but I'm rational enough to know what I saw."

Barrett stared intently at him. Sure, he thought. Take a crazy man's word for it, when the crazy man tells you in a nice calm voice that he's perfectly sane. Sure.

He said in a milder tone, "All right, Don. Maybe so. I want you to stay by the door, anyway. I'll run a quick check, just to see what's what."

He went into the building, planning to make a circuit of the dome, beginning with the room where the Hammer was mounted. He entered it. Everything seemed to be in perfect order there. No Hawksbill Field glow was in evidence, nor could Barrett see any indication that anything had been disturbed.

The receiving room had no closets or cupboards or alcoves or crannies in which Hahn could be hiding. When he had inspected the room thoroughly, Barrett moved on down the corridor, looking into the infirmary, the mess hall, the kitchen, the reception room. He checked every likely hiding place. He looked high and he looked low.

No Hahn. Not anywhere.

Of course, there were plenty of places in those rooms where Hahn might have secreted himself. Maybe he was sitting in the refrigerator on top of a pile of frigid trilobites. Maybe he was under all the equipment in the recreation room. Maybe he was in the drug closet.

But Barrett doubted that Hahn was in the building at all. Very likely he was down by the waterfront, taking a moody stroll, and hadn't set foot in the place since evening. Very likely this entire episode had been some feverish fantasy of Latimer's, nothing more. Knowing that Barrett was worried about Hahn's interest in the Hammer, Latimer and Altman had nudged themselves into imagining that they saw him snooping here, and had succeeded in convincing themselves of it.

Barrett completed the route through the building's circling corridor and found himself back at the main entrance. Latimer still stood guard there. He had been joined by a sleepy Quesada, his face bruised and puffy from his battle with Valdosto. Altman, pale and shaky-looking, was just outside the door.

"What's going on?" Quesada asked.

"I'm not sure," Barrett said. "Don and Ned had the idea that they saw Lew Hahn fooling around with the time equipment. I've checked through the whole building, and he doesn't seem to be in here, so maybe they made a little mistake. I suggest you take them both into the infirmary and give them a shot of something to settle their nerves, and then we'll all try to get back to sleep."

Latimer said thinly, "I tell you, I swear I saw—"

"Shut up!" Altman broke in. "Listen! Listen! What's that noise?"

Barrett listened. The sound was clear and loud: the hissing whine of ionization. It was the sound produced by a functioning Hawksbill Field. Suddenly goosepimples were breaking out on his skin.

In a low voice, he said, "The Field's on. We're probably getting some supplies."

"At this hour?" said Latimer.

"We don't know what time it is Up Front. All of you stay here. I'll check the Hammer."

"Perhaps I ought to go with you, Jim," Quesada suggested gently.

"*Stay* here!" Barrett thundered. He paused, embarrassed at his own explosive show of wrath. Nerves. Nerves. He said more quietly, "It only takes one of us to check things. You wait. I'll be right back."

Without staying around to hear further dissent, Barrett pivoted and limped down the hall to the Hammer room. He shouldered the door open and looked in. There was no need for him to switch on the light. The deep red glow of the Hawksbill Field illuminated everything.

He stationed himself just within the door. Hardly daring to breathe, he stared fixedly at the metallic bulk of the Hammer, watching the play of colors against its shafts and power rods and fuses. The glow of the Field deepened through various shades of pink toward crimson, and then spread until it enfolded the waiting Anvil beneath it. An endless moment passed.

Then came the implosive thunderclap, and Lew Hahn dropped out of nowhere and lay for a moment in temporal shock on the broad plate of the Anvil.

They had arrested Barrett on a beautiful day in October 2006, when the leaves were crisp and yellowing, when the air was clear and cool, when the cloudless blue sky seemed to reflect all the glory of autumn. He was in Boston that day, as he had been on a day ten years previous when they had arrested Janet at his New York apartment. He was walking down Boylston Street on his way to an appointment when two alert-looking young men in neutral gray business suits matched their strides to his, kept pace with him for perhaps ten feet, and moved in to flank him.

"James Edward Barrett?" the one on the left said.

"That's right." Why pretend?

"We'd like you to come with us," said the one on the right.

"Please don't attempt any violence," said his partner.

"It'll be better for all of us if you don't. Especially for you."

"I won't make trouble," Barrett said.

They had a car parked on the corner. Keeping close to him at every step, they walked him to the car and guided him within it. When they closed the doors, they didn't just lock them, but sealed them with a radio block.

"May I make a phone call?" Barrett asked.

"Sorry. No."

The agent who sat at his left produced a degausser and quickly voided any recording device Barrett might be carrying. The agent at his right checked him out for communication instruments, found the telephone mounted against his ear, and deftly removed it. They locked Barrett in place with a microwave restraining field that left him enough freedom to yawn or stretch, but not enough to touch either of the agents beside him. The car moved away from the curb.

"So this is it," Barrett said. "I've been expecting it for so long that I began to believe it would never happen."

"It happens eventually," said the left-hand one.

"To all of you," said the right-hand one. "It just takes time."

Time. Yes. In '85, '86, '87, the first years of the resistance movement, an adolescent Jim Barrett had lived in perpetual expectation of arrest. Arrest or worse: a laser beam whistling out of nowhere to penetrate his skull, maybe. In those years he saw the new government as omniscient and all-threatening, and saw himself in constant peril. But the arrests had been few, and in time Barrett had swung to the opposite extreme, confidently assuming that the secret police would leave him untouched. He had even convinced himself that a decision had been taken not to molest him—that he was being spared deliberately, as a symbol of the regime's tolerance of dissent. After Chancellor Dantell had replaced Chancellor Arnold, Barrett had lost some of that naïve confidence of personal grace. But yet he had not fully come to terms with the possibility

Hawksbill Station

of arrest until the day they took Janet away. One does not believe one can be struck by lightning until a bolt blasts the person at one's side. And after that one expects the heavens to open again whenever a cloud appears.

There had been arrests all through the harsh years of the middle '90s, but he had never even been called in for questioning. Eventually he came once again to believe that he was immune. Having lived with the possibility of arrest, on and off, for more than twenty years, Barrett simply pushed that possibility into a distant corner of his mind and forgot about it. And now they had come for him at last.

He searched his soul for a reaction, and was puzzled at the only reaction he found: relief. The suspense was over. So was the toil. Now he could rest.

He was thirty-eight years old. He was Supreme Commander of the Eastern Division of the Continental Liberation Front. Since boyhood he had labored to bring about the overthrow of the government, taking a million tiny steps that covered no territory whatever. Of those who had been present at his first underground meeting, that day in 1984, he alone remained. Janet was missing and presumed dead. Jack Bernstein, his mentor in revolutionary affairs, had gone over cheerfully to the enemy. Hawksbill had died, bloated and hypothyroid at forty-three, just a few years ago. His work on time travel, so they said, had been a success: He had built a workable time machine and turned it over to the government. There was a rumor that the government was conducting experiments with the machine, using political prisoners as subjects. Barrett had heard that old Norman Pleyel had been one of the subjects. They had arrested him in March of '05, at any rate, and no one knew where he was now. Pleyel's arrest had left Barrett in command of the sector in title as well as in fact; but he had expected to have a little more time before they picked him up too.

So they were all gone, those revolutionaries of '84, dead or missing or on the other side. He alone was left, and now he was about to be dead or missing too. Strangely, he had few regrets. He was willing to let others carry on the dreary task of preparing for The Revolution.

The Revolution that would never come, he thought bitterly. The Revolution had been lost before it ever began. Jack Bernstein's words drifted across time to him out of 1987: "We're going to lose unless we grab the kids growing up! The syndicalists are getting them, and educating them to think that syndicalism is true and good and beautiful, and the longer that goes on, the longer it's going to go on. It's self-perpetuating. Anybody who wants the old constitution back, or who wants the new constitution amended, is going to look like a dangerous fire-breathing radical, and the syndicalists will be the nice, safe, conservative boys we've always had and always want. At which point everything is over and done with." Yes. Jack had been right. The Front had grabbed some of the kids growing up, but not enough. Despite an ever more sophisticated propaganda campaign, despite a cunning interleaving of revolutionary agitation with popular entertainment, despite the financial support of some of the nation's finest minds, they had achieved nothing. They had been unable to move that vast placid mass of citizens, the ones who were satisfied with the government, whatever sort of government it might happen to be, the ones who feared rocking the boat more than they feared being devoured by the boat.

They might as well arrest me, then, Barrett told himself. I'm used up. I've got nothing left to offer the Front. I've admitted inward defeat, and if I stick around, I'll poison all the younger ones with my pessimism.

It was true. He had ceased to be a revolutionary agitator years ago. He was nothing but a bureaucrat of revolution now, a shuffler of papers, a representative of entrenched interests. If The Revolution actually broke out, now, would he rejoice or would he be terrified of it? He had grown accustomed to living on the brink of revolution. He was comfortable there. His commitment to change had eroded.

"You're very quiet," said the agent at his left.

"Should I be screaming and sobbing?"

"We expected more trouble with you," said the agent at his right. "A top leader like you—"

"You don't know me very well," Barrett said. "I'm past the stage of caring what you do with me."

"Oh, really? That's not the profile we've got on you. You're a dedicated revolutionary from way back, Barrett. You're a dangerous radical. We've been watching you."

"Why did you wait so long to arrest me, then?"

"We don't believe in picking up everybody right away. We have a long-range program of arrest. Everything's programmed for impact. We get one leader this year, one the next, one five years afterward—"

"Sure," Barrett said. "You can afford to wait, because we don't represent any real threat anyway. We're just a bunch of frauds."

"You sound almost serious," said the agent at his left.

Barrett laughed.

"You're a funny one," said the agent at his right. "We've never had one quite like you before. You don't even look like an agitator. You could almost be a lawyer, or something. Something respectable."

"Are you sure you've got the right man, then?" Barrett asked.

The two agents eyed each other. The man on Barrett's right stopped the car and deactivated the restraining field in which Barrett was caged. He seized Barrett's right hand and pushed it against the data plate on the dashboard. He punched for computer time. A moment passed while the central computer checked Barrett's fingerprints against its master files.

"You're Barrett, all right," the agent said in obvious relief.

"I never denied it, did I? I just asked if you were sure."

"Well, now we're even surer."

"Good."

"You're a funny one, Barrett."

They took him to the airport. A small government plane was waiting there. The flight lasted two hours, which would have been enough to take him nearly across the continent, but Barrett had no assurance that he had gone any such distance. They could have been flying in circles over Boston all that time; the government, he knew, did things like that. When the plane landed, nightfall had come. He did not catch more than a glimpse of the airport, for a sealed transport capsule was pushed up against the plane and he was hustled into it. That single glimpse was not enough to tell Barrett where he might be.

But he did not need to be told his destination. He ended his journey in one of the government's interrogation camps. A blank, smooth black metal door closed behind him. Within, all was sleek, brightly lit, antiseptic. It might have been a hospital. Corridors receded in many directions; recessed lighting gave a pleasant greenish-yellow glow.

They fed him. They gave him a seamless uniform made of some imperishable-looking fabric. They put him in a cell.

Barrett was surprised and vaguely pleased to discover that he had not landed in a maximum-security block. His cell was a comfortable room, about ten by fourteen, with a bunk, a toilet, an ultrasonic bath, and a video eye behind a nearly invisible barrier in the ceiling. There was a grillwork in the cell door through which he could carry on conversations with the prisoners in the facing cells. He did not recognize their names; some of them belonged to underground groups he had never heard of, and he thought he had heard of them all. Probably at least a few of his neighbors here were government spies, but Barrett did not mind that, since he expected it.

"How often do the interrogators come?" Barrett asked.

"They don't," said the stocky, bearded man across the way. His name was Fulks. "I've been here a month and I haven't been interrogated yet."

"They don't come here to interrogate," said the man next to Fulks. "They take you away and question you somewhere else. Then you never come back here. They're in no hurry, either. I've been here a month and a half.'

A week passed, and no one took official notice of Barrett. He was fed regularly, allowed to requisition certain reading matter, and taken from his cell every third day for exercise in the courtyard. But there was no indication that he was going to be interrogated or placed on trial or even indicted. Under the law of preventive detention, he could be held indefinitely without an arraignment, if he were deemed dangerous to the continuity of the state.

Some of the prisoners were led away. They did not return. New prisoners arrived each day.

Hawksbill Station

A good deal of the talk was about the time-travel program. "They're doing the experiments," reported a thin, tough-faced newcomer named Anderson. "They got a process, it lets them send back rabbits and monkeys a couple of years in time. They got it almost perfect now. And then they're going to start sending prisoners back. They'll send us a million years back and let us get eaten by dinosaurs."

It sounded unlikely to Barrett, even though he had discussed this project with its inventor six years before. Well, Hawksbill was dead now, and his work was the property of those who had footed the bill for it, and God help us all if these wild stories are true. A million years into the past? The government piously declared that it had renounced capital punishment; but perhaps it could stick a man into Hawksbill's machine, ship him off to who knew where or when, and maintain a clear conscience.

Barrett thought he had been in custody for four weeks when they took him from his cell and transferred him to the interrogation department. He was not sure, because he had been having some difficulty keeping an accurate count of the passing days, but he thought it was about four weeks. He had never known twenty-eight days to pass so slowly. He would not have been amazed at all to learn that he had been in his cell four years before they came for him.

A snub-nosed little electric runabout took him through endless mazes and delivered him to a cheerful office, where he went through an elaborate registration process. When the routines were completed, two monitors escorted him to a small, austere room containing a desk, a couch, and a chair.

"Lie down," one monitor said. Barrett obeyed. He was aware of a restraining shield taking form about him. He studied the ceiling. It was gray and perfectly smooth, as though the entire room had been squirted from a nozzle as a single bubble. They let him examine the perfection of the ceiling for several hours, and then, just as he was beginning to get hungry, a section of the wall slid away long enough to admit the lean figure of Jack Bernstein.

"I knew it would be you, Jack," Barrett said calmly.

"Please call me Jacob."

"You never let anyone call you Jacob when we were kids," Barrett said. "You insisted your name was Jack, right on your birth certificate. Remember when a bunch of our classmates got bothered with you and chased you halfway across the schoolyard, yelling, Jacob, Jacob, Jacob? I had to save you then. That was, how long, Jack, twenty-five years ago? Two thirds of our lives ago, Jack."

"Jacob."

"Do you mind if I go on calling you Jack? I can't break the habit after all this time."

"You'd be wiser to call me Jacob," Bernstein said. "I have great power over your future."

"I've got no future. I'm a prisoner for keeps."

"That isn't necessarily so."

"Don't tease me, Jack. The only power you have is to decide, maybe, whether I'll get tortured or just left to rot in boredom. And, frankly, I don't give a damn. I'm beyond your reach, Jack. There's nothing you can do to me that matters."

"Nevertheless," Bernstein said, "it might prove to your advantage to cooperate with me, in the small things as well as in the big ones. Regardless of how desperate you think your present situation is, you're still alive, and you might conceivably discover that we mean you no harm. But it all depends on your attitude. I find that it pleases me to be called Jacob these days, and it shouldn't be that difficult for you to adapt."

"As long as you wanted to change your name, Jack," said Barrett amiably, "why didn't you make it Judas?"

Bernstein did not reply at once. He crossed the room and stood beside the couch on which Barrett lay, and stared down at him in an impersonal, abstracted manner. His face, thought Barrett, looks calm and relaxed for the first time I can recall. But he's lost more weight. His cheekbones are like knives. He can't weigh more than a hundred pounds. And his eyes are so bright...so bright....

Bernstein said, "You were always such a big fool, Jim."

"Yes. I didn't have the sense to be radical when you were joining the underground. Then I didn't have the sense to jump to the other side when the jumping was good."

"And now you don't have the sense to accommodate yourself to your interrogator."

"I'm not much on selling out, Jack. Jacob."

"To save yourself?"

"Suppose I'm not interested in saving myself?"

"The Revolution needs you, doesn't it?" Bernstein asked. "It's your duty to get out of our clutches and continue your sacred task of working toward the overthrow of the government."

"Is it?"

"I think so."

"I don't, Jack. I'm tired of being a revolutionary. I think I'd just like to lie here and rest for the next forty or fifty years. As prisons go, this one's pretty comfortable."

"I can arrange your release," Bernstein said. "But only if you cooperate."

Barrett smiled. "All right, Jacob. Tell me what you want to know, and I'll see if I can't give you the answers you want."

"I have no questions now."

"None?"

"None."

"That's a lousy way to interrogate a man, no?"

"You're still full of resistance, Jim. I'll come back another time, and we'll talk again."

Bernstein went out. They left Barrett alone for a couple of hours, until he thought he would split apart in boredom, and then they brought him a meal. He expected Bernstein to return after dinner. But, in fact, Barrett did not see the interrogator again for quite some time.

They put him in an interrogation tank late that evening.

The theory, and it was a reasonable one, held that total sensory deprivation lessens a man's individuality, and hence reduces his tendency toward stubbornness. Plug his ears, cap his eyes, put him in a warm nutrient bath, pipe food and air to him along plastic conduits, let him float in idleness, in womblike ease, day after day, until the spirit decays and the ego corrodes. Barrett entered the tank. He could not hear. He could not see. Before long, he could not sleep.

As he lay in his tank he dictated his autobiography to himself, a document several volumes long. He invented mathematical games of great intricacy. He recited the names of the states of the old United States of America, and tried to recall the names of their capitals. He reenacted scenes that had been climactic in his life, altering the script here and there.

Then it became too much trouble even to think, and he merely drifted on the amniotic tide. He came to believe that he was dead, and that this was the afterlife, eternal relaxation. Soon his mind twitched into renewed activity, and he waited eagerly to be taken from the tank and questioned, and then he waited desperately, and then he waited furiously, and then he ceased to wait at all.

After what could have been eight hundred years, they took him from the interrogation tank.

"How do you feel?" a guard asked. His voice was like a shriek. Barrett clapped his hands to his ears and dropped to the floor. They picked him up.

"You get used to the sound of voices again eventually," the guard said.

"Stop it," Barrett whispered. "Stop talking!"

He could not abide even the sound of his own voice. His heartbeat was merciless thunder in his ears. His breathing made a ferocious rustling sound, like the tearing down of forests by gusts of wind. His eyes were numbed by the flood of visual impressions. He shivered. He quaked.

Jacob Bernstein came to him an hour after he had been brought from the tank.

"Feel rested?" Bernstein asked. "Relaxed, happy, cooperative?"

"How long was I in there?"

"I'm not prepared to tell you that."

"A week? A month? A year? What's today's date?"

"It doesn't matter, Jim."

"Please stop talking. Your voice hurts my ears."

Bernstein smiled. "You'll adjust. I hope you've been reviewing your memory while you've rested, Jim. Answer some questions, now. The names of people in your group, to begin with. Not everybody—just those in positions of responsibility."

"You know all the names," Barrett murmured.

"I want to hear them from you."

"What for?"

"Perhaps we took you from the tank too soon."

"So put me back," Barrett said.

"Don't be stubborn. List some names for me."

"It hurts my ears when I talk."

Bernstein folded his arms. "Let the names go, for now. I have here a statement describing the extent of your counterrevolutionary activities."

"*Counter*revolutionary?"

"Yes. In opposition to the continuing work of the founders of the Revolution of 1984."

"I haven't heard us described as counterrevolutionaries in a long time, Jack."

"Jacob."

"Jacob."

"Thank you. I'll read the statement. You may amend it if you find it incorrect in any details. Then you'll sign it, please." He opened a lengthy document and read a concise, dry account of Barrett's career in the underground, substantially accurate, covering everything from that first meeting in 1984 to date. When he finished he said, "Any criticisms or suggestions?"

"No."

"Sign it, then."

"My muscular coordination is lousy right now. I can't hold a pen. I guess I was in your tank too long."

"Dictate a verbal adherence to the statements of the confession, then. We'll take a voiceprint, and it'll serve as admissible evidence."

"No."

"You deny that this is an accurate summary of your career?"

"I take the Fifth Amendment."

"There is no such concept as the Fifth Amendment," Bernstein said. "Will you admit that you've worked for the conscious overthrow of the present legally constituted government of this nation?"

"Doesn't it make you sick to hear words like that coming out of your mouth, Jack?"

"I warn you not to launch a personal attack on my integrity," said Bernstein quietly. "You can't possibly understand the motivations that caused me to transfer my allegiance from the underground to the government, and I'm not about to discuss them with you. This is your interrogation, not mine."

"I hope your turn comes soon."

"I doubt that it will."

Barrett said, "When we were sixteen, you spoke of this government as wolves eating the world. You warned me that unless I woke up, I'd be one more slave in a world full of slaves. And I said I'd rather be a live slave than a dead subversive, remember, and you took me apart for saying something like that. Now here you are on the team of the wolves. You're a live slave and I'm going to be a dead subversive."

"This government has renounced capital punishment," said Bernstein. "I regard myself as neither a wolf nor a slave. And by your own words you've just demonstrated the fallacy of trying to uphold your opinions-aged-sixteen into adulthood."

"What do you want from me, Jack?"

"Two things. Your acceptance of the résumé I've just read you. And your cooperation in our attempt to gain information about the leadership of the Continental Liberation Front."

"You're forgetting one thing. You also want me to call you Jacob, Jacob."

Bernstein did not smile. "If you cooperate, I can promise you a satisfactory end to this interrogation."

"And if not?"

"We are not vindictive. But we take action to maintain the security of the citizens by removing from their environment those who threaten national stability."

"But you don't kill people," Barrett said. "Hell, you must have awfully crowded prisons by now. Unless the time-travel business is true."

Bernstein's armor of self-containment seemed to be pierced for the first time.

Barrett said, "Is it? Did Hawksbill build a machine that lets you toss prisoners back in time? Are you feeding us to the dinosaurs?"

"I'll give you another opportunity to answer my questions," said Bernstein, looking nettled. "Will you tell me—"

"You know, Jack, a funny thing's been happening to me in this interrogation camp. When the police picked me up that day in Boston, I honestly didn't mind. I had lost interest in The Revolution. I was as uncommitted that day as I had been when I was sixteen and you dragged me into the whole business. What it was, my faith in the revolutionary process had burned out. I had stopped believing we could ever overthrow the government, and I saw that I was just going through the motions, getting older and older, using up my life in a futile Bolshevik dream, keeping up appearances so I wouldn't discourage the kids in the movement. I had just discovered that my whole life was empty. So what difference did it make to me if you arrested me? I was nothing. I bet that if you came and questioned me my first day in jail, I would have told you anything you wanted to know, simply because I was too bored to go on resisting. But now I've been in interrogation for six months, a year, I can't tell how long, and the effect's been quite interesting. I'm stubborn again. I came in here flaccid-willed, and you've built up my will until it's stronger than ever. Isn't that interesting, Jack? I guess it doesn't make you look like such a hotshot interrogator, and I'm sorry about that, but I thought you'd like to know how the process has been affecting me."

"Are you asking to be tortured, Jim?"

"I'm not asking anything. Just telling."

They took Barrett back to the tank. As before, he had no idea how long he was left in it, but it seemed longer this time than the first time, and he felt weaker when he came out. He could not be interrogated for three hours afterward, because he could not tolerate noise. Bernstein tried, but gave up and waited until his pain threshold had improved. Barrett failed to be cooperative. Bernstein was distressed.

They inflicted a moderate amount of physical torture on Barrett next. He withstood it.

Bernstein tried to be friendly. He offered cigarettes, had Barrett released from restraint, chatted about old times. They argued ideology from all viewpoints. They laughed together. They joked.

"Will you help me now, Jim?" Bernstein asked. "Just answer a few questions."

"You don't need the information I could give you. It's all on file. You're only after a symbolic capitulation. Well, I'm going to hold out forever. You might as well give up and bring me to trial."

"Your trial can't begin until you've signed the statement," Bernstein said.

"In that case you'll have to go on interrogating."

But in the end, boredom got the better of him. He was tired of his immersions in the tank, tired of the bright lights, the electronic probes, the subcutaneous shocks, the jabbing questions, tired of Bernstein's haggard face peering into his own. Coming to trial seemed the only way out. Barrett signed the résumé Bernstein offered him. He delivered up a list of names of Continental Liberation Front officers. The names were imaginary, and Bernstein knew it; but he was satisfied. It was the appearance of capitulation they were after.

"You will be tried next week," said Bernstein.

"Congratulations," Barrett said. "You did a masterly job of breaking my spirit. I'm utterly defeated now. My will is shattered. I've surrendered in all respects. You're a credit to your profession—Jack."

The look that Jacob Bernstein gave him was tipped with acid.

The trial duly took place: no jury, no attorneys, merely a government functionary sitting before a bank of computer inputs and outputs. Barrett's confession was entered into the records. Barrett himself supplied a verbal statement. The interrogator's report was delivered. In the course of proceedings, it was necessary for a date to be affixed to all these reports, and so Barrett learned that it was now the summer of 2008. He had been in the interrogation camp for twenty months.

Hawksbill Station

"The verdict is guilty as charged. James Edward Barrett, we sentence you to imprisonment for life, the place of your internment to be Hawksbill Station."

"Where?"

No reply. They led him away.

Hawksbill Station? What was that? Something to do with the time machine, perhaps?

Barrett found out soon enough.

He was brought to a vast room filled with improbable machinery. At the center of everything was a gleaming metallic plate twenty feet in diameter. Above it, descending from the distant ceiling, was a conglomeration of apparatus weighing many tons, an arrangement of colossal pistons and power cores that looked like a prehistoric monster about to strike...or perhaps like a gigantic hammer. The room was crowded with hard-eyed technicians, busy at dials and screens. No one spoke to Barrett. He was thrust up onto the huge anvil-like plate beneath the monstrous hammer. All about him, the room throbbed with activity. This was a lot of fuss, he told himself, for one weary political prisoner. Were they going to send him to Hawksbill Station now?

There was a red glow in the room.

But nothing happened for a long while. Barrett stood patiently, feeling faintly absurd. A voice said in the background, "How's the calibration?"

"Fine. We'll toss him exactly a billion years back."

"Wait a second!" Barrett yelled. "A billion years—"

They ignored him. He could not move. There was a high whining sound, a strange odor in the air. And then he felt pain, the most intense, the most dislocating pain he had ever experienced. Had the hammer descended and crushed him flat? He could not see. He was nowhere. He was—

—falling—

—landing—

—sitting up, dazed, sweating, bewildered. He was in another room with some of the same sort of equipment around him, but the faces here were not the hard faces of impersonal technicians.

He recognized these faces. Members of the Continental Liberation Front...men he had not seen for years, men who had been arrested, whose whereabouts had been unknown.

There was Norman Pleyel, with tears in his gentle eyes.

"Jim—Jim Barrett—so they finally sent you here too, Jim! Don't try to get up. You're in temporal shock now, but it passes fast."

Barrett said hoarsely, "Is this Hawksbill Station?"

"This is Hawksbill Station. Such that it is."

"Where is it?"

"Not where, Jim. When. We're a billion years back in time."

"No. No." He shook his foggy head. So Hawksbill's machine did work, and the rumors were true, and this was where they sent the troublesome ones. Was Janet here too? He asked. No, Pleyel said. There were only men here. Twenty or thirty prisoners, managing somehow to survive.

Barrett was reluctant to believe any of this. But then they helped him down from the Anvil, and took him outside to show him what the world was like, and he stared in slowly spreading wonder at the curve of bare rock slanting into the gray sea, at the unmarred, uninhabited coast, and the reality of his exile sank in with a blow more painful than the one the Hammer had dealt him.

14

In the darkness, Hahn did not notice Barrett at first. He sat up slowly, shaking off the stunning effects of a trip through time. After a few seconds he pushed himself toward the lip of the Anvil and let his legs dangle over it. He swung them to get the circulation going. He took a series of deep breaths. Finally he slipped to the floor. The glow of the field had gone out in the moment of his arrival, and so he moved warily, as though not wanting to bump into anything.

Abruptly Barrett switched on the light and said, "What have you been up to, Hahn?"

The younger man recoiled as though he had been jabbed in the gut. He gasped, hopped backward a few steps, and flung up both hands in a defensive gesture. "Answer me," Barrett said.

Hahn seemed to regain his equilibrium. He shot a quick glance past Barrett's bulky form toward the hallway and said, "Let me go, will you? I can't explain now."

"You'd better explain now."

"It'll be easier for everyone if I don't," said Hahn. "Please. Let me pass."

Barrett continued to block the door. "I want to know where you've been this evening. And what you've been doing with the Hammer."

"Nothing. Just studying it a little."

"You weren't in this room a minute ago. Then you appeared out of nowhere. Where did you come from, Hahn?"

"You're mistaken. I was standing right behind the Hammer. I didn't—"

"I saw you drop down on the Anvil. You took a time trip, didn't you?"

"No."

"Don't lie to me! I don't know how you do it, but you've got some way of going forward in time, isn't that so? You've been spying on us, and you just went somewhere to file your report—somewhen—and now you're back."

Hahn's pale forehead was glistening. He said tautly, "I warn you, Barrett, don't ask too many questions right now. You'll know everything you want to know in due time. This isn't the time. Please, now. Let me pass."

"I want answers first," Barrett said.

He realized that he was trembling. He already knew the answers, and they were answers that shook him to the core of his soul. He knew where Hahn had been.

But Hahn had to admit it himself.

Hahn said nothing. He took a couple of hesitant steps toward Barrett, who did not move. Hahn seemed to be gathering momentum for a sudden rush at the doorway.

Barrett said, "You aren't getting out of this room until you've told me what I want to know."

Hahn charged.

Barrett planted himself squarely, crutch braced against the doorframe, his good leg flat on the floor, and waited for the younger man to reach him. He figured that he outweighed Hahn by at least eighty pounds. That might be just enough to balance the fact that he was spotting Hahn some thirty years and one leg. They came together, and Barrett drove his hands down onto Hahn's shoulders, trying to hold him, to force him back into the room.

Hahn gave an inch or two. He looked up at Barrett without saying a word and pushed forward again.

"Don't—don't—" Barrett grunted. "I—won't—let— you—"

"I don't want to do this," Hahn said.

He pushed again. Barrett felt himself buckling under the impact. He dug his hands as hard as he could into Hahn's shoulders, and tried to shove the other man backward into the room. But Hahn held firm, and all of Barrett's energy was converted into a backward thrust rebounding on himself. He lost control of his crutch. It scraped along the doorframe and slithered out from under his arm. For one agonizing moment Barrett's full weight rested on the crushed uselessness of his left foot, and then, as though his limbs were melting away beneath him, he began to sink toward the floor. He landed with a reverberating crash.

Quesada, Altman, and Latimer came rushing into the room. Barrett writhed in pain on the floor, digging his fingers into the thigh of his crippled leg. Hahn stood over him, looking unhappy, his hands locked together.

"I'm sorry," he said. "You shouldn't have tried to muscle me like that."

Barrett glowered at him. "You were traveling in time, weren't you? You can answer me now!"

"Yes," Hahn said at last. "I went Up Front."

Hawksbill Station

An hour later, after Quesada had pumped him with enough shots of neural depressant to keep him from jumping out of his skin with pain, Barrett got the full story. Hahn hadn't wanted to reveal it so soon, but he had changed his mind after his little scuffle.

It was all very simple. Time travel now worked in both directions. The glib, impressive noises about the flow of entropy had turned out to be just noises.

"No," Barrett said. "I discussed it with Hawksbill myself, in—let's see—it was 1998. Hawksbill and I knew each other. I said, can people go back and forth in time, with your machine, and he said no, only back. Forward motion was impossible according to his equations."

"His equations were incomplete," said Hahn. "Obviously. He never worked out the forward-motion part."

"How could a man like Hawksbill make a mistake?"

"He made at least one. There's been further research, and we know now how to move in both directions. Even Einstein had to be amended later on. Why not Hawksbill?"

Barrett shook his head. Well, why not Hawksbill, he asked himself? But he had taken it as an article of faith that Hawksbill's work had been perfect, that he was condemned to live out his days here at the dawn of time.

"How long has this two-way thing been known?" Barrett asked.

"At least five years," Hahn said. "We aren't sure yet exactly when the breakthrough came. After we're finished going through all the secret records of the former government—"

"The former government?"

Hahn nodded. "The revolution came in January. Of '29. It wasn't really a violent one, either. The syndicalists just mildewed from within, and when they got the first push they fell over. There was a revolutionary government waiting in the wings to take over and restore the old constitutional guarantees."

"Was it mildew?" Barrett asked, coloring. "Or termites? Keep your metaphors straight."

Hahn glanced away. "Anyway, the old government fell. We've got a provisional liberal regime in office now, and there's going to be an open election in six months or so. Don't ask me much about the philosophy of the new administration. I'm not a political theorist. I'm not even an economist. You guessed as much."

"What are you, then?"

"A policeman," Hahn said. "Part of the commission that's investigating the prison system of the former government. Including this prison."

Barrett said, "What's happening to the prisoners Up Front? The politicals."

"They're being freed. We review their cases and generally let them go fast."

Barrett nodded. "And the syndicalists? What's becoming of them? I wonder if you could tell me about one in particular, an interrogator, name of Jacob Bernstein. Maybe you know of him."

"Bernstein? Sure. One of the Council of Syndics, he was. Head of interrogation."

"Was?"

"Committed suicide," said Hahn. "A lot of the Syndics did that when the regime fell apart. Bernstein was the first."

"It figures," Barrett said, feeling oddly moved, somehow.

There was a long moment of silence.

"There was a girl," Barrett said. "Long ago—she disappeared—they arrested her in 1994, and no one ever could find out what happened to her. I wonder if—if—"

Hahn shook his head. "I'm sorry," he said gently. "That was thirty-five years ago. We didn't find any prisoners who had been in jail more than six or seven years. The hard core opposition all got sent to Hawksbill Station, and the others—well, if she was a special friend of yours, it's not likely that she's going to turn up."

"No," Barrett said. "You're right. She's been dead a long time, probably. But I couldn't help asking—just in case—"

He looked at Quesada, then at Hahn. Thoughts were streaming turbulently through him, and he could not remember when he had last been so overwhelmed by events. He had to work hard to keep from breaking into the shakes again. His voice quavered a little as he said to Hahn, "You came back to observe Hawksbill Station, right, to see how we were getting along? And you went Up Front tonight to tell them what you saw here. You must think we're a pretty sad bunch, eh?"

"You've all been under extraordinary stress here," Hahn said. "Considering the circumstances of your imprisonment—to be sent to this remote era—"

Quesada broke in. "If there's a liberal government in power, now, and it's possible to travel both ways in time, then am I right in assuming that the Hawksbill prisoners are going to be sent back Up Front?"

"Of course," said Hahn. "It'll be done as soon as possible, as soon as we can take care of the logistics end. That's been the whole purpose of my reconnaissance mission. To find out if you people were still alive, first—we didn't even know if anyone had ever survived being sent back in time. And then to see what shape you're in, how badly in need of treatment you are. You'll be given every available benefit of modern therapy, naturally. No expense spared to—"

Barrett scarcely paid attention to Hahn's words. He had been fearing something like this all night, ever since Altman had told him that Hahn was monkeying with the Hammer. But he had never fully allowed himself to believe that it could really be possible. He saw his kingdom crumbling, now. He saw himself returned to a world he could not begin to comprehend—a lame Rip van Winkle, coming back after twenty years.

And he saw himself being taken from a place that had become his home.

Barrett said tiredly, "You know, some of the men aren't going to be able to adapt to the shock of freedom. It might just kill them to be dumped into the real world again. We've got a lot of advanced psychos here. You've seen them. You saw what Valdosto did this afternoon."

"Yes," Hahn said. "I've mentioned such cases in my report."

"It'll be necessary for the sick ones to be prepared in gradual stages to the idea of going back," Barrett said. "It might even take longer than that."

"I'm no therapist," said Hahn. "Whatever the doctors think is right for them is what will be done. Maybe it'll be necessary to keep them here indefinitely, some of them. I can see where it would be a pretty potent upheaval to send them back, after they've spent all these years believing there's no return."

"More than that," said Barrett. "There's a lot of work that can be done here. I mean, scientific work. Exploration. Going across this world, and even up and down the time-lines using this place as a base of operations. I don't think Hawksbill Station ought to be closed down."

"No one said it would be. We have every intention of keeping it going, more or less as you suggest. There's going to be a tremendous program of time exploration getting underway, and a base like this in the past will be invaluable. But the Station won't be a prison any more. The prison concept is out. Completely out."

"Good," Barrett said. He fumbled for his crutch, found it, and got heavily to his feet, swaying a little. Quesada moved toward him as though to steady him, but Barrett brusquely shook him off.

"Let's go outside," he said.

They left the building. A gray mist had come in over the Station, and a fine drizzle was beginning to fall. Barrett looked around at the scattering of huts. He looked at the ocean, dimly visible to the east in the faint moonlight. He looked toward the west and the distant sea. He thought of Charley Norton and the party that had gone on the annual expedition to the Inland Sea. That bunch is going to be in for a real surprise, he thought. When they come back here in a few weeks and discover that everybody is free to go home.

Very strangely, Barrett felt a sudden pressure forming around his eyelids, as of tears trying to force their way out into the open.

He turned to Hahn and Quesada. In a low voice he said, "Have you followed what I've been trying to tell you? Someone's got to stay here and ease the transition for the sick men who won't be able to stand the shock of return. Someone's got to keep the base running. Someone's got to explain things to the new men who'll be coming back here, the scientists."

"Naturally," Hahn said.

Hawksbill Station

"The one who does that—the one who stays behind after the others go—I think it ought to be someone who knows the Station well. Someone who's fit to return Up Front right away, but who's willing to make the sacrifice and stay behind. Do you follow me? A volunteer." They were smiling at him now. Barrett wondered if there might not be something patronizing about those smiles. He wondered if he might not be a little too transparent. To hell with both of them, he thought. He sucked the Cambrian air into his lungs until his chest swelled grandly.

"I'm offering to stay," Barrett said in a loud tone. He glared at them to keep them from objecting. But they wouldn't dare object, he knew. In Hawksbill Station, he was the king. And he meant to keep it that way. "I'll be the volunteer," he said. "I'll be the one who stays." They went on smiling at him. Barrett could not stand those smiles. He turned away from them.

He looked out over his kingdom from the top of the hill.

Up the LINE

For Anne McCaffrey
a friend in deed

I

Sam the guru was a black man, and his people up the line had been slaves—and before that, kings. I wondered about mine. Generations of sweaty peasants, dying weary? Or conspirators, rebels, great seducers, swordsmen, thieves, traitors, pimps, dukes, scholars, failed priests, translators from the Gheg and the Tosk, courtesans, dealers in used ivories, short-order cooks, butlers, stockbrokers, coin-trimmers? All those people I had never known and would never be, whose blood and lymph and genes I carry—I wanted to know them. I couldn't bear the thought of being separated from my own past. I hungered to drag my past about with me like a hump on my back, dipping into it when the dry seasons came.

"Ride the time-winds, then," said Sam the guru.

I listened to him. That was how I got into the time-traveling business.

Now I have been up the line. I have seen those who wait for me in the millennia gone by. My past hugs me as a hump.

Pulcheria!

Great-great-multi-great-grandmother!

If we had never met—

If I had stayed out of the shop of sweets and spices—

If dark eyes and olive skin and high breasts had meant nothing to me, Pulcheria—

My love. My lustful ancestress. You ache me in my dreams. You sing to me from up the line.

He was really black. The family had been working at it for five or six generations now, since the Afro Revival period. The idea was to purge the gonads of the hated slave-master genes, which of course had become liberally entangled in Sam's lineage over the years. There was plenty of time for Massa to dip the wick between centuries seventeen and nineteen. Starting about 1960, though, Sam's people had begun to undo the work of the white devils by mating only with the ebony of hue and woolly of hair. Judging by the family portraits Sam showed me, the starting point was a café-au-lait great-great-grandmother. But she married an ace-of-spades exchange student from Zambia or one of those funny little temporary countries, and their eldest son picked himself a Nubian princess, whose daughter married an elegant ebony buck from Mississippi, who—

"Well, my grandfather looked decently brown as a result of all this," Sam said, "but you could see the strain of the mongrel all over him. We had darkened the family hue by three shades, but we couldn't pass for pure. Then my father was born and his genes reverted. In spite of everything. Light skin and a high-bridged nose and thin lips—a mingler, a monster. Genetics must play its little joke on an earnest family of displaced Africans. So Daddo went to a helix parlor and had the Caucasoid genes edited, accomplishing in four hours what the ancestors hadn't managed to do in eighty years, and here I be. Black and beautiful."

Sam was about thirty-five years old. I was twenty-four. In the spring of '59 we shared a two-room suite in Under New Orleans. It was Sam's suite, really, but he invited me to split it with him when he found out I had no place to stay. He was working then part time as an attendant in a sniffer palace.

I was fresh off the pod out of Newer York, where I was supposed to have been third assistant statutory law clerk to Judge Mattachine of the Manhattan County More Supreme Court, Upper. Political patronage got me the job, of course, not brains. Statutory law clerks aren't supposed to have brains; it gets the computers upset. After eight days with Judge Mattachine my patience eroded and I hopped the first pod southbound, taking with me all my earthly possessions, consisting of my toothflash and blackhead remover, my key to the master information output, my most recent thumb-account statement, two changes of clothing, and my lucky piece, a Byzantine gold coin, a nomisma of Alexius I. When I reached New Orleans I got out and wandered down through the underlevels until my feet took me into the sniffer palace on Under Bourbon Street, Level Three. I confess that what attracted me inside were the two jiggly girls who swam fully submerged in a tank of what looked like and turned out to be cognac. Their names were Helen and Betsy and for a while I got to know them quite well. They were the sniffer palace's lead-in vectors, what they used to call come-ons in the atomic days. Wearing gillmasks, they displayed their pretty nudities to the by-passers, promising but never quite delivering orgiastic frenzies. I watched them paddling in slow circles, each gripping the other's left breast, and now and then a smooth thigh slid between the thighs of Helen or Betsy as the case may have been, and they smiled beckoningly at me and finally I went in.

Sam came up to greet me. He was maybe three meters tall in his build-ups, and wore a jock and a lot of oil. Judge Mattachine would have loved him. Sam said, "Evening, white folks, want to buy a dream?"

"What do you have going?"

"Sado, maso, homo, lesbo, inter, outer, upper, downer and all the variants and deviants." He indicated the charge plate. "Take your pick and put your thumb right here."

"Can I try samples first?"

He looked closely. "What's a nice Jewish boy like you doing in a place like this?"

"Funny. I was just going to ask you the same thing."

"I'm hiding out from the Gestapo," Sam said. "In blackface. *Yisgadal v'yiskadash—*"

"*—adonai elohainu,*" I said. "I'm a Revised Episcopalian, really."

"I'm First Church of Christ Voudoun. Shall I sing a nigger hymn?"

"Spare me," I told him. "Can you introduce me to the girls in the tank?"

"We don't sell flesh here, white folks, only dreams."

"I don't buy flesh, I just borrow it a little while."

"The one with the bosom is Betsy. The one with the backside is Helen. Quite frequently they're virgins, and then the price is higher. Try a dream instead. Look at those lovely masks. You sure you don't want a sniff?"

"Sure I'm sure."

"Where'd you get that Newer York accent?"

I said, "In Vermont, on summer vacation. Where'd you get that shiny black skin?"

"My daddy bought it for me in a helix parlor. What's your name?"

"Jud Elliott. What's yours?"

"Sambo Sambo."

"Sounds repetitious. Mind if I call you Sam?"

"Many people do. You live in Under New Orleans now?"

"Just off the pod. Haven't found a place."

"I get off work at 0400. So do Helen and Betsy. Let's all go home with me," said Sam.

Up the Line

I found out a lot later that he also worked part time in the Time Service. That was a real shocker, because I always thought of Time Servicemen as stuffy, upright, hopelessly virtuous types, square-jawed and clean-cut—overgrown Boy Scouts. And my black guru was and is anything but that. Of course, I had a lot to learn about the Time Service, as well as about Sam.

Since I had a few hours to kill in the sniffer palace he let me have a mask, free, and piped cheery hallucinations to me. When I came up and out, Sam and Helen and Betsy were dressed and ready to go. I had trouble recognizing the girls with their clothes on. Betsy for bosoms, was my mnemonic, but in their Missionary sheaths they were indistinguishable. We all went down three levels to Sam's place and plugged in. As the good fumes rose and clothes dropped away, I found Betsy again and we did what you might have expected us to do, and I discovered that eight nightly hours of total immersion in a tank of cognac gave her skin a certain burnished glow and did not affect her sensory responses in any negative way.

Then we sat in a droopy circle and smoked weed and the guru drew me out.

"I am a graduate student in Byzantine history," I declared.

"Fine, fine. Been there?"

"To Istanbul? Five trips."

"Not Istanbul. Constantinople."

"Same place," I said.

"Is it?"

"Oh," I said. "*Constantinople.* Very expensive."

"Not always," said black Sam. He touched his thumb to the ignition of a new weed, leaned forward tenderly, put it between my lips. "Have you come to Under New Orleans to study Byzantine history?"

"I came to run away from my job."

"Tired of Byzantium so soon?"

"Tired of being third assistant statutory law clerk to Judge Mattachine of the Manhattan County More Supreme Court, Upper."

"You said you were—"

"I know. Byzantine is what I *study*. Law clerk is what I *do*. Did."

"Why?"

"My uncle is Justice Elliott of the U.S. Higher Supreme Court. He thought I ought to get into a decent line of work."

"You don't have to go to law school to be a law clerk?"

"Not any more," I explained. "The machines do all the data retrieval, anyway. The clerks are just courtiers. They congratulate the judge on his brilliance, procure for him, submit to him, and so forth. I stuck it for eight days and podded out."

"You have troubles," Sam said sagely.

"Yes. I've got a simultaneous attack of restlessness, Weltschmerz, tax liens, and unfocused ambition."

"Want to try for tertiary syphilis?" Helen asked.

"Not just now."

"If you had a chance to attain your heart's desire," said Sam, "would you take it?"

"I don't know what my heart's desire is."

"Is that what you mean when you say you're suffering from unfocused ambitions?"

"Part of it."

"If you knew what your heart's desire was, would you lift a finger to seize it?"

"I would," I said.

"I hope you mean that," Sam told me, "because if you don't, you'll have your bluff called. Just stick around here."

He said it very aggressively. He was going to force happiness on me whether I liked it or not.

We switched partners and I made it with Helen, who had a firm white tight backside and was a virtuoso of the interior muscles. Nevertheless she was not my heart's desire. Sam gave me a three-hour sleepo and took the girls home. In the morning, after a scrub, I inspected the suite and observed that it was decorated with artifacts of many times and places: a Sumerian clay tablet, a stirrup cup from Perú, a goblet of Roman glass, a string of Egyptian faience beads, a medieval mace and suit of chain mail, several copies of *The New-York Times* from 1852 and 1853, a shelf of books bound in blind-stamped calf, two Iroquois false-face masks, an immense array of Africana, and a good deal else, cluttering every available alcove, aperture, and orifice. In my fuddled way I assumed that Sam had antiquarian leanings and drew no deeper conclusions. A week later I noticed that everything in his collection seemed newly made. He is a forger of antiquities, I told myself. "I am a part-time employee of the Time Service," black Sam insisted.

"The Time Service," I said, "is populated by square-jawed Boy Scouts. Your jaw is round."

"And my nose is flat, yes. And I am no Boy Scout. However, I am a part-time employee of the Time Service."

"I don't believe it. The Time Service is staffed entirely by nice boys from Indiana and Texas. Nice white boys of all races, creeds, and colors."

"That's the Time Patrol," said Sam. "I'm a Time Courier."

"There's a difference?"

"There's a difference."

"Pardon my ignorance."

"Ignorance can't be pardoned. Only cured."

"Tell me about the Time Service."

"There are two divisions," Sam said. "The Time Patrol and the Time Couriers. The people who tell ethnic jokes end up in the Time Patrol. The people who invent ethnic jokes end up as Time Couriers. *Capisce?*"

"Not really."

"Man, if you're so dumb, why ain't you black?" Sam asked gently. "Time Patrolmen do the policing of paradoxes. Time Couriers take the tourists up the line. Couriers hate the Patrol, Patrol hates

Couriers. I'm a Courier. I do the Mali-Ghana-Gao-Kush-Aksum-Kongo route in January and February, and in October and November I do Sumer, Pharaonic Egypt, and sometimes the Nazca-Mochica-Inca run. When they're shorthanded I fill in on Crusades, Magna Carta, 1066, and Agincourt. Three times now I've done the Fourth Crusade taking Constantinople, and twice the Turks in 1453. Eat your heart out, white folks."

"You're making this up, Sam!"

"Sure I am, sure. You see all this stuff here? Smuggled right down the line by yours truly, out past the Time Patrol, not a thing they suspected except once. Time Patrol tried to arrest me in Istanbul, 1563, I cut his balls off and sold him to the Sultan for ten bezants. Threw his timer in the Bosphorus and left him to rot as a eunuch."

"You didn't!"

"No, I didn't," Sam said. "Would have, though."

My eyes glistened. I sensed my unknown heart's desire vibrating just beyond my grasp. "Smuggle me up the line to Byzantium, Sam!"

"Go smuggle yourself. Sign on as a Courier."

"Could I?"

"They're always hiring. Boy, where's your *sense*? A graduate student in history, you call yourself, and you've never even thought of a Time Service job?"

"I've thought of it," I said indignantly. "It's just that I never thought of it seriously. It seems—well, too *easy*. To strap on a timer and visit any era that ever was—that's cheating, Sam, do you know what I mean?"

"I know what you mean, but you don't know what you mean. I'll tell you your trouble, Jud. You're a compulsive loser."

I knew that. How did he know it so soon?

He said, "What you want most of all is to go up the line, like any other kid with two synapses and a healthy honker. So you turn your back on that, and instead of signing up you let them nail you with a fake job, which you run away from at the earliest possible opportunity. Where are you now? What's ahead? You're, what, twenty-two years old—"

"—twenty-four—"

"—and you've just unmade one career, and you haven't made move one on the other, and when I get tired of you I'll toss you out on your thumb, and what happens when the money runs dry?"

I didn't answer.

He went on, "I figure you'll run out of stash in six months, Jud. At that point you can sign up as stoker for a rich widow, pick a good one out of the Throbbing Crotch Registry—"

"Yigg."

"Or you can join the Hallucination Police and help to preserve objective reality—"

"Yech."

"Or you can return to the More Supreme Court and surrender your lily-white to Judge Mattachine—"

"Blugh."

"Or you can do what you should have done all along, which is to enroll as a Time Courier. Of course, you won't do that, because you're a loser, and losers infallibly choose the least desirable alternative. Right?"

"Wrong, Sam."

"Balls."

"Are you trying to make me angry?"

"No, love." He lit a weed for me. "I go on duty at the sniffer palace in half an hour. Would you mind oiling me?"

"Oil yourself, you anthropoid. I'm not laying a hand on your lovely black flesh."

"Ah! Aggressive heterosexuality rears its ugly head!"

He stripped to his jock and poured oil into his bath machine. The machine's arms moved in spidery circles and started to polish him to a high gloss.

"Sam," I said, "I want to join the Time Service."

5

PLEASE ANSWER ALL QUESTIONS

Name: Judson Daniel Elliott III
Place of Birth: Newer York
Date of Birth: 11 October 2055
Sex (M or F): M
Citizen Registry Number: 070=28=5479=xx5=100089891
Academic Degrees—Bachelor: Columbia '55
    Master: Columbia '56
    Doctor: Harvard, Yale, Princeton, incomplete
    Scholar Magistrate: --
    Other: --

Height: 1 meter (s) 88 centimeters
Weight: 78 kg.
Hair Color: black
Eye Color: black
Racial Index: 8.5 C+
Blood Group: BB 132

Marriages (List Temporary and Permanent Liaisons, in order of registration, and duration of each): none
Acknowledged Offspring: none

Reason for Entering Time Service (limit: 100 words): To improve my knowledge of Byzantine culture, which is my special study area; to enlarge my acquaintance with human customs and behavior; to deepen my relationship to other individuals through constructive service; to offer the benefits of my education thus far to those in need of information; to satisfy certain romantic longings common to young men.

Names of Blood Relatives Currently Employed by Time Service: none

Up the Line

Very little of the foregoing really mattered. I was supposed to keep the application on my person, like a talisman, in case anybody in the Time Service bureaucracy really wanted to see it as I moved through the stages of enrolling; but all that was actually necessary was my Citizen Registry Number, which gave the Time Service folk full access to everything else I had put on the form except my Reason for Entering Time Service, and much more besides. At the push of a node the master data center would disgorge not only my height, weight, date of birth, hair color, eye color, racial index, blood group, and academic background, but also a full list of all illnesses I had suffered, vaccinations, my medical and psychological checkups, sperm count, mean body temperature by seasons, size of all bodily organs including penis both flaccid and erect, all my places of residence, my kin to the fifth degree and the fourth generation, current bank balance, pattern of financial behavior, tax status, voting performance, record of arrests if any, preference in pets, shoe size, etcetera. Privacy is out of fashion, they tell me.

Sam waited in the waiting room, molesting the hired help, while I was filling out my application. When I had finished my paperwork he rose and conducted me down a spiraling ramp into the depths of the Time Service building. Squat hammerheaded robots laden with equipment and documents rolled beside us on the ramp. A door in the wall opened and a secretary emerged; as she crossed our path Sam gave her a lusty tweaking of the nipples and she ran away shrieking. He goosed one of the robots, too. They call it appetite for life. "Abandon all hope, ye who enter here," Sam said. "I play the part well, don't I?"

"What part? Satan?"

"Virgil," he said. "Your friendly spade guide to nether regions. Turn left here."

We stepped onto a dropshaft and went down a long way.

We appeared in a large steamy room at least fifty meters high and crossed a swaying rope bridge far above the floor. "How," I asked, "is a new man who doesn't have a guide supposed to find his way around in this building?"

"With difficulty," said Sam.

The bridge led us into a glossy corridor lined with gaudy doors. One door had SAMUEL HERSHKOWITZ lettered on it in cutesy psychedelic lettering, real antiquarian stuff. Sam jammed his face into the scanner slot and the door instantly opened. We peered into a long narrow room, furnished in archaic fashion with blowup plastic couches, a spindly desk, even a typewriter, for God sake. Samuel Hershkowitz was a long, long, lean individual with a deeply tanned face, curling mustachios, sideburns, and a yard of chin. At the sight of Sam he came capering across the desk and they embraced furiously.

"Soul brother!" cried Samuel Hershkowitz.

"*Landsmann!*" yelled Sam the guru.

They kissed cheekwise. They hugged. They pounded shoulders. Then they split and Hershkowitz looked at me and said, "Who?"

"New recruit. Jud Elliott. Naïve, but he'll do for Byzantium run. Knows his stuff."

"You have an application, Elliott?" Hershkowitz asked.

I produced it. He scanned it briefly and said, "Never married, eh? You a pervo-deviant?"

"No, sir."

"Just an ordinary queer?"

"No, sir."

"Scared of girls?"

"Hardly, sir. I'm just not interested in taking on the permanent responsibilities of marriage."

"But you *are* hetero?"

"Mainly, sir," I said, wondering if I had said the wrong thing.

Samuel Hershkowitz tugged at his sideburns. "Our Byzantium Couriers have to be above reproach, you understand. The prevailing climate up that particular line is, well, steamy. You can futz around all you want in the year 2059, but when you're a Courier you need to maintain a sense of perspective. Amen. Sam, you vouch for this kid?"

"I do."

Up the Line

"That's good enough for me. But let's just run a check, to be sure he isn't wanted for a capital crime. We had a sweet, clean-cut kid apply last week, asking to do the Golgotha run, which of course requires real tact and saintliness, and when I looked into him I found he was wanted for causing protoplasmic decay in Indiana. And several other offenses. So, thus. We check." He activated his data outlet, fed in my identification number, and got my dossier on his screen. It must have matched what I had put on my application, because after a quick inspection he blanked it, nodded, keyed in some notations of his own, and opened his desk. He took from it a smooth flat tawny thing that looked like a truss and tossed it to me. "Drop your pants and put this on," he said. "Show him how, Sam."

I pressed the snap and my trousers fell. Sam wrapped the truss around my hips and clasped it in place; it closed seamlessly upon itself as though it had always been one piece. "This," said Sam, "is your timer. It's cued in to the master shunt system, synchronized to pick up the waves of transport impulses as they come forth. As long as you don't let it run out of phlogiston, this little device is capable of moving you to any point in time within the last seven thousand years."

"No earlier?"

"Not with this model. They aren't allowing unrestricted travel to the prehistoric yet, anyway. We've got to open this thing up era by era, with care. Attend to me, now. The operating controls are simplicity itself. Right here, just over your left-hand Fallopian tubes, is a microswitch that controls backward and forward motion. In order to travel, you merely describe a semicircle with your thumb against this pressure point: from hip toward navel to go back in time, from navel toward hip to go forward. On this side is your fine tuning, which takes some training to use. You see the laminated dial—year, month, day, hour, minute? Yes, you've got to squint a little to read it; that can't be helped. The years are calibrated in B.P.—Before Present—and the months are numbered, and so on. The trick lies in being able to make an instant calculation of your destination—843 years B.P., five months, eleven days, and so on—and setting the dials. It's mostly arithmetic, but you'd be surprised how many people can't translate

February 11, 1192 into a quantity of years, months, and days ago. Naturally you'll have to master the knack if you're going to be a Courier, but don't worry about that now."

He paused and looked up at Hershkowitz, who said to me, "Sam is now going to give you your preliminary disorientation tests. If you pass, you're in."

Sam strapped on a timer also.

"Ever shunted before?" he asked.

"Never."

"We gonna have some fun, baby." He leered. "I'll set your dial for you. You wait till I give the signal, then use the left-hand switch to turn the timer on. Don't forget to pull your pants back up."

"Before or after I shunt?"

"Before," he said. "You can work the switch through your clothes. It's never a good idea to arrive in the past with your pants around your knees. You can't run fast enough that way. And sometimes you've got to be ready to run the second you get there."

Sam set my dial. I pulled up my pants. He touched his hand lightly to the left-hand side of his abdomen and vanished. I described an arc from my hip to my navel on my own belly with two fingertips. I didn't vanish. Samuel Hershkowitz did.

He went wherever candle flames go when they're snuffed, and in the same instant Sam popped back into view beside me, and the two of us stood looking at each other in Hershkowitz' empty office. "What happened?" I said. "Where is he?"

"It's half-past eleven at night," said Sam. "He doesn't work overtime, you know. We left him two weeks down the line when we made our shunt. We're riding the time-winds now, boy."

"We've gone back two weeks into the past?"

"We've gone two weeks up the line," Sam corrected. "Also half a day, which is why it's nighttime now. Let's go take a walk around the city."

Up the Line

We left the Time Service building and rose to the third level of Under New Orleans. Sam didn't seem to have any special destination in mind. We stopped at a bar for a dozen oysters apiece; we downed a couple of beers; we winked at tourists. Then we reached Under Bourbon Street and I realized suddenly why Sam had chosen to go back to this night, and I felt the tingle of fear in my scrotum and started suddenly to sweat. Sam laughed. "It always gets the new ones right around this point, Jud-baby. This is where most of the washouts wash out."

"I'm going to meet myself!" I cried.

"You're going to *see* yourself," he corrected. "You better take good care not to *meet* yourself, not ever, or it'll be all up for you. The Time Patrol will use you up if you pull any such trick."

"Suppose my earlier self happens to see me, though?"

"Then you've had it. This is a test of your nervous system, man, and you better have the juice turned on. Here we go. You recognize that dumb-looking honky coming up the street?"

"That's Judson Daniel Elliott III."

"Yeah, man! Ever see anything so stupid in your life? Back in the shadows, man. Back in the shadows. White folks there, he ain't smart, but he ain't *blind*."

We huddled in a pool of darkness and I watched, sick-bellied, as Judson Daniel Elliott III, fresh off the pod out of Newer York, came wandering up the street toward the sniffer palace on the corner, suitcase in hand. I observed the slight slackness of his posture and the hayseed out-turning of his toes as he walked. His ears seemed amazingly large and his right shoulder was a trifle lower than his left. He looked gawky; he looked like a rube. He went past us and paused before the sniffer palace, staring intently at the two nude girls in the tank of cognac. His tongue slid forth and caressed his upper lip. He rocked on the balls of his toes. He rubbed his chin. He was wondering what his chances were of spreading the legs of one or the other of those bare beauties before the night was over. I could have told him that his chances were pretty good.

He entered the sniffer palace. "How do you feel?" Sam asked me.

"Shaky."

"At least you're honest. It always hits them hard, the first time they go up the line and see themselves. You get used to it, after a while. How does he look to you?"

"Like a clod."

"That's standard too. Be gentle with him. He can't help not knowing all the things you know. He's younger than you are, after all."

Sam laughed softly. I didn't. I was still dazed by the impact of seeing myself come up that street. I felt like my own ghost. Preliminary disorientations, Hershkowitz had said. Yes.

"Don't worry," said Sam. "You're doing fine."

His hand slipped familiarly into the front of my pants and I felt him make a small adjustment on my timer. He did the same to himself. He said, "Let's shunt up the line."

He vanished. I followed him up the line. A blurry half instant later we stood side by side again, on the same street, at the same time of night.

"When are we?" I asked.

"Twenty-four hours previous to your arrival in New Orleans. There's one of you here and one of you in Newer York, getting ready to take the pod south. How does that catch you?"

"Crosswise," I said. "But I'm adapting."

"There's more to come. Let's go home now."

He took me to his flat. There was nobody there, because the Sam of this time slot was at work at the sniffer palace. We went into the bathroom and Sam adjusted my timer again, setting it 31 hours forward. "Shunt," he said, and we went down the line together and came out still in Sam's bathroom, on the next night. I heard the sound of drunken laughter coming from the next room; I heard hoarse gulping cries of lust. Swiftly Sam shut the bathroom door and palmed the seal. I realized that I was in the next room sexing with Betsy or Helen, and I felt fear return.

"Wait here," Sam said crisply, "and don't let anybody in unless he knocks two longs and a short. I'll be right back, maybe."

He went out. I locked the bathroom door after him. Two or three minutes passed. There came two long knocks and a short, and

Up the Line

I opened up. Grinning, Sam said, "It's safe to peek. Nobody's in any shape to notice us. Come on."

"Do I have to?"

"If you want to get into the Time Service you do."

We slipped out of the bathroom and went to sightsee the orgy. I had to fight to keep from coughing as the fumes hit my unready nostrils. In Sam's living room I confronted acres of bare writhing flesh. To my left I saw Sam's huge black body pounding against Helen's sleek whiteness; all that was visible of her beneath him was her face, her arms (clasped across his broad back) and one leg (hooked around his butt). To my right I saw my own prior self down on the floor entwined with busty Betsy. We lay in a kamasutroid posture, she on her right hip, I on my left, her upper leg arched over me, my body curved and pivoted at an oblique angle to hers. In a kind of cold terror I watched myself having her. Although I've seen plenty of copulation scenes before, in the tridim shows, on the beaches, occasionally at parties, this was the first time I had ever witnessed myself in the act, and I was shattered by the grotesqueness of it, the idiot gaspings, the contorted features, the sweaty humpings. Betsy made bleating sounds of passion; our thrashing limbs rearranged themselves several times; my clutching fingers dug deep into her meaty buttocks; the mechanical thrustings went on and on and on. And my terror ebbed as I grew accustomed to the sight, and I found a cold clinical detachment stealing over me, and my fear-born perspiration dried and at last I stood there with my arms folded, coolly studying the activities on the floor. Sam smiled and nodded as if to tell me that I had passed a test. He reset my timer once more and we shunted together.

The living room was empty of fornicators and free of fumes. "When are we now?" I asked.

He said, "We're back thirty-one hours and thirty minutes. In a little while now, you and I are going to come walking into the bathroom, but we won't stay around to wait for that. Let's go up on top of the town."

We journeyed uplevel to Old New Orleans, under the starry sky.

The robot who monitors the comings and goings of the eccentrics who like to go outdoors made note of us, and we passed through, into the quiet streets. Here was the real Bourbon Street; here were the crumbling buildings of the authentic French quarter. Spy-eyes mounted on the lacy grillwork balconies watched us, for in this deserted area the innocent are at the mercy of the depraved, and tourists are protected, through constant surveillance, against the marauders who prowl the surface city. We didn't stay long enough to get into trouble, though. Sam looked around, considering things a bit, and positioned us against a building wall. As he adjusted my timer for another shunt, I said, "What happens if we materialize in space that's already occupied by somebody or something?"

"Can't," Sam said. "The automatic buffers cut in and we get kicked back instantly to our starting point. But it wastes energy, and the Time Service doesn't like that, so we always try to find a nonconflicting area before we jump. Up against a building wall is usually pretty good, provided you can be fairly sure that the wall was in the same position at the time you're shunting to."

"When are we going to now?"

"Shunt and see," he said, and jumped. I followed.

The city came to life. People in twentieth-century clothes strolled the streets: men wearing neckties, women with skirts that came down to their knees, no real flesh showing, not even a nipple. Automobiles crashing along emitting fumes that made me want to vomit. Horns honking. Drills digging up the ground. Noise, stench, ugliness. "Welcome to 1961," Sam said. "John F. Kennedy has just been sworn in as President. The very first Kennedy, dig? That thing up there is a jet airplane. That's a traffic light. It tells when it's safe for you to cross the street. Those up here are street lights. They work by electricity. There are no underlevels. This is the whole thing, the city of New Orleans, right here. How do you like it?"

"It's an interesting place to visit. I wouldn't want to live here."

"You feel dizzy? Sick? Revolted?"

"I'm not sure."

"You're allowed. You always feel a little temporal shock on your first look at the past. It somehow seems smellier and more chaotic than you expect. Some applicants cave in the moment they get into a decently distant shunt up the line."

Up the Line

"I'm not caving."

"Good boy."

I studied the scene, the women with their breasts and rumps encased in tight exoskeletons under their clothing, the men with their strangled, florid faces, the squalling children. Be objective, I told myself. You are a student of other times, other cultures.

Someone pointed at us and screamed, "Hey, looka the beatniks!"

"Onward," Sam said. "They've noticed us."

He adjusted my timer. We jumped.

Same city. A century earlier. Same buildings, genteel and timeless in their pastels. No traffic lights, no drills, no street lights. Instead of automobiles zooming along the streets that bordered the old quarter, there were buggies.

"We can't stay," said Sam. "It's 1858. Our clothes are too weird, and I don't feel like pretending I'm a slave. Onward." We shunted.

The city vanished. We stood in a kind of swamp. Mists rose in the south. Spanish moss clung to graceful trees. A flight of birds darkened the sky.

"The year is 1382," said the guru. "Those are passenger pigeons overhead. Columbus' grandfather is still a virgin."

Back and back we hopped. 897. 441. 97. Very little changed. A couple of naked Indians wandered by at one point. Sam bowed in a courteous way. They nodded affably to us, scratched their genitals, and sauntered on. Visitors from the future did not excite them greatly. We shunted. "This is the year A.D. 1," said Sam. We shunted. "We have gone back an additional twelve months and are now in 1 B.C. The possibilities for arithmetical confusion are great. But if you think of the year as 2059 B.P., and the coming year as 2058 B.P., you won't get into any trouble."

He took me back to 5800 B.P. I observed minor changes in climate; things were drier at some points than at others, drier and cooler. Then we came forward, hopping in easy stages, five hundred years at a time. He apologized for the unvarying nature of the environment; things are more exciting, he promised me, when you go up the line in the Old World. We reached 2058 and made our way to the Time Service building. Entering Hershkowitz' empty office, we halted for a moment while Sam made a final adjustment on our timers.

"This has to be done carefully," he explained. "I want us to land in Hershkowitz' office thirty seconds after we left it. If I'm off even a little, we'll meet our departing selves and I'll be in real trouble."

"Why not play it safe and set the dial to bring us back five minutes later, then?"

"Professional pride," Sam said.

We shunted down the line from an empty Hershkowitz office to one in which Hershkowitz sat behind his desk, peering forward at the place where we had been—for him—thirty seconds earlier.

"Well?" he said.

Sam beamed. "The kid has balls. I say hire him."

And so they took me on as a novice Time Serviceman, in the Time Courier division. The pay wasn't bad; the opportunities were limitless. First, though, I had to undergo my training. They don't let novices schlep tourists around the past just like that.

For a week nothing much happened. Sam went back to work at the sniffer palace and I lounged around. Then I was called down to the Time Service headquarters to begin taking instruction.

There were eight in my class, all of us novices. We made a pretty disreputable crew. In age we ranged from early twenties to—I think—late seventies; in sex we ranged from male to female with every possible gradation between; in mental outlook we were all something on the rapacious side. Our instructor, Najeeb Dajani, wasn't much better. He was a Syrian whose family had converted to Judaism after the Israeli conquest, for business reasons, and he wore a glittering, conspicuous Star of David as an insignia of his faith; but in moments of abstraction or stress he was known to evoke Allah or swear by the Prophet's beard, and I don't know if I'd really trust him on the board of directors of my synagogue, if I had a synagogue. Dajani looked like a stage Arab, swarthy and sinister, with

Up the Line

dark sunglasses at all times, an array of massive gold rings on twelve or thirteen of his fingers, and a quick, amiable smile that showed several rows of very white teeth. I later found out that he had been taken off the lucrative Crucifixion run and demoted to this instructorship for a period of six months, by orders of the Time Patrol, by way of punishment. It seems he had been conducting a side business in fragments of the True Cross, peddling them all up and down the time lines. The rules don't allow a Courier to take advantage of his position for private profit. What the Patrol especially objected to was not that Dajani was selling fake relics, but that he was selling authentic ones. We began with a history lesson.

"Commercial time-travel," Dajani said, "has been functioning about twenty years now. Of course, research into the Benchley Effect began toward the end of the last century, but you understand that the government could not permit private citizens to venture into temponautics until it was ruled to be perfectly safe. In this way the government benevolently oversees the welfare of all."

Dajani emitted a broad wink, visible through the dark glasses as a corrugation of his brow.

Miss Dalessandro in the front row belched in contempt.

"You disagree?" Dajani asked.

Miss Dalessandro, who was a plump but curiously small-breasted woman with black hair, distinct Sapphic urges, and a degree in the history of the industrial revolution, began to reply, but Dajani smoothly cut her off and continued, "The Time Service, in one of whose divisions you have enrolled, performs several important functions. To us is entrusted the care and maintenance of all Benchley Effect devices. Also, our research division constantly endeavors to improve the technological substructure of time transport, and in fact the timer now in use was introduced only four years ago. To our own division—the Time Couriers—is assigned the task of escorting citizens into the past." He folded his hands complacently over his paunch and studied the interlocking patterns of his gold rings. "Much of our activity is concerned with the tourist trade. This provides our economic basis. For large fees, we take groups of eight or ten sightseers on carefully conducted trips to the past, usually accompanied by one Courier, although two may be sent in unusually complex situations. At any given moment in now-time, there may be a hundred thousand tourists scattered over the previous millennia, observing the Crucifixion, the signing of the Magna Carta, the assassination of Lincoln, and such events. Because of the paradoxes inherent in creating a cumulative audience for an event located at a fixed position in the time stream, we are faced with an increasingly difficult task, and limit our tours accordingly."

"Would you explain that, sir?" said Miss Dalessandro.

"At a later meeting," Dajani replied. He went on, "Naturally, we must not confine time travel exclusively to tourists. Historians must have access to all significant events of the past, since it is necessary to revise all existing views of history in the light of the revelation of the real story. We set aside out of the profits of our tourist business a certain number of scholarships for qualified historians, enabling them to visit periods of their research without cost. These tours, too, are conducted by Courier. However, you will not be concerned with this aspect of our work. We anticipate assigning all of you who qualify as Couriers to the tourist division.

"The other division of the Time Service is the Time Patrol, whose task it is to prevent abuses of Benchley Effect devices and to guard against the emergence of paradoxes. At our next lesson we will consider in detail the nature of these paradoxes and how they may be avoided. Dismissed."

We had a small social session after Dajani left the room. Miss Dalessandro, moving in a determined whirl of hairy armpits, closed in on blonde, delicate Miss Chambers, who promptly fled toward Mr. Chudnik, a brawny, towering gentleman with the vaguely noble look of a Roman bronze. Mr. Chudnik, however, was in the process of trying to reach an accommodation with Mr. Burlingame, a dapper young man who could not possibly have been as homosexual as he looked and acted. And so, seeking some other shelter from the predatory Miss Dalessandro, Miss Chambers turned to me and invited me to take her home. I accepted. It developed that Miss Chambers was a student of later Roman imperial history, which meant that her field of interest dovetailed with mine. We sexed in a perfunctory and mechanical way, since she was not really very interested in sex but was just doing it out of politeness, and then we talked about the conversion of Constantine to Christianity until the early hours of the morning. I think she fell in love with me. I gave her no encouragement, though, and it didn't last. I admired her scholarship but her pale little body was quite a bore.

9

At our next lesson we considered in detail the nature of the time-travel paradoxes and how they may be avoided.

"Our greatest challenge," Dajani began, "lies in maintaining the sanctity of now-time. The development of Benchley Effect devices has opened a Pandora's Box of potential paradoxes. No longer is the past a fixed quantity, since we are free now to travel up the line to any given point and alter the so-called 'real' events. The results of such alteration would of course be catastrophic, creating a widening vector of disruption that, by the time it had reached our own era, might transform every aspect of society." Dajani yawned politely. "Consider, if you will, the consequences of permitting a time-traveler to journey to the year 600 and assassinate the youthful Mohammed. The whole dynamic movement of Islam will thus be arrested at its starting point; there will be no Arab conquest of the Near East and southern Europe; the Crusades will not have taken place; millions who died as a result of the Islamic invasions will now not have died, and numerous lines of progeny that would not otherwise have existed at all will come into being, with incalculable effects. All this stems simply from the slaying of a certain young merchant of Mecca. And therefore—"

"Perhaps," suggested Miss Dalessandro, "there's a Law of Conservation of History which would provide that if Mohammed didn't happen, some other charismatic Arab would arise and play precisely the same role?"

Dajani glowered at her.

"We do not care to risk it," he said. "We prefer to see to it that all 'past' events, as recorded in the annals of history as compiled prior to the era of time-travel, go untouched. For the past fifty years of now-time the entire previous span of history, thought to be fixed, has been potentially fluid; yet we struggle to keep it fixed. Thus we employ the Time Patrol to make certain that everything will happen in the past exactly as it *did* happen, no matter how unfortunate an event it might be. Disasters, assassinations, tragedies of all kinds must occur on schedule, for otherwise the future—our now-time—may be irreparably changed."

Miss Chambers said, "But isn't the very fact of our presence in the past a changing of the past?"

"I was about to reach that point," said Dajani, displeased. "If we assume that the past and present form a single continuum, then obviously visitors from the twenty-first century *were* present at all the great events of the past, unobtrusively enough so that no mention of them found its way into the annals of the fixed-time era. So we take great care to camouflage everyone who goes up the line in the costume of the time being visited. One must watch the past without meddling, as a silent bystander, as inconspicuous as possible. This is a rule that the Time Patrol enforces with absolute inflexibility. I will discuss the nature of that enforcement shortly.

"I spoke the other day of cumulative audience paradox. This is a severe philosophical problem which has not yet been resolved, and which I will present to you now purely as a theoretical exercise, to give you some insight into the complexities of our undertaking. Consider this: the first time-traveler to go up the line to view the Crucifixion of Jesus was the experimentalist Barney Navarre, in 2012. Over the succeeding two decades, another fifteen or twenty experimentalists made the same journey. Since the commencement of commercial excursions to Golgotha in 2041, approximately one tourist group a month—or 100 tourists a year—has viewed the scene. Thus about 1800 individuals of the twenty-first century, so far, have observed the Crucifixion. Now, then: each of these groups is leaving from a different month, but *every one of them is converging on the same day!* If tourists continue to go up the line at a rate of 100 a year to see the Crucifixion, the crowd at

Up the Line

Golgotha will consist of at least 10,000 time-travelers by the middle of the twenty-second century, and—assuming no increase in the permissible tourist trade—by the early thirtieth century, some 100,000 time-travelers will have made the trip, all of them necessarily congregating simultaneously at the site of the Passion. Yet obviously no such crowds are present there now, only a few thousand Palestinians—when I say 'now,' I mean of course the time of the Crucifixion relative to now-time 2059—and just as obviously those crowds will continue to grow in the centuries of now-time. Taken to its ultimate, the cumulative audience paradox yields us the picture of an audience of billions of time-travelers piled up in the past to witness the Crucifixion, filling all the Holy Land and spreading out into Turkey, into Arabia, even to India and Iran. Similarly for every other significant event in human history: as commercial time-travel progresses, it must inevitably smother every event in a horde of spectators, yet at the original occurrence of those events, *no such hordes were present*! How is this paradox to be resolved?"

Miss Dalessandro had no suggestions. For once, she was stumped. So were the rest of us. So was Dajani. So are the finest minds of our era.

Meanwhile, the past fills up with time-traveling sightseers.

Dajani tossed one final twister at us before he let us go. "I may add," he said, "that I myself, as a Courier, have done the Crucifixion run twenty-two times, with twenty-two different groups. If you were to attend the Crucifixion yourselves tomorrow, you would find twenty-two Najeeb Dajanis at the hill of Golgotha simultaneously, each of me occupying a different position at the event explaining the happening to my clients. Is this multiplication of Dajanis not a fascinating thing to consider? Why are there not twenty-two Dajanis at loose in now-time? It stretches the intellect to revolve such thoughts. Dismissed, dear ladies and gentlemen, dismissed."

10

I was troubled about those twenty-one extra Dajanis, but the smart alecks in the class quickly figured out why they hadn't all jammed up together here in now-time. It had to do with the fundamental limitations of the Benchley Effect in achieving down-the-line, or forward, travel.

My classmate Mr. Burlingame explained it all to me after class. It was his quaint way of trying to seduce me. He didn't score, but I learned a little time theory.

When you go down the line, he told me, you can come forward only as far as you had previously jumped up the line, *plus* the amount of absolute time elapsed during your stay up the line. That is, if you jump from March 20, 2059, say, to the spring of 1801, and spend three months in 1801, you can come forward again as far as June 20, 2059. But you can't jump down the line to August, 2059, nor can you jump to 2159 or 20590.

There is no way at all to get into your own future.

I don't know why this is so. Mr. Burlingame placed his pale palm on my knee and gave me the theoretical substructure for it, but I was too busy fending him off to follow it.

In fact, although Dajani later spent three sessions simply instructing us on the mechanics of the Benchley Effect, I still can't say for sure how the whole thing works, or why, or even if. At times I suspect I've dreamed it all.

Anyway, there aren't twenty-two Dajanis in now-time because whenever Dajani made the Crucifixion run, he always jumped back to now-time at a point somewhat prior to his next departure for the past. He couldn't help himself about that; if you go up the line in January, spend a couple of weeks in an earlier era, and come back, you've got to land in January or maybe February of the year you started from. And if your next jump isn't scheduled until March, there's no way you can overlap yourself.

So the Dajani who escorted tourists to Golgotha was always the "same" one, from the point of view of people in now-time. At the other end of the jump, though, a couple dozen Dajanis have been piling up, since he keeps jumping from different points in now-time to the same point in then-time. The same happens to anybody who makes repeated jumps to one spot up the line. This is the Paradox of Temporal Accumulation. You can have it.

When not wrestling with such paradoxes I passed my time pleasantly in pleasure, as usual. There were always plenty of willing girls hanging around Sam's place.

In those days I chased crotch quite a bit. Obsessively, even. The pursuit of cunt occupied all my idle hours; it seemed a night wasted if I hadn't slid down that slippery slope at least once. It never occurred to me that it might be worthwhile for me to seek a relationship with a member of the opposite sex that was more than six inches deep. What they call "love."

Shallow, callow youth that I was, I wasn't interested in "love."

On the other hand, maybe I wasn't so shallow. For now I've tried "love" and I don't see where I'm the happier for it. I'm a lot worse off than before, as a matter of fact.

Of course, nobody told me to fall in love with someone who lived up the line.

11

Lieutenant Bruce Sanderson of the Time Patrol came to our class one day to explain to us the perils of daring to meddle with the fixity of past time.

The lieutenant looked his part. He was the tallest man I had ever seen, with the widest shoulders and the squarest jaw. Most of the girls in the class had instant orgasms when he entered, as did Mr. Chudnik and Mr. Burlingame. He took a spread-legged stance, back to the wall, ready for trouble. His uniform was gray. His hair was red and cut very short. His eyes were a soulless blue.

Dajani, himself guilty of transgressing, himself a victim of the Time Patrol's diligence, slithered into a corner of the classroom and yielded the floor. I saw him peering balefully at the lieutenant through his dark glasses.

"Now then," Lieutenant Sanderson said, "you know that our big job involves maintaining the sanctity of now-time. We can't let all kinds of random changes get introduced into our past, because that'll mess up our present. So we have a Time Patrol that monitors the whole territory up the line and makes sure that everything happens according to the books. And I want to say, God bless the men who legislated the Time Patrol into existence."

"Amen," said the penitent Dajani.

"Mind you, it isn't that I'm thankful for the job I have," the lieutenant continued. "Although I am, because I think it's the most important job a human being can have, preserving the sanctity of his now-time. But when I say God bless the men who said we had to have a Time Patrol, it's because those men are responsible for saving everything that is true and good and precious about our existence. Do you know what might have happened without a Time Patrol? What sort of things unscrupulous villains might have done? Let me give you a few examples.

"Such as going back and killing Jesus, Mohammed, Buddha, all our great religious leaders, when they were still children and hadn't had time to formulate their wonderful and inspiring ideas.

"Such as warning the great villains of our history of trouble in store for them, and thus allowing them to cheat destiny and continue doing harm to humanity.

"Such as stealing the art treasures of the past and preventing millions of people over many centuries from enjoying them.

"Such as engaging in fraudulent financial operations resulting in the bankrupting of millions of innocent investors who happened not to have information on future stock prices.

"Such as giving false advice to great rulers and leading them into terrible traps.

"I mention all these examples, my friends, because they are things that have *actually happened*. They all come from the files of the Time Patrol, believe it or not! In April, 2052, a young man from Bucharest used an illegally obtained timer to shunt up the line to A.D. 11 and poison Jesus Christ. In October, 2043, a citizen of Berlin traveled back to the year 1945 and rescued Adolf Hider just before the Russians entered the city. In August, 2049, a woman from Nice jumped to the era of Leonardo da Vinci, stole the unfinished *Mona Lisa*, and hid it in her beach cabana. In September, 2055, a New York man journeyed to the summer of 1929 and netted close to a billion dollars by selling stock short. In January, 2051, a professor of military history from Quebec journeyed to 1815 and, by marketing to the British what purported to the French strategic program, caused the defeat of the Duke of Wellington by the forces of Napoleon at the Battle of Waterloo. And therefore—"

"Wait a second!" I heard myself say. "Napoleon *didn't* win at Waterloo. Christ *wasn't* poisoned in A.D. 11. If the past was really changed as you just said, how come no effects of it have been felt in now-time?"

"*Aha!*" cried Lieutenant Sanderson. He was the best crier of "*Aha!*" I have ever heard. "The fluidity of the past, my friend, is a double-edged blade. If the past can be changed once, it can be changed many times. Now we come to the role of the Time Patrol.

"Let us consider the case of the deranged person who assassinated the young Jesus. As a result of this shocking deed, Christianity did not emerge, and much of the Roman Empire was ultimately converted to Judaism. The Jewish leaders of Rome were able to steer the empire away from its collapse of the fourth and fifth centuries A.D., turning it into a monolithic theocratic state that controlled all of western Europe. However, the Byzantine Empire did not develop in the East, which instead was ruled from Jerusalem by a schismatic Hebrew sect. In the tenth century a cataclysmic war between the forces of Rome and those of Jerusalem resulted in the annihilation of civilization and in the takeover of all of Europe and Asia by Turkish nomads, who proceeded to construct a totalitarian state that, by the twenty-first century, had become the most repressive in human history.

"You can see from this how devastating it can be to meddle with the past."

"Yes," I said, "but—"

Lieutenant Sanderson gave me a frigid smile. "You are about to observe that we do not, in fact, live under a repressive Turkish tyranny. I agree. Our present pattern of existence was saved by the following procedure:

"The murder of the young Jesus was detected by a Time Courier who went up the line late in April 2052, escorting a party of tourists to witness the Crucifixion. When the group arrived at the time and place of the Crucifixion, they found two thieves undergoing execution; no one, however, had heard of Jesus of Nazareth. The Courier instantly notified the Time Patrol, which began a paradox search. Jesus' time line was followed from birth through boyhood and was seen to be unchanged; but no trace of him could be found after mid-adolescence, and inquiry in the neighborhood finally turned up the information that he had died suddenly and mysteriously in the year 11. It was a simple matter then to maintain surveillance until we observed the arrival of the illegal time-traveler.

"What do you think we did then?"

Hands went up. Lieutenant Sanderson recognized Mr. Chudnik, who said, "You arrested the criminal five minutes before he could give the poison to Jesus, thus preventing the changing of history, and took him back down the line for trial."

Lieutenant Sanderson smiled genially. "Wrong," he said. "We let him give the poison to Jesus."

Uproar.

The Time Patrol man said benignly, "As you surely know, the maximum penalty for unauthorized interference in past events is death—the only capital offense now recognized in law. But before so severe a penalty can be invoked, absolute proof of the crime is necessary. Therefore, whenever a crime of this kind is detected, Time Patrolmen allow it to proceed and surreptitiously make a full record of it."

"But how," Miss Dalessandro demanded, "does the past get unchanged that way?"

"Aha!" cried Lieutenant Sanderson. "Once we have a proper record of the commission of the crime, we can obtain a quick conviction and secure permission to carry out sentence. This was done. The Time Patrol investigators returned with their evidence to the

Up the Line

night of April 4, 2052. *This* was the date of the departure up the line of the would-be murderer of Jesus. They presented their proof of crime to the Time Patrol commissioners, who ordered execution of the criminal. Time Patrol executioners were dispatched to the home of the criminal, seized his timer, and painlessly put him to death an hour before *his* intended trip into the past. Thus he was erased from the time-stream and the main current of the past was served, for in fact he did not make his trip and Jesus lived on to preach his creed. In this way—through detection of unlawful changes and eradication of the changers advance of their departure up the line—we preserve sanctity of now-time." How beautiful, I thought.

I'm too easily satisfied. Miss Dalessandro, that arch-troublemaker, put up her fleshy hand, and when called said, "I'd like one clarification, though. Presumably when your Time Patrolmen returned to April, 2052, with the evidence of the crime, they were returning to a changed world run by Turkish dictators. Where would they find Time Patrol commissioners? Where would they then find the murderer? He might have ceased to exist as a consequence of his own crime, because by murdering Jesus he set in motion some train of events that eliminated his own ancestors. For that matter, maybe time-travel itself was never invented in that world where Jesus didn't live, and so the moment Jesus was killed all Time Patrolmen and Time Couriers and tourists would become impossibilities, and cease to exist." Lieutenant Sanderson did not look pleased. "You bring up," he said slowly, "a number of interesting subsidiary paradoxes. I'm afraid that the time at my disposal isn't sufficient to deal with them properly. Briefly, though: if the timecrime of 11 A.D. had not been detected relatively quickly, the focus of change would indeed have widened over the centuries and eventually transformed the entire future, possibly preventing the *emergence of the Benchley Effect* and the Time Patrol itself, leading to what we call the Ultimate Paradox, in which time-travel becomes its own negation. In fact, though, the vast potential consequences of the poisoning of Jesus never occurred because of the detection of the crime by the Time Courier visiting the Crucifixion. Since that event took place in A.D. 33, only the years 11 to 33 were ever affected by the timecrime, and the changes created by the absence of Jesus from those years were insignificant, because Jesus' influence on history emerged only long after the Crucifixion. Meanwhile the retroactive deletion of the timecrime canceled even the slight changes that had taken place in the 22-year period affected; those two decades were pinched off into another track of time, inaccessible to us and in effect nonexistent, and the basic and authentic track was restored in full continuity from A.D. 11 to the present."

Miss Dalessandro wasn't satisfied. "There's something circular here. Shouldn't the Ultimate Paradox have occurred all the way down the line, the instant Jesus was poisoned? How did any of the Couriers and Patrolmen manage to continue to exist, let alone to remember how the past *should* have gone? It seems to me that there ought not to be any way of correcting a timecrime sweeping enough to bring on the Ultimate Paradox."

"You forget, or perhaps you don't yet know," said Sanderson, "that time-travelers currently up the line at the moment of a timecrime are unaffected by *any* change in the past, since they're detached from their time matrices. A time-traveler in transit is a drifting bubble of now-time ripped loose from the matrix of the continuum, immune to the transformations of paradox. This means that anyone currently up the line may observe and correct an alteration of the true past, and will continue to retain memories both of the temporary false condition and of his role in correcting it. Of course, any time-traveler leaving the sanctuary of the transit state is vulnerable once he comes back to his starting point down the line. That is, if you go up the line and kill your grandfather before his marriage, you won't instantaneously wink out of existence, since you're shielded from paradox by the Benchley Effect. But the moment you return to the present you will cease *ever to have existed*, since as a result of your alteration of your own past you no longer have a time-link to the present. Clear?" No, I thought. But I kept quiet.

Miss Dalessandro pressed onward. "Those in transit are protected by—"

"The Paradox of Transit Displacement, we call it."

"The Paradox of Transit Displacement. They're encapsulated, and as they travel they're free to compare what they see with what they remember true time to have been once, and if necessary they can make changes to restore true order if it's been changed."

"Yes."

"Why? Why *should* they be immune? I know I keep coming back to this point, but—"

Lieutenant Sanderson sighed. "Because," he said, "if they were affected by a past-change while they were in the past themselves, this would be the Ultimate Paradox: a time-traveler changing the era that produced time-travel. This is even more paradoxical than the Paradox of Transit Displacement. By the Law of Lesser Paradoxes, the Paradox of Transit Displacement, being less improbable, holds precedence. Do you see?"

"No, but—"

"I'm afraid I can't dwell on this in greater detail," said the Patrolman. "However, no doubt Mr. Dajani will go into these matters at later instruction sessions."

He gave Dajani a sickly smile and excused himself fast.

Dajani, you can bet on it, didn't deal with Miss Dalessandro's paradoxes properly, or at all. He found cunning ways to sidetrack her every time she brought up the issue.

"You can be sure," he said, "that the past *is* restored whenever it is changed. The hypothetical worlds created by unlawful change cease retroactively to exist the moment the changer is apprehended. Q.E.D."

That didn't explain a damned thing. But it was the best explanation we ever got.

12

One thing they made clear to us was that *good* changes in the past are also forbidden. Dozens of people have been eliminated for trying to persuade Abe Lincoln to stay home from the theater that night, or for trying to tell Jack Kennedy that he should for God's sake put the bulletproof bubble on his car.

They get wiped out, just like the murderers of Jesus and the rescuers of Hitler. Because it's just as deadly to the fabric of now-time to help Kennedy serve out his term as it would be to help Hitler rebuild the Third Reich. Change is change, and even the virtuous changes can have unpredictably catastrophic results. "Just imagine," said Dajani, "that because Kennedy was not assassinated in 1963, the escalation of the Vietnamese War that in fact did take place under his successor did not occur, and so the lives of thousands of servicemen were spared. Suppose now that one of those men, who otherwise would have died in 1965 or 1966, remained alive, became President of the United States in 1992, and embarked on an atomic war that brought about the destruction of civilization. You see why even supposedly beneficial alterations of the past must be prevented?"

We saw. We saw it over and over again.

We saw it until we were scared toothless of going into the Time Service, because it seemed inevitable that we would sooner or later do something up the line that would bring down on us the fatal wrath of the Time Patrol.

"Don't worry about it," Sam said. "The way they talk, the death penalty is inflicted a million times a day. Actually I don't think there have been fifty executions for timecrime in the past ten years. And all of those were real nuts, the kind whose mission it is to murder Mohammed."

"Then how does the Patrol keep the past from being changed?"

"They don't," said Sam. "It gets changed all the time. Despite the Time Patrol."

"Why doesn't our world change?"

"It does. In little ways." Sam laughed. "If a Time Courier gives Alexander the Great antibiotics and helps him live to a ripe old age, that would be an intolerable change, and the Time Patrol would prevent it. But a lot of other stuff goes on all the time. Couriers recovering lost manuscripts, sleeping with Catherine the Great, collecting artifacts for resale in other eras. Your man Dajani was peddling the True Cross, wasn't he? They found out about him, but they didn't execute him. They just suspended him from his profitable run for a while and stuck him in a classroom. Most of the petty tinkering never even gets discovered." He let his glance rove meaningfully over his collection of artifacts from the past. "As you get into this business, Jud, you'll find out that we're in constant intersection with past events. Every time a Time Cornier steps on an ant in 2000 B.C., he's changing the past. Somehow we survive. The dumb bastards in the Time Patrol watch out for structural changes in history, but they leave the little crap alone. They have to. There aren't enough Patrolmen to handle everything."

"But that means," I said, "that we're building up a lot of tiny alterations in history, bit by bit, an ant here and a butterfly there, and the accumulation may someday cause a major change, and nobody will then be able to trace all the causes and put things back the way they ought to be!"

"Exactly."

"You don't sound worried about it," I said.

"Why should I be? Do I own the world? Do I give a damn if history gets changed?"

"You would if the change involved seeing to it that you had never existed."

"There are bigger things to worry about, Jud. Like having a good time from day to day."

"Doesn't it scare you that someday you might just pop out of existence?"

"Someday I will," Sam said. "No maybes about it. If not sooner, then later. Meanwhile I enjoy myself. Eat, drink, and be merry, kid. Let the yesterdays fall where they will."

13

When they were finished hammering the rules into our heads, they sent us on trial runs up the line. All of us had already been into the past, of course, before beginning the instruction sessions; they had tested us to see if we had any psychological hangups about time-traveling. Now they wanted us to observe Couriers in actual service, and so they let us go along as hitchhikers with tour groups.

They split us up, so there wouldn't be more than two of us to each six or eight tourists. To save expense, they assigned us all to visit events right in New Orleans. (In order to shoot us back to the Battle of Hastings, say, they would have had to fly us to London first. Time-travel doesn't include space travel; you have to be physically present in the place you want to reach, before you jump.)

New Orleans is a fine city, but it hasn't had all that many important events in its history, and I'm not sure why anybody would want to pay *very* good money to go up the line there when for about the same fee he could witness the signing of the Declaration of Independence, the fall of Constantinople, or the assassination of Julius Caesar. But the Time Service is willing to provide transport to any major historical event whatever—within certain limits of taste, I mean—for any group of at least eight tourists who have the stash for tickets, and I suppose the patriotic residents of New Orleans have every right to sightsee their city's own past, if they prefer.

So Mr. Chudnik and Miss Dalessandro were shipped to 1815 to cheer for Andrew Jackson at the Battle of New Orleans. Mr. Burlingame and Mr. Oliveira were transported to 1877 to watch the last of the carpetbaggers thrown out. Mr. Hotchkiss and Mrs. Notabene went off to 1803 to see the United States take possession of Louisiana after buying it from the French. And Miss Chambers and I went up the line to 1935 to view the assassination of Huey Long.

Assassinations are usually over in a hurry, and nobody goes up the line just to watch a quick burst of gunfire. What the Time Service was really offering these people was a five-day tour of Louisiana in the early twentieth century, with the gunning down of the Kingfish as its climax. We had six fellow travelers: three well-to-do Louisiana couples in their late fifties and early sixties. One of the men was a lawyer, one a doctor, one a big executive of Louisiana Power & Light Company. Our Time Courier was the right sort to shepherd these pillars of the establishment around: a sleek, bland character named Madison Jefferson Monroe. "Call me Jeff," he invited.

We had several orientation meetings before we went anywhere.

"These are your timers," said Jeff Monroe. "You keep them next to your skin at all times. Once you put them on in Time Service headquarters, you don't remove them again until you come back down the line. You bathe with them, sleep with them, perform—ah—all intimate functions while wearing them. The reason for this should be obvious. It would be highly disruptive to history if a timer were to fall into the hands of a twentieth-century person; therefore we don't allow the devices out of your physical possession even for an instant."

("He's lying," Sam told me when I repeated this to him. "Somebody up the line wouldn't know what the hell to do with a timer. The real reason is that sometimes the tourists have to get out of an area in a hurry, maybe to avoid being lynched, and the Courier can't take the risk that some of his people may have left their timers in the hotel room. But he doesn't dare tell them that.")

The timers that Jeff Monroe distributed were a little different from the one I had worn the night Sam and I went jumping up the line. The controls were sealed, and functioned only when the Courier sounded a master frequency. Sensible enough: the Time Service doesn't want tourists slipping away for time-jaunts on their own.

Our Courier spelled out at great length the consequences of changing the past, and begged us repetitiously not to rock any boats. "Don't speak unless spoken to," he said, "and even then confine any conversations with strangers to a minimum of words. Don't use slang; it won't be comprehensible. You may recognize other time-tourists; under no condition are you to speak to them or greet them in any way, and you should ignore any attention you may get from them. Anyone who breaks these regulations, no matter how innocently, may have his shunting permit revoked on the spot and may be returned at once to now-time. Understood?" We nodded solemnly.

Jeff Monroe added, "Think of yourselves as Christians in disguise who have been smuggled into the holy Moslem city of Mecca. You're in no danger so long as you're not discovered; but if those about you find out what you are, you're in big trouble. Therefore it's to your advantage to keep your mouths shut while you're up the line, to do a lot of seeing and a minimum of saying. You'll be all right as long as you don't call attention to yourselves."

(I learned from Sam that time-tourists very frequently get themselves into muddles with people living up the line, no matter how hard their Couriers try to avoid such incidents. Sometimes the trouble can be patched up with a few diplomatic words, often when the Courier explains apologetically to the offended party that the stranger is really a mental case. Sometimes it's not so easy, and the Courier has to order a quick evacuation of all the tourists; the Courier must remain behind until he has sent all his people safely down the line, and there have been several fatalities to Couriers in the line of duty as a result. In extreme cases of tourist bungling, the Time Patrol steps in and cancels the jump retroactively, plucking the careless traveler from the tour and thereby undoing the damage. Sam said, "It can really get one of these rich bastards furious when a Patrolman shows up at the last minute and tells him that he can't make the shunt, because if he does he'll commit some ferocious faux pas up the line. They just can't understand it. They promise to be good, and won't believe that their promise is worthless because their conduct is already a matter of record. The trouble with most of the dumb tourists is that they can't think four-dimensionally." "Neither can I, Sam," I said, baffled. "You will. You'd better," said Sam.)

Before we set out for 1935 we were given a quick hypnocourse in the social background of the era. Pumped into us were data on the Depression, the New Deal, the Long family of Louisiana, Huey Long's rise to fame, his "Share Our Wealth" program of taking from the rich and giving to the poor, his feud with President Franklin Roosevelt, his dream of taking the Presidency himself in 1936, his flamboyant disregard for traditions, his demagogic appeal to the masses. We also got enough incidental details on life in 1935—celebrities, sports developments, the stock market—so we wouldn't feel hopelessly out of context there.

Lastly, they fitted us out in 1935 wardrobes. We strutted around giggling and quipping at the sight of ourselves in those quaint rigs. Jeff Monroe, checking us out, reminded the men about zipper flies and how to use them, reminded the women that it was sternly prohibited to reveal the breasts from the nipple down, and urged us strenuously to keep in mind at all times that we were entering a staunchly puritanical era where neurotic repression was regarded as a virtue and our normal freedoms of behavior were looked upon as sinful and shameless.

Finally, we were ready.

They took us uplevel to Old New Orleans, since it wouldn't have been healthy to make our jump from one of the underlevels. They had set up a room in a boarding-house on North Rampart Street for shunting to the twentieth century.

"Here we go up the line," said Madison Jefferson Monroe, and gave the signal that activated our timers.

Suddenly, it was 1935.

We didn't notice any changes in the dingy room were in, but yet we knew we were up the line.

We wore tight shoes and funny clothes, and we carried real cash money, United States dollars, because our thumbprints weren't legal tender here. The advance man of the tour had booked us into a big New Orleans hotel on Canal just at the edge of the old French quarter, for the first part of our stay, and after Jeff Monroe had given us a final warning to be circumspect, we went out and walked around the corner to it.

The automobile traffic was fantastic for this supposedly "depressed" year. So was the din. We strolled along, two by two, Jeff leading the way. We stared at things a lot, but no one would get suspicious about that. The locals would simply guess that we were tourists just down from Indiana. Nothing about our curiosity marked us particularly as tourists just down from 2059.

Thibodeaux, the power company man, couldn't get over the sight of power lines right out in the open, dangling from post to post. "I've read about such things," he said several times, "but I never really believed them!"

The womenfolk clucked a lot about the fashions. It was a hot, sticky September day and yet everybody was all covered up. They couldn't understand that.

The weather gave us trouble. We had never been exposed to real humidity before; there isn't any in the undercities, of course, and only a lunatic goes up to surface level when the climate is sour. So we sweated and labored.

There wasn't any air-conditioning in the hotel, either. I think it may not have been invented yet.

Jeff checked us all in at the hotel. When he was through signing the register, the desk clerk, who of course was human and not a computer terminal, banged a bell and yelled, "Front!" and a platoon of friendly black bellhops came over to get our luggage.

I overheard Mrs. Bienvenu, the lawyer's wife, whisper to her husband, "Do you think they're slaves?"

"Not here!" he said fiercely. "The slaves were freed seventy years ago!"

The desk clerk must have overheard that. I wonder what he made of it.

The Courier had booked Flora Chambers and me into one room. He explained that he had registered us as Mr. and Mrs. Elliott, because it wasn't permissible to let an unmarried couple share the same hotel room even if they were part of the same tour party. Flora gave me a pale but hopeful smile and said, "We'll pretend we're on a temporary."

Monroe glared at her. "We don't talk about down-the-line customs here!"

"They don't have temporary liaisons in 1935?"

"Shut *up*!" he hissed.

We unpacked and bathed and went out to see the town. We did Basin Street and heard some respectable primitive jazz. Then we walked a few blocks over to Bourbon Street for drinks and a striptease. The place was full; and it amazed us all that grown men and women would sit around for a full hour, enduring a lot of indifferent music and polluted atmosphere, simply to wait for a girl to come out and take off some of her clothes.

When she got undressed, finally, she kept little shiny caps on her nipples and a triangular patch of cloth over her pubic region, too. Anybody who has a serious interest in nudity can see more than that any day at a public bathhouse. But of course this was a repressive, sexually strangled era, we reminded ourselves.

Our drinks and other nightclub charges were all put on one bill, which Jeff Monroe always paid. The Time Service didn't want us ignorant tourists handling unfamiliar currencies except when absolutely necessary. The Courier also deftly fended off drunks who kept invading our group, beggars, soliciting prostitutes, and other challenges to our ability to handle the social situations 1935 presented.

"It's hard work," Flora Chambers observed, "being a Courier."

"But think of all the free traveling you get to do," I said.

We were profoundly awed by the ugliness of the people up the line. We realized that there were no helix parlors here, that cosmetic microsurgery was unknown, and that esthetic genetics, if it had been heard of at all in 1935, would have been regarded as a Fascist or Communist conspiracy against the right of free men to have ugly children. Nevertheless, we couldn't help registering surprise and dismay at the mismatched ears, the pockmarked skins, the distorted teeth, the bulging noses, of these un-programmed and unedited people. The plainest member of our group was a theatrical beauty, compared to the 1935 norm.

We pitied them for having to live in their cramped, dark little era.

When we got back to our hotel room, Flora took all her clothing off, and sprawled out wildly on the bed with legs spread. "Do me!" she shrieked. "I'm drunk!"

I was a little drunk too, so I did her.

Madison Jefferson Monroe had carefully allotted each of us one alcoholic drink during the whole evening. Despite all temptations, we weren't allowed a second, and had to stick to soft drinks the rest of the time. He couldn't take the risk that we might say something dangerous under the influence of alcohol, a substance we weren't really accustomed to. As it is, even that one drink was enough to loosen some tongues and melt some brains, and a few remarks slipped out which, if they had been overheard, could have caused trouble.

It astounded me to see the twentieth-century people drink so much without collapsing.

("Get used to alcohol," Sam had urged me. "It's the favorite mind-poison in most places up the line. Develop a tolerance for it or you may have problems." "No drugs?" I asked. "Well, you'll find some weed here and there, but nothing really psychedelic. No sniffer palaces anywhere. Learn to drink, Jud. Learn to drink.")

Later that night Jeff Monroe came to our room. Flora lay in an exhausted heap, unconscious; Jeff and I talked for a long while about the problems of being a Courier. I rather got to like him for all his slickness and blandness.

He seemed to enjoy his work. His specialty was twentieth-century United States, and the only thing he regretted was the wearying routine of covering the assassinations. "Nobody wants to see anything else," he complained. "Dallas, Los Angeles, Memphis, New York, Chicago, Baton Rouge, Cleveland, over and over again. I can't tell you how sick I am of muscling into the crowd by that overpass, and pointing out that window on the sixth floor, and watching that poor woman crawling onto the back of that car. At least the Huey Long thing is reasonably untouched. But there are twenty of me in Dallas by now. Don't people want to see the *happy* parts of the twentieth century?"

"Were there any?" I asked.

We had breakfast at Brennan's and dinner at Antoine's, and had a tour of the Garden District, and came back to the old town to visit the cathedral in Jackson Square, and then we walked down to have a look at the Mississippi. We also went to see Clark Gable and Jean Harlow in *Red Dust* at a movie house, visited the post office and the public library, bought a lot of newspapers (which are permissible souvenirs), and spent a few hours listening to the radio. We rode the Streetcar Named Desire, and Jeff took us motoring in a hired automobile. He offered to let us drive, but we were all terrified of taking the wheel after watching him going through the intricate routines of changing gears. And we did a lot of other twentieth-century things. We really soaked up the flavor of the era.

Up the Line

Then we went up to Baton Rouge to watch Senator Long get killed.

We got there on Saturday, September 7, and took rooms in what Jeff swore was the finest hotel in the city. The legislature was in session, and Senator Huey had come down from Washington to run things. We hovered around town aimlessly until late Sunday afternoon. Then Jeff got us ready to see the show.

He had donned a thermoplastic disguise. His pink, regular face was now pocked and sallow, he had a mustache, and he wore dark glasses that he might have borrowed from Dajani. "This is the third time I've conducted this tour," he explained to us. "I think it might look bad if somebody noticed identical triplets standing in the corridor when Huey gets shot." He warned us to pay no attention to any of the other Jeff Monroes we might see at the assassination; he, pockmarks and mustache and glasses, was our authentic Courier and the other two were not to be approached.

Toward evening we strolled over to the colossal 34-story state capitol building and casually wandered in—sightseers, here to admire Huey's $5,000,000 edifice. Unobtrusively we entered. Jeff checked the time every few seconds.

He positioned us where we'd have a good view while still keeping out of range of the bullets.

We couldn't help noticing other groups of sightseers slouching into positions nearby. I saw a man who was unmistakably Jeff Monroe standing with one group; another group was clustered around a man of the same size and physique who, however, wore metal-rimmed glasses and had a plum-colored birthmark on one cheek. We made an elaborate show of not looking at these other people. They worked hard at not looking at us.

I worried about the Cumulative Paradox. It seemed to me that everybody who would ever come up the line to witness Huey Long's assassination should be right here now—thousands of people, maybe, all crowding round, jostling for a view. Yet there were only a few dozen, representing those who had set out from 2059 and earlier. Why weren't the others here? Was time so fluid that the same event could be played off infinitely often, for a larger audience each time?

"Here he comes," Jeff whispered.

The Kingfish hurried toward us, his bodyguard close behind. He was short and chubby, with a florid face, a snub nose, orange hair, heavy lips, a deeply cleft chin. I told myself that I could sense the power of the man, and wondered if I might be deluding myself. As he approached he scratched his left buttock, said something to a man to his left, and coughed. His suit was slightly rumpled; his hair was unruly.

Since we had been coached by our Courier, we knew where to look for the assassin. On a murmured signal from Jeff—not before!—we turned our heads and saw Dr. Carl Austin Weiss detach himself from the crowd, step up to the Senator, and push a .22 automatic pistol into his stomach. He fired one shot. Huey, surprised, fell back, mortally wounded. His bodyguards instantly drew their guns and killed the assassin. Gleaming puddles of blood began to form; people screamed; the red-faced bodyguards pushed at us, hammered at us, told us to get back, get back, get back!

That was it. The event we had come to see was over.

It had seemed unreal, a playback of ancient history, a clever but not quite convincing tridim. We were impressed with the ingenuity of the process, but we were not awed by the impact of the event.

Even while the bullets had been flying, none of it had seemed completely true to us.

Yet those bullets had been real bullets, and if they had hit us, we would have died real deaths.

And for the two men lying on the capitol's polished floor, it had been an extremely real event.

16

I went on four more training missions before they certified me as a Time Courier. All my jumps were made in the New Orleans area. I got to know the history of that area a lot better than I ever thought I would.

The third of these trips was to 1803, the Louisiana Purchase run. I was the only trainee. There were seven tourists. Our Courier was

Up the Line

a hard-faced little man named Sid Buonocore. When I mentioned his name to Sam, Sam guffawed and said, "That shady character!"

"What's shady about him?"

"They used to have him on the Renaissance run. Then the Time Patrol caught him pimping lady tourists to Cesare Borgia. The tourist gals paid him nicely, and so did Cesare. Buonocore claimed he was just doing his job—letting his girls get a deeper experience of the Renaissance, you know. But they pulled him back here and stuck him on Louisiana Purchase."

"Is a Courier supposed to supervise the sex life of his tourists?" I asked.

"No, but he isn't supposed to encourage transtemporal fornication, either."

I found the encourager of transtemporal fornication to be an engaging rakish sort. Buonocore was a long way from handsome, but he had an aura of omnivorous sexuality about him that I had to admire. And his high regard for his own welfare was so obvious that it had a certain rapacious charm. You can't applaud a skulking pickpocket, but you can cheer an out-and-out brigand. That was what Sid Buonocore was.

He was a capable Courier, besides. He slipped us cunningly into 1803 New Orleans in the guise of a party of Dutch traders making a market tour; as long as we didn't meet a real Hollander we were safe, and our "Dutch" label covered the oddities of our futuristic accents. We strode around town uncomfortably garbed in early nineteenth-century clothing, feeling like refugees from a costume drama, and Sid showed us the sights in fine fashion.

On the side, I quickly discovered, he was carrying on a flourishing trade in gold doubloons and Spanish eight-real pieces. He didn't bother to conceal what he was doing from me, but he didn't talk about it, either, and I never really figured out all the intricate details. It had something to do—maybe—with taking advantage of variable exchange rates. All I know is that he swapped United States silver dollars for British gold guineas, used the guineas to buy French silver currency at a big discount, and met with Caribbean buccaneers by night on the banks of the Mississippi to trade the French coins for Spanish gold and silver. What he did with his doubloons and eight-real pieces I never knew. Nor could I see where the profit in the deal was coming from. My best theory was that he simply was trying to switch as many currencies around as possible, in order to build up a stock of coins for sale to collectors down the line; but somehow that seemed too simple-minded an operation for someone of his style. He didn't offer explanations and I was too shy to ask.

He was also a busy sexman. That isn't unusual for a Courier. ("The lady tourists are fair game," Sam said. "They fall all over themselves to submit to us. It's like the white-hunter thing in Africa.") But Sid Buonocore didn't just confine himself to plugging romance-hungry tourists, I discovered.

Late one night in our 1803 trip I was bothered with some procedural point and went to the Courier's bedroom to ask him about it. I knocked and he said, "Come in," so I went in, but he wasn't alone. A tawny maiden with long black hair was sprawled on the bed, naked, sweat-shiny, rumpled. Her breasts were hard and heavy and her nipples were chocolate-colored. "Excuse me," I said. "I didn't mean to intrude." Sid Buonocore laughed. "Crap," he said. "We're finished for now. You aren't interrupting things. This is Maria."

"Hello, Maria," I said tentatively.

She giggled drunkenly. Sid spoke to her in the Creole patois and she giggled again. Rising from the bed, she performed an elegant nude curtsy before me and murmured, *"Bon soir, m'sieu."* Then she fell on her face with a gentle swooning fall.

"She's lovely, isn't she?" Sid asked proudly. "Half Indian, half Spanish, half French. Have some rum."

I took a gulp from the flask he proffered. "That's too many halves," I said.

"Maria doesn't do anything in a petty way."

"So I see."

"I met her on my last trip through here. I'm timing things very carefully so that I can have her for a little while each night, and still not deprive my other selves of her. I mean, I can't predict how often I'll be doing this goddam run, Jud, but I might as well set myself up nicely each time I go up the line."

"Should you be saying such things in front of—"

Up the Line

"Doesn't speak a word of English. Absolutely safe."

Maria stirred and moaned. Sid took the rum flask from me and let some splash down onto her chest. She giggled again, and sleepily began to rub it into her breasts like a magic growth ointment. She didn't need any ointment.

Sid said, "She's quite passionate."

"I'm sure."

He said something to her and she lurched to her feet and came toward me. Her breasts swayed like bells. Fumes of rum and fumes of lust rose from her. Unsteadily she reached her hands toward me, but she lost her balance and slipped once again to the planked floor. She lay there chuckling.

"Want to try her?" Sid asked. "Let her sober up a little, and take her back to your room and have some fun."

I said something about the interesting diseases she might be carrying. Sometimes I break out all over with fastidiousness at funny moments.

Buonocore spat scornfully. "You've had your shots. What are you worrying about?"

"They immunized us against typhoid and diphtheria and yellow fever and all that," I said. "But syphilis?"

"She's clean. Believe me. Anyway, if you're nervous, you can take a thermobath the minute you go down the line." He shrugged. "If something like that scares you, maybe you better not be a Courier."

"I didn't—"

"You saw that *I* was willing to ball her, didn't you? Jud, do you think I'm an ordinary fool or a goddam fool? Would I go to bed with a syphilitic? And then offer her to you?"

"Well—"

"There's only one thing you do have to worry about," he said. "Have you had your pill?"

"My pill?"

"Your *pill*, stupid! Your monthly pill!"

"Oh. Yes. Yes, of course."

"That's vital, if you're going to go up the line. You don't want to run around fertilizing other people's ancestors. The Time Patrol will really scrape you for a thing like that. You can get away with a little fraternization with up-the-line people—you can do some business with them, you can go to bed with them—but you damned well better not plant any babies in them. Got it?"

"Sure, Sid."

"Remember, just because I fool around a little, that doesn't mean I'm willing to risk changing the past in a big way. Like fouling up the genetic flow by making babies up the line. Go you and do likewise, kid. Don't forget your pills. Now take Maria and clear out."

I took Maria and cleared out.

She sobered up fast in my room. She couldn't speak a word of any language I understood. I couldn't speak a word of any language she understood. But we made out all right anyway.

Even though she was 250 years older than me, there was nothing wrong with any aspect of her performance. Some things don't change much.

17

After I qualified as a Time Courier, and just before I departed to go on the Byzantium run, Sam gave a farewell party for me. Just about everyone I had known in Under New Orleans was invited, and we all crammed into Sam's two rooms. The girls from the sniffer palace were there, and an unemployed oral poet named Shigemitsu who spoke only in iambic pentameter, and five or six Time Service people, and a peddler of floaters, and a wild green-haired girl who worked as a splitter in a helix parlor, and others. Sam even invited Flora Chambers, but she had shipped out the day before to fill in on the Sack of Rome run.

Everyone was given a floater as he arrived. So things turned on fast. Instants after the buzz of the floater's snout against my arm I felt my consciousness expanding like a balloon, stretching until my body could no longer contain it, bursting the confines of my skin. With a *pop!* I broke free and floated. The others were going through the same experience. Liberated from our chains of flesh, we drifted around the ceiling in an ectoplasmic haze, enjoying the slinkiness of the sensation.

Up the Line

I sent foggy tentacles off to curl around the floating forms of Betsy and Helen, and we enjoyed a tranquil triple conjugation of the psychedelic sort. Meanwhile, music came seeping from a thousand outputs in the wall paint, and the ceiling screen was tuned to the abstraction channel to enhance the effects. It was a very sweet scene.

"We grieve that you must take your leave of us," said Shigemitsu tenderly. "Your absence here creates an aching void. Though all the world now opens to your knock—"

He went on like that for at least five minutes. The poetry got really erotic toward the end. I wish I could remember that part of it.

We floated higher and higher. Sam, hosting it to the full, saw to it that nobody wore off even for a minute. His huge black body gleamed with oil. One young couple from the Time Service had brought their own coffin along; it was a lovely job, silk-lined, with all the sanitary attachments. They climbed in and let us monitor them on the telemetry line. Afterward, the rest of us tried it, in twos or threes, and there was a great deal of laughter over some of the couplings. My partner was the floater peddler, and right in the middle of things we turned on all over again.

The sniffer palace girls danced for us, and three of the Time Couriers—two men and a fragile-looking young woman in an ermine loincloth—put on an exhibition of biological acrobatics, very charming. They had learned the steps in Knossos, where they watched Minos's dancers perform, and had simply adapted the movements to modern tastes by grafting in the copulations at the right moments. During the performance Sam distributed input scramblers to everybody. We plugged them in and beautiful synesthesia took hold. For me this time, touch became smell; I caressed Betsy's cool buttocks and the fragrance of April lilacs came to me; I squeezed a cube of ice and smelled the sea at high tide; I stroked the ribbed wall fabric and my lungs filled with the dizzying flavor of a pine forest on fire. Then we did the pivot and for me sound became texture; Helen made passion-sounds in my ear and they became furry moss; music roared from the speakers as a torrent of thick cream; Shigemitsu began to moan in blank verse and the stabbing rhythms of his voice reached me as pyramids of ice. We went on to do things with color, taste, and duration. Of all the kinds of sensory pleasures invented in the last hundred years, I think scrambling is by far my favorite.

Later Emily, the helix-parlor girl, came over. She was starvation-slim, with painfully sharp cheekbones, a scraggly mop of tangled green hair, and the most beautiful piercing green eyes I have ever seen. Though she was high on everything simultaneously, she seemed cool and self-possessed—an illusion, I quickly discovered. She was floating. "Listen carefully to what she says," Sam advised me. "She goes clairvoyant under the influence of floaters. I mean it: she's the real thing."

She toppled into my arms. I supported her uncertainly a moment while her mouth sought mine. Her teeth nipped lightly into my lips. Delicately we toppled to the carpet, which emitted little thrumming sounds when we landed. Emily wore a cloak of copper mesh strips interlaced at her throat. I searched patiently beneath it for her breasts. She said in a hollow, prophetic voice, "You will soon begin a long journey."

"Yes."

"You will go up the line."

"That's right."

"In—Byzantium."

"Byzantium, yes."

"That is no country for old men!" cried a voice from the far side of the room. "The young in one another's arms, birds in the trees—"

"Byzantium," murmured an exhausted dancer spread-eagled near my feet.

"The golden smithies of the Emperor!" Shigemitsu screamed. "Spirit after spirit! The smithies break the flood! Flames that no faggot feeds, nor steel has lit!"

"The Emperor's drunken soldiery are abed," I said.

Emily, quivering, bit my ear and said, "You will find your heart's desire in Byzantium."

"Sam said the same thing to me."

"And lose it there. And you will suffer, and regret, and repent, and you will not be the same as you were before."

"That sounds serious," I said.

Up the Line

"Beware love in Byzantium!" the prophetess shrilled. "Beware! Beware!"

"... the jaws that bite, the claws that catch!" sang Shigemitsu.

I promised Emily that I would be careful.

But the light of prophecy was gone from her eyes. She sat up, blinked several times, smiled uncertainly, and said, "Who are you?" Her thighs were tightly clasped around my left hand.

"I'm the guest of honor. Jud Elliott."

"I don't know you. What do you do?"

"Time Courier. Will be. I'm leaving to start service tomorrow."

"I think I remember now. I'm Emily."

"Yes, I know. You're with a helix parlor?"

"Someone's been talking about me!"

"Not much. What do you do there?"

"I'm a splitter," she said. "I separate genes. You see, when somebody is carrying the gene for red hair, and wants to transmit that to his children, but the gene is linked to, let's say, the gene for hemophilia, I split off the unwanted gene and edit it out."

"It sounds like very difficult work," I ventured.

"Not if you know what you're doing. There's a six-month training course."

"I see."

"It's interesting work. It tells you a lot about human nature, seeing how people want their children to come out. You know, not everybody wants improvements edited in. We get some amazing requests."

"I guess it depends on what you mean by improvements," I said.

"Well, there *are* certain norms of appearance. We assume that it's better to have thick, lustrous hair than none at all. Better for a man to be two meters tall than one meter tall. Better to have straight teeth than crooked ones. But what would you say if a woman comes in and tells you to design a son with undescended testicles?"

"Why would anybody want a child like that?"

"She doesn't like the idea of his fooling around with girls," Emily said.

"Did you do it?"

"The request was two full points below the mark on the genetic deviation index. We have to refer all such requests to the Board of Genetic Review."

"Would they approve it?" I asked.

"Oh, no, never. They don't authorize counterproductive mutations of that sort."

"I guess the poor woman is just going to have a baby with balls, then."

Emily smiled. "She can go to bootleg helixers, if she likes. They'll do anything for anybody. Don't you know about them?"

"Not really."

"They produce the far-out mutations for the avant-garde set. The children with gills and scales, the children with twenty fingers, the ones with zebra-striped skin. The bootleggers will notch any gene at all—for the right price. They're terribly expensive. But they're the wave of the future."

"They are?"

"Cosmetic mutations are on the way in," Emily declared. "Don't misunderstand—*our* parlor won't touch the things. But this is the last generation of uniformity the human race is going to have. Variety of genotype and phenotype—that's what's ahead!" Her eyes sparkled with sudden lunacy, and I realized that a slow-acting floater must have exploded in her veins in the last few minutes. Drawing close to me, she whispered, "What do you think of this idea? Let's make a baby right now, and I'll redesign it after hours at the parlor! We'll keep up with the trends!"

"I'm sorry," I said. "I've had my pill this month."

"Let's try anyway," she said, and slipped her eager hand into my pants.

18

I reached Istanbul on a murky summer afternoon and caught an express pod across the Bosphorus to the Time Service headquarters, on the Asian side. The city hadn't changed much since my last visit

Up the Line

a year before. That was no surprise. Istanbul hasn't really changed since Kemal Ataturk's time, and that was 150 years ago. The same gray buildings, the same archaic clutter of unlabeled streets, the same overlay of grit and grime. And the same heavenly mosques floating above the dilapidation.

I admire the mosques tremendously. They show that the Turks were good for *something*. But to me, Istanbul is a black joke of a city that someone has painted over the wounded stump of my beloved Constantinople. The little pieces of the Byzantine city that remain hold more magic for me than Sultan Ahmed's mosque, the Suleimaniye, and the mosque of Beyazit, all taken together.

The thought that I would soon be seeing Constantinople as a living city, with all the Turkish excrescences swept away, almost made me stain my pants with glee.

The Time Service had set up shop in a squat, formidable building of the late twentieth century, far up the Bosphorus, practically facing the Turkish fortress of Rumeli Hisari, from which the Conqueror strangled Byzantium in 1453. I was expected; even so, I had to spend fifteen minutes milling in an anteroom, surrounded by angry tourists complaining about some foulup in scheduling. One red-faced man kept shouting, "Where's the computer input? I want all this on record in the computer!" And a tired, angelic-looking secretary kept telling him wearily that everything he was saying *was* going on record, down to the ultimate bleat. Two swaggering giants in Time Patrol uniforms cut coolly through the mêlée, their faces grimly set, their minds no doubt riveted to duty. I could almost hear them thinking, "Aha! *Aha!*" A thin woman with a wedge-shaped face rushed up to them, waved papers at their deep-cleft chins, and yelled, "Seven months ago I confirmed these reservations, yet! Right after Christmas it was! And now they tell me—" The Time Patrolmen kept walking. A robot vendor entered the waiting room and started to sell lottery tickets. Behind it came a haggard, unshaven Turk in a rumpled black jacket, peddling honeycakes from a greasy tray.

I admired the quality of the confusion. It showed genius.

Still, I wasn't unhappy to be rescued. A Levantine type who might have been a cousin of my fondly remembered instructor

Najeeb Dajani appeared, introduced himself to me as Spiros Protopopolos, and led me hastily through a sphincter door I had not noticed. "You should have come through the side way," he said. "I apologize for this delay. We didn't realize you were here."

He was about thirty, plump, sleek, with sunglasses and a great many white teeth. As we shot upshaft to the Couriers' lounge he said, "You have never worked as a Courier before, yes?"

"Yes," I said. "Never. My first time."

"You will love it! The Byzantium run especially. Byzantium, it is so—how shall I express it?" He pressed his pudgy palms rapturously together. "Surely you must feel some of it. But only a Greek like myself can respond fully. Byzantium! Ah, Byzantium!"

"I'm Greek also," I said.

He halted the shaft and raised his glasses. "You are not Judson Daniel Elliott III?"

"I am."

"This is Greek?"

"My mother's name was originally Passilidis. She was born in Athens. My maternal grandfather was mayor of Sparta. On his mother's side he was descended from the Markezinis family."

"You are my brother!" cried Spiros Protopopolos.

It turned out that six of the nine other Time Couriers assigned to the Byzantium run were Greeks by nationality or descent; there were two Germans, Herschel and Melamed, while the tenth man was a slick, dark-haired Spaniard named Capistrano who later on, when deep in his cups, confided to me that his great-grandmother had been a Turk. He may have invented that so I'd despise him; Capistrano had a distinct streak of masochism.

Five of my nine colleagues were currently up the line and four were here in now-time Istanbul, thanks to the scheduling mishap that was causing so much dismay in the anteroom. Protopopolos made the introductions: Melamed, Capistrano, Pappas, meet Elliott. Melamed was fair-haired and hid behind a dense sandy beard; Pappas had hollow cheeks, sad eyes, and a drooping mustache. They were both about forty. Capistrano looked a little younger.

Up the Line

An illuminated board monitored the doings of the other members of the team: Herschel, Kolettis, Plastiras, Metaxas, and Gompers. "Gompers?" I said. Protopopolos replied, "His grandmother was pure Hellene." The five of them were scattered over ten centuries, according to that board, with Kolettis in 1651 B.P., and Metaxas in 606 B.P.—that is, in A.D. 408 and 1453—and the others in between. As I stared at the board, Kolettis moved down the line by more than a century. "They have gone to see the riots," Melamed said softly, and Capistrano nodded, sighing.

Pappas brewed strong coffee for me. Capistrano uncorked a bottle of Turkish brandy, which I found a little hard to ingest. He prodded me encouragingly, saying, "Drink, drink, it's the best you'll taste in the last fifteen centuries!" I remembered Sam's advice that I should learn how to drink, and forced the stuff down, longing for a weed, a floater, a fume, anything decent.

While I relaxed with my new comrades, a Time Patrolman came into the room. He didn't use the scanner to get entry permission, or even knock; he just barged in. "Can't you ever be polite?" Pappas growled.

"Up yours," said the Time Patrolman. He sank down into a web and unbuttoned his uniform shirt. He was a chunky Aryan-looking sort with a hairy chest; what looked like golden wire curled toward his clavicles. "New man?" he said, jerking his head at me.

"Jud Elliott," I said. "Courier."

"Dave Van Dam," he said. "Patrol." His huge hand enfolded mine. "Don't let me catch you screwing around up the line. Nothing personal, but I'm a tough bastard. It's so easy to hate us: we're incorruptible. Try me and see."

"This is the lounge for Couriers," said Capistrano thinly.

"You don't need to tell me that," said Van Dam. "Believe it or not, I can read."

"Are you now a Courier, then?"

"Do you mind if I relax a little with the opposition?" The Patrolman grinned, scratched his chest, and put the brandy bottle to his lips. He drank copiously and belched resonantly. "Christ, what a killer of a day! You know where I was today?"

Nobody seemed to care.

He continued anyway, "I spent the whole day in 1962! Nineteen goddam sixty-two! Checking out every floor of the Istanbul Goddam Hilton for two alleged timecrimers running an alleged artifact siphon. What we heard was they were bringing gold coins and Roman glass down from 1400 B.P. and selling them to American tourists in the Hilton, then investing the proceeds on the stock market and hiding the stash in a Swiss bank for pickup in now-time. Christ! You know, you can make *billions* that way? You buy in a bear-market year and stick it away for a century and you end up owning the world. Well, maybe so, but we didn't see a thing in the whole goddam Hilton except plenty of legitimate free enterprise based in then-time. Crap on it!" He took another pull on the brandy bottle. "Let them run a recheck upstairs. Find their own goddam timecrimers."

"This is the lounge for Couriers," Capistrano said once more.

The Patrolman took no notice. When he finally left, five minutes later, I said, "Are they all like that?"

Protopopolos said, "This was one of the refined ones. Most of the others are boors."

They put me to bed with a hypnosleep course in Byzantine Greek, and when I woke up I not only could order a meal, buy a tunic, and seduce a virgin in Byzantine argot, but I knew some phrases that could make the mosaics of Haghia Sophia peel from the walls in shame. I hadn't known about those phrases when I was a graduate student at Harvard, Yale, and Princeton. Good stuff, hypnosleep.

I still wasn't ready to go out solo as a Courier. Protopopolos, who was serving as staff router this month, arranged to team me with Capistrano for my first time out. If everything went smoothly, I'd be put on my own in a few weeks.

The Byzantium run, which is one of the most popular that the Time Service offers, is pretty standard stuff. Every tour is taken to see the coronation of an emperor, a chariot race in the Hippodrome,

Up the Line

the dedication of Haghia Sophia, the sack of the city by the Fourth Crusade, and the Turkish conquest. A tour like that stays up the line for seven days. The fourteen-day tour covers all that plus the arrival of the First Crusade in Constantinople, the riots of 532, an imperial wedding, and a couple of lesser events. The Courier has his options about which coronations, emperors, or chariot races to go to; the idea is to avoid contributing to the Cumulative Paradox by cluttering any one event with too many tourists. Just about every major period between Justinian and the Turks gets visited, although we're cautioned to avoid the years of bad earthquakes, and absolutely prohibited, under penalty of obliteration by the Time Patrol, from entering the bubonic plague years of 745-47.

On my last night in now-time I was so excited I couldn't sleep. Partly I was keyed up over the fear of blundering somehow on my first assignment as a Courier; it's a big responsibility to be a Courier, even with a colleague along, and I was afraid of committing some terrible mistake. The thought of having to be rescued by the Time Patrol upset me. What a humiliation!

But mainly I was worried about Constantinople. Would it live up to my dream of it? Or would it let me down? All my life I had cherished an image of that golden, glittering city of the past; now, on the verge of going up the line to it, I trembled.

I got up and stumbled around the little room they had given me, feeling drawn and tense. I was off all drugs and wasn't allowed to smoke—Couriers have to taper off such things ahead of time, since it's obviously an illegal anachronism to light up a weed in a tenth-century street. Capistrano had given me the dregs of his brandy, but that was small consolation. He heard me walking into furniture, though, and came to see what the trouble was. "Restless?" he asked.

"Very."

"I always am, before a jump. It never wears off."

He talked me into going out with him to soothe our nerves. We crossed to the European side and wandered at random through the silent streets of the new city, up from Dolmabahce Palace at the shore to the old Hilton, and down past Taksim to the Galata Bridge and into Istanbul proper. We walked tirelessly. We seemed to be the only ones awake in the city. Through the winding maze of a market we wound, emerging on one of those streets leading to Haghia Sophia, where we stood awhile in front of the majestic old building. I imprinted its features on my brain—the extraneous minarets, the late buttresses—and tried to make myself believe that in the morning I'd *see* it in its true form, serene mistress of the city, no longer compelled to share its grand plaza with the alien loveliness of the Blue Mosque across the way.

On and on we went, scrambling over the fragments of the Hippodrome, circling Topkapi, making our way to the sea and the old sea wall. Dawn found us outside the Yedikule fortress, in the shadow of the crumbling Byzantine rampart. We were half asleep. A Turkish boy of about fifteen approached us politely and asked, first in French and then in English, if we were in the market for anything— old coins, his sister, hashish, Israeli currency, gold jewelry, his brother, a carpet. We thanked him and said we weren't. Undaunted, he summoned his sister, who may have been fourteen but looked four or five years older.

"Virgin," he said. "You like her? Nice figure, eh? What are you, American, English, German? Here, you look, eh?" She unsnapped her blouse at a harsh command from him, and displayed attractive taut round breasts. Dangling on a string between them was a heavy Byzantine bronze coin, possibly a *follis*. I peered close for a better look. The boy, breathing garlic at me, realized suddenly that it was the coin and not the breasts that I was studying, and made a smooth switch, saying, "You like old coins, eh? We find plenty under wall in a pot. You wait here, I show you, yes?" He ran off. The sister sullenly closed her blouse. Capistrano and I walked away. The girl followed us, calling out to us to stay, but by the time we had gone twenty meters she lost interest. We were back at the Time Service building in an hour, by pod.

After breakfast we got into costume: long silk tunics, Roman sandals, light cloaks. Capistrano solemnly handed me my timer. By now I had been well trained in its use. I slipped it in place against my skin and felt a dazzling surge of power, knowing that now I was free to transport myself to any era, and was accountable to no one so long as I kept in mind the preservation of the sanctity of now-time. Capistrano winked at me.

"Up the line," he said.

"Up the line," I said.

We went downstairs to meet our eight tourists.

The jumping-off place for the Byzantium run is almost always the same: the plaza in front of Haghia Sophia. The ten of us, feeling faintly foolish in our robes, were taken there by bus, arriving about ten that morning. More conventional tourists, merely there to see Istanbul, flocked back and forth between the great cathedral and nearby Sultan Ahmed. Capistrano and I made sure that everybody's timer was in place and that the rules of time-travel had been thoroughly nagged into everyone's skull.

Our group included a pair of pretty young men from London, a couple of maidenly German schoolteachers, and two elderly American husband-and-wife outfits. Everybody had had the hypnocourse in Byzantine Greek, and for the next sixty days or so would be as fluent in that as in their native languages, but Capistrano and I had to keep reminding the Americans and one of the German girls to speak it.

We jumped.

I felt the momentary disorientation that always comes when you go up the line. Then I got my bearings and discovered that I had departed from Istanbul and had reached Constantinople.

Constantinople did not let me down.

The grime was gone. The minarets were gone. The mosques were gone. The Turks were gone.

The air was blue and sweet and clear. We stood in the great plaza, the Augusteum, in front of Haghia Sophia. To my right, where there should have been bleak gray office buildings, I saw open fields. Ahead of me, where the blue fantasy of Sultan Ahmed's mosque should have been, I saw a rambling conglomeration of low marble palaces. To the side rose the flank of the Hippodrome. Figures in colorful robes, looking like fugitives from Byzantine mosaics, sauntered through the spacious square.

I swung around for my first view of Haghia Sophia without her minarets.

Haghia Sophia was not there.

On the familiar site I saw the charred and tumbled ruins of an unfamiliar rectangular basilica. The stone walls stood but precariously; the roof was gone. Three soldiers drowsed in the shadow of its facade. I was lost.

Capistrano said droningly, "We have journeyed sixteen centuries up the line. The year is 408; we have come to behold the baptismal procession of Emperor Arcadius' son, who will one day rule as Theodosius II. To our rear, on the site of the well-known cathedral of Haghia Sophia, we may see the ruins of the original basilica, built during the reign of the Emperor Constantius, son of Constantine the Great, and opened for prayer on the 15th of December, 360. This building was burned on the 20th of June, 404, during a rebellion, and as you can see, reconstruction has not yet begun. The church will be rebuilt about thirty years down the line by Emperor Theodosius II, and you will view it on our next stop. Come this way."

As though in a dream I followed, as much a tourist as our eight charges. Capistrano did all the work. He lectured us in a perfunctory but comprehensive way about the marble buildings ahead, which were the beginning of the Great Palace. I couldn't reconcile what I saw with the ground plans I had memorized at Harvard; but of course the Constantinople I had studied was the later, greater, post-Justinian city, and now I stood in the city at its dawn. We turned inland, away from the palace district, into a residential district where the houses of the rich, blank-fronted and courtyarded, mixed helter-skelter with the rush-roofed hovels of the poor. And then we emerged on the Mese, the grand processional street, lined by arcaded shops, and on this day, in honor of the baptism of the prince, decked with silk hangings adorned with gold. All the citizens of Byzantium were here, packing the street elbow to elbow in anticipation of the grand parade. Food shops were busy; we smelled grilled ham and

Up the Line

baked lamb, and eyed stalls laden with cheeses, nuts, unfamiliar fruits. One of the German girls said she was hungry, and Capistrano laughed and bought spitted lamb for us all, paying for it with bright copper coins worth a fortune to a numismatist. A one-eyed man sold us wine out of a huge cool amphora, letting us drink right from the ladle. Once it became obvious to the other peddlers in the vicinity that we were susceptible customers, they crowded around by the dozens, offering us souvenirs, candied sweets, elderly-looking hard-boiled eggs, pans of salted nuts, trays of miscellaneous animal organs, eyeballs and other balls. This was the real thing, the genuinely archaic past; that array of vended oddities and the reek of sweat and garlic coming from the mob of vendors told us that we were a long way from 2059.

"Foreigners?" asked a bearded man who was selling little clay oil lamps. "Where from? Cyprus? Egypt?"

"Spain," said Capistrano.

The oil-lamp man eyed us in awe, as though we had claimed to come from Mars. "Spain," he repeated. "Spain! Wonderful! To travel so far, to see our city—" He gave our whole group a detailed survey, taking a quick inventory and fastening on blonde and breasty Clotilde, the more voluptuous of our two German schoolteachers. "Your slavegirl is a Saxon?" he asked me, feeling the merchandise through Clotilde's loose robes. "Ah, very nice! You are a man of taste!" Clotilde gasped and pried his fingers from her thigh. Coldly Capistrano seized the man, pushing him up against the wall of a shop so roughly that a dozen of his clay lamps tumbled to the pavement and shattered. The vendor winked, but Capistrano said something chilly under his breath and gave the man a terrible glare. "I meant no harm," the vendor protested. "I thought she was a slave!" He muttered a curt apology and limped away. Clotilde was trembling—whether from outrage or excitement, it was hard to tell. Her companion, Lise, looked a little envious. No Byzantine street peddler had ever fondled her bare flesh!

Capistrano spat. "That could have been troublesome. We must always be on our guard; innocent pinching can turn quickly to complications and catastrophe."

The peddlers edged away from us. We found places near the front of the mob, facing the street. It seemed to me that many of the faces in the crowd were un-Byzantine, and I wondered if they were the faces of time-travelers. A time is coming, I thought, when we from down the line will throng the past to the choking point. We will fill all our yesterdays with ourselves and crowd out our own ancestors.

"Here they come!" a thousand voices shouted.

Trumpets blared in several different keys. In the distance there appeared a procession of nobles, clean-cut and close-cropped in the Roman fashion, for this was still as much a Roman city as it was a Greek one. Everyone wore white silk—imported at great cost by caravan from China, Capistrano murmured; the Byzantines had not yet stolen the secret of silk manufacture—and the late afternoon sun, striking the splendid robes at a steep angle, gave the procession such a glow of beauty that even Capistrano, who had seen it all before, was moved. Slowly, slowly, the high dignitaries advanced.

"They look like snowflakes," whispered a man behind me. "Dancing snowflakes!"

It took nearly an hour for these high ones to pass us. Twilight came. Following the priests and dukes of Byzantium were the imperial troops, carrying lighted candles that flickered in the deepening dusk like an infinity of stars. Then came more priests, bearing medallions and icons; and then a prince of the royal blood, carrying a gurgling, plump infant who would be the mighty Emperor Theodosius II; and then the reigning emperor Arcadius, clad in imperial purple. The Emperor of Byzantium! I repeated that to myself a thousand times. I, Judson Daniel Elliott III, stood bareheaded under the Byzantine sky, here in A.D. 408, while the Emperor of Byzantium, robes aswish, walked past me! Even though the monarch was merely the trifling Arcadius, the insignificant interpolation between the two Theodosii, I trembled. I swayed. The pavement heaved and bucked beneath me. "Are you ill?" whispered Clotilde anxiously. I sucked breath and begged the universe to stand still. I was overwhelmed, and by Arcadius. What if this had been Justinian? Constantine? Alexius?

You know how it is. Eventually I got to see even those great ones. But by then I had seen too much up the line, and though I was impressed, I wasn't engulfed with awe. Of Justinian my clearest memory is that he sneezed; but when I think of Arcadius, I hear trumpets and see stars whirling in the sky.

21

We stayed that night in an inn overlooking the Golden Horn; on the other side of the water, where Hiltons and countinghouses one day would rise, was only an impenetrable darkness. The inn was a substantial wooden building with a dining hall on the ground floor and huge, rough, dormitory-style rooms above. Somehow I expected to be asked to sleep on the floor in a strew of rushes, but no, there were beds of a recognizable sort, and mattresses stuffed with rags. Sanitary facilities were outside, behind the building. There were no baths; we were expected to use the public bathhouses if we craved cleanliness. The ten of us shared one room, but fortunately none of us minded that. Clotilde, when she undressed, indignantly went around showing us the purpling bruises left by the vendor's grip on her soft white thigh; her angular friend Lise looked gloomy again, for having nothing to show.

That night we did little sleeping. There was too much noise, for one thing, since the celebration of the imperial baptism went on raucously throughout the city until almost dawn. But who could sleep, anyway, knowing that the world of the early fifth century lay just beyond the door?

One night before and sixteen centuries down the line, Capistrano had kindly seen me through a siege of sleeplessness. Now he did it again. I rose and stood by the little slit of a window, peering at the bonfires in the city, and when he noticed me he came over and said, "I understand. Sleeping is hard at first."

"Yes."

"Shall I get a woman for you?"

"No."

"We'll take a walk, then?"

"Can we leave them?" I asked, looking at our eight tourists.

"We won't go far. We'll stay just outside, within reach if some trouble starts."

The air was heavy and mild. Snatches of obscene song floated up from the tavern district. We walked toward it; the taverns were still open and full of drunken soldiers. Swarthy prostitutes offered their wares. One girl, hardly sixteen, had a coin on a string between her bare breasts. Capistrano nudged me to notice it, and we laughed. "The same coin, maybe?" he asked. "But different breasts?" I shrugged. "Perhaps the same breasts, too," I said, thinking of the unborn girl who had been for sale at the Yedikule a night ago. Capistrano bought two flasks of oily Greek wine and we returned to the inn, to sit quietly downstairs and drink the darkness away.

He did most of the talking. Like many Time Couriers, his life had been a complex, jagged one full of detours, and he let his autobiography dribble out between gulps of wine. Noble Spanish ancestors, he said (he didn't tell me about the Turkish great-grandmother until months later, when he was far more thoroughly drunk); early marriage to a virgin of high family; education at the best universities of Europe. Then inexplicable decline, loss of ambition, loss of fortune, loss of wife. "My life," said Capistrano, "broke in half when I was twenty-seven years of age. I required total reintegration of personality. As you see, the effort was not a true success." He spoke of a series of temporary marriages, adventures in criminality, experiments with hallucinatory drugs that made weeds and floaters look innocent. When he enrolled as a Time Courier, it was only as an alternative to suicide. "I keyed to an output and asked for a bit at random," he said. "Positive, and I become a Courier. Negative, and I drink poison. The bit came up positive. Here I am." He drained his wine.

To me that night he seemed a wonderful mixture of the desperate, tragic romantic and the self-dramatizing charlatan. Of course, I was drunk myself, and very young. But I told him how much I admired his quest for identity, and secretly wished that I could learn the knack of seeming so appealingly destroyed, so interestingly lost.

"Come," he said, when the last of the wine was gone. "To dispose of the corpses."

Up the Line

We hurled our flasks into the Golden Horn. Streaks of dawn were emerging. As we walked slowly back to the inn, Capistrano said, "I have made a little hobby of tracing my ancestors, do you know? It is my own private research. Here—look at these names." He produced a small, thick notebook. "In each era I visit," he said, "I seek out my ancestors and list them here. Already I know several hundred of them, going back to the fourteenth century. Do you realize how immense the number of one's ancestors is? We have two parents, and each of them has two parents, and each of them two parents—go back only four generations and you have already thirty ancestors!"

"An interesting hobby," I said.

Capistrano's eyes blazed. "More than a hobby! More than a hobby! A matter of death and life! Look, my friend, whenever I grow more tired than usual of existence, all I must do is find one of these people, *one*, and destroy him! Take his life when he is still a child, perhaps. Then return to now-time. And in that moment, swiftly, without pain, my own tiresome life ceases ever to have been!"

"But the Time Patrol—"

"Helpless," said Capistrano. "What can the Patrol do? If my crime is discovered, I am seized and erased from history for timecrime, right? If my crime is not discovered—and why should it be?—then I have erased myself. Either way I am gone. Is this not the most charming way of suicide?"

"In eliminating your own ancestor," I said, "you might be changing now-time to a greater degree. You'd also eliminate your own brothers and sisters—uncles—grandparents and all of *their* brothers and sisters—all by removing one prop from the past!"

He nodded solemnly. "I am aware of this. And so I compile these genealogies, you see, in order to determine how best to effect my own erasure. I am not Samson; I have no wish to bring the temple crashing down with myself. I will look for the strategic person to eliminate—one who is himself sinful, incidentally, for I will not slay the truly innocent—and I will remove that person and thus myself, and perhaps the changes in now-time will not be terribly great. If they are, the Patrol will discover and undo them, and still give me the exit I crave."

I wondered if he was crazy or just drunk. A little of both, I decided.

I felt like telling him that if he really wanted to kill himself that badly, it would be a whole lot less trouble for everybody else if he'd just go jump in the Bosphorus.

I felt a twinge of terror at the thought that the whole Time Service might be permeated by Capistranos, all shopping around for the most interestingly self-destructive way of changing the past.

Upstairs, the early light revealed eight sleepers, huddled two by two. Our elderly married folks slept peacefully; the two pretty boys from London looked sweaty and tousled after some busy buggery; Clotilde, smiling, slept with her hand tucked between Lise's pale thighs, and Lise's left hand was cupped cozily about Clotilde's maidenly but firm right breast. I lay down on my lonely bed and slipped quickly into sleep. Soon Capistrano woke me, and we woke the others. I felt ten thousand years old.

We had a breakfast of cold lamb and went out for a quick daylight walking tour of the city. Most of the interesting things had not yet been built, or else were still in early forms; we didn't stay long. At noon we went to the Augusteum to shunt. "Our next stop," Capistrano announced, "will be A.D. 532, where we will see the city of Justinian's time and witness the riots which destroyed it, making possible the construction of the finer and more grand city that won such eternal fame." We backed into the shadows of the ruined original Haghia Sophia, so that no passersby would be startled by the sight of ten people vanishing. I set all the timers. Capistrano produced his pitchpipe and gave the master signal. We shunted.

Two weeks later we all returned down the line to 2059. I was dizzied, intoxicated, my soul full of Byzantium. I had seen the highlights of a thousand years of greatness. The city of my dreams had come to life for me. The meat and wine of Byzantium had passed through my bowels.

Up the Line

From a Courier's professional point of view, the trip had been a good one, that is, uneventful. Our tourists had not entangled themselves in trouble, nor had any paradoxes been created, as far as we could tell. There had been a little friction only one night, when Capistrano, very drunk, tried to seduce Clotilde; he wasn't subtle about it, letting seduction shade into rape when she resisted, but I managed to separate them before her nails got into his eyes. In the morning he wouldn't believe it. "The blonde lesbian?" he asked. "I would stoop so low? You must dream it!" And then he insisted on going eight hours up the line to see if it had really happened. I had visions of a sober Capistrano taking his earlier sozzled self to task, and it scared me. I had to argue him out of it in a blunt and direct way, reminding him of the Time Patrol's regulation prohibiting anyone from engaging in conversation with himself of a different now-time basis, and threatening to report him if he tried it. Capistrano looked wounded, but he let the matter drop. And when we came down the line and he filed a report of his own, upon request, concerning my behavior as a Courier, he gave me the highest rating. Protopopolos told me that afterward.

"Your next trip," said Protopopolos, "will be as assistant to Metaxas, on the one-week tour."

"When do I leave?"

"In two weeks," he said. "Your layoff comes first, remember? And after you return from the trip with Metaxas, you begin soloing. Where will you spend your layoff?"

"I think I'll go down to Crete or Mykonos," I said, "and get a little rest on the beach."

The Time Service insists that Couriers take two-week vacations between trips. The Time Service doesn't believe in pushing its Couriers too hard. During layoffs, Couriers are completely at liberty. They can spend the whole time relaxing in now-time, as I proposed to do, or they can sign up with a time tour, or they can simply go hopping by themselves to any era that may interest them.

There's no charge for timer use when a Courier makes jumps up the line in his layoff periods. The Time Service wants to encourage its employees to feel at home in all periods of the past, and what better way than to allow unlimited free shunting?

Protopopolos looked a little disappointed when I said I'd spend my vacation sunning myself in the islands. "Don't you want to do some jumping?" he asked.

The idea of making time-jumps on my own at this stage of my career scared me, frankly. But I couldn't tell Protopopolos that. I also considered the point that in another month he'd be handing me the responsibility for the lives of an entire tour group. Maybe this conversation was part of the test of my qualifications. Were they trying to see if I had the guts to go jumping on my own?

Protopopolos seemed to be fishing for an answer.

I said, "On second thought, why waste a chance to do some jumping? I'll have a peek at post-Byzantine Istanbul."

"With a tour group?"

"On my own," I said.

So I went jumping, smack into the Paradox of Discontinuity.

My first stop was the wardrobe department. I needed costumes suited for Istanbul of the sixteenth through nineteenth centuries. Instead of giving me a whole sequence of clothes to fit the changing fashions, they decked me out in an all-purpose Moslem rig, simple white robes of no particular era, nondescript sandals, long hair, and a straggly youthful beard. By way of pocket money they supplied me with a nice assortment of gold and silver pieces of the right eras, a little of everything that might have been circulating in medieval Turkey, including some bezants of Greek-ruled times, miscellaneous coinage of the sultans, and a good deal of Venetian gold. All this was installed in a currency belt that I wore just above my timer, the coins segregated from left to right according to centuries, so that I wouldn't get into trouble by offering an eighteenth-century dinar in a sixteenth-century market place. There was no charge for the money; the Time Service runs a continuous siphon

Up the Line

of its own, circulating coinage between now-time and then-time for the benefit of its personnel, and a Courier going on holiday can sign out any reasonable amount to cover his expenses. To the Service it's only play money, anyway, infinitely replenishible at will. I like the system.

I took hypnosleep courses in Turkish and Arabic before I left. The Special Requests department fabricated a quick cover identity for me that would work well in any era of my intended visit: if questioned, I was supposed to identify myself as a Portuguese national who had been kidnapped on the high seas by Algerian pirates when ten years old, and raised as a Moslem in Algiers. That would account for flaws in my accent and for my vagueness about my background; if I had the misfortune to be interrogated by a real Portuguese, which wasn't likely, I could simply say that I couldn't remember much about my life in Lisbon and had forgotten the names of my forebears. So long as I kept my mouth shut, prayed toward Mecca five times a day, and watched my step, I wasn't likely to get into trouble. (Of course, if I landed in a really serious mess, I could escape by using my timer, but in the Time Service that's considered a coward's route, and also undesirable because of the implications of witchcraft that you leave behind when you vanish.)

All these preparations took a day and a half. Then they told me I was ready to jump. I set my timer for 500 B.P., picking the era at random, and jumped.

I arrived on August 14, 1559, at nine-thirty in the evening. The reigning sultan was the great Suleiman I, nearing the close of his epoch. Turkish armies threatened the peace of Europe; Istanbul was bursting with the wealth of conquest. I couldn't respond to this city as I had to the sparkling Constantinople of Justinian or Alexius, but that was a personal matter having to do with ancestry, chemistry, and historical affinity. Taken on its own merits, Suleiman's Istanbul was a city among cities.

I spent half the day roaming it. For an hour I watched a lovely mosque under construction, hoping it was the Suleimaniye, but later in the day I found the Suleimaniye, brand-new and glistening in the noon light. I made a special pilgrimage, covertly consulting a map I had smuggled with me, to find the mosque of Mehmet the Conqueror, which an earthquake would bring down in 1766. It was worth the walk. Toward midafternoon, after an inspection of the mosquified Haghia Sophia and the sad ruins of the Great Palace of Byzantium across the plaza (Sultan Ahmed's mosque would be rising there fifty years down the line), I made my way to the Covered Bazaar, thinking to buy a few small trinkets as souvenirs, and when I was no more than ten paces past the entrance I caught sight of my beloved guru Sam.

Consider the odds against that: with thousands of years in which to roam, the two of us coming on holiday to the same year and the same day and the same city, and meeting under the same roof!

He was clad in Moorish costume, straight out of Othello. There was no mistaking him; he was by far the tallest man in sight, and his coal-black skin glistened brilliantly against his white robes. I rushed up to him.

"Sam!" I cried. "Sam, you old black bastard, what luck to meet you *here*."

He whirled in surprise, frowned at me, looked puzzled. "I know you not," he said coldly.

"Don't let the beard fool you. It's me, Sam. Jud Elliott."

He glared. He growled. A crowd began to gather. I wondered if I had been wrong. Maybe this wasn't Sam, but Sam's multi-great-grandfather, made to look like his twin by a genetic fluke. No, I told myself, this is the authentic Sambo.

But then why is he pulling out that scimitar?

We had been talking in Turkish. I switched to English and said, "Listen, Sam, I don't know what's going on, but I'm willing to ride along with your act. Suppose we meet in half an hour outside Haghia Sophia, and we can—"

"Infidel dog!" he roared. "Beggar's spawn! Masturbator of pigs! Away from me! Away, cutpurse!"

He swished the scimitar menacingly above my head and continued to rave in Turkish. Suddenly in a lower voice he muttered, "I don't know who the hell you are, pal, but if you don't clear out of here fast I'm going to have to slice you in half." That much was in

Up the Line

English. In Turkish again he cried, "Molester of infants! Drinker of toad's milk! Devourer of cameldung!"

This was no act. He genuinely didn't recognize me, and he genuinely didn't want anything to do with me. Baffled, I backed away from him, hustled down one of the subsidiary corridors of the bazaar, stepped out into the open, and hastily shunted myself ten years down the line. A couple of people saw me go, but faex on them; to a Turk of 1559 the world must have been full of efreets and jinni, and I was just one more phantom.

I didn't stay in 1569 more than five minutes. Sam's wild reaction to my greeting had me so mystified that I couldn't relax and see the sights. I had to have an explanation. So I hurried on down the line to 2059, materializing a block from the Covered Bazaar and nearly getting smeared by a taxi. A few latter-day Turks grinned and pointed at my medieval Turkish robes. The unsophisticated apes hadn't yet learned to take returning time-travelers for granted, I guess.

I went quickly to the nearest public communications booth, thumbed the plate, and put through a call to Sam.

"He is not at his home number," the master information output told me. "Should we trace him?"

"Yes, please," I said automatically.

A moment later I slapped myself for stupidity. Of course he won't be home, you idiot! He's up the line in 1559!

But the master communications network had already begun tracing him. Instead of doing the sensible thing and hanging up, I stood there like a moron, waiting for the inevitable news that the master communications network couldn't find him anywhere.

About three minutes went by. Then the bland voice said, "We have traced your party to Nairobi and he is standing by for your call. Please notify if you wish to proceed."

"Go ahead," I said, and Sam's ebony features blossomed on the screen.

"Is there trouble, child?" he asked.

"What are you doing in Nairobi?" I screamed.

"A little holiday among my own people. Should I not be here?"

"Look," I said, "I'm on my layoff between Courier jobs, and I've just been up the line to 1559 Istanbul, and I met you there."

"So?"

"How can you be there if you're in Nairobi?"

"The same way that there can be twenty-two specimens of your Arab instructor back there watching the Romans nail up Jesus," Sam said. "Sheet, man, when will you learn to think four-dimensionally?"

"So that's a different you up the line in 1559?"

"It better be, buster! He's there and I'm here!" Sam laughed. "A little thing like that shouldn't upset you, man. You're a Courier now, remember?"

"Wait. Wait. Here's what happened. I walked into the Covered Bazaar, see, and there you were in Moorish robes, and I let out this big whoop and ran up to you to say hello. And you didn't know me, Sam! You started waving your scimitar, and cursing me out, and you told me in English to get the hell away from you, and —"

"Well, hey, man, you know it's against regulations to talk to other time-travelers when you're up the line. Unless you set out from the same now-time as the other man, you're supposed to ignore him even if you see through his cover. Fraternization is prohibited because—"

"Yeah, sure, but it was *me*, Sam. I didn't think you'd pull rules on *me*. You didn't even know me, Sam!"

"That's obvious. But why are you so upset, kid?"

"It was like you had amnesia. It scared me."

"But I *couldn't* have known you."

"What are you talking about?"

Sam began to laugh. "The Paradox of Discontinuity! Don't tell me they never taught you that one!"

"They said something about it, but I never paid much attention to a lot of that stuff, Sam."

"Well, pay attention now. You know what year it was I took that Istanbul trip?"

"No."

"It was 2056, '55, someplace back there. And I didn't meet you until three or four years later—this spring, it was. So the Sam you found in 1559 never saw you before. Discontinuity, see? You were working from a now-time basis of 2059, and I was working from a basis of maybe '55, and so you were a stranger to me, but I wasn't a stranger to you. That's one reason why Couriers aren't supposed to talk to friends they run into by accident up the line."

I began to see.

"I begin to see," I said.

"To me," said Sam, "you were some dumb fresh kid trying to make trouble, maybe even a Time Patrol fink. I didn't know you and I didn't want anything to do with you. Now that I think about it a little, I remember something like that happening when I was there. Somebody from down the line bothering me in the bazaar. Funny that I never connected him with you, though!"

"I had a fake beard on, up the line."

"That must have been it. Well, listen, are you all straightened out now?"

"The Paradox of Discontinuity, Sam. Sure."

"You'll remember to keep clear of old friends when you're up the line?"

"You bet. Christ, Sam, you really terrified me with that scimitar!"

"Otherwise, how's it going?"

"Great," I said. "It's really great."

"Watch those paradoxes, kid," Sam said, and blew me a kiss.

Much relieved, I stepped out of the booth and went up the line to 1550 to watch them build the mosque of Suleiman the Magnificent.

24

Themistoklis Metaxas was the chief Courier for my second time-tour of Byzantium. From the moment I met him I sensed that this man was going to play a major role in my destiny, and I was right.

Metaxas was bantam-sized, maybe 1.5 meters tall. His skull was triangular, flat on top and pointed at the chin. His hair, thick and curly, was going gray. I guess he was about fifty years old. He had small glossy dark eyes, heavy brows, and a big sharp slab of a nose. He kept his lips curled inward so that he didn't seem to have lips at all. There was no fat on him anywhere. He was unusually strong. His voice was low and compelling.

Metaxas had charisma. Or should I call it chutzpah?

A little of both, I think. For him the whole universe revolved around Themistoklis Metaxas; suns were born only that they might shed starlight on Themistoklis Metaxas; the Benchley Effect had been invented solely to enable Themistoklis Metaxas to walk through the ages. If he ever died, the cosmos would crumble.

He had been one of the first Time Couriers ever hired, more than fifteen years ago. If he had cared to have the job, he could have been the head of the entire Courier Service by now, with a platoon of wanton secretaries and no need to battle fleas in old Byzantium. By choice, though, Metaxas remained a Courier on active duty, doing nothing but the Byzantium run. He practically regarded himself as a Byzantine citizen, and even spent his layoffs there, in a villa he had acquired in the suburbs of the early twelfth century.

He was engaged on the side in a variety of small and large illegalities; they might be interrupted if he retired as a Courier, so he didn't retire. The Time Patrol was terrified of him and let him have his own way in everything. Of course, Metaxas had more sense than to meddle with the past in any way that might cause serious changes in now-time, but aside from that his plunderings up the line were totally uninhibited.

When I met him for the first time, he said to me, "You haven't lived until you've laid one of your own ancestors."

It was a big group: twelve tourists, Metaxas, and me. They always loaded a few extras into his tours because he was such an unusually capable Courier and in such great demand. I tagged along as an assistant, soaking up experience against my first solo trip, which would be coming next time.

Up the Line

Our dozen included three young and pretty single girls, Princeton co-eds making the Byzantium trip on gifts from their parents, who wanted them to learn something; two of the customary well-to-do middle-aged couples, one from Indianapolis and one from Milan; two youngish interior decorators, male and queer, from Beirut; a recently divorced response manipulator from New York, around forty-five and hungry for women; a puffy-faced little high-school teacher from Milwaukee, trying to improve his mind, and his wife; in short, the customary sampling.

At the end of the first introductory session all three of the Princeton girls, both interior decorators, and the Indianapolis wife were visibly hungering to go to bed with Metaxas. Nobody paid much attention to me.

"It will be different after the tour starts," said Metaxas consolingly. "Several of the girls will become available to you. You *do* want the girls, don't you?"

He was right. On our first night up the line he picked one of the Princeton girls for himself, and the other two resigned themselves speedily to accepting the second best. For some reason, Metaxas chose a pugnosed redhead with splashy freckles and big feet. He left for me a long, cool, sleek brunette, so flawless in every way that she was obviously the product of one of the world's finest helix men, and a cute, cheerful honey-blonde with warm eyes, smooth flesh, and the breasts of a twelve-year-old. I picked the brunette and regretted it; she came on in bed like something made of plastic. Toward dawn I traded her for the blonde and had a better time.

Metaxas was a tremendous Courier. He knew everybody and everything, and maneuvered us into superb positions for the big events.

"We are now," he said, "in January, 532. The Emperor Justinian rules. His ambition is to conquer the world and govern it from Constantinople, but most of his great achievements lie ahead. The city, as you see, still looks much as it did in the last century. In front of you is the Great Palace; to the rear is the rebuilt Haghia Sophia of Theodosius II, following the old basilica plan, not yet reconstructed with the familiar domes. The city is tense; there will soon be civil disorder. Come this way."

Shivering in the cold, we followed Metaxas through the city, down byways and avenues I had not traveled when I came this way earlier with Capistrano. Never once on this trip did I catch sight of my other self or Capistrano or any of that group; one of Metaxas' legendary skills was his ability to find new approaches to the standard scenes.

Of course, he had to. At this moment there were fifty or a hundred Metaxases leading tours through Justinian's city. As a matter of professional pride he wouldn't want to intersect any of those other selves.

"There are two factions in Constantinople now," said Metaxas. "The Blues and the Greens, they are called. They consist of perhaps a thousand men on each side, all troublemakers, and far more influential than their numbers indicate. The factions are something less than political parties, something more than mere supporters of sports teams, but they have characteristics of both. The Blues are more aristocratic; the Greens have links to the lower classes and the commercial strata. Each faction backs a team in the Hippodrome games, and each backs a certain course of governmental policies. Justinian has long been sympathetic to the Blues, and the Greens mistrust him. But as emperor he has tried to appear neutral. He would actually like to suppress both factions as threats to his power. Each night now the factions run wild in the streets. Look: those are the Blues."

Metaxas nodded at a cluster of insolent-looking bravos across the way: eight or nine idling men with long tumbles of thick hair to their shoulders, and festoons of beards and mustaches. They had cut back only the hair on the front of their heads. Their tunics were drawn in tight at the wrists, but flared out enormously from there to the shoulders; they wore gaudy capes and breeches and carried short two-edged swords. They looked brutal and dangerous.

"Wait here," said Metaxas, and went over to them.

The Blues greeted him like an old friend. They clapped him on the back, laughed, shouted in glee. I couldn't hear the conversation, but I saw Metaxas grasping hands, talking quickly, articulately, confidently. One of the Blues offered him a flask of wine and he took a deep drink; then, hugging the man in mock tipsiness, Metaxas cunningly whisked the Blue's sword from its sheath and pretended to run him through. The rowdies capered and applauded. Now Metaxas pointed at us; there were nods of agreement, oglings of the girls, winks, gestures. Finally we were summoned across the street.

"Our friends invite us to the Hippodrome as their guests," said Metaxas. "The races begin next week. Tonight we are permitted to join them in their revels."

I could hardly believe it. When I'd been here with Capistrano, we skulked about, keeping out of sight, for this was a time of rape and murder by night and all laws ceased to function after dark. How did Metaxas dare to bring us so close to the criminals?

He dared. And that night we roamed Constantinople, watching the Blues rob, ravish, and kill. For other citizens, death lay just around any corner; we were immune, privileged witnesses to the reign of terror. Metaxas presided over the nightmare prowl like a sawed-off Satan, cavorting with his Blue friends and even fingering one or two victims for them.

In the morning it seemed like a dream. The phantoms of violence vanished with the night; by pale winter sunlight we inspected the city and listened to Metaxas' historical commentary.

"Justinian," he said, "was a great conqueror, a great lawgiver, a great diplomat and a great builder. This is history's verdict. We also have the *Secret History* of Procopius, which says that Justinian was both a knave and a fool, and that his wife Theodora was a demonic whorish villainess. I know this Procopius: a good man, a clever writer, something of a puritan, a little too gullible. But he's right about Justinian and Theodora. Justinian is a great man in the great things and a terribly evil man in the petty things. Theodora"—he spat—"is a whore among whores. She dances naked at dinners of state; she exhibits her body in public; she sleeps with her servants. I've heard she gives herself to dogs and donkeys, too. She's every bit as depraved as Procopius claims."

Metaxas' eyes twinkled. I knew without being told that he must have shared Theodora's bed.

Later that day he whispered, "I can arrange it for you. The risks are slight. Did you ever dream you could sleep with the Empress of Byzantium?"

"The risks—"

"What risks? You have your timer! You can get free! Listen to me, boy, she's an acrobat! She wraps her heels around your ears. She *consumes* you. I can fix it up for you. The Empress of Byzantium! Justinian's wife!"

"Not this trip," I blurted. "Some other time. I'm still too new at this business."

"You're afraid of her."

"I'm not ready to fuck an empress just yet," I said solemnly.

"Everybody else does it!"

"Couriers?"

"Most of them."

"On my next trip," I promised. The idea appalled me. I had to turn it off somehow. Metaxas misunderstood; I wasn't shy, or afraid of being caught by Justinian, or anything like that; but I couldn't bring myself to intersect with history that way. Traveling up the line was still fantasy for me; humping the celebrated monstress Theodora would make the fantasy all too real. Metaxas laughed at me, and for a while I think he felt contempt for me. But afterward he said, "It's okay. Don't let me rush you into things. When you're ready for her, though, don't miss her. I recommend her personally."

We stayed around for a couple of days to watch the early phases of the riots. The New Year's Games were about to begin, and the Blues and Greens were growing more unruly. Their roughnecking was verging on anarchy; no one was safe in the streets after dark. Justinian worriedly ordered the factions to halt their maraudings, and various ringleaders were arrested. Seven were condemned to death, four by decapitation because they were caught carrying weapons, three by hanging on grounds of conspiracy.

Metaxas took us to see the performance. One of the Blues survived his first hanging when the rope broke under his weight. The imperial guards put him up there again, and again the gallows couldn't finish him, though the rope left fiery marks on his throat. So they put him aside for a while and strung up a Green, and bungled that job twice too; they were about to put the battered victims through a third hanging apiece when some outraged monks came boiling out of their monastery, grabbed the men in the midst of the confusion, and spirited them across the Golden Horn by rowboat to sanctuary in some church. Metaxas, who had seen all this before, cackled wildly at the fun. It seemed to me that his face peered at me from a thousand places in the crowd that had turned out for the executions.

Then the racing season began at the Hippodrome, and we went as guests of Metaxas' friendly gang of Blues. We had plenty of company; 100,000 Byzantines were in the stands. The tiers of marble seats were crowded far past capacity, but space had been saved for us.

I hunted for myself in the stands, knowing that I sat somewhere else here with Capistrano and that tour; but in the crush I couldn't catch a glimpse of myself. I saw plenty of Metaxas, though.

The blonde Princetonian gasped when we got to our seats. "Look there!" she said. "The things from Istanbul!" Down the center of the arena was a row of familiar monuments, marking the boundary between the outward and inward courses of the track. The serpent column from Delphi, brought here by Constantine, was there, and the great obelisk of Thutmose III, stolen out of Egypt by the first Theodosius. The blonde remembered them from Istanbul down the line, where they still stand, though the Hippodrome itself is gone.

"But where's the third one?" she asked.

Metaxas said softly, "The other obelisk has not yet been erected. Best not to talk about it."

It was the third day of the races—the fatal day. An ugly mood gripped this arena where emperors had been made and unmade. Yesterday and the day before, I knew, there had been nasty outcries when Justinian appeared in the imperial box; the crowd had yelled to him to free the imprisoned ringleaders of the factions, but he had ignored the shouts and let the races proceed. Today, January 13, Constantinople would erupt. Time-tourists love catastrophes; this would be a good one. I knew. I had seen it already.

Below, officials were completing the preliminary rituals. Imperial guards, standards flying, paraded grandly. Those leaders of the Blues and Greens who were not in jail exchanged chilly ceremonial greetings. Now the mob stirred, and Justinian entered his box, a man of middle height, rather plump, with a round, florid face. Empress Theodora followed. She wore clinging, diaphanous silks, and she had rouged her nipples; they blazed through the fabric like beacons.

Justinian mounted the steps of his box. The cries began: "Free them! Let them out!" Serenely he lifted a fold of his purple robe and blessed the audience with the sign of the Cross, three times, once toward the center block of seats, then to the right, then to the left. The uproar grew. He threw a white kerchief down. Let the games begin! Theodora stretched and yawned and pulled up her robe to study the contours of her thighs. The stable doors burst open. Out came the first four chariots.

They were quadrigas, four-horse vehicles; the audience forgot about politics as, wheel to wheel, the chariots went into action. Metaxas said pleasantly, "Theodora has been to bed with each of the drivers. I wonder which one is her favorite." The empress looked profoundly bored. I had been surprised to find her here, the last time: I had thought that empresses were barred from the Hippodrome. As indeed they were, but Theodora made her own rules.

The charioteers hustled down to the spina, the row of monuments, and came round and back up the course. A race ran seven rounds; seven ostrich eggs were set out on a stand, and as each round was completed one egg was removed. We watched two races. Then Metaxas said, "Let us shunt forward by one hour and get to the climax of this." Only Metaxas would pull a bit like that: we adjusted all the timers and shunted, en masse, in casual disregard of the rules for public jumping. When we reappeared in the Hippodrome, the sixth race was about to begin.

"Now starts the trouble," said Metaxas happily.

The race was run. But as the victor came forth to receive his crown, a booming voice bellowed from out of a group of Blues, "Long live the Greens and Blues!"

Up the Line

An instant later, from the seats of the Greens, cams the answering cry: "Long live the Blues and Greens!"

"The factions are uniting against Justinian," Metaxas said, quietly, schoolmasterishly. The chaos that was engulfing the stadium didn't ruffle him.

"Long live the Greens and Blues!"

"Long live the Blues and Greens!"

"Long live the Greens and Blues!"

"Victory!"

"Victory!"

"Victory!"

And the one word, "Victory!" became a mighty cry from thousands of throats. "*Nika! Nika!* Victory!"

Theodora laughed. Justinian, scowling, conferred with officers of his imperial guard. Greens and Blues marched from the Hippodrome, followed by a happy, screaming mob bent on destruction. We hung back, keeping a judicious distance; I caught sight of other equally cautious little groups of spectators, and knew they were no Byzantines.

Torches flared in the streets. The imperial prison was aflame. The prisoners were free, the jailers were burning. Justinian's own guard, afraid to interfere, looked on soberly. The rioters piled faggots against the gate of the Great Palace, across the plaza from the Hippodrome. Soon the palace was on fire. Theodosius' Haghia Sophia was aflame; bearded priests, waving precious icons, appeared on its blazing roof and toppled back into the inferno. The senate house caught fire. It was a glorious orgy of destruction. Whenever snarling rioters approached us, we adjusted timers and shunted down the line, taking care to jump no more than ten or fifteen minutes at a hop, so that we wouldn't reappear right inside some fire that hadn't been set when we shunted.

"*Nika! Nika!*"

Constantinople's sky was black with oily smoke, and flames danced on the horizon. Metaxas, his wedge-shaped face smudged and sooty, his eyes glinting with excitement, seemed constantly on the verge of breaking away from us and going to join the destroyers.

"The firemen themselves are looting," he called to us. "And look—the Blues burn the houses of the Greens, and the Greens burn the houses of the Blues!"

A tremendous exodus was under way, as terrified citizens streamed toward the docks and begged the boatmen to ferry them to the Asian side. Unharmed, invulnerable, we moved through the holocaust, witnessing the walls of the old Haghia Sophia collapse, watching flames sweep the Great Palace, observing the behavior of the looters and the arsonists and the rapists who paused in fire-spattered alleys to pump some screaming silk-clad noblewoman full of proletarian jissom.

Metaxas skillfully edited the riots for us; he had timed everything dozens of visits ago, and he knew exactly which highlights to hit.

"Now we shunt forward six hours and forty minutes," he said.

"Now we jump three hours and eight minutes."

"Now we jump an hour and a half."

"Now we jump two days."

We saw everything that mattered. With the city still aflame, Justinian sent bishops and priests forth bearing sacred relics, a piece of the True Cross, the rod of Moses, the horn of Abraham's ram, the bones of martyrs; the frightened clerics paraded bravely about, asking for a miracle, but no miracles came, only cascades of brickbats and stones. A general led forty guardsmen out to protect the holy men. "That is the famous Belisarius," said Metaxas. Messages came from the emperor, announcing the deposing of unpopular officials; but churches were sacked, the imperial library given the torch, the baths of Zeuxippus were destroyed.

On January 18, Justinian was bold enough to appear publicly in the Hippodrome to call for peace. He was hissed down by the Greens and fled as stone-throwing began. We saw a worthless prince named Hypatius proclaimed as emperor by the rebels in the Square of Constantine; we saw General Belisarius march through the smoldering city in defense of Justinian; we saw the butchery of the insurgents.

We saw everything. I understood why Metaxas was the most coveted of Couriers. Capistrano had done his best to give his people an exciting show, but he had wasted too much time in the early phases. Metaxas, leaping brilliantly over hours and days, unveiled the entire catastrophe for us, and brought us at last to the morning when order was restored and a shaken Justinian rode through the charred ruins of Constantinople. By a red dawn we saw the clouds of ash still dancing in the air. Justinian studied the blackened hull of Haghia Sophia, and we studied Justinian.

Metaxas said, "He is planning the new cathedral. He will make it the greatest shrine since Solomon's Temple in Jerusalem. Come: we have seen enough destruction. Now let us see the birth of beauty. Down the line, all of you! Five years and ten months down the line, and behold Haghia Sophia!"

27

"On your next layoff," said Metaxas, "visit me at my villa. I live there now in 1105. It is a good time to be in Byzantium; Alexius Comnenus rules and rules wisely. I'll have a lusty wench ready for you, and plenty of wine. You'll come?"

I was lost in admiration for the sharp-faced little man. We were nearing the end of our tour, with only the Turkish Conquest yet to do, and he had revealed to me in a stunning way the difference between an inspired Courier and a merely competent one.

Only a lifetime of dedication to the task could achieve such results, could provide such a show.

Metaxas hadn't just taken us to the standard highlights. He had shown us any number of minor events, splicing us in for an hour here, two hours there, creating for us a glorious mosaic of Byzantine history that dimmed the luster of the mosaics of Haghia Sophia. Other Couriers made a dozen stops, perhaps; Metaxas made more than fifty.

He had a special fondness for the foolish emperors. We had listened to a speech of Michael II, the Stammerer, and we had watched the antics of Michael III, the Drunkard, and we had attended the baptism of the fifth Constantine, who had the misfortune to soil the font and was known for the rest of his life as Constantine Copronymus, Constantine the Pisser. Metaxas was completely at home in Byzantium in any one of a thousand years. Coolly, easily, confidently, he ranged through the eras.

The villa he maintained was a mark of his confidence and his audacity. No other Courier had ever dared to create a second identity for himself up the line, spending his holidays as a citizen of the past. Metaxas ran his villa on a now-time basis; when he had to leave it for two weeks to run a tour, he took care to return to it two weeks after his departure. He never overlapped, never let himself go to it at a time when he was already in residence; there was only one Metaxas permitted to it, and that was the now-time Metaxas. He had bought the villa ten years ago in his double now-time: 2049 down the line, 1095 in Byzantium. And he had maintained his basis with precision; it was ten years later for him in both places. I promised to visit him in 1105. It would be an honor, I said.

He grinned and said, "I'll introduce you to my great-great-multi-great-grandmother when you come, too. She's a terrific lay. You remember what I told you about screwing your own ancestors? There's nothing finer!"

I was stunned. "Does she know who you are?"

"Don't talk nonsense," said Metaxas. "Would I break the first rule of the Time Service? Would I even hint to anyone up the line that I came from the future? *Would I?* Even Themistoklis Metaxas abides by *that* rule!"

Like the moody Capistrano, Metaxas had devoted much effort to hunting out his ancestors. His motives were altogether different, though. Capistrano was plotting an elaborate suicide, but Metaxas was obsessed with trans-temporal incest.

"Isn't it risky?" I asked.

"Just take your pills and you're safe, and so is she."

"I mean the Time Patrol—"

"You make sure they don't find out," said Metaxas. "That way it isn't risky."

"If you happen to get her pregnant, you might become your own ancestor."

Up the Line

"Groovy," said Metaxas.

"But—"

"People don't get people pregnant by accident anymore, boy. Of course," he added, "someday I might want to knock her up on purpose."

I felt the time-winds blowing up a gale. I said, "You're talking anarchy!"

"Nihilism, to be more accurate. Look here, Jud, look at this book. I've got all my female ancestors listed, hundreds of them, from the nineteenth century back to the tenth. Nobody else in the world has a book like this except maybe some snotty ex-kings and queens, and even they don't have it this complete."

"There's Capistrano," I said.

"He goes back only to the fourteenth century! Anyway, he's sick in the head. You know why he does his genealogies?"

"Yes."

"He's pretty sick, isn't he?"

"Yes," I said. "But tell me, why are you so eager to sleep with your own ancestors?"

"Do you really want to know?"

"Really."

Metaxas said, "My father was a cold, hateful man. He beat his children every morning before breakfast for exercise. *His* father was a cold, hateful man. He forced his children to live like slaves. *His* father—I come from a long line of tyrannical authoritarian dictatorial males. I despise them all. It is my form of rebellion against the father-image. I go on and on through the past, seducing the wives and sisters and daughters of these men whom I loathe. Thus I puncture their icy smugness."

"In that case, then, to be perfectly consistent, you must have—your own mother—begun with—"

"I draw the line at abominations," said Metaxas.

"I see."

"But my grandmother, yes! And several great-grandmothers! And on and on and on!" His eyes glowed. It was a divine mission with him. "I have ploughed through twenty, thirty generations already, and I will keep on for thirty more!" Metaxas laughed his shrill, satanic laugh. "Besides," he said, "I enjoy a good lay as much as the next man. Others seduce at random; Metaxas seduces *systematically*! It gives meaning and structure to my life. This interests you, eh?"

"Well—"

"It is life's most intense joy, what I do."

I pictured a row of naked women lying side by side, reaching off to infinity. Every one of them had the wedge-shaped head and sharp features of Themistoklis Metaxas. And Metaxas was moving patiently up the line, pausing to stick it into this one, and the one next to her, and the next, and the next, and in his tireless fashion he balled right up the line until the spread-legged women grew hairy and chinless, the womenfolk of Pithecanthropus erectus, and there was Metaxas erectus still jazzing his way back to the beginning of time. Bravo, Metaxas! Bravo!

"Why don't you try it sometime?" he asked.

"Well—"

"They tell me you are of Greek descent."

"On my mother's side, yes."

"Then probably your ancestors lived right here in Constantinople. No Greek worth anything would have lived in Greece itself at this time. At this very moment a luscious ancestress of yours is in this very city!"

"Well—"

"Find her!" cried Metaxas. "Fuck her! It is joy! It is ecstasy! Defy space and time! Stick your finger in God's eye!"

"I'm not sure I really want to," I said. But I did.

28

As I say, Metaxas transformed my life. He changed my destinies in many ways, not all of them good. But one good thing he did for me was to give me confidence. His charisma and his chutzpah both rubbed off on me. I learned arrogance from Metaxas.

Up the Line

Up until this point I had been a modest and self-effacing young man, at least while I was around my elders.

Especially in my Time Service aspect I had been unpushy and callow. I did a lot of forelock-tugging and no doubt came across even more naïve than I really was. I acted this way because I was young and had a lot to learn, not only about myself, which everybody does, but also about the workings of the Time Service. So far I had met a lot of men who were older, smarter, slicker, and more corrupt than myself, and I had treated them with deference: Sam, Dajani, Jeff Monroe, Sid Buonocore, Capistrano. But now I was with Metaxas, who was the oldest, smartest, slickest and most corrupt of them all, and he imparted momentum to me, so that I stopped orbiting other men and took up a trajectory of my own.

Later I found out that this is one of Metaxas' functions in the Time Service. He takes moist-eyed young Couriers-in-training and fills them full of the swagger they need to be successful operators in their own right.

When I got back from my tour with Metaxas I no longer feared my first solo as a Courier. I was ready to go. Metaxas had showed me how a Courier can be a kind of artist, assembling a portrait of the past for his clients, and that was what I wanted to be. The risks and responsibilities didn't trouble me now.

Protopopolos said, "When you come back from your layoff, you'll take six people out on the one-week tour."

"I'll skip the layoff. I'm ready to leave right now!"

"Well, your tourists aren't. Anyway, the law says you've got to rest between trips. So rest. I'll see you back here in two weeks, Jud."

So I had a holiday against my will. I was tempted to accept Metaxas' invitation to his villa in 1105, but it occurred to me that maybe Metaxas had had enough of my company for a while. Then I toyed with the idea of signing up with a time-tour to Hastings or Waterloo or even back to the Crucifixion to count the Dajanis. But I passed that up, too. Now that I was on the threshold of leading a tour myself, I didn't want to have to be led by somebody else, not just at the moment. I needed to be more secure in my new-found confidence before I dropped down under some other Courier's leadership again.

I dithered around in now-time Istanbul for three days, doing nothing special. Mainly I hung around the Time Service headquarters, playing stochastic chess with Kolettis and Melamed, who also happened to be off duty at this time. On the fourth day I hopped a shortshot for Athens. I didn't know why I was going there until I got there.

I was up on the Acropolis when I realized what my mission was. I was wandering around the ruins, fending off the peddlers of hologram slides and the guided-tour hucksters, when an advert globe came drifting toward me. It hovered about four feet away from me at eye level, radiating a flickering green glow designed to compel my attention, and said, "Good afternoon. We hope you're enjoying your visit to twenty-first-century Athens. Now that you've seen the picturesque ruins, how would you like to see the Parthenon as it *really* looked? See the Greece of Socrates and Aristophanes? Your local Time Service office is on Aeolou Street, just opposite the Central Post Office, and—"

Half an hour later I checked in at the Aeolou Street headquarters, identified myself as a Courier on vacation, and outfitted myself for a shunt up the line.

Not to the Greece of Socrates and Aristophanes, though.

I was heading for the Greece of the prosaic year 1997, when Konstantin Passalidis was elected mayor of Sparta.

Konstantin Passalidis was my mother's father. I was about to start tracing my ancestral seed back to its sprouting place.

Dressed in the stark, itchy clothes of the late twentieth century, and carrying crisp and colorful obsolete banknotes, I shunted back sixty years and caught the first pod from Athens to Sparta. Pod service was brand new in Greece in 1997, and I was in mortal terror of a phaseout all the way down, but the alignment held true and I got to Sparta in one piece.

Sparta was remarkably hideous.

The present Sparta is not, of course, a linear descendant of the old militaristic place that caused so much trouble for Athens. That Sparta faded away gradually, and vanished altogether in medieval times. The new Sparta was founded in the early nineteenth century on the old site. In Grandfather Passilidis' heyday it was a city of

Up the Line

about 80,000 people, having grown rapidly after the installation of Greece's first fusion-power plant there in the 1980's.

It consisted of hundreds of identical apartment houses of gray brick, arranged in perfectly straight rows. Every one of them was ten stories high, decked with lemon-colored balconies on every floor, and about as appealing as a jail. At one end of this barracks-like city was the shining dome of the power plant; at the other was a downtown section of taverns, banks, and municipal offices. It was quite charming, if you find brutality charming.

I got off the pod and walked downtown. There weren't any master information outputs to be seen on the streets—I guess the network hadn't yet gone into operation here—but I had no trouble finding Mayor Passilidis. I stopped at a tavern for a quick ouzo and said, "Where can I find Mayor Passilidis?" and a dozen friendly Spartans escorted me to City Hall.

His receptionist was a dark-haired girl of about twenty with big breasts and a faint mustache. Her Minoan Revival bodice was neatly calculated to distract a man's attention from the shortcomings of her face. Wiggling those pink-tipped meaty globes at me, she said huskily, "Can I help you?"

"I'd like to see Mayor Passilidis. I'm from an American newspaper. We're doing an article on Greece's ten most dynamic young men, and we feel that Mr. Passilidis—"

It didn't sound convincing even to me. I stood there studying the beads of sweat on the white mounds of her bosom, waiting for her to turn me away. But she bought the story unhesitatingly, and with a minimum of delay was escorted into His Honor's office.

"A pleasure to have you here," my grandfather said in perfect English. "Won't you sit down? Can I get you a martini, maybe? Or if you'd prefer a weed—"

I froze. I panicked. I didn't even take his hand when he offered it to me.

The sight of Konstantin Passilidis terrified me.

I had never seen my grandfather before, of course. He was gunned down by an Abolitionist hoodlum in 2010, long before I was born—one of the many victims of the Year of Assassins.

257

Time-travel had never seemed so frighteningly real to me as it did right now. Justinian in the imperial box at the Hippodrome was nothing at all compared to Konstantin Passilidis greeting me in his office in Sparta.

He was in his early thirties, a boy wonder of his time. His hair was dark and curly, just beginning to gray at the fringes, and he wore a little clipped mustache and a ring in his left ear. What terrified me so much was our physical resemblance. He could have been my older brother.

After an endless moment I snapped out of my freeze. He was a little puzzled, I guess, but he courteously offered me refreshment again, and I declined, telling him I didn't indulge, and somehow I found enough poise to launch my "interview" of him.

We talked about his political career and all the wonderful things he planned to do for Sparta and for Greece. Just as I was starting to work the conversation around to the personal side, to his family background, he looked at his watch and said, "It's time for lunch. Will you be my guest?"

What he had in mind was a typical Mediterranean siesta, closing the office down for three hours and going home. We drove there in his little electric runabout, with the mayor himself at the steering rod. He lived in one of the gray apartment houses, like any ordinary citizen: four humble rooms on the fifth floor.

"I'd like you to meet my wife," Mayor Passilidis said. "Katina, this is an American newspaperman, Jud Elliott. He wants to write about my career."

I stared at my grandmother.

My grandmother stared at me.

We both gasped. We were both amazed.

She was beautiful, the way the girls on the Minoan murals are beautiful. Dark, very dark, with black hair, olive skin, dark eyes. Peasant strength to her. She didn't expose her breasts the way the fashionable mustachioed receptionist had done, but her thin blouse wasn't very concealing. They were high and round. Her hips were broad. She was lush, fertile, abundant. I suppose she was about twenty-three years old, perhaps twenty-four.

It was lust at first sight. Her beauty, her simplicity, her warmth, captivated me instantly. I felt a familiar tickling in the scrotum and a familiar tightening of the glutei. I longed to rip away her clothing and sink myself deep into her hot tangled black shrubbery.

This was not a Metaxian incestuous wish. It was an innocent and purely animal reaction.

In that onrushing tide of yearning I didn't even think of her as my grandmother. I thought of her only as a young and fantastically desirable woman. A couple of ticks later I realized on an emotional level who she was, and I went limp at once.

She was Grandma Passilidis. And I remembered Grandma Passilidis.

I used to visit her at the senior citizens' camp near Tampa. She died when I was fourteen, in '49, and though she was only in her seventies then, she had always seemed terribly old and decrepit to me, a withered, shrunken, palsied little woman who wore black clothing all the time. Only her eyes—my God, her dark, liquid, warm, shining eyes!—had ever given any hint that she might once have been a healthy and vital human being.

Grandma Passilidis had had all kinds of diseases, feminine things first—prolapses of the uterus or whatever it is they get—and then kidney breakdowns and the rest. She had been through a dozen or more organ transplants, but nothing had helped, and all through my childhood she had inexorably declined. I was always hearing of some new crisis on her road to the grave, the poor old lady!

Here was the same poor old lady, miraculously relieved of her burden of years. And here was I, mentally snuggling between the thighs of my mother's mother. O vile impiety, that man should travel backward through time and think such thoughts!

Young Mrs. Passilidis' reaction to me was equally potent, although not at all lustful. For her, sex began and ended with the mayoral pecker. She stared at me not in desire but in astonishment and blurted finally, "Konstantin, he looks just like you!"

"Indeed?" said Mayor Passilidis. He hadn't noticed it before.

His wife propelled us both toward the living-room mirror, giggling and excited. The soft masses of her bosom jostled up against me and I began to sweat. "Look!" she cried. "Look there? Like brothers you are!"

"Amazing," said Mayor Passilidis.

"An incredible coincidence," I said. "Your hair is thicker, and I'm a little taller, but—"

"Yes! Yes!" The mayor clapped his hands. "Can it be that we are related?"

"Impossible," I said solemnly. "My family's from Boston. Old New England stock. Nevertheless it *is* amazing. You're sure you didn't have ancestors on the Mayflower, Mr. Passilidis?"

"Not unless there was a Greek steward on board."

"I doubt that."

"So do I. I am pure Greek on both sides for many generations," he said.

"I'd like to talk about that with you a little if I could," I said casually. "For example, I'd like to know—"

Just then a sleepy and completely naked five-year-old girl came out of one of the bedrooms. She planted herself shamelessly before me and asked me who I was. How sweet, I thought. That saucy little rump, that pink little slit—how *clean* little girls always look when they're naked. Before puberty messes them up.

Passilidis said proudly, "This is my daughter Diana."

A voice of thunder said in my brain, "THE NAKEDNESS OF THY MOTHER SHALT THOU NOT UNCOVER."

I looked away, shattered, and covered my confusion with a coughing fit. Little Diana's fleeceless labia blazed in my soul. As though sensing that I saw something improper about the child's bareness, Katina Passilidis hustled a pair of panties onto her.

I was still shaking. Passilidis, puzzled, uncorked some retsina. We sat on the balcony in the bright midday light. Below, some schoolchildren waved and shouted greetings to the mayor. Little

Up the Line

Diana toddled out to be played with, and I tousled her fluffy hair and pressed the tip of her nose and felt very, very strange about all of this.

My grandmother provided a handsome lunch of boiled lamb and pastitsio. We went through a bottle and a half of retsina. I finished pumping the mayor about politics and shifted to the topic of his ancestors. "Have your people always lived in Sparta?" I asked.

"Oh, no," he said. "My grandfather's people came here a century ago from Cyprus. That is, on my father's side. On my mother's side I am Athenian, for many generations back."

"That's the Markezinis family?" I said.

He gave me a queer look. "Why, yes! How did you—"

"Something I came across while I was reading up on you," I said hurriedly.

Passilidis let the point pass. Now that he was on the subject of his family he grew expansive—maybe it was the wine—and favored me with the genealogical details. "My father's people were on Cyprus for at least a thousand years," he said. "There was a Passilidis there when the Crusaders came. On the other hand, my mother's ancestors came to Athens only in the nineteenth century, after the defeat of the Turks. Before that they lived in Shqiperi."

"Shqiperi?"

"Albania. They settled there in the thirteenth century when the Latins seized Constantinople. And then they remained, through the Serbians, through the Turks, through the time of Skanderbeg the rebel, always retaining their Greek heritage against all difficulties."

My ears prickled. "You mentioned Constantinople? You can trace your ancestry there?"

Passilidis smiled. "Do you know Byzantine history?"

"Slightly," I said.

"Perhaps you know that in the year 1204 the Crusaders seized Constantinople and ruled it for a while as a Latin kingdom. The Byzantine nobility fled, and several new Byzantine splinter states formed—one in Asia Minor, one on the Black Sea, and one in the west, in Albania. My ancestors followed Michael Angelus Comnenus into Albania, rather than submit to the rule of the Crusaders."

"I see." I was trembling again. "And the family name? It was Markezinis even back then?"

"Oh, no, Markezinis is a late Greek name! In Byzantium we were of the Ducas family."

"You *were?*" I gasped. It was as if he had been a German claiming Hohenzollern blood, or an Englishman laying claim to Plantagenet genes. "Ducas! Really?"

I had seen the gleaming palaces of the Ducas family. I had watched forty proud Ducases march clad in cloth of gold through the streets of Constantinople, to celebrate the rise of their cousin Constantine to the imperial throne. If Passilidis was a Ducas, *I* was a Ducas.

"Of course," he said, "the family was very large, and I believe we were of a minor branch. Still, it is something to take pride in, descent from such a family."

"It certainly is. Could you give me the names of any of your Byzantine ancestors, maybe? The first names?"

I must have sounded as though I planned to look them up the next time I was in Byzantium. Which I did, but Passilidis wasn't supposed to suspect that, because time-travel hadn't been invented yet.

He frowned and said, "Do you need this for the article you are writing?"

"No, not really. I'm just curious."

"You seem to know more than a little about Byzantium." It worried him that an American barbarian would recognize the name of a famous Byzantine family.

I said, "Just casual knowledge. I studied it in school."

"Sadly, I can give you no names. This information has not come down to us. But perhaps someday, when I have retired from politics, I will search the old records—"

My grandmother poured us more wine, and I stole a quick, guilty peek at her full, swaying breasts. My mother climbed on my knee and made little trilling noises. My grandfather shook his head and said, "It is very surprising, the way you resemble me. Can I take your photograph?"

I wondered if it went against Time Patrol regulations. I decided that it probably did. But also I saw no polite way to refuse such a trifling request.

My grandmother produced a camera. Passilidis and I stood side by side and she took a picture of us for him, and then one for me. She pulled them from the camera when they were developed and we studied them intently.

"Like brothers," she said over and over. "Like brothers!"

I destroyed my print as soon as I was out of the apartment. But I suppose that somewhere in my mother's papers there is an old and faded flattie photograph showing her father as a young man, standing beside a somewhat younger man who looks very much like him, and whom my mother probably assumed was some forgotten uncle of hers. Perhaps the photograph still exists. I'd be afraid to look.

Grandfather Passilidis had saved me a great deal of trouble. He had lopped almost eight centuries off what I was already starting to think of as my quest.

I jumped down the line to now-time, did some research in the Time Service headquarters at Athens, and had myself outfitted as a Byzantine noble of the late twelfth century, with a sumptuous silk tunic, black cloak, and white bonnet. Then I podded up north to Albania, getting off the town of Gjinokaster. In the old days this town was known as Argyrokastro, in the district of Epirus.

From Gjinokaster I went up the line to the year 1205.

The peasant folk of Argyrokastro were awed by my princely garb. I told them I was seeking the court of Michael Angelus Comnenus, and they told me the way and sold me a donkey to help me get there. I found Michael and the rest of the exiled Byzantines holding a chariot race in an improvised Hippodrome at the foot of a range of jagged hills. Quietly I affiliated myself with the crowd.

"I'm looking for Ducas," I told a harmless-looking old man who was passing around some wine.

"Ducas? Which one?"

"Are there many here? I bear a message from Constantinople for a Ducas, but they did not tell me there was more than one."

The old man laughed. "Just before me," he said, "Is Nicephorus Ducas, John Ducas, Leo Ducas, George Ducas, Nicephorus Ducas the Younger, Michael Ducas, Simeon Ducas, and Dimitrios Ducas. I am unable to find at the moment Eftimios Ducas, Leontios Ducas, Simeon Ducas the Tall, Constantine Ducas, and— let me think— Andronicus Ducas. Which member of the family, pray, do you seek?"

I thanked him and moved down the line.

In sixteenth century Gjinokaster I asked about the Markezinis family. My Byzantine garb earned me some strange glances, but the Byzantine gold pieces I carried got me all the information I needed. One bezant and I was given the location of the Markezinis estate. Two bezants more and I had an introduction to the foreman of the Markezinis vineyard. Five bezants—a steep price—and I found myself nibbling grapes in the guest-hall of Gregory Markezinis, the head of the clan. He was a distinguished man of middle years with a flowing gray beard and burning eyes; he was stern but hospitable. As we talked, his daughters moved serenely about us, refilling cups, bringing more grapes, cold legs of lamb, mounds of rice. There were three girls, possibly thirteen, fifteen, and seventeen years old. I took good care not to look too closely at them, knowing the jealous temperament of mountain chieftains.

They were beauties: olive skin, dark eyes, high breasts, full lips. They might have been sisters of my radiant grandmother Katina Passilidis. My mother Diana, I believe, looked this way in girlhood. The family genes are powerful ones.

Unless I happened to be climbing on the wrong branch of the tree, one of these girls was my great-great-multi-great-grandmother. And Gregory Markezinis was my great-great-great-multi-great-grandfather.

I introduced myself as a wealthy young Cypriote of Byzantine descent who was traveling the world in search of pleasure and adventure. Gregory, whose Greek was slightly contaminated by Albanian words (did his serfs speak Gheg or Tosk? I forget) had evidently never met a Cypriote before, since he accepted my accent as authentic. "Where have you been?" he asked.

Up the Line

Oh, I said, Syria and Libya and Egypt, and Rome and Paris and Lisbon, and to London to attend the coronation of Henry VIII, and Prague, and Vienna. And now I was working my way eastward again, into the Turkish domain, determined despite all risks to visit the graves of my ancestors in Constantinople.

He raised an eyebrow at the mention of ancestors. Energetically hacking off a slice of lamb with his dagger, he said, "Was your family a high one in the old days?"

"I am of the Ducas line."

"*Ducas?*"

"Ducas," I said blandly.

"I am of the Ducas line as well."

"Indeed!"

"Beyond doubt!"

"A Ducas in Epirus!" I cried. "How did it happen?"

"We came here with the Comneni, after the Latin pigs took Constantinople."

"Indeed!"

"Beyond doubt!"

He called for more wine, the best in the house. When his daughters appeared, he did a little dance, crying, "A kinsman! A kinsman! The stranger is a kinsman! Give him proper greeting!"

I found myself engulfed in Markezinis daughters, overwhelmed by taut youthful breasts and sweet musky bodies. Chastely I embraced them, as a long-lost cousin would.

Over thick, elderly wine we talked genealogy. I went first, picking a Ducas at random—Theodoros—and claiming that he had escaped to Cyprus after the debacle in Constantinople in 1204, to found my line. Markezinis had no way of disproving that, and in fact he accepted it at face value. I unreeled a long list of Ducas forebears up the line between myself and distant Theodoros, using customary Byzantine names. When I concluded I said, "And you, Gregory?"

Using his knife to scratch family trees into the tabletop at some of the difficult points, Markezinis traced his line back to a Nicholas Markezinis of the late fourteenth century who had married the eldest daughter of Manuel Ducas of Argyrokastro, that Ducas having had only daughters and therefore bringing his immediate line to an end. From Manuel, then, Markezinis took things back in a leisurely way to the expulsion of the Byzantines from Constantinople by the Fourth Crusade. The particular Ducas of his direct line who had fled to Albania was, he said, Simeon.

My gonads plunged in despair.

"Simeon?" I said. "Do you mean Simeon Ducas the Tall, or the other one?"

"Were there two? How could you know?"

Cheeks flaming, I improvised, "I have to confess that I something of a student of the family. Two Simeon Ducases followed the Comneni to this land, Simeon the Tall and a man of shorter stature."

"Of this I know nothing," said Markezinis. "I have been taught that my ancestor's name was Simeon. And his father was Nicephorus, whose palace was close to the church of St. Theodosia, by the Golden Horn. The Venetians burned the palace of Nicephorus when they took the city in 1204. And the father of Nicephorus—" He hesitated, shaking his head slowly and sadly from side to side like an aging buffalo. "I do not remember the name of the father of Nicephorus. I have forgotten the name of the father of Nicephorus. Was it Leo? Michael? Basil? I forget. My head is full of wine."

"It does not matter that much," I said. With the ancestry traced into Constantinople, there would be no further difficulties.

"Romanos? John? Isaac? It is right here, inside my head, but there are so many names—so many names—" Still muttering names, he fell asleep at the table. A dark-eyed daughter showed me to a drafty bedroom. I could have shunted instead, having learned all here that had come to know; but it seemed civil to spend the night under my multi-great-grandfather's roof, rather than shunting like a thief. I stripped, snuffed the candle, got into bed.

In the darkness a soft-bodied wench joined me under he blankets.

Her breasts nicely filled my hands and her fragrance was sweetly musky. I couldn't see her, but I assumed she must be one of the Markezinis' three daughters, coming to show how hospitable the family could be. My palm slid down her smoothly rounded belly to its base, and when I reached the junction of her thighs, her legs opened to me, and I found her ready for love.

I felt obscurely disappointed at the thought that Markezinis' daughters would give themselves so freely to strangers—even a noble stranger claiming to be a cousin. After all, these were my *ancestors*. Was my line of descent muddied by the sperm of casual wayfarers?

That thought led logically to the really troublesome one, which was, if this girl is really my great-great-multi-great-grandmother, what am *I* doing in bed with her? To hell with sleeping with strangers—should she sleep with descendants? When I began this quest at Metaxas' prodding, it wasn't really with the intent of committing trans-temporal incest—but yet here I was doing it, it seemed.

Guilt blossomed in me and I became so nervous that it made me momentarily impotent.

But my bedmate slithered down to my waist and restored my virility with busy lips. A fine old Byzantine trick, I thought, and, rigid again, I slipped into her and pronged her with gusto. I soothed my conscience by telling myself that the chances were two out of three that this girl was merely my great-great-multi-great-*aunt*, in which case the incest must surely be far less serious. So far as bloodlines went, the connection between myself and any sixteenth-century aunt must be exceedingly cloudy.

My conscience let me alone after that, and the girl and I gasped our way to completion. And then she rose, and went from the room, and as she passed the window a sliver of moonlight illuminated her white buttocks and her pale thighs and her long blonde hair, and I realized what I should have known all along, which is that the Markezinis girls would not come like Eskimo wenches to sleep with guests, but that someone had thoughtfully sent in a slave-girl for my amusement. So much for the prickings of conscience. Absolved even of the most tenuous incest, I slept soundly.

In the morning, over a breakfast of cold lamb and rice, Gregory Markezinis said, "Word reaches me that the Spaniards have found a new world beyond the Ocean Sea. Do you think there's truth in it?" This was the year A.D. 1556.

I said, "Beyond all doubt it's true. I saw the proof in Spain, at the court of King Charles. It's a world of gold and jade and spices—of red-skinned men—"

"Red-skinned men? Oh, no, cousin Ducas, no, no, I can never believe that!" Markezinis roared in delight, and summoned his daughters. "The new world of the Spaniards—its men have red skins! Cousin Ducas tells us so!"

"Well, copper-colored, really," I murmured, but Markezinis scarcely heard.

"Red skins! Red skins! And no heads, but eyes and mouths in their chests! And men with a single leg, which they raise above their heads at midday to shield themselves from the sun! Yes! Yes! Oh, wonderful new world! Cousin, you amuse me!"

I told him I was glad to bring him such pleasure. I thanked him for his gracious hospitality, and chastely embraced each of his daughters, and prepared to take my leave. And suddenly it struck me that if my ancestors' name had been Markezinis from the fourteenth century through the twentieth, then none of these girls could possibly be ancestral to me. My priggish pangs of conscience had been pointless, except insofar as they taught me where my inhibitions lay. "Do you have sons?" I asked my host.

"Oh, yes," he said, "six sons!"

"May your line increase and prosper," I said, and departed, and rode my donkey a dozen kilometers out into the countryside, and tethered it to an olive tree, and shunted down the line.

31

At the end of my layoff I reported for duty, and set out for the first time solo as a Time Courier.

I had six people to take on the one-week tour. They didn't know it was my first solo. Protopopolos didn't see any point in telling them, and I agreed. But I didn't feel as though it were my first solo. I was full of Metaxian chutzpah. I emanated charisma. I feared nothing except fear itself.

Up the Line

At the preliminary meeting I told my six the rules of time-touring in crisp, staccato phrases. I invoked the dread menace of the Time Patrol as I warned against changing the past either carelessly or by design. I explained how they could best keep out of trouble. Then I handed out timers and set them.

"Here we go," I said. "Up the line."

Charisma. Chutzpah.

Jud Elliott, Time Courier, on his own!

Up the line!

"We have arrived," I said, "in 1659 B.P., better known to you as the year 400. I've picked it as a typical early Byzantine time. The ruling emperor is Arcadius. You remember from now-time Istanbul that Haghia Sophia should be back there, and the mosque of Sultan Ahmed should be there. Well, of course, Sultan Ahmed and his mosque are currently a dozen centuries in the future, and the church behind us is the original Haghia Sophia, constructed forty years ago when the city was still very young. Four years from now it'll burn down during a rebellion caused by the exiling of Bishop John Chrysostorios by Emperor Arcadius after he had criticized Arcadius' wife Eudoxia. Let's go inside. You see that the walls are of stone but the roof is wooden—"

My six tourists included a real-estate developer from Ohio, his wife, their gawky daughter and her husband, plus a Sicilian shrink and his bowlegged temporary wife: typical assortment of prosperous citizens. They didn't know a nave from a narthex, but I gave them a good look at the church, and then marched them through Arcadius' Constantinople to set the background for what they'd see later. After two hours of this I jumped down the line to 408 to watch the baptism of little Theodosius again, and caught sight of myself on the far side of the street, standing close to Capistrano. I didn't wave. My other self did not appear to see me. I wondered if this present self of mine had been standing here that other time, when I was with Capistrano. The intricacies of the Cumulative Paradox oppressed me. I banished them from mind. "You see the ruins of the old Haghia Sophia," I said. It will be rebuilt under the auspices of this infant, the future Theodosius II, and opened to prayer in October, 445—"

We shunted down the line to 445 and watched the ceremony of dedication. There are two schools of thought about the proper way to conduct a time-tour. The Capistrano method is to take tourists to four or five high spots a week, letting them spend plenty of time in taverns, inns, back alleys, and marketplaces, and moving in such a leisurely way that the flavor of each period soaks in deeply. The Metaxas method is to construct an elaborate mosaic of events, hitting the same high spots but also twenty or thirty or forty other events, spending half an hour here and two hours there. I had experienced both methods and I preferred Metaxas' approach. The serious student of Byzantium wants depth, not breadth; but these folk were not serious students. Better to make a pageant of Byzantium for them, hurry them breathless through the eras, show them riots and coronations, chariot races, the rise and fall of monuments and kings.

And so I took my people from time to time in imitation of my idol Metaxas. I gave them a full day in early Byzantium, as Capistrano would have done, but I split it into six shunts. We ended our day's work in 537, in the city Justinian had built on the charred ruin of the one destroyed by the rioting Blues and Greens.

"We've come to December 27," I said. "Justinian will inaugurate the new Haghia Sophia today. You see how much larger the cathedral is than the ones that preceded it—a gigantic building, one of the wonders of the world. Justinian has poured the equivalent of hundreds of millions of dollars into it."

"Is this the one they have in Istanbul now?" asked Mr. Real Estate's son-in-law doubtfully.

"Basically, yes. Except that you don't see any minarets here—the Moslems tacked those on, of course, after they turned the place into a mosque—and the gothic buttresses haven't been built yet, either. Also the great dome here is not the one you're familiar with. This one is slightly flatter and wider than the present one. It turned out that the architect's calculations of thrust were wrong, and half the dome will collapse in 558 after weakening of the arches by earthquakes. You'll see that tomorrow. Look, here comes Justinian."

A little earlier that day I had shown them the harried Justinian of 532 attempting to cope with the Nika riots. The emperor who now appeared, riding in a chariot drawn by four immense black horses, looked a good deal more than five years older, far more plump and florid of face, but he also seemed vastly more sure of himself, a figure of total command. As well he should be, having surmounted the tremendous challenge to his power that the riots presented, and having rebuilt the city into something uniquely glorious.

Senators and dukes lined the approach; we remained respectfully to one side, amid the commoners. Priests, deacons, deaconesses, subdeacons, and cantors awaited the imperial procession, all in costly robes. Hymns in the ancient mode rose to heaven. The Patriarch Menos appeared at the colossal imperial door of the cathedral; Justinian dismounted; the patriarch and the emperor, hand in hand, entered the building, followed by the high officials of state.

"According to a tenth-century chronicle," I said, "Justinian was overcome by emotion when he entered his new Haghia Sophia. Rushing to the apse, he gave thanks to God who had allowed him to achieve such a building, and cried out, 'O Solomon, I have surpassed thee.' The Time Service thought it might be interesting for visitors to this era to hear this famous line, and so some years back we planted an Ear just beside the altar." I reached into my robes. "I've brought along a pickup speaker which will transmit Justinian's words to us as he nears the apse. Listen."

I switched on the speaker. At this moment, any number of other Couriers in the crowd were doing the same thing. A time will come when so many of us are clustered in this moment that Justinian's voice, amplified by a thousand tiny speakers, will boom majestically across the whole city.

From the speaker in my palm came the sound of footsteps.

"The emperor is walking down the aisle," I said.

The footsteps halted abruptly. Justinian's words came to us—his first exclamation upon entering the architectural masterpiece of the ages.

Thick-voiced with rage, the emperor bellowed, "Look up there, you sodomitic simpleton! Find me the mother-humper who left that scaffold hanging in the dome! I want his balls in an alabaster vase before mass begins!" Then he sneezed in imperial wrath.

I said to my six tourists, "The development of time travel has made it necessary for us to revise many of our most inspiring anecdotes in the light of new evidence."

That night as my tired tourists slept, I slipped away from them to carry out some private research.

This was strictly against regulations. A Courier is supposed to remain with the clients at all times, in case an emergency occurs. The clients, after all, don't know how to operate their timers, so only the Courier can help them make a quick escape from trouble.

Despite this I jumped six centuries down the line, while my tourists slept, and I visited the era of my prosperous ancestor Nicephorus Ducas.

Which took chutzpah, of course, considering that this was my first solo trip. But actually I wasn't running any serious risks.

The safe way to carry out such side trips, as Metaxas had explained to me, is to set your timer carefully and make sure that your net absence from your tourists is one minute or less. I was departing from December 27, 537, at 2345 hours. I could go up or down the line from there and spend hours, days, weeks, or months elsewhere. When I had finished with my business, all I had to do was set my timer to bring me back to December 27, 537, at 2346 hours. From the point of view of my sleeping tourists I'd have been gone only sixty seconds.

Of course, it wouldn't be proper to land at 2344 hours on the return trip, which is to say to come back a minute before I had left. There would then be two of me in the same room, which produces the Paradox of Duplication, a subspecies of the Cumulative Paradox, and is certain to bring a reprimand or worse if the Time Patrol hears of it. No: precise coordination is necessary.

Another problem is the difficulty of making an exact point-to-point shunt. The inn where my group was lodged in 537 would almost certainly no longer exist by 1175, the year of my immediate

Up the Line

destination. I couldn't blindly shunt forward from the room, because I might find myself materializing in some awkward place later constructed on the site—a dungeon, say.

The only safe way would be to go out in the street and shunt from there, both coming and going. This, though, requires you to be away from your tourists more than sixty seconds, just figuring the time necessary to go downstairs, find a safe and quiet place for your shunt, etc. And if a Time Patrolman comes along on a routine checkup and recognizes you in the street and asks you why the hell you aren't with the clients, you're in trouble.

Nevertheless I shunted down the line and got away with it.

I hadn't been in 1175 before. It was probably the last really good year Byzantium had.

It seemed to me that an atmosphere of gathering trouble hung over Constantinople. Even the clouds looked ominous. The air had the tang of impending calamity.

Subjective garbage. Being able to move freely along the line distorts your perspective and colors your interpretation. I knew what lay ahead for these people; they didn't. Byzantium in 1175 was cocky and optimistic; I was imagining all the omens.

Manuel I Comnenus was on the throne, a good man, coming to the end of a long, brilliant career. Disaster was closing in on him. The Comnenus emperors had spent the whole twelfth century recapturing Asia Minor from the Turks, who had grabbed it the century before. I knew that one year down the line, in 1176, Manuel was going to lose his entire Asian empire in a single day, at the battle of Myriocephalon. After that it would be downhill all the way for Byzantium. But Manuel didn't know that yet. Nobody here did. Except me.

I headed up toward the Golden Horn. The upper end of town was the most important in this period; the center of things had shifted from the Haghia Sophia/Hippodrome/Augusteum section to the Blachernae quarter, in the northernmost corner of the city at the angle where the city walls met. Here, for some reason, Emperor Alexius I had moved the court at the end of the eleventh century, abandoning the jumbled old Great Palace. Now his grandson

Manuel reigned here in splendor, and the big feudal families had built new palaces nearby, all along the Golden Horn.

One of the finest of these marble edifices belonged to Nicephorus Ducas, my many-times-removed-great-grandfather.

I spent half the morning prowling around the palace grounds, getting drunk on the magnificence of it all. Toward midday the palace gate opened and I saw Nicephorus himself emerge in his chariot for his noontime drive: a stately figure with a long, ornately braided black beard and elaborate gold-trimmed robes. On his breast he wore a pendant cross, gilded and studded with huge jewels; his fingers glistened with rings. A crowd had gathered to watch the noble Nicephorus leave his palace.

Gracefully he scattered coins to the multitude as he rode forth. I caught one: a thin, shabby bezant of Alexius I, nicked and filed at the edges. The Comnenus family had debased the currency badly. Still, it's no small thing to be able to toss even debased gold coins to a mob of miscellaneous onlookers.

I have that worn and oily-looking bezant to this day. I think of it as my inheritance from my Byzantine multi-great-grandfather.

Nicephorus' chariot vanished in the direction of the imperial palace. A filthy old man standing beside me sighed, crossed himself many times, and murmured, "May the Savior bless the blessed Nicephorus! Such a wonderful person!"

The old man's nose had been lopped off at the base. He had also lost his left hand. The kindly Byzantines of this latter-day era had made mutilation the penalty for many minor crimes. A step forward; the Code of Justinian called for death in such cases. Better to lose eye or tongue or nose than life.

"Twenty years I spent in the service of Nicephorus Ducas!" the old man went on. "The finest years of my life, they were."

"Why did you leave?" I asked.

He held forth the stump of his arm. "They caught me stealing books. I was a scribe, and I hungered to keep some of the books I copied. Nicephorus has so many! He would not have missed five or six! But they caught me and I lost my hand and also my employment, ten years ago."

Up the Line

"And your nose?"

"In that very harsh winter six years back I stole a barrel of fish. I am a very poor thief, always getting caught."

"How do you support yourself?"

He smiled. "By public charity. And by begging. Can you spare a silver nomisma for an unhappy old man?"

I inspected the coins I carried. By ill luck all my silver pieces were early ones, of the fifth and sixth centuries, long out of circulation; if the old man tried to pass one, he'd be arrested on charges of robbing some aristocratic collector, and probably would lose his other hand. So I pressed a fine gold bezant of the early eleventh century into his palm. He stared at it in amazement. "I am yours, noble sir!" he cried. "I am wholly yours!"

"Come with me to the nearest tavern, then, and answer a few questions," I said.

"Gladly! Gladly!"

I bought us wine and pumped him on the Ducas genealogy. It was hard for me to look at his mutilated face, and so as we talked I kept my eyes trained on his shoulder; but he seemed accustomed to that. He had all the information I was seeking, for one of his duties while in the service of the Ducases had been to copy out the family records.

Nicephorus, he said, was then forty-five years old, having been born in 1130. The wife of Nicephorus was the former Zoe Catacalon, and they had seven children: Simeon, John, Leo, Basil, Helena, Theodosia, and Zoe. Nicephorus was the eldest son of Nicetas Ducas, born in 1106; the wife of Nicetas was the former Irene Cerularius, whom he had married in 1129. Nicetas and Irene had had five other children: Michael, Isaac, John, Romanos, and Anna. Nicetas' father had been Leo Ducas, born in 1070; Leo had married the former Pulcheria Botaniates in 1100, and their children, other than Nicetas, included Simeon, John, Alexander—

The recitation went on and on, carrying the Ducases back through the generations of Byzantium, into the tenth century, the ninth, the eighth, names growing cloudy now, gaps appearing in the record, the old man frowning, fumbling, apologizing for scanty data. I tried a couple of times to stop him, but he would not be stopped, until finally he sputtered out with a Tiberius Ducas of the seventh century whose existence, he said, was possibly apocryphal.

"This, you understand, is merely the lineage of Nicephorus Ducas," he said. "The imperial family is a distinct branch, which I can trace back for you through the Comneni to Emperor Constantine X and his ancestors, who—"

Those Ducases didn't interest me, even though they were distantly related to me in some way. If I wanted to know the lineage of the imperial Ducases, I could find it in Gibbon. I cared only for my own humbler branch of the family, the collateral offshoot from the imperial line. Thanks to this hideous outcast scribe I was able to secure the path of those Ducases through three Byzantine centuries, down to Nicephorus. And I already knew the rest of the line, from Nicephorus's son Simeon of Albania to Simeon's several-times-grandson Manuel Ducas of Argyrokastro, whose eldest daughter married Nicholas Markezinis, and through the Markezinis line until a Markezinis daughter married a Passilidis son and produced my estimable grandfather Konstantin, whose daughter Diana wed Judson Daniel Elliott II and brought forth into the world my own ultimate self.

"For your trouble," I said, and gave the filthy scribe another gold piece, and fled from the tavern while he still was muttering dazed thanks.

I knew Metaxas would be proud of me. A little jealous, even—for in short order I had put together a lengthier family tree than his own. *His* went back to the tenth century, mine (a little shakily) to the seventh. Of course, he had an annotated list of hundreds of ancestors, and I knew details of only a few dozen, but he had started years ahead of me.

I set my timer carefully and shunted back to December 27, 537. The street was dark and silent. I hurried into the inn. Less than three minutes had elapsed since my departure, even though I had spent eight hours down the line in 1175. My tourists slept soundly. All was well.

I was pleased with myself. By candlelight I sketched the details of the Ducas line on a scrap of old vellum. I wasn't really planning to do anything with the genealogy. I wasn't looking for ancestors to kill, like Capistrano, or ancestors to seduce, like Metaxas. I just wanted to gloat a little over the fact that my ancestors were Ducases. Some people don't have ancestors at all.

33

I don't think I was quite the equal of Metaxas as a Courier, but I gave my people a respectable view of Byzantium. I did a damned good job, especially for a first try.

We shunted through all the highlights and some of the lowlights. I showed them the baptism of Constantine the Pisser; the smashing of the icons under Leo III; the invasion by the Bulgars in 813; the trees of gilded bronze in the Magnaura Hall of Theophilus; the debaucheries of Michael the Drunkard; the arrival of the First Crusade in 1096 and 1097; the much more disastrous arrival of the Fourth Crusade in 1204; the reconquest of Constantinople by the Byzantines in 1261, and the coronation of Michael VIII; in short, all that counted.

My people loved it. Like most time-tourists, they particularly loved the riots, insurrections, rebellions, sieges, massacres, invasions, and fires.

"When do you show us the Turks come bustin' in?" the Ohio real-estate-man kept asking. "I want to see those goddam Turks wreck the place!"

"We're moving toward it," I told him.

First I gave them a look at Byzantium in the sunset years, under the dynasty of the Palaeologi. "Most of the empire is gone," I said, as we dropped down the line into 1275. "The Byzantines think and build on a small scale now. Intimacy is the key word. This is the little Church of St. Mary of the Mongols, built for a bastard daughter of Michael VIII who for a short while was married to a Mongol khan. See the charm? The simplicity?"

We glided on down the line to 1330 to look in on the Church of Our Savior in Chora. The tourists had already seen it down the line in Istanbul under its Turkish name, Kariye Camii; now they saw it in its pre-mosquified condition, with all its stunning mosaics intact and new. "See, there," I said. "There's the Mary who married the Mongol. She's still there down the line. And this—the early life and miracles of Christ—that one's gone from our time, but you can see how superb it was here."

The Sicilian shrink holographed the whole church; he was carrying a palm camera that the Time Service regards as permissible, since nobody up the line is likely to notice it or comprehend its function. His bowlegged tempie waddled around oohing at everything. The Ohio people looked bored, as I knew they would. No matter. I'd give them culture if I had to shove it up them.

"When do we see the Turks?" the Ohioans asked restlessly.

We skipped lithely over the Black Death years of 1347 and 1348. "I can't take you there," I said, when the protests came. "You've got to sign up for a special plague tour if you want to see any of the great epidemics."

Mr. Ohio's son-in-law grumbled, "We've had all our vaccinations."

"But five billion people down the line in now-time are unprotected," I explained. "You might pick up some contamination and bring it back with you, and start a worldwide epidemic. And then we'd have to edit your whole time-trip out of the flow of history to keep the disaster from happening. You wouldn't want that, would you?"

Bafflement.

"Look, I'd take you there if I could," I said. "But I can't. It's the law. Nobody can enter a plague era except under special supervision, which I'm not licensed to give."

I brought them down in 1385 and showed them the withering of Constantinople, a shrunken population within the great walls, whole districts deserted, churches falling into ruins. The Turks were devouring the surrounding countryside. I took my people up on the walls back of the Blachernae quarter and showed them the horsemen of the Turkish sultan prowling in the countryside beyond the city limits. My Ohio friend shook his fist at them. "Barbarian bastards!" he cried. "Scum of the earth!"

Up the Line

Down the line to 1398 we came. I showed them Anadolu Hisari, Sultan Beyazit's fortress on the Asiatic side of the Bosphorus. A summer haze made it a trifle hard to see, so we shunted a few months into autumn and looked again. Surreptitiously we passed around a little pair of field glasses. Two elderly Byzantine monks appeared, saw the field glasses before I could get hold of them and hide them, and wanted to know what we were looking through.

"It helps the eyes," I said, and we got out of there fast.

In the summer of 1422 we watched Sultan Murat II's army bashing at the city walls. About 20,000 Turks had burned the villages and fields around Constantinople, massacred the inhabitants, uprooted the vines and olive trees, and now we saw them trying to get into the city. They moved siege machines up to the walls, went to work with battering rams, giant catapults, all the heavy artillery of the time. I got my people right up close to the battle line to see the fun.

The standard technique for doing this is to masquerade as holy pilgrims. Pilgrims can go anywhere, even into front lines. I distributed crosses and icons, taught everybody how to look devout, and led them forward, chanting and intoning. There was no hope of getting them to chant genuine Byzantine hymns, of course, and so I told them to chant anything they liked, just making sure it sounded somber and pious. The Ohio people did *The Star Spangled Banner* over and over, and the shrink and his friend sang arias from Verdi and Puccini. The Byzantine defenders paused in their work to wave to us. We waved back and made the sign of the Cross.

"What if we get killed?" asked the son-in-law.

"No chance of it. Not permanently, anyway. If a stray shot gets you, I'll summon the Time Patrol, and they'll pull you out of here five minutes ago."

The son-in-law looked puzzled.

"*Celeste Aida, forma divina—*"

"*...so proudly we hailed—*"

The Byzantines fought like hell to keep the Turks out. They dumped Greek fire and boiling oil on them, hacked off every head that peered over the wall, withstood the fury of the artillery.

Nevertheless it seemed certain that the city would fall by sunset. The evening shadows gathered.

"Watch this," I said.

Flames burst forth at several points along the wall. The Turks were burning their own siege machines and pulling back!

"Why?" I was asked. "Another hour and they'll have the city."

"Byzantine historians," I said, "later wrote that a miracle had taken place. The Virgin Mary had appeared, clad in a violet mantle, dazzlingly bright, and had walked along the walls. The Turks, in terror, withdrew."

"Where?" the son-in-law demanded. "I didn't see any miracle! I didn't see any Virgin Mary!"

"Maybe we ought to go back half an hour and look again," said his wife vaguely.

I explained that the Virgin Mary had not in fact been seen on the battlements; rather, messengers had brought word to Sultan Murad of an uprising against him in Asia Minor, and, fearing he might be cut off and besieged in Constantinople if he succeeded in taking it, the sultan had halted operations at once to deal with the rebels in the east. The Ohioans looked disappointed. I think they genuinely had wanted to see the Virgin Mary. "We saw her on last year's trip," the son-in-law muttered.

"That was different," said his wife. "That was the *real* one, not a miracle!"

I adjusted timers and we shunted down the line.

Dawn, April 5, 1453. We waited for sunrise on the rampart of Byzantium. "The city is isolated now," I said. "Sultan Mehmet the Conqueror has built the fortress of Rumeli Hisari up along the European side of the Bosphorus. The Turks are moving in. Come, look, listen to this."

Sunrise broke. We peered over the top of the wall. A deafening shout went up. "Across the Golden Horn are the tents of the Turks—200,000 of them. In the Bosphorus are 493 Turkish ships. There are 8,000 Byzantine defenders, 15 ships. No help has come from Christian Europe for Christian Byzantium, except 700 Genoese soldiers and sailors under the command of Giovanni Giustiniani."

Up the Line

I lingered on the name of Byzantium's last bulwark, stressing the rich echoes of the past: "Giustiniani.... Justinian—" No one noticed. "Byzantium is to be thrown to the wolves," I went on. "Listen to the Turks roar!"

The famous Byzantine chain-boom was stretched across the Golden Horn and anchored at each bank: great rounded logs joined by iron hooks, designed to close the harbor to invaders. It had failed once before, in 1204; now it was stronger.

We jumped down the line to April 9, and watched the Turks creep closer to the walls. We skipped to April 12, and saw the great Turkish cannon, the Royal One, go into action. A turncoat Christian named Urban of Hungary had built it for the Turks; 100 pair of oxen had dragged it to the city; its barrel, three feet across, fired 1,500-pound granite projectiles. We saw a burst of flame, a puff of smoke, and then a monstrous ball of stone rise sleepily, slowly, and slam with earthshaking force against the wall, sending up a cloud of dust. The thud jarred the whole city; the explosion lingered in our ears. "They can fire the Royal One only seven times a day," I said. "It takes a while to load it. And now see this." We shunted forward by a week. The invaders were clustered about the giant cannon, readying it to fire. They touched it off; it exploded with a frightful blare of flame, sending huge chunks of its barrel slewing through the Turks. Bodies lay everywhere. The Byzantines cheered from the walls. "Among the dead," I said, "is Urban of Hungary. But soon the Turks will build a new cannon."

That evening the Turks rushed the walls, and we watched, singing *America the Beautiful* and arias from *Otello*, as the brave Genoese of Giovanni Giustiniani drove them off. Arrows whistled overhead; a few of the Byzantines fired clumsy, inaccurate rifles.

I did the final siege so brilliantly that I wept at my own virtuosity. I gave my people naval battles, hand-to-hand encounters at the walls, ceremonies of prayer in Haghia Sophia. I showed them the Turks slyly hauling their ships overland on wooden rollers from the Bosphorus to the Golden Horn, in order to get around the famous chain-boom, and I showed them the terror of the Byzantines when dawn on April 23 revealed 72 Turkish warships at anchor inside the harbor, and I showed them the gallant defeat of those ships by the Genoese.

We skipped forward through the days of the siege, watching the walls diminishing but remaining unbreached, watching the fortitude of the defenders grow and the determination of the attackers lessen. On May 28 we went by night to Haghia Sophia, to attend the last Christian service ever to be held there. It seemed that all the city was in the cathedral: Emperor Constantine XI and his court, beggars and thieves, merchants, pimps, Roman Catholics from Genoa and Venice, soldiers and sailors, dukes and prelates, and also a good many disguised visitors from the future, more, perhaps, than all the rest combined. We listened to the bells tolling, and to the melancholy *Kyrie*, and we dropped to our knees, and many, even some of the time-travelers, wept for Byzantium, and when the service ended the lights were dimmed, veiling the glittering mosaics and frescoes.

And then it was May 29, and we saw a world on its last day.

At two in the morning the Turks rushed St. Romanus Gate. Giustiniani was wounded; the fighting was terrible, and I had to keep my people back from it; the rhythmic *"Allah! Allah!"* grew until it filled the universe with noise, and the defenders panicked and fled, and the Turks burst into the city.

"All is over," I said. "Emperor Constantine perishes in battle. Thousands flee the city; thousands take refuge behind the barred doors of Haghia Sophia. Look now: the pillaging, the slaughter!" We jumped frantically, vanishing and reappearing, so that we would not be run down by the horsemen galloping joyously through the streets. Probably we startled a good many Turks, but in all that frenzy the miraculous vanishing of a few pilgrims would attract no excitement. For a climax I swept them into May 30, and we watched Sultan Mehmet ride in triumph into Byzantium, flanked by viziers and pashas and janissaries.

"He halts outside Haghia Sophia," I whispered. "He scoops up dirt, drops it on his turban; it is his act of contrition before Allah, who has given him such a glorious victory. Now he goes in. It would not be safe for us to follow him there. Inside he finds a Turk hacking up the mosaic floor, which he regards as impious; the sultan will strike the man and forbid him to harm the cathedral, and then he will go to the altar and climb upon it and make his Salaam. Haghia Sophia becomes Ayasofya, the mosque. There is no more Byzantium. Come. Now we go down the line."

Dazed by what they had seen, my six tourists let me adjust their timers. I sounded the note on my pitchpipe, and down the line we went to 2059.

In the Time Service office afterward, the Ohio real-estate man approached me. He stuck out his thumb in the vulgar way that vulgar people do, when they're offering a tip. "Son," he said, "I just want to tell you, that was one hell of a job you did! Come on over with me and let me stick this thumb on the input plate and give you a little bit of appreciation, okay?"

"I'm sorry," I said. "We're not permitted to accept gratuities."

"Crap on that, son. Suppose you don't pay any attention, and I just get some stash thumbed into your account, okay? Let's say you don't know a thing about it."

"I can't prevent a transfer of funds that I don't know about," I said.

"Good deal. By damn, when those Turks came into the city, what a show! What a show!"

When I got next month's account statement I found he had thumbed a cool thousand into my credit. I didn't report myself to my superiors. I figured I had earned it, rules or not.

34

I figured I had also earned the right to spend my layoff at Metaxas' villa in 1105. No longer a pest, a driveling apprentice, I was a full member of the brotherhood of Time Couriers. And one of the best in the business, in my opinion. I didn't have to fear that I'd be unwelcome at Metaxas' place.

Checking the assignment board, I found that Metaxas, like myself, had just finished a tour. That meant he'd be at his villa.

I picked up a fresh outfit of Byzantine clothes, requisitioned a pouch of gold bezants, and got ready to jump to 1105.

Then I remembered the Paradox of Discontinuity.

I didn't know *when* in 1105 I was supposed to arrive. And I had to allow for Metaxas' now-time basis up there. In now-time for me it was currently November, 2059. Metaxas had just jumped up the line to some point in 1105 that corresponded, for him, to November of 2059. Suppose that point was in July, 1105. If, not knowing that, I shunted back to—say—March, 1105, the Metaxas I'd find wouldn't know me at all. I'd be just some uninvited snot barging in on the party. If I jumped to—say—June, 1105, I'd be the young newcomer, not yet a proven quantity, whom Metaxas had just taken out on a training trip. And if I jumped to—say—October, 1105, I'd meet a Metaxas who was three months ahead of me on a now-time basis, and who therefore knew details of my own future. That would be the Paradox of Discontinuity in the other direction, and I wasn't eager to experience it; it's dangerous and a little frightening to run into someone who has lived through a period that you haven't reached yet, and no Time Serviceman enjoys it.

I needed help.

I went to Spiros Protopopolos and said, "Metaxas invited me to visit him during my layoff, but I don't know when he is."

Cautiously Protopopolos said, "Why do you think I know? He doesn't confide in me."

"I thought he might have left some record with you of his now-time basis."

"What the hell are you talking about?"

I wondered if I had made some hideous blunder. Bulling ahead, I winked and said, "You know where Metaxas is now. And maybe you know when, too. Come on, Proto. I'm in on the story. You don't need to be cagey with me."

He went into the next room and consulted Plastiras and Herschel. They must have vouched for me. Protopopolos, returning, whispered in my ear, "August 17, 1105. Say hello for me."

I thanked him and got on my way.

Up the Line

Metaxas lived in the suburbs, outside the walls of Constantinople. Land was cheap out there in the early twelfth century, thanks to such disturbances as the invasion of the marauding Patzinak barbarians in 1090 and the arrival of the disorderly rabble of Crusaders six years later. The settlers outside the walls had suffered badly then. Many fine estates had gone on the market. Metaxas had bought in 1095, when the landowners were still in shock over their injuries at the hands of the Patzinaks and were starting to worry about the next set of invaders.

He had one advantage denied to the sellers: he had already looked down the line and seen how stable things would be in the years just ahead, under Alexius I Comnenus. He knew that the countryside in which his villa was set would be spared from harm all during the twelfth century.

I crossed into Old Istanbul and cabbed out to the ruins of the city wall, and beyond it for about five kilometers. Naturally, this wasn't any suburban countryside in now-time, but just a gray sprawling extension of the modern city.

When I figured I was the proper distance out of town, I thumbed the plate and dismissed my cab. Then I took up a position on the sidewalk, checking things out for my jump. Some kids saw me in my Byzantine costume and came over to watch, knowing that I must be going to go back in time. They called gaily to me in Turkish, maybe asking me to take them along.

One angelically grimy little boy said in recognizable French, "I hope they cut your head off."

Children are so sweetly frank, aren't they? And so charmingly hostile, in all eras.

I set my timer, gestured obscenely at my well-wisher, and went up the line.

The gray buildings vanished. The November bleakness gave way to the sunny glow of August. The air I breathed was suddenly fresh and fragrant. I stood beside a broad cobbled road running between two green meadows. A modest chariot drawn by two horses came clopping up and halted before me.

A lean young man in simple country clothes leaned out and said, "Sir, Metaxas has sent me to fetch you to him."

"But—he wasn't expecting—"

I shut up fast, before I said something out of line. Obviously Metaxas *was* expecting me. Had I hit the Paradox of Discontinuity, somehow? Shrugging, I climbed up into the chariot. As we rode into the west, my driver nodded to the acres of grapevines to the left of the road and the groves of fig trees to the right. "All this," he said proudly, "belongs to Metaxas. Have you ever been here before?"

"No, never," I said.

"He is a great man, my master. He is a friend to the poor and an ally to the mighty. Everyone respects him. Emperor Alexius himself was here last month."

I felt queasy about that. Bad enough that Metaxas had carved out a now-time identity for himself ten centuries up the line; what would the Time Patrol say about his hobnobbing with emperors? Giving advice, no doubt; altering the future by his foreknowledge of events; cementing himself into the historical matrix of this era as a valued adviser to royalty! Could anyone match him for gall?

Figs and grapes gave way to fields of wheat. "This, too, belongs to Metaxas," said the driver. I had pictured Metaxas living in some comfortable little villa on a hectare or two of land, with a garden in front and perhaps a vegetable plot in the rear. I hadn't realized that he was a major landowner on such a scale.

We passed grazing cattle, and a mill worked by plodding oxen, and a pond no doubt well stocked with fish, and then we came to a double row of cypress trees that guarded a side road branching from the main highway, and took that road, and a splendid villa appeared, and at its entrance waited Metaxas, garbed in raiment suitable for the companion of an emperor.

"Jud!" he cried, and we embraced. "My friend! My brother! Jud, they tell me about the tour you led! Magnificent! Your tourists, they never stopped praising you?"

"Who told you?"

"Kolettis and Pappas. They're here. Come in, come in, come in! Wine for my guest! A change of robes for him! Come in, Jud, come in!"

35

The villa was classical in style, atrium-and-peristyle, with a huge central courtyard, colonnaded walkways, mosaic floors, frescoed walls, a great apsed reception room, a pond in the courtyard, a library bulging with scrolls, a dining room whose round gold-inlaid ivory table could have seated three dozen, a statuary hall, and a marble bathroom. Metaxas' slaves hustled me toward the bathroom, and Metaxas called out that he'd see me later. I got the royal treatment.

Three dark-haired slave wenches—Persians, Metaxas said later—ministered to me in the bath. All they wore were loinstrings, and in a moment I was wearing less than that, for in a giggling jiggle of breasts they stripped me and went to work buffing and soaping me until I gleamed. Steam bath, hot bath, cold bath—my pores got the full workout. When I emerged they dried me most detailedly and robed me in the most elegant tunic I ever expect to wear. Then they vanished, with a saucy wigwag of bare bottoms as they disappeared through some subterranean passageway. A middle-aged butler appeared and conveyed me to the atrium, where Metaxas awaited me with beakers of wine.

"You like it?" he asked.

"I feel I'm in a dream."

"You are. And I'm the dreamer. You saw the farms? Wheat, olives, cattle, figs, everything. I own. My tenants farm. Each year I acquire new land on the profits of last year's work."

"It's incredible," I said. "And what's even more incredible is that you get away with it."

"I have earned my invulnerability," said Metaxas simply. "The Time Patrol knows I must not be persecuted."

"They realize you're here?"

"I believe they do," he said. "They stay away, though. I take care to make no significant changes in the fabric of history. I'm no villain. I'm merely self-indulgent."

"But you *are* changing history just by being here! Some other landowner must have held these lands in the real 1105."

"This is the real 1105."

"I mean the original, before Benchley Effect visitors began coming here. You've interpolated yourself into the landowner rolls, and—my God, the chariot driver spoke of you as Metaxas! Is that the name you use here?"

"Themistoklis Metaxas. Why not? It is a good Greek name."

"Yes, but—look, it must be in all the documents, the tax records, everything! You've certainly changed the Byzantine archives that have come down to us, putting yourself in where you weren't in before. What—"

"There is no danger," Metaxas said. "So long as I take no life and create no life here, so long as I cause no one to change a previously decided course of action, all is well. You know, making a real alteration in the time flow is a difficult thing. You have to do something big, like killing a monarch. Simply being here, I introduce tiny changes, but they are damped out by ten centuries of time, and no real change results down the line. Do you follow?"

I shrugged. "Just tell me one thing, at least. How did you know I was coming?"

Laughing, he said, "I looked two days down the line and you were here. Therefore I checked for your time of arrival and arranged to have Nicholas meet you. It saved you a long walk, yes?"

Of course. I just hadn't been thinking four-dimensionally. It stood to reason that Metaxas would habitually scan his immediate future here, so he'd never be the victim of some unpleasant surprise in this sometimes unpredictable era.

"Come," Metaxas said. "Join the others."

They were lounging on divans by the courtyard pool, nibbling bits of roasted meat that slavegirls in diaphanous robes popped into their mouths. Two of my fellow Couriers were there, Kolettis and Pappas, both enjoying layoffs. Pappas, of the drooping mustache, managed to look sad even while pinching a firm Persian buttock, but Kolettis, plump and boisterous, was in high form, singing and laughing. A third man, whom I didn't know, was peering at the fish in the pool. Though dressed in twelfth-century robes, he had a face that was instantly recognizable as modern, I thought. And I was right.

Up the Line

"This is Scholar Magistrate Paul Speer," said Metaxas to me in English. "A visiting academic. Meet Time Courier Jud Elliott, Dr. Speer."

We touched hands formally. Speer was about fifty, somewhat desiccated, a pale little man with an angular face and quick, nervous eyes. "Pleased," he said.

"And this," said Metaxas, "is Eudocia."

I had noticed her the instant I entered the courtyard, of course. She was a slim, auburn-haired girl, fair-skinned but with dark eyes, nineteen or twenty years old. She was heavily laden with jewelry, and so obviously was not just one of the slavegirls; yet her costume was daring by Byzantine standards, consisting only of a light double winding of translucent silk. As the fabric pulled taut against her, it displayed small high breasts, boyish buttocks, a shallow navel, even a hint of the triangular tuft at her loins. I prefer my women dark of hair and complexion and voluptuous of figure, but even so this Eudocia was enormously attractive to me. She seemed tense, coiled, full of pent-up fury and fervor.

She studied me in cool boldness and indicated her approval by placing her hands at her thighs and arching her back. The movement pulled her robes closer and showed me her nakedness in greater detail. She smiled. Her eyes sparkled wantonly.

In English, Metaxas said to me, "I've told you of her. She's my great-great-multi-great-grandmother. Try her in your bed tonight. The hip action is incredible!"

Eudocia smiled more warmly. She didn't know what Metaxas was saying, but she must have known he was talking about her. I tried not to stare too intently at the exposed beauties of the fair Eudocia. Is a man supposed to ogle his host's great-great-multi-great-grandmother?

A bare and beautiful slave offered me lamb and olives en brochette. I swallowed without tasting. My nostrils were filled with the perfume of Eudocia.

Metaxas gave me wine and led me away from her. "Dr. Speer," he said, "is here on a collecting trip. He's a student of classical Greek drama, in search of lost plays."

Dr. Speer clicked his heels. He was the sort of Teutonic pedant who, you automatically know, would use his full academic title on all occasions. *Achtung! Herr Scholar Magistrate Speer!* Scholar Magistrate Speer said, "It has been most successful for me so far. Of course, my search is just beginning, yet already from Byzantine libraries I have obtained the *Nausicaa* and *Triptolemus* of Sophocles, and of Euripides the *Andromeda,* the *Peliades,* the *Phaethon,* and the *Oedipus,* and also of Aeschylus a nearly complete manuscript of *The Women of Aetna.* So you see I have done well." He clicked heels again.

I knew better than to remind him that the Time Patrol frowns on the recovery of lost masterpieces. Here in Metaxas' villa we were all ipso facto breakers of Patrol regulations, and accessories before and after the fact to any number of timecrimes.

I said, "Do you plan to bring these manuscripts down to now-time?"

"Yes, of course."

"But you can't publish them! What will you do with them?"

"Study them," said Scholar Magistrate Speer. "Increase the depth of my understanding of the Greek drama. And in time I will plant each manuscript in some place where archaeologists are likely to discover it, and so these plays will be restored to the world. It is a minor crime, is it not? Can I be called evil for wishing to enlarge our scanty stock of Sophocles?"

It seemed quite all right to me.

To me it has always seemed like numbnoggin uprightness to have made it illegal to go up the line to discover lost manuscripts or paintings. I can see where it wouldn't be desirable to let somebody go back to 1600 and make off with Michelangelo's *Pietá* or Leonardo's *Leda.* That would be timechange and timecrime, since the *Pietá* and the *Leda* must make their way year by year toward our now-time, and not leapfrog over four and a half centuries. But why not allow us to obtain works of art that we don't already have? Who's injured by it?

Kolettis said, "Doc Speer, you're absolutely right! Hell, they let historians inspect the past to make corrections in the historical record, don't they? And when they bring out their revisionist books, it goddam well alters the state of knowledge!"

"Yes," said Pappas. "As for example when it was noticed that Lady Macbeth was in fact a tender woman who struggled in vain to limit the insane ambitions of her bloodthirsty husband. Or we could consider the case of the Moses story. Or what we know now about Richard III. Or the truth about Joan of Arc. We've patched up standard history in a million places since Benchley Effect travel began, and—"

"—and so why not patch up some of the holes in literary history?" Kolettis asked. "Here's to Doc Speer! Steal every goddam play there is, Doc!"

"The risks are great," said Speer. "If I am caught I will be severely punished, perhaps stripped of my academic standing." He said it as though he'd prefer to be parted from his genitals. "The law is so foolish—they are such frightened men, these Time Patrol, worried about changes even that are virtuous."

To the Time Patrol no change is virtuous. They accept historical revisions because they can't help themselves; the enabling legislation specifically permits that kind of research. But the same law prohibits the transportation of any tangible object from up the line, except as required for the functions of the Time Service itself, and the Patrol sticks to the letter of it.

I said, "If you're looking for Greek plays, why don't you check out the Alexandria Library? You're bound to find a dozen there for every one that's survived into the Byzantine period."

Scholar Magistrate Speer gave me the smile one gives to clever but naïve children.

"The Library of Alexandria," he explained ponderously, "is of course a prime target for scholars such as myself. Therefore it is guarded perpetually by a man of the Time Patrol in the guise of a scribe. He makes several arrests a month, I hear. I take no risk such as that. Here in Byzantium my goal is more hard but my exposure is not so much. I will look more. I still hope to find some ninety plays of Sophocles, and at least so many of Aeschylus, and—"

36

Dinner that night was a gaudy feast. We gorged on soups, stews, grilled duck, fish, pork, lamb, asparagus, mushrooms, apples, figs, artichokes, hard-boiled eggs served in blue enamel egg cups, cheese, salads, and wine. Out of courtesy to Eudocia, who was at table with us, we conversed in Greek and therefore spoke not at all of time-travel or the iniquities of the Time Patrol.

After dinner, while dwarf jesters performed, I called Metaxas aside. "I have something to show you," I said, and handed him the roll of vellum on which I had inscribed my genealogy. He glanced at it and frowned.

"What is it?"

"My ancestry. Back to the seventh century."

"When did you do all this?" he asked, laughing.

"On my last layoff." I told him of my visits to Grandfather Passilidis, to Gregory Markezinis, to the time of Nicephorus Ducas.

Metaxas studied the list more carefully.

"*Ducas?* What is this, Ducas?"

"That's me. I'm a Ducas. The scribe gave me the details right back to the seventh century."

"Impossible. Nobody knows who the Ducases were, that early! It's false!"

"Maybe that part is. But from 950 on, it's legitimate. Those are my people. I followed them right out of Byzantium into Albania and on to twentieth-century Greece."

"This is the truth?"

"I swear it!"

"You clever little cockeater," Metaxas said fondly. "All in one layoff, you learned this. And a Ducas, no less! A Ducas!" He consulted the list again. "Nicephorus Ducas, son of Nicetas Ducas, son of—hmm—Leo Ducas! Pulcheria Botaniates.'"

"What's wrong?"

"I know them," Metaxas cried. "They've been my guests here, and I've stayed with them. He's one of the richest men in Byzantium, do you know that? And his wife Pulcheria—such a beautiful girl—" He gripped my arm fiercely. "You'd swear? These are your ancestors?"

"I'm positive."

"Wonderful," Metaxas said. "Let me tell you about Pulcheria, now. She's—oh, seventeen years old. Leo married her when she was just a child; they do a lot of that here. She's got a waist like *this*, but breasts out to *here*, and a flat belly and eyes that turn you afire, and—"

I shook free of his grasp and jammed my face close to his.

"Metaxas, have you—" I couldn't say it.

"—slept with Pulcheria? No, no, I haven't. God's truth, Jud! I've got enough women here. But look, boy, here's *your* opportunity! I can help you to meet her. She's ripe for seduction. Young, childless, beautiful, bored, her husband so busy with business matters that he hardly notices her—and she's your own great-great-multi-grandmother besides!"

"That part is your clutchup, not mine," I reminded him. "For me it might be a reason to stay away from her, in fact."

"Don't be an idiot. I'll fix it all up for you in two, three days. An introduction to the Ducases, a night as a guest in their palace in town, a word to Pulcheria's lady in waiting—"

"No," I said.

"No?"

"No. I don't want to get mixed up in any of this."

"You're a hard man to make happy, Jud. You don't want to fuck Empress Theodora, you don't want to lay Pulcheria Ducas, you—say, next thing you'll tell me you don't want Eudocia either."

"I don't mind screwing one of *your* ancestors," I said. I grinned. "I wouldn't even mind putting a baby in Eudocia's belly. How would you feel if I turned out to be your multi-great-grandfather?"

"You can't," said Metaxas.

"Why not?"

"Because Eudocia remains unmarried and childless until 1109. Then she weds Basil Stratiocus and has seven sons and three daughters in the following fifteen years, including one who is ancestral to me. Christ, does she get fat!"

"All of that can be changed," I reminded him.

"Like holy crap it can," said Metaxas. "Don't you think I guard my own line of descent? Don't you think I'd obliterate you from history if I caught you making a timechange on Eudocia's marriage? She'll stay childless until Basil Stratiocus fills her up, and that's that. But she's yours for tonight."

And she was. Giving me the highest degree of hospitality in his lexicon, Metaxas sent his ancestress Eudocia into my bedroom. Her lean, supple body was a trifle meager for me; her hard little breasts barely filled my hands. But she was a tigress. She was all energy and all passion, and she clambered on top of me and rocked herself to ecstasy in twenty quick rotations, and that was only the beginning. It was dawn before she let me sleep.

And in my dreams I saw Metaxas escort me to the palace of the Ducases, and introduce me to my multi-great-grandfather Leo, who said serenely, "This is my wife Pulcheria," and in my dream it seemed to me that she was the loveliest woman I had ever seen.

37

I had my first troublesome moment as a Courier on my next tour. Because I was too proud to call in the Time Patrol for help, I got myself involved in the Paradox of Duplication and also caught a taste of the Paradox of Transit Displacement. But I think I came out of it looking pretty good.

I was escorting nine tourists through the arrival of the First Crusade in Byzantium when the mess happened.

"In 1095," I told my people, "Pope Urban II called for the liberation of the Holy Land from the Saracens. Very shortly, the knights of Europe began to enroll in the Crusade. Among those who welcomed such a war of liberation was Emperor Alexius of Byzantium, who saw in it a way of regaining the territories in the Near East that Byzantium had lost to the Turks and the Arabs. Alexius sent word that he wouldn't mind getting a few hundred experienced knights to help him clean the infidels out. But he got a good deal more than that, as we'll see in moment, down the line in 1096."

We shunted to August 1, 1096.

Ascending the walls of Constantinople, we peered out into the countryside and saw it full of troops: not mailed knights but a raggle-taggle band of tattered peasants.

"This," I said, "is the People's Crusade. While the professional soldiers were working out the logistics of their march, a scrawny, foul-smelling little charismatic named Peter the Hermit rounded up thousands of paupers and farmers and led them across Europe to Byzantium. They looted and pillaged along the way, cleaned out the harvest of half of Europe, and burned Belgrade in a dispute with the Byzantine administrators. But finally they got here, 30,000 of them."

"Which one is Peter the Hermit?" asked the most obstreperous member of the group, a full-blown, fortyish bachelor lady from Des Moines named Marge Hefferin.

I checked the time. "You'll see him in another minute and a half. Alexius has sent a couple of officials to invite Peter to court. He wants Peter and his rabble to wait in Constantinople until the knights and barons get here, since these people will get slaughtered by the Turks if they go over into Asia Minor without a military escort. Look: there's Peter now."

Two dandified Byzantine grandees emerged from the mob, obviously holding their breath and looking as though they'd like to hold their noses too. Between them marched a scruffy, barefoot, ragclad, filthy, long-chinned, gnomish man with blazing eyes and a pockmarked face.

"Peter the Hermit," I said, "on his way to see the emperor."

We shunted forward three days. The People's Crusade was inside Constantinople and playing hell with Alexius' city. A good many buildings were aflame. Ten Crusaders were atop one of the churches, stripping the lead from the roof for resale. A highborn-looking Byzantine woman emerged from Haghia Sophia and was stripped bare and raped by a pack of Peter's pious pilgrims before our eyes.

I said, "Alexius has miscalculated by letting this riffraff into the city. Now he's making arrangements to get them out the other side, by offering free ferry service across the Bosphorus to Asia. On August 6 they'll start on their way. The Crusaders will begin by massacring the Byzantine settlements in western Asia Minor; then they'll attack the Turks and be wiped out almost completely. If we had time, I'd take you down to 1097 and across to see the mountain of bones along the road. That's what happened to the People's Crusade. However, the pros are on their way, so let's watch them."

I explained about the four armies of Crusaders: the army of Raymond of Toulouse, the army of Duke Robert of Normandy, the army of Bohemond and Tancred, and the army of Godfrey of Bouillon, Eustace of Boulogne, and Baldwin of Lorraine. Some of my people had read up on their Crusader history and nodded in recognition of the names.

We shunted to the final week of 1096. "Alexius," I said, "has learned his lesson from the People's Crusade. He doesn't plan to let the real Crusaders linger long in Constantinople. They all have to pass through Byzantium on their way to the Holy Land, but he's going to hustle them through in a hurry, and he'll make their leader swear allegiance to him before he admits them."

We watched the army of Godfrey of Bouillon pitch camp outside the walls of Constantinople. We observed the envoys going back and forth, Alexius requesting the oath of allegiance, Godfrey refusing. With careful editing I covered four months in less than an hour, showing how mistrust and enmity were building up between the Christian Crusaders and the Christian Byzantines who were supposed to collaborate in the liberation of the Holy Land. Godfrey still refused to swear allegiance; Alexius not only kept the Crusaders sealed out of Constantinople, but now was blockading their camp, hoping to starve them into going away. Baldwin of Lorraine began to raid the suburbs; Godfrey captured a platoon of Byzantine soldiers and put them to death in view of the city walls. And on April 2 the Crusaders began to lay siege to the city.

"Observe how easily the Byzantines drive them off," I said. "Alexius, losing patience, has sent his best troops into battle. The

Up the Line

Crusaders, not yet accustomed to fighting together, flee. On Easter Sunday, Godfrey and Baldwin submit, and swear allegiance to Alexius. All now is well. The emperor will give a banquet for the Crusaders in Constantinople, and then swiftly will ship them across the Bosphorus. More Crusaders, he knows, will arrive in a few days—the army of Bohemond and Tancred."

Marge Hefferin emitted a little gasping squeak at the sound of those names. I should have been warned.

We skipped forward to April 10 for a look at the next batch of Crusaders. Thousands of soldiers again camped outside Constantinople. They strolled around arrogantly in chain mail and surcoats, and playfully swatted each other with swords or maces when things got dull.

"Which one is Bohemond?" asked Marge Hefferin.

I scanned the field. "There," I said.

"Ooooh."

He *was* impressive. About two meters tall, a giant for his times, head and shoulders above everyone else around him. Broad shoulders, deep chest, close-cropped hair. Strangely white of skin. Swaggering posture. A grim customer, tough and savage.

He was cleverer than the other leaders, too. Instead of quarreling with Alexius over the business of swearing allegiance, Bohemond gave in immediately. Oaths, to him, were only words, and it was foolish to waste time bickering with the Byzantines when there were empires to be won in Asia. So Bohemond got quick entry to Constantinople. I took my people to the gate where he'd be passing into the city, so they could have a close look at him. A mistake.

The Crusaders came striding grandly in on foot, six abreast.

When Bohemond appeared, Marge Hefferin broke from the group. She ripped open her tunic and let her big pale breasts bobble into the open. An advertisement, I suppose.

She rushed toward Bohemond, squealing, "Bohemond, Bohemond, I love you, I've always loved you, Bohemond! Take me! Make me your slave, beloved!" And other words to that effect.

Bohemond turned and peered at her in bewilderment. I guess the sight of a hefty, shrieking, half-naked female running wildly in his direction must have puzzled him. But Marge didn't get within five meters of him.

A knight just in front of Bohemond, deciding that an assassination plot was unfolding, pulled out his dagger and jammed it right between Marge's big breasts. The impact halted her mad charge, and she staggered back, frowning. Blood burbled from her lips. As she toppled, another knight swung at her with a broadsword and just about cut her in half at the waist. Entrails went spilling all over the pavement.

The whole thing took about fifteen seconds. I had no chance to move. I stood aghast, realizing that my career as a Time Courier might just have come to an end. Losing a tourist is about the worst thing a Courier can do, short of committing timecrime itself.

I had to act quickly.

I said to my tourists, "Don't any of you move from the spot! That's an order!" It wasn't likely that they'd disobey. They were huddled together in hysteria, sobbing and puking and shivering. The shock alone would hold them in place for a few minutes—more time than I'd need. I set my timer for a two-minute jump up the line and bunted fast.

Instantly I found myself standing right behind myself. There I was, big ears and all, watching Bohemond saunter up the street. My tourists were standing on both sides of me. Marge Hefferin, breathing hard, rearing up on tiptoes for a better view of her idol, was already starting to undo her tunic.

I moved into position in back of her. Just as she made the first movement toward the street, my hands shot out. I clamped my left hand on her ass and got the right hand on her breast and hissed in her ear, "Stay where you are or you'll be sorriest." She squirmed and twisted. I dug my fingertips deep into the meat of her quivering rump and hung on. She writhed around to see who her attacker was, saw it was me, and stared in amazement at the other me a few paces her left. All the fight went out of her. She sagged, and I whispered another reminder for her to stay put, and then Bohemond was past us and well up the street.

I released her, set my timer, and shunted down the line by sixty seconds.

Up the Line

My net absence from my tourists had been less than a minute. I half expected to find them still gagging and retching over the bloody smiting of Marge Hefferin. But the editing had succeeded. There was no corpse in the street now. No intestines were spilled beneath the boots of the marching Crusaders. Marge stood with the group, shaking her head in confusion and rubbing her backside. Her tunic still hung open and I could see the red imprints of my fingers on the soft globe of her right breast.

Did any of them suspect what had happened? No. No. Not even a phantom memory. My tourists did not experience the Paradox of Transit Displacement, for they had not made the jump-within-a-jump that I had; and so only I remembered what now was gone from their minds, could recall clearly the bloody event that I had transformed into a nonevent.

"Down the line!" I yelled, and shunted them all into 1098.

The street was quiet. The Crusaders were long since gone, and at the moment were hung up in Syria at the siege of Antioch. It was dusk on a sticky summer day and there were no witnesses to our sudden arrival.

Marge was the only one who realized that something funny had gone on; the others had not seen anything unusual occurring, but she clearly knew that an extra Jud Elliott had materialized behind her and prevented her from rushing out into the street.

"What the hell do you think you were doing?" I asked her. "You were about to run out into the street and throw yourself at Bohemond, weren't you?"

"I couldn't help it. It was a sudden compulsion. I've always loved Bohemond, don't you see? He's been my hero, my god—I've read every word anyone's written about him—and then there he was, right in front of me—"

"Let me tell you how events really unfolded," I said, and described the way she had been killed. Then I told her how I had edited the past, how I had pinched the episode of her death into a parallel line. I said, "I want you to know that the only reason I got you unkilled was to save my own job. It looks bad for a Courier if he can't keep control of his people. Otherwise I'd have been happy to leave you disemboweled. Didn't I tell you a million times *never* to break from cover?"

I warned her to forget every shred of my admission that I had changed events to save her life.

"The next time you disobey me in any way, though," I told her, "I'll—"

I was going to say that I'd ram her head up her tail and make a Moebius strip out of her. Then I realized that a Courier can't talk to a client that way, no matter what the provocation.

"—cancel your tour and send you down the line to now-time immediately, you hear me?"

"I won't ever try that again," she murmured. "I swear it. You know, now that you've told me about it, I can almost feel it happening. That dagger going into me—"

"It never happened."

"It never happened," she said doubtfully.

"Put some conviction into it. *It never happened.*"

"*It never happened,*" she repeated. "But I can almost feel it!"

38

We all spent the night in an inn in 1098. Feeling tense and stale after so much delicate work, I decided to jump down to 1105, while my people slept, and drop in on Metaxas. I didn't even know if he'd be at his villa, but it was worth the try. I needed desperately to unwind.

I calibrated the timing with care.

Metaxas' last layoff had begun in early November, 2059, and he had jumped to mid-August, 1105. I figured he had spent ten or twelve days there. That schedule would have returned him to 2059 toward the end of November; and then, assuming he had taken out a group on a two-week tour, he'd have been able to get back to his villa by September 15 or so, 1105.

I played it safe and shunted down to September 20.

Now I had to find a way to get to his villa.

Up the Line

It is one of the oddities of the era of the Benchley Effect that I would find it easier to jump across seven years of time than to get myself a few dozen kilometers into the Byzantine countryside. But I did have that problem. I had no access to a chariot, and there aren't any cabs for hire in the twelfth century.

Walk? Ridiculous idea!

I contemplated heading for the nearest inn and dangling bezants in front of freelance charioteers until I found one willing to make the trip to Metaxas' place. As I considered this I heard a familiar voice yelling, "Herr Courier Elliott! Herr Courier Elliott!"

I turned. Scholar Magistrate Speer.

"*Guten Tag*, Herr Courier Elliott!" said Scholar Magistrate Speer.

"*Guten*—" I scowled, cut myself short, greeted him in a more Byzantine way. He smiled indulgently at my observance of the rules.

"I have a very successful visit been having," he said. "Since last I enjoyed with you company, have I found the *Thamyras* of Sophocles and also the *Melanippe* of Euripides, and further a partial text of what I believe is the *Archelaus* of Euripides. And then there is besides the text of a play that is claiming to be of Aeschylus the *Helios,* of which there is in the records no reference for. So perhaps is a forgery or otherwise is maybe a new discovery. I will see which only upon reading. Eh? A good visit, eh, Herr Courier!"

"Splendid," I said.

"And now I am returning to the villa of our friend Metaxas, just as soon as I complete a small purchase in this shop of spices. Would you accompany me?"

"You have wheels?" I asked.

"*Was meinen Sie mit* 'wheels'?"

"Transportation. A chariot."

"*Naturlich!* Over there. It waits for me, a chariot *mit* driver, from Metaxas."

"Swell," I said. "Take care of your business in the spice shop and then we can ride out to Metaxas' place together, okay?"

The shop was dark and fragrant. In barrels, jugs, flasks, and baskets it displayed its wares: olives, nuts, dates, figs, raisins, pistachios, cheeses, and spices both ground and whole of many different sorts. Speer, apparently running some errand for Metaxas' chef, selected a few items and pulled forth a purse of bezants to pay for them. While this was going on, an ornate chariot pulled up outside the shop and three figures dismounted and entered. One was a slavegirl—to carry the merchandise to the chariot, evidently. The second was a woman of mature years and simple dress—a duenna, I supposed, just the right kind of dragon to escort a Byzantine wife on a shopping expedition. The third person was the wife herself, obviously a woman of the very highest class making a tour of the town.

She was fantastically beautiful.

I knew at once that she was no more than seventeen. She had a supple, liquid Mediterranean beauty; her eyes were dark and large and glossy, with long lashes, and her skin was light olive in hue, and her lips were full and her nose aquiline, and her bearing was elegant and aristocratic. Her robes of white silk revealed the outlines of high, sumptuous breasts, curving flanks, voluptuous buttocks. She was all the women I had ever desired, united into one ideal form.

I stared at her without shame.

She stared back. Without shame.

Our eyes met and held, and a current of pure force passed between us, and I quivered as the full surge hit me. She smiled only on the left side of her mouth, quirking the lips in, revealing two glistening teeth. It was a smile of invitation, a smile of lust.

She nodded almost imperceptibly to me.

Then she turned away, and pointed to the bins, ordering this and this and this, and I continued to stare, until the duenna, noticing it, shot me a furious look of warning.

"Come," Speer said impatiently. "The chariot is waiting—"

"Let it wait a little longer."

I made him stay in the store with me until the three women had completed their transaction. I watched them leave, my eyes riveted to the subtle sway of my beloved's silk-sheathed tail. Then I whirled and pounced on the proprietor of the shop, seizing his wrist and barking, "That woman! What's her name?"

"Milord, I—that is—"

I flipped a gold piece to the counter. "Her name!"

"That is Pulcheria Ducas," he gasped. "The wife of the well-known Leo Ducas, who—"

I groaned and rushed out of the store.

Her chariot clattered off toward the Golden Horn.

Speer emerged. "Are you in good health, Herr Courier Elliott?"

"I'm sick as a pig," I muttered. "Pulcheria Ducas— that was Pulcheria Ducas—"

"And so?"

"I love her, Speer, can you understand that?"

Looking blankfaced, he said, "The chariot is ready."

"Never mind. I'm not going with you. Give Metaxas my best regards."

In anguish I ran down the street, aimlessly, my mind and my crotch inflamed with the vision of Pulcheria. I trembled. I streamed with sweat. I sobbed. Finally I came up against the wall of some church, and pressed my cheek to the cold stone, and touched my timer and shunted back to the tourists I had left sleeping in 1098.

I was a lousy Courier for the rest of that trip.

Moody, withdrawn, lovesick, confused, I shuttled my people through the standard events, the Venetian invasion of 1204 and the Turkish conquest of 1453, in a routine, mechanical way. Maybe they didn't realize they were getting a minimum job, or didn't care. Maybe they blamed it on the trouble Marge Hefferin had caused. For better or for worse I gave them their tour and delivered them safely down the line in now-time and was rid of them.

I was on layoff again, and my soul was infected by desire.

Go to 1105? Accept Metaxas' offer, let him introduce me to Pulcheria? I recoiled at the idea.

Time Patrol rules specifically forbid any kind of fraternization between Couriers (or other time-travelers) and people who live up the line. The only contact we are supposed to have with the residents of the past is casual and incidental—buying a bag of olives, asking how to get to Haghia Sophia from here, like that. We are not permitted to strike up friendships, get into long philosophical discussions, or have sexual intercourse with inhabitants of previous eras.

Especially with our own ancestors.

The incest taboo per se didn't scare me much; like all taboos, it isn't worth a whole lot any more, and while I'd hesitate at bedding my sister or my mother, I couldn't see any very convincing reason to abstain from bedding Pulcheria. I felt a little lingering Puritanism, maybe, but I knew it would fade in a minute if Pulcheria became available.

What held me back, though, was the universal deterrent, fear of retribution. If the Time Patrol caught me sexing around with my multi-great-grandmother, they'd certainly fire me from the Time Service, might imprison me, might even try to invoke the death penalty for first-degree timecrime on the grounds that I had tried to become my own ancestor. I was terrified of the possibilities.

How could they catch me?

Plenty of scenarios presented themselves. For example:

I wangle introduction to Pulcheria. Somehow get into situation of privacy with her. Reach for her fair flesh; she screams; family bodyguards seize me and put me to death. Time Patrol, when I don't check in after my layoff, traces me, finds out what has happened, rescues me, then brings charges of timecrime.

Or:

I wangle introduction, etc., and seduce Pulcheria. Just at moment of mutual climax husband bursts into bedroom and impales me. Rest of scenario follows.

Or:

I fall so desperately in love with Pulcheria that I abscond with her to some distant point in time, say 400 B.C. or A.D. 1600, and we live happily ever after until Time Patrol catches us, returns her to proper moment of 1105, brings charges of timecrime against me.

Or:

A dozen other possibilities, all of them ending in the same melancholy way. So I resisted all temptation to spend my layoff in 1105

Up the Line

sniffing after Pulcheria. Instead, to suit the darkness of my mood in this time of unrequited lust, I signed up to do the Black Death tour.

Only the weirds, the freaks, the sickos, and the pervos would take a tour like that, which is to say the demand is always pretty heavy. But as a vacationing Courier, I was able to bump a paying customer and get into the next group leaving.

There are four regular Black Death outings. One sets out from the Crimea for 1347 and shows you the plague as it spills out of Asia. The highlight of that tour is the siege of Kaffa, a Genoese trading port on the Black Sea, by Khan Janibeg of the Kipchak Mongols. Janibeg's men were rotten with plague, and he catapulted their corpses into the town to infect the Genoese. You have to book a reservation a year in advance for that one.

The Genoese carried the Black Death westward into the Mediterranean, and the second tour takes you to Italy, autumn of 1347, to watch it spread inland. You see a mass burning of Jews, who were thought to have caused the epidemic by poisoning the wells. The third tour brings you to France in 1348, and the fourth to England in the late spring of 1349.

The booking office got me on the England trip. I made a noon hop to London and joined the group two hours before it was about to leave. Our Courier was a tall, cadaverous man named Riley, with bushy eyebrows and bad teeth. He was a little strange, as you have to be to specialize in this particular tour. He welcomed me in friendly if moody fashion and got me fitted for a plague suit.

A plague suit is more or less a spacesuit, done up in black trim. You carry a standard fourteen-day rebreathing unit, you eat via an intake pipe, and you eliminate wastes with difficulty and complexity. The idea, naturally, is to keep you totally sealed off from the infectious environment. Tourists are told that if they open their suits even for ten seconds, they'll be marooned permanently in the plague era; and although this is not true at all, there hasn't been a case yet of a tourist calling the Time Service's bluff.

This is one of the few tours that operates to and from fixed points. We don't want returning groups materializing all over the place, carrying plague on their spacesuits, and so the Service has marked off jumping areas in red paint at the medieval end of each of the four plague tours. When your group is ready to come back, you go to a jumping area and shunt down the line from there. This materializes you within a sealed sterile dome; your suit is taken from you and you are thoroughly fumigated before you're allowed to rejoin the twenty-first century.

"What you are about to see," said Riley portentously, "is neither a reconstruction nor a simulation nor an approximation. It is the real thing, exaggerated in no way."

We shunted up the line.

Clad in our black plastic suits, we marched single file through a land of the dead.

Nobody paid any attention to us. At such a time as this our costume didn't even seem outlandish; the black was logical, the airtight sealing of our suits even more logical. And though the fabric was a little on the anachronistic side for the fourteenth century, no one was curious. At this time, wise men stayed indoors and kept their curiosities on tight leashes.

Those who saw us must have assumed that we were priests going on a pilgrimage of prayer. Our somber suits, our single-file array, the fearlessness with which we paraded through the worst areas of infestation, all marked us as God's men, or else Satan's, and, either way, who would dare to interfere with us?

Bells tolled a leaden dirge, donging all day and half the night. The world was a perpetual funeral. A grim haze hung over London; the sky was never anything but gray and ashen all the time we were there. Not that nature was reinforcing the dolefulness, that old pathetic fallacy; no, the haze was man-made, for thousands of small fires were burning in England, consuming the clothes and the homes and the bodies of the stricken.

We saw plague victims in all stages, from the early staggering to the later trembling and sweating and falling and convulsing. "The onset of the disease," said Riley calmly, dispassionately, "is marked by hardenings and swellings of the glands in the armpits and the groin. The swellings rapidly grow to the size of eggs or apples. See, this woman here—" She was young, haggard, terror-stricken. She clutched desperately at the sprouting buboes and lurched past us through the smoky streets.

"Next," he said, "come the black blotches, first on the arms and thighs, then all over the body. And the carbuncles which, when lanced, give no relief. And then delirium, insanity, death always on the third day after the swellings appear. Observe here—" A victim in the late stages, groaning in the street, abandoned. "And here—" Pale faces looking down from a window. "Over here—" Heaped corpses at the door of a stable.

Houses were locked. Shops were barred. The only people in the streets were those already infected, roaming desperately about searching for a doctor, a priest, a miracle-worker.

Fractured, tormented music came to us from the distance: pipes, drums, viols, lutes, sackbuts, shawms, clarions, krummhorns, all the medieval instruments at once but giving forth not the pretty buzz and tootle of the middle ages, but rather a harsh, discordant, keyless whine and screech. Riley looked pleased. "A procession of flagellants is coming!" he cried, elated. "Follow me! By all means, let's not miss it!"

And through the winding streets the flagellants came, men and women, naked to the waist, grimy, bloody, some playing on instruments, most wielding knotted whips, lashing, lashing, tirelessly bringing down the lash across bare backs, breasts, cheeks, arms, foreheads. They droned toneless hymns; they groaned in agony; they stumbled forward, a few of the whippers and some of the whipped already showing the buboes of the plague, and without looking at us they went by, down some dismal alley leading to a deserted church.

And we happy time-tourists picked our way over the dead and the dying and marched on, for our Courier wished us to drink this experience to the deepest.

We saw the bonfired bodies of the dead blackening and splitting open.

We saw other heaps of the unburied left in fields to rot. We saw ghouls searching cadavers for items of value. We saw a plague-smitten man fall upon a half-conscious plague-smitten woman in the streets, and part her thighs for one last desperate act of lust.

We saw priests on horseback fleeing from parishioners begging for Heaven's mercy.

We entered an unguarded palace to watch terrified surgeons letting blood from some dying duke.

We saw another procession of strange black-clad beings cross our street at an angle, their faces hidden behind mirrorlike plates, and we shivered at the grotesque sight of these nightmare marchers, these demons without faces, and we realized only slowly that we had intersected some other party of tourists.

Riley was ready with cool statistics. "The mortality rate of the Black Death," he announced, "was anywhere from one-eighth to two-thirds of the population in a given area. In Europe it is estimated that twenty-five per cent of the entire population perished; worldwide, the mortality was about thirty-three per cent. That is to say, a similar plague today would take the lives of more than two billion people."

We watched a woman emerge from a thatched house and, one by one, arrange the bodies of five children in the street so that they might be taken away by the department of sanitation.

Riley said, "The aristocracy was annihilated, causing great shifts in patterns of inheritance. There were permanent cultural effects as a result of the wholesale death of painters of a single school, of poets, of learned monks. The psychological impact was long-lasting; for generations it was thought that the mid-fourteenth century had done something to earn the wrath of God, and a return of His wrath was momentarily expected."

We formed the audience for a mass funeral at which two young and frightened priests muttered words over a hundred blotched and swollen corpses, tolled their little bells, sprinkled holy water, and signaled to the sextons to start the bonfire.

"Not until the early sixteenth century," said Riley, "will the population reach its pre-1348 level."

Up the Line

It was impossible for me to tell how the others were affected by these horrors, since we all were hidden in our suits. Probably most of my companions were fascinated and thrilled. I'm told that it's customary for a dedicated plague aficionado to take all four Black Death tours in succession, starting in the Crimea; many have gone through the set five or six times. My own reaction was one of diminishing shock. You accommodate to monstrous horror. I think that by the tenth time through I'd have been as cool and dispassionate as Courier Riley, that brimming fount of statistics.

At the end of our journey through hell we made our way to Westminster. On the pavement outside the palace, Time Service personnel had painted a red circle five meters in diameter. This was our jumping point. We gathered close in the middle. I helped Riley make the timer adjustments—on this tour, the timers are mounted on the outside of the suits. He gave the signal and we shunted.

A couple of plague victims, shambling past the palace, were witnesses to our departure. I doubt that it troubled them much. In a time when all the world is perishing, who can get excited over the sight of ten black demons vanishing?

41

We emerged under a shimmering dome, yielded up our polluted suits, and came forth purged and purified and ennobled by what we had seen. But images of Pulcheria still obsessed me. Restless, tormented, I fought with temptation.

Go back to 1105? Let Metaxas insinuate me into the Ducas household? Bed Pulcheria and ease my yearnings? No. No. No. No.

Fight temptation. Sublimate. Fuck an empress instead.

I hurried back to Istanbul and shunted up the line to 537. I went over to Haghia Sophia to look for Metaxas at the dedication ceremony.

Metaxas was there, in many parts of the throng. I spotted at least ten of him. (I also saw two Jud Elliotts, and I wasn't half trying.) On my first two approaches, though, I ran into the Paradox of

Discontinuity; neither Metaxas knew me. One shook me off with a scowl of irritation, and the other simply said, "Whoever you are, we haven't met yet. Beat it." On the third try I found a Metaxas who recognized me, and we arranged to meet that evening at the inn where he was lodging his tour. He was staying down the line in 610 to show his people the coronation of Emperor Heraclius.

"Well?" he said. "What's your now-time basis, anyway?"

"Early December, 2059."

"I'm ahead of you," said Metaxas. "I'm out of the middle of February, 2060. We're discontinuous."

That scared me. This man knew two and a half months of my future. Etiquette required him to keep his knowledge to himself; it was quite possible that I would be/had been killed in January, 2060, and that this Metaxas knew all the details, but he couldn't drop a hint of that to this me. Still, the gap frightened me.

He saw it. "Do you want to go back and find a different one?" he asked.

"No. That's all right. I think we can manage."

His face was a frozen mask. He played by the rules; neither by inflection nor expression was he going to react to anything I said in a way that might reveal my own future to me.

"You once said you'd help me get into Empress Theodora."

"I remember that, yes."

"I turned you down then. Now I'd like to try her."

"No problem," said Metaxas. "Let's jump up to 535. Justinian will be preoccupied with building Haghia Sophia. Theodora's available."

"How easily?"

"Nothing to it," he said.

We shunted. On a cool spring day in 535 I went with Metaxas to the Great Palace, where he sought and found a plump, eunuchoid individual named Anastasius and had a long, animated discussion with him. Evidently Anastasius was chief procurer to the empress this year, and had the responsibility of finding her anywhere from one to ten young men a night. The conversation was carried on in low muttered tones, punctuated by angry outbursts, but from what

Up the Line

I could hear of it I gathered that Anastasius was offering me an hour with Theodora, and that Metaxas was holding out for a whole night. I felt edgy about that. Virile I am, yes, but would I be able to entertain one of history's most celebrated nymphomaniacs from darkness to dawn? I signaled to Metaxas to accept something less grandiose, but he persisted, and in the end Anastasius agreed to let me have four hours with the empress.

"If he qualifies," the plump one said.

The test for qualification was administered by a ferocious little wench named Photia, one of the imperial ladies in waiting. Anastasius complacently watched us in action; Metaxas at least had the good taste to leave the room. Watching, I guess, was how Anastasius got his kickies.

Photia was black-haired, thin-lipped, busty, voracious. Have you ever seen a starfish devour an oyster? No? Well, imagine it, anyway. Photia was a starfish of sex. The suction was fantastic. I stayed with her, wrestled her into submission, pronged her off to ecstasy. And—I suppose—I passed my test with something to spare, because Anastasius gave me his seal of approval and set up my assignation with Theodora. Four hours.

I thanked Metaxas and he left, jumping down to his tour in 610.

Anastasius took charge of me. I was bathed, groomed, curried, required to swallow an oily, bitter potion that he claimed was an aphrodisiac. And an hour before midnight I was ushered into the bedchambers of the Empress Theodora.

Cleopatra... Delilah... Harlow... Lucrezia Borgia... Theodora...

Had any of them ever existed? Was their legendary wantonness real? Could this truly be Judson Daniel Elliott III standing before the bed of the depraved Empress of Byzantium?

I knew the tales Procopius told of her. The orgies at dinners of state. The exhibitionist performances in the theater. The repeated illegitimate pregnancies and the annual abortions. The friends and lovers betrayed and tortured. The severed ears, noses, testicles, penes, limbs, and lips of those who displeased her. The offerings on the altar of Aphrodite of every orifice she owned. If only one story out of ten were true, her vileness was unequaled.

She was pale, fair-skinned, big-breasted, narrow-waisted, and surprisingly short, the top of her head barely reaching my chest. Perfumes drenched her skin, yet unmistakable fleshy reeks came through. Her eyes were fierce, cold, hard, slightly hyperthyroid: nymphomaniacal eyes.

She didn't ask my name. She ordered me to strip, and inspected me, and nodded. A wench brought us thick greasy wine in an enormous amphora. We drank a good deal of it, and then Theodora anointed herself with the rest, coating her skin with it from forehead to toes.

"Lick it off," she said.

I obeyed. I obeyed other commands too. Her tastes were remarkably various, and in my four hours I satisfied most of them. It may not have been the kinkiest four hours I ever spent, but came close. And yet her pyrotechnics chilled me. There was something mechanical and empty about the way Theodora presented now this, now that, now the other thing, for me to deal with. It was as if she were running through a script that she had played out a million times.

It was interesting in a strenuous way. But it wasn't overwhelming. I mean, I expected more, somehow, from being in bed with one of history's most famous sinners.

When I was fourteen years old, an old man who taught me a great deal about the way of the world said to me, "Son, when you've jazzed one snatch you've jazzed them all."

I was barely out of my virginity then, but I dared to disagree with him. I still do, in a way, but less and less each year. Women do vary—in figure, in passion, in technique, in approach. But I've had the Empress of Byzantium, mind you, Theodora herself. I'm beginning to think, after Theodora, that that old man was right. When you've jazzed one snatch you've jazzed them all.

I went back down to Istanbul and reported for duty, and took a party of eight out on the two-week tour.

Up the Line

Neither the Black Death nor Theodora had burned away my passion for Pulcheria Ducas. I hoped now that I'd shake free of that dangerous obsession by getting back to work.

My tour group included the following people:

J. Frederick Gostaman of Biloxi, Mississippi, a retail dealer in pharmaceuticals and transplant organs, along with his wife, Louise, his sixteen-year-old daughter Palmyra, and his fourteen-year-old son Bilbo.

Conrad Sauerabend of St. Louis, Missouri, a stockbroker, traveling alone.

Miss Hester Pistil of Brooklyn, New York, a young schoolteacher.

Leopold Haggins of St. Petersburg, Florida, a retired manufacturer of power cores, and his wife Chrystal.

In short, the usual batch of overcapitalized and undereducated idlers. Sauerabend, who was fat and jowly and sullen, took an immediate dislike to Gostaman, who was fat and jowly and jovial, because Gostaman made a joking remark about the way Sauerabend was peering down the neckline of Gostaman's daughter at one of our orientation sessions. I think Gostaman was joking, anyway, but Sauerabend got red-faced and furious, and Palmyra, who though sixteen was underdeveloped enough to pass for a skinny thirteen, ran out of the room in tears. I patched things up, but Sauerabend continued to glare at Gostaman. Miss Pistil, the schoolteacher, who was a vacant-eyed blonde with an augmented bosom and an expression that managed to be both tense and languid, established at our first meeting that she is the sort of girl who takes these trips in order to get laid by Couriers; even if I hadn't been preoccupied with Pulcheria, I don't think I'd have taken advantage of her availability, but as things stood I felt very little urge to explore Miss Pistil's pelvis. This was not the case with young Bilbo Gostaman, who was such a fashion-plate that he was wearing knickers with padded groin (if they can revive Cretan bodices, why not the codpiece?) and who got his hand under Miss Pistil's skirt during our second orientation session. He thought he was being surreptitious about it, but I saw him, and so did old man Gostaman, who beamed in paternal pride, and so did Mrs. Chrystal Haggins, who was shocked into catalepsy. Miss Pistil looked thrilled, and squirmed a little to afford Bilbo a better angle for groping. Mr. Leopold Haggins, who was eighty-five and pretty leathery, meanwhile winked hopefully at Mrs. Louise Gostaman, a placid and matronly sort of woman who was destined to spend most of our tour fighting off the old scoundrel's quivering advances. You can see how it was.

Off we went for two happy weeks together.

I was, again, a second-rate Courier. I couldn't summon up the divine spark. I showed them everything I was supposed to show them, but I wasn't able to do the extra things, the leaping, cavorting, charismatic, Metaxian things, that I had vowed I would do on every trip.

Part of the trouble was my edginess over the Pulcheria situation. She danced in and out of my mind a thousand times a day. I pictured myself dropping down to 1105 or thereabouts and getting to work with her; surely she'd remember me from the spice shop, and surely that was an open invitation she had given me then.

Part of the trouble was the ebbing of my own sense of wonder. I had been on the Byzantium run for almost half a year, and the thrill was gone. A gifted Courier—a Metaxas—could derive as much excitement from his thousandth imperial coronation as from his third. And transmit that excitement to his people. Maybe I just wasn't a naturally gifted Courier. I was becoming bored with the dedication of Haghia Sophia and the baptism of Theodosius II, the way an usher in a stimmo house gets weary of watching orgies.

Part of the trouble was the presence of Conrad Sauerabend in the group. That fat, sweaty, untidy man was an instant turnoff for me every time he opened his mouth.

He wasn't stupid. But he was gross and coarse and crude. He was a leerer, a gaper, a gawker. I could count on him to make some blunt and inappropriate remark anywhere.

At the Augusteum he whistled and said, "What a parking lot this would make!"

Inside Haghia Sophia he clapped a white-bearded priest on the back and said, "I just got to tell you what a swell church you got here, priesto."

Up the Line

During a visit to the icon-smashings of Leo the Isaurian, when Byzantium's finest works of art were being destroyed as idols, he interrupted an earnest iconoclastic fanatic and said, "Don't be such a dumb prick. You know that you're hurting this city's tourist trade?"

Sauerabend was also a molester of little girls, and proud of it. "I can't help it," he explained. "It's my particular personal clutchup. The shrink calls it the Lolita complex. I like 'em twelve, thirteen years old. You know, old enough to bleed, maybe to have a little hair on it, but still kind of unripe. Get 'em before the tits grow, that's my ideal. I can't stand all that swinging meat on a woman. Pretty sick, huh?"

Pretty sick, yes. And also pretty annoying, because we had Palmyra Gostaman with us; Sauerabend couldn't stop staring at her. The lodgings provided on a time-tour don't always give the tourists much privacy, and Sauerabend ogled the poor girl into despair. He drooled over her constantly, forcing her to dress and undress under a blanket as if this was the nineteenth or twentieth century; and when her father wasn't looking, he'd get his fat paws on her behind or the little bumps of her breasts and whisper lewd propositions in her ear. Finally I had to tell him that if he didn't stop bothering her, I'd bounce him from the tour. That settled him down for a few days. The girl's father, incidentally, thought the whole incident was very funny. "Maybe what that girl needs is a good banging," he said to me. "Get the body juices flowing, huh?" Papa Gostaman also approved of his son Bilbo's affair with Miss Pistil, which also became a nuisance, since we wasted a terrific amount of time waiting for them to finish their current copulations. I'd be giving a preliminary talk on what we were to see this morning, get me, and Bilbo would be standing behind Miss Pistil, and suddenly she'd get this transfigured look on her face and I'd know he'd done it again, up with her skirt in back, *wham!* Bilbo looked pleased as hell all the time, which I suppose was reasonable enough for a fourteen-year-old boy having an affair with a woman ten years his senior. Miss Pistil looked guilty. Her sore conscience, though, didn't keep her from opening the gate for Bilbo three or four times a day.

I didn't find all this conducive to creative Couriering.

Then there were minor annoyances, such as the ineffectual lecheries of old Mr. Haggins, who persecuted the dim Mrs. Gostaman mercilessly. Or the insistence of Sauerabend on fiddling around with his timer. "You know," he said several times, "I bet I could ungimmick this thing so I could run it myself. Used to be an engineer, you know, before I took up stockbroking." I told him to leave his timer alone. Behind my back, he went on tinkering with it.

Still another headache was Capistrano, whom I met by chance in 1097 while Bohemond's Crusaders were entering Constantinople. He showed up while I was concentrating on the replay of the Marge Hefferin scene. I wanted to see how permanent my correction of the past had been.

This time I lined my people up on the opposite side of the street. Yes, there I was; and there was Marge, eager and impatient and hot for Bohemond; and there was the rest of the group. As the Crusaders paraded toward us, I felt almost dizzy with suspense. Would I see myself save Marge? Or would I see Marge leap toward Bohemond and be cut down? Or would some third alternative unreel? The fluidity, the mutability, of the time stream, that was what terrified me now.

Bohemond neared. Marge was undoing her tunic. Heavy creamy breasts were visible. She tensed and readied herself for the dash into the street. And a second Jud Elliott materialized out of nowhere across the way, right behind her. I saw the look of shock on Marge's face as my alter ego's steely fingers clamped tight to her ass. I saw his hand splay wide to seize her breast. I saw her whirl, struggle, sag; and as Bohemond went by, I saw myself vanish, leaving only the two of me, one on each side of the processional avenue.

I was awash with relief. Yet I was also troubled, because I knew now that my editing of this scene was embedded in the time-flow for anyone to see. Including some passing Time Patrolman, perhaps, who might happen to observe the brief presence of a doubled Courier and wonder what was going on. At any time in the next million millennia the Patrol might monitor that scene—and then, no matter if it went undiscovered until the year 8,000,000,000,008, I would be called to account for my unauthorized correction of the record.

I could expect to feel the hand on my shoulder, the voice calling my name—I felt a hand on my shoulder. A voice called my name.

I spun around. *"Capistrano!"*

"Sure, Capistrano. Did you expect someone else?"

"I—I—you surprised me, that's all." I was shaking. My knees were watery.

I was so upset that it took me a few seconds to realize how awful Capistrano looked.

He was frayed and haggard; his glossy dark hair was graying and stringy; he had lost weight and looked twenty years older than the Capistrano I knew. I sensed discontinuity and felt the fear that I always felt when confronted with someone out of my own future. "What's the trouble?" I asked.

"I'm coming apart. Breaking up. Look, there's my tour over there." He indicated a clump of time-travelers who peered intently at the Crusaders. "I can't stay with them anymore. They sicken me. Everything sickens me. It's the end for me, Elliott, absolutely the end."

"Why? What's wrong?"

"I can't talk about it here. When are you staying tonight?"

"Right here in 1097. The inn by the Golden Horn."

"I'll see you at midnight," Capistrano said. He clutched my arm for a moment. "It's the end, Elliott. Really the end. God have mercy on my soul!"

43

Capistrano appeared at the inn just before midnight. Under his cloak he carried a lopsided bottle, which he uncorked and handed to me. "Cognac," he said. "From 1825, bottled in 1775. I just brought it up the line."

I tasted it. He slumped down in front of me. He looked worse than ever: old, drained, hollow. He took the cognac from me and gulped it greedily.

"Before you say anything," I told him, "I want to know what your now-time basis is. Discontinuities scare me."

"There's no discontinuity."

"There isn't?"

"My basis is December, 2059. The same as yours."

"Impossible!"

"Impossible?" he repeated. "How can you say that?"

"Last time I saw you, you weren't even forty. Now you're easily past fifty. Don't fool me, Capistrano. Your basis is somewhere in 2070, isn't it? And if it is, for God's sake don't tell me anything about the years still ahead for me!"

"My basis is 2059," said Capistrano in a ragged voice. I realized from the thickness of his tone that this bottle of cognac was not the first for him tonight. "I am no older now than I ought to be, for you," he said. "The trouble is that I'm a dead man."

"I don't understand."

"Last month I told you of my great-grandmother, the Turk?"

"Yes."

"This morning I went down the line to Istanbul of 1955. My great-grandmother was then seventeen years old and unmarried. In a moment of wild despair I choked her and threw her into the Bosphorus. It was at night, in the rain; no one saw us. I am dead, Elliott. Dead."

"No, Capistrano!"

"I told you, long ago, that when the time came, I would make my exit that way. A Turkish slut—she who beguiled my great-grandfather into a shameful marriage —gone now. And so am I. Once I return to now-time, I have never existed. What shall I do, Elliott? You decide. Shall I jump down the line now and end the comedy?"

Sweating, I said, after a deep pull of the cognac, "Give me the exact date of your stopoff in 1955. I'll go down the line right now and keep you from harming her."

"You will not."

"Then you do it. Arrive in the nick of time and save her, Capistrano!"

He looked at me sadly. "What's the point? Sooner or later I'll kill her again. I have to. It's my destiny. I'm going to shunt down now. Will you look after my people?"

"I've got a tour of my own," I reminded him.

"Of course. Of course. You can't handle more. Just see that mine aren't stranded. I have to go—have to—" His hand was on his timer.

"*Capis—*"

He took the cognac with him when he jumped.

Gone. Extinct. A victim of suicide by timecrime. Blotted out of history's pages. I didn't know how to handle the situation. Suppose I went down to 1955 and prevented him from murdering his great-grandmother. He was already a nonperson in now-time; could I retroactively restore him to existence? How did the Paradox of Transit Displacement function in reverse? This was a case I had not studied. I wanted to do whatever was best for Capistrano; I also had his stranded tourists to think about.

I brooded over it for an hour. Finally I came to a sane if not romantic conclusion: this is none of my business, I decided, and I'd better call in the Time Patrol. Reluctantly I touched the alarm stud on my timer, the signal which is supposed to summon a Patrolman at once.

Instantly a Patrolman materialized. Dave Van Dam, the belching blond boor I had met on my first day in Istanbul.

"So?" he said.

"Timecrime suicide," I told him. "Capistrano just murdered his great-grandmother and jumped back to now-time."

"Son of a goddam bitch. Why do we have to put up with these unstable motherfuckers?"

I didn't bother to tell him that his choice of obscenity was inappropriate. I said, "He also left a party of tourists marooned here. That's why I called you in."

Van Dam spat elaborately. "Son of a goddam bitch," he said again. "Okay, I'm with it." He timed out of my room.

I was sick with grief over the stupid waste of a valuable life. I thought of Capistrano's charm, his grace, his sensitivity, all squandered because in a drunken moment of misery he had to timecrime himself. I didn't weep, but I felt like kicking furniture around, and I did. The noise woke up Miss Pistil, who gasped and murmured, "Are we being attacked?"

"You are," I said, and to ease my rage and anguish I dropped down on her bed and rammed myself into her. She was a little startled, but began to cooperate once she realized what was up. I came in half a minute and left her, throbbing, to be finished off by Bilbo Gostaman. Still in a black mood, I awakened the innkeeper and demanded his best wine, and drank myself into a foggy stupor.

Much later I learned that my dramatics had all been pointless. That slippery bastard Capistrano had had a change of heart at the last minute. Instead of shunting to 2059 and obliterating himself, he clung to his Transit Displacement invulnerability and stayed up the line in 1600, marrying a Turkish pasha's daughter and fathering three kids on her. The Time Patrol didn't succeed in tracing him until 1607, at which point they picked him up for multiple timecrime, hoisted him down to 2060, and sentenced him to obliteration. So he got his exit anyway, but not in a very heroic way. The Patrol also had to un-murder Capistrano's great-grandmother, unmarry him from the pasha's daughter in 1600, and uncreate those three kids, as well as find and rescue his stranded tourists, so all in all he was a great deal of trouble for everybody. "If a man wants to commit suicide," said Dave Van Dam, "why in hell can't he just drink carniphage in now-time and make it easier on the rest of us?" I had to agree. It was the only time in my life when the Time Patrol and I saw things the same way.

44

The mess over Capistrano and the general unsavoriness of this batch of tourists combined to push me into abysses of gloom.

I moved grimly along from epoch to epoch, but my heart wasn't in it. And by the time, midway through the second week, that we reached 1204, I knew I was going to do something disastrous.

Doggedly I delivered the usual orientation lecture.

"The old spirit of the Crusaders is reviving," I said, scowling at Bilbo, who was fondling Miss Pistil again, and scowling at Sauerabend, who was visibly dreaming of Palmyra Gostaman's

Up the Line

meager breasts. "Jerusalem, which the Crusaders conquered a century ago, has been recaptured by the Saracens, but various Crusader dynasties still control most of the Mediterranean coast of the Holy Land. The Arabs now are feuding among themselves, and since 1199, Pope Innocent III has been calling for a new Crusade."

I explained how various barons answered the Pope's call.

I told how the Crusaders were unwilling to make the traditional land journey across all of Europe and down through Asia Minor into Syria. I told how they preferred to go by sea, landing at one of the Palestinian ports.

I discussed how in 1202 they applied to Venice, Europe's leading naval power of the time, for transportation.

I described the terms by which the ancient and crafty Doge Enrico Dandolo of Venice agreed to provide ships.

"Dandolo," I said, "contracted to transport 4,500 knights with their horses, 9,000 squires, and 20,000 infantrymen, along with nine months' provisions. He offered to throw in fifty armed galleys to escort the convoy. For these services he asked 85,000 silver marks, or about $20,000,000 in our money. Plus half of all the territory or treasure that the Crusaders won in battle."

I told how the Crusaders agreed to this stiff price, planning to cheat the blind old Doge.

I told how the blind old Doge, once he had the Crusaders hung up in Venice, gripped them by the throats until they paid him every mark due him.

I told how the venerable monster seized control of the Crusade and set off in command of the fleet on Easter Monday, 1203—heading not for the Holy Land but for Constantinople.

"Byzantium," I said, "is Venice's great maritime rival. Dandolo doesn't care warm spit for Jerusalem, but wants very badly to get control of Constantinople."

I explicated the dynastic situation. The Comnenus dynasty had come to a bad end. When Manuel II died in 1180, his successor was his young son Alexius H, who shortly was murdered by his father's amoral cousin, Andronicus. The elegantly depraved Andronicus was himself destroyed in a particularly ghastly way by an enraged mob, after he had ruled harshly for a few years, and in 1185 there came to the throne Isaac Angelus, an elderly and bumbling grandson of Alexius I, by the female line. Isaac ruled for ten haphazard years, until he was dethroned, blinded, and imprisoned by his brother, who became Emperor Alexius III.

"Alexius III still rules," I said, "and Isaac Angelus is still in prison. But Isaac's son, also Alexius, has escaped and is in Venice. He has promised Dandolo huge sums of money if Dandolo will restore his father to the throne. And so Dandolo is coming to Constantinople to overthrow Alexius III and make Isaac into an imperial puppet."

They didn't follow the intricacy of it. I didn't care. They'd figure it out as they saw things taking place.

I showed them the Fourth Crusade arriving at Constantinople at the end of June, 1203. I let them see Dandolo directing the capture of Scutari, Constantinople's suburb on the Asian side of the Bosphorus. I pointed out how the entrance to the port of Constantinople was guarded by a great tower and twenty Byzantine galleys, and blocked by a huge iron chain. I called their attention to the scene in which Venetian sailors boarded and took the Byzantine galleys while one of Dandolo's ships, equipped with monstrous steel shears, cut through the chain and opened the Golden Horn to the invaders. I allowed them to watch the superhuman Dandolo, ninety years old, lead the attackers over the ramparts of Constantinople. "Never before," I said, "have invaders broken into this city."

From a distance, part of a cheering mob, we watched Dandolo bring Isaac Angelus forth from his dungeon and name him Emperor of Byzantium, with his son crowned as co-emperor, by the style of Alexius IV.

"Alexius IV," I said, "now invites the Crusaders to spend the winter in Constantinople at his expense, preparing for their attack on the Holy Land. It is a rash offer. It dooms him."

We shunted down the line to the spring of 1204.

"Alexius IV," I said, "has discovered that housing thousands of Crusaders is bankrupting Byzantium. He tells Dandolo that he is out of money and will no longer underwrite their expenses. A furious dispute begins. While it proceeds, a fire starts in the city. No one knows who caused it, but Alexius suspects the Venetians. He sets seven decrepit ships on fire and lets them drift into the Venetian fleet. Look."

We saw the fire. We saw the Venetians using boat-hooks to drag the blazing hulks away from their own ships. We saw sudden revolution break out in Constantinople, the Byzantines denouncing Alexius IV as the tool of Venice, and putting him to death. "Old Isaac Angelus dies a few days later," I said. "The Byzantines find the son-in-law of the expelled Emperor Alexius III, and put him on the throne as Alexius V. This son-in-law is a member of the famous Ducas family. Dandolo has lost both his puppet emperors, and he is furious. The Venetians and the Crusaders decide now to conquer Constantinople and rule it themselves."

Once again I took a pack of tourists through scenes of battle as, on April 8, the struggle began. Fire, slaughter, rape, Alexius V in flight, the invaders plundering the city. April 13, in Haghia Sophia: Crusaders demolish the choir stalls with their twelve columns of silver, and pull apart the altar, and seize forty chalices and scores of silver candelabra. They take the Gospel, and the Crosses, and the altar cloth, and forty incense burners of pure gold. Boniface of Montferrat, the leader of the Crusade, seizes the imperial palace. Dandolo takes the four great bronze horses that the Emperor Constantine had brought from Egypt 900 years before; he will carry them to Venice and place them over the entrance to St. Mark's Cathedral, where they still are. The priests of the Crusaders scurry after relics: two chunks of the True Cross, the head of the Holy Lance, the nails that had held Christ on the Cross, and many similar objects, long revered by the Byzantines.

From the scenes of plunder we jumped to mid-May.

"A new Emperor of Byzantium is to be elected," I said. "He will not be a Byzantine. He will be a westerner, a Frank, a Latin. The conquerors choose Count Baldwin of Flanders. We can see his coronation procession."

We waited outside Haghia Sophia. Within, Baldwin of Flanders is donning a mantle covered with jewels and embroidered with eagle figures; he is handed a scepter and a golden orb; he kneels before the altar and is anointed; he is crowned; he mounts the throne.

"Here he comes," I said.

On a white horse, clad in glittering clothes that blaze as if on fire, Emperor Baldwin of Byzantium rides forth from the cathedral to the palace. Unwillingly, sullenly, the people of Byzantium pay homage to their alien master.

"Most of the Byzantine nobility has fled," I told my tourists, who were yearning for more battles, more fires. "The aristocracy has scattered to Asia Minor, to Albania, to Bulgaria, to Greece. For fifty-seven years the Latins will rule here, though Emperor Baldwin's reign will be brief. In ten months he will lead an army against Byzantine rebels and will be captured by them, never to return."

Chrystal Haggins said, "When do the Crusaders go to Jerusalem?"

"Not these. They never bother to go. Some of them stay here, ruling pieces of the former Byzantine Empire. The rest go home stuffed with Byzantine loot."

"How fascinating," said Mrs. Haggins.

We went to our lodgings. A terrible weariness had me in its grip. I had done my job; I had shown them the Latin conquest of Byzantium, as advertised in the brochures. Suddenly I couldn't stand their faces any longer. We dined, and they went to sleep, or at least to bed. I stood a while, listening to the passionate groans of Miss Pistil and the eager snorts of Bilbo Gostaman, listening to the protests of Palmyra as Conrad Sauerabend sneakily stroked her thighs in the dark, and then I choked back tears of fury and surrendered to my temptations, and touched my timer, and shunted up the line. To 1105. To Pulcheria Ducas.

45

Metaxas, as always, was glad to help.

"It'll take a few days," he said. "Communications are slow here. Messengers going back and forth."

"Should I wait here?"

Up the Line

"Why bother?" Metaxas asked. "You've got a timer. Jump down three days, and maybe by then everything will be arranged."

I jumped down three days. Metaxas said, "Everything is arranged."

He had managed to get me invited to a soiree at the Ducas palace. Just about everyone of importance would be there, from Emperor Alexius Comnenus down. As my cover identity, I was to claim that I was Metaxas' cousin from the provinces, from Epirus. "Speak with a backwoods accent," Metaxas instructed me. "Dribble wine on your chin and make noises when you chew. Your name will be—ah—Nicetas Hyrtacenus."

I shook my head. "Too fancy. It isn't *me*."

"Well then, George Hyrtacenus?"

"George Markezinis," I said.

"It sounds too twentieth century."

"To them it'll sound provincial," I said, and as George Markezinis I went to the Ducas soiree.

Outside the gleaming marble walls of the Ducas palace I saw two dozen Varangian guards stationed. The presence of these yellow-bearded Norse barbarians, the core of the imperial bodyguard, told me that Alexius was already within. We entered. Metaxas had brought his fair and wanton ancestress Eudocia to the party.

Within, a dazzling scene. Musicians. Slaves. Tables heaped with food. Wine. Gorgeously dressed men and women. Superb mosaic floors; tapestried walls, heavy with cloth of gold. The tinkle of sophisticated laughter; the shimmer of female flesh beneath nearly transparent silks.

I saw Pulcheria at once.

Pulcheria saw me.

Our eyes met, as they had met in the shop of sweets and spices, and she recognized me, and smiled enigmatically, and again the current surged between us. In a later era she would have fluttered her fan at me. Here, she withdrew her jeweled gloves and slapped them lightly across her left wrist. Some token of encouragement? She wore a golden circlet on her high, smooth forehead. Her lips were rouged.

"That's her husband to her left," Metaxas whispered. "Come. I'll introduce you."

I stared at Leo Ducas, my great-great-great-multi-great-grandfather, and my pride in having so distinguished an ancestor was tinged by the envy I felt for this man, who each night caressed the breasts of Pulcheria.

He was, I knew from my genealogical studies, thirty-five years old, twice the age of his wife. A tall man, graying at the temples, with unByzantine blue eyes, a neatly clipped little beard, a high-bridged, narrow nose, and thin, tightly compressed lips, he seemed austere, remote, unutterably dignified. I suspected that he might be boringly noble. He did make an impressive sight, and there was no austerity about his tunic of fine cut, nor about his jewelry, his rings and pendants and pins.

Leo presided over the gathering in serene style, befitting a man who was one of the premier nobles of the realm, and who headed his branch of the great house of Ducas. Of course, Leo's house was empty, and perhaps that accounted for the faint trace of despair that I imagined I saw on his handsome face. As Metaxas and I approached him, I picked up a stray exchange of conversation from two court ladies to my left:

"...no children, and such a pity, when all of Leo's brothers have so many. And he the eldest!"

"Pulcheria's still young, though. She looks as if she'll be a good breeder."

"If she ever gets started. Why, she's close to eighteen!"

I wanted to reassure Leo, to tell him that his seed would descend even unto the twenty-first century, to let him know that in only a year's time Pulcheria would give him a son, Nicetas, and then Simeon, John, Alexander, and more, and that Nicetas would sire six children, among them the princely Nicephorus whom I had seen seventy years down the line, and the son of Nicephorus would follow an exiled leader into Albania, and then, and then, and then—

Metaxas said, "Your grace, this is my mother's sister's third son, George Markezinis, of Epirus, now a guest at my villa during the harvest season."

"You've come a long way," said Leo Ducas. "Have you been to Constantinople before?"

"Never," I said. "A wonderful city! The churches! The palaces! The bathhouses! The food, the wine, the clothes! The women, the beautiful women!"

Pulcheria glowed. She gave me that sidewise smile of hers again, on the side away from her husband. I knew she was mine. The sweet fragrance of her drifted toward me. I began to ache and throb.

Leo said, "You know the emperor, of course?"

With a grand sweep of his arm he indicated Alexius, holding court at the far end of the room. I had seen him before: a short, stocky man of clearly imperial bearing. A circle of lords and ladies surrounded him. He seemed gracious, sophisticated, relaxed in manner, the true heir to the Caesars, the defender of civilization in these dark times. At Leo's insistence I was presented to him. He greeted me warmly, crying out that the cousin of Metaxas was as dear to him as Metaxas himself. We talked for a while, the emperor and I; I was nervous, but I carried myself well, and Leo Ducas said, finally, "You speak with emperors as though you've known a dozen of them, young man."

I smiled. I did not say that I had several times glimpsed Justinian, that I had attended the baptisms of Theodosius II, Constantine V, the yet unborn Manuel Comnenus, and many more, that I had knelt in Haghia Sophia not far from Constantine XI on Byzantium's last night, that I had watched Leo the Isaurian direct the iconoclasms. I did not say that I was one of the many pluggers of the hungry hole of the Empress Theodora, five centuries previously. I looked shy and said, "Thank you, your grace."

46

Byzantine parties consisted of music, a dance of slavegirls, some dining, and a great deal of wine. The night wore on; the candles burned low; the assembled notables grew tipsy. In the gathering darkness I mingled easily with members of the famed families, meeting men and women named Comnenus, Phocas, Skleros, Dalassenes, Diogenes, Botaniates, Tzimisces and Ducas. I made courtly conversation and impressed myself with my glibness. I watched arrangements for adultery being made subtly, but not subtly enough, behind the backs of drunken husbands. I bade goodnight to Emperor Alexius and received an invitation to visit him at Blachernae, just up the road. I fended off Metaxas' Eudocia, who had had too much to drink and wanted a quick balling in a back room. (She finally selected one Basil Diogenes, who must have been seventy years old.) I answered, evasively, a great many questions about my "cousin" Metaxas, whom everybody knew, but whose origins were a mystery to all. And then, three hours after my arrival, I found that I was at last speaking with Pulcheria.

We stood quietly together in an angle of the great hall. Two flickering candles gave us light. She looked flushed, excited, even agitated; her breasts heaved and a line of sweat-beads stippled her upper lip. I had never beheld such beauty before.

"Look," she said. "Leo dozes. He loves his wine more than most other things."

"He must love beauty," I said. "He has surrounded himself with so much of it."

"Flatterer!"

"No. I try to speak the truth."

"You don't often succeed," she said. "Who are you?"

"Markezinis of Epirus, cousin to Metaxas."

"That tells me very little. I mean, what are you looking for in Constantinople?"

I took a deep breath. "To fulfill my destiny, by finding the one whom I am meant to find, the one whom I love."

That got through to her. Seventeen-year-old girls are susceptible to that kind of thing, even in Byzantium, where girls mature early and marry at twelve. Call me Heathcliff.

Pulcheria gasped, crossed her arms chastely over the high mounds of her breasts, and shivered. I think her pupils may have momentarily dilated.

"It's impossible," she said.

"Nothing's impossible."

"My husband—"

"Asleep," I said. "Tonight—under this roof—"
"No. We can't."
"You're trying to fight destiny, Pulcheria."
"George!"
"A bond holds us together—a bond stretching across all of time—"
"Yes, George!"

Easy, now, great-great-multi-great-grandson, don't talk too much. It's cheap timecrime to brag that you're from the future.

"This was fated," I whispered. "It had to be!"
"Yes! Yes!"
"Tonight."
"Tonight, yes."
"Here."
"Here," said Pulcheria.
"Soon."
"When the guests leave. When Leo is in bed. I'll have you hidden in a room where it's safe—I'll come to you—"
"You knew this would happen," I said, "that day when we met in the shop."
"Yes. I knew. Instantly. What magic did you work on me?"
"None, Pulcheria. The magic rules us both. Drawing us together, shaping this moment, spinning the strands of destiny toward our meeting, upsetting the boundaries of time itself—"
"You speak so strangely, George. So beautifully. You must be a poet!"
"Perhaps."
"In two hours you'll be mine."
"And you mine," I said. "And for always."

I shivered, thinking of the Time Patrol swordlike above me. "For always, Pulcheria."

47

She spoke to a servant, telling him that the young man from Epirus had had too much to drink, and wished to lie down in one of the guest chambers. I acted appropriately woozy. Metaxas found me and wished me well. Then I made a candlelight pilgrimage through the maze of the Ducas palace and was shown to a simple room somewhere far in the rear. A low bed was the only article of furniture. A rectangular mosaic in the center of the floor was the only decoration. The single narrow window admitted a shaft of moonlight. The servant brought me a washbasin of water, wished me a good night's rest, and let me alone. I waited a billion years.

Sounds of distant revelry floated to me. Pulcheria did not come.

It's all a joke, I thought. A hoax. The young but sophisticated mistress of the house is having some fun with the country cousin. She'll let me fidget and fret in here alone until morning, and then send a servant to give me breakfast and show me out. Or maybe after a couple of hours she'll tell one of her slavegirls to come in here and pretend she's Pulcheria. Or send in a toothless crone, while her guests watch through concealed slots in the wall. Or—

A thousand times I considered fleeing. Just touch the timer, and shoot up the line to 1204, where Conrad Sauerabend and Palmyra Gostaman and Mr. and Mrs. Haggins and the rest of my tourists lie sleeping and unguarded.

Clear out? Now? When everything had gone so neatly so far? What would Metaxas say to me when he found out I had lost my nerve?

I remembered my guru, black Sam, asking me, "If you had a chance to attain your heart's desire, would you take it?"

Pulcheria was my heart's desire; I knew that now.

I remembered Sam Spade telling me, "You're a compulsive loser. Losers infallibly choose the least desirable alternative."

Go ahead, great-great-multi-great-grandson. Skip out of here before the luscious primordial ancestress can offer her dark musky loins to you.

I remembered Emily, the helix-parlor girl with the gift of prophecy, crying shrilly, "Beware love in Byzantium! Beware! Beware!"

I loved. In Byzantium.

Rising, I paced the room a thousand times, and stood at the door listening to the faint laughter and the far-off songs, and then

Up the Line

I removed all of my clothing, carefully folding each garment and placing it on the floor beside my bed. I stood naked except for my timer, and I debated removing that too. What would Pulcheria say when she saw that tawny plastic band at my waist? How could I explain it?

I unfastened the timer too, separating myself from it for the first time in my career up the line. Waves of real terror burst over me. I felt more naked than naked, without it; I felt stripped down to my bones. Without my timer around my hips I was the slave of time, like all these others. I had no means of quick escape. If Pulcheria planned some cruel joke and I was caught without my timer in easy reach, I was doomed.

Hastily I put the timer back on.

Then I washed myself, meticulously, everywhere, cleansing myself for Pulcheria. And stood naked beside the bed, waiting another billion years. And thought longingly of the dark swollen tips of Pulcheria's full breasts, and the softness of the skin inside her thighs. And my manhood came to life, rising to such extravagant proportions that I was both proud and embarrassed.

I didn't want Pulcheria to walk in and find me like this, beside the bed with this tree of flesh sprouting between my legs. I looked like a tipped tripod; to greet her this way was too blunt, too direct. Quickly I dressed again, feeling foolish. And waited a billion years more. And saw dawnlight beginning to blend with moonlight in my slit of a window.

And the door opened, and Pulcheria came into the room, and bolted the door behind her.

She had wiped away her heavy makeup and had taken off all her jewelry except a single gold pectoral, and she had changed from her party clothes into a light silken wrap. Even by the dim light I saw she was nude beneath and the soft curves of her body inflamed me almost to insanity. She glided toward me.

I took her in my arms and tried to kiss her. She didn't understand kissing. The posture one must adopt for mouth-to-mouth contact was alien to her. I had to arrange her. I tilted her head gently. She smiled, puzzled but willing.

Our lips touched. My tongue wiggled forth. She quivered and flattened her body tight against mine. She picked up the theory of kissing in a hurry. My hands slid down her shoulders. I drew off her wrap; she trembled a little as I bared her. I counted her breasts. Two. Rosy pink nipples. I measured her hind cheeks with my outspread hands. A good size. I ran fingertips over her thighs. Excellent thighs. I admired the two deep dimples in the small of her back. She was at once shy and wanton, a superb combination.

When I undressed, she saw the timer and touched it, plucked at it, but asked for no explanation, and her hands slipped lower. We tumbled down together on the bed.

You know, sex is really a ridiculous thing. The physical act of it, I mean. What they call "making love" in twentieth-century novels; what they call "sleeping together." I mean, consider all the literary effort that has gone into writing rhapsodies to screwing. And what does it amount to, anyway? You take this short rigid fleshy rod and you put it into the lubricated groove, and you rub it back and forth until enough of a charge is built up so that discharge is possible. Like making a fire by twirling a stick against a plank.

Really, there's nothing to it; Stick Tenon A into Mortise B. Vibrate until finished.

Look upon the act and you *know* it's preposterous. The buttocks humping up and down, the thrashing legs, the muffled groans, the speedings up and slowing down—can anything be sillier, as a central act governing human emotions?

Of course not. Yet why was this sweaty transaction with Pulcheria so important to me? (And maybe to her.)

My theory is that the real significance of sex, good sex, is a symbolic one. It's something beyond the fact that you get a tickle of "pleasure" for a short while during the ramming and butting. The same pleasure is available without the bother of finding a partner, after all, and yet it isn't the same, is it?

No, what sex is about is more than a twitch in the loins; it's a celebration of spiritual union, of mutual trust. We say to each other in bed, here, I give myself to you in the expectation that you'll give me pleasure, and I will attempt to give you pleasure too. The social contract, let's call it. And the thrill lies in the contract, not in the pleasure that is its payoff.

Also you say, here is my naked body with all its flaws, which I expose trustingly to you, knowing you will not mock it. Also you say, I accept this intimate contact with you even though I know you may transmit to me a loathsome disease. I am willing to take this risk, because you are you. And also the woman used to say—at least up until the nineteenth or early twentieth century—I will open myself to you even though there may be all sorts of biological consequences nine months from now.

All these things are much more vital than quick kickies. This is why mechanical masturbating devices have never replaced sex and never will.

This is why what happened between myself and Pulcheria Ducas on that Byzantine morning in 1105 was far more significant a transaction than what happened between myself and the Empress Theodora half a millennium earlier, and more significant than what had happened between myself and any number of girls a full millennium later. Into Theodora, into Pulcheria, and into those many girls down the line I poured roughly the same number of cubic centimeters of salty fluid; but with Pulcheria it was different. With Pulcheria, our orgasm was only the symbolic sealing of something greater. For me, Pulcheria was the embodiment of beauty and grace, and her easy surrender to me made me an emperor more mighty than Alexius, and neither the spurting of my jet nor her quiver of response mattered a tenth as much as the fact that she and I had come together in trust, in faith, in shared desire, in—love. There you have the heart of my philosophy. I stand revealed as a naked romantic. This is the profundity I've distilled from all my experience: sex with love is better than sex without love. Q.E.D. I can also show, if you like, that to be healthy is better than to be ill, and that having money is superior to being poor. My capacity for abstract thought is limitless.

48

Nevertheless, even though we had proven the philosophical point quite adequately, we went on to prove it all over again half an hour later. Redundancy is the soul of understanding.

Afterward we lay side by side, glowing sweetly. It was the moment to offer my partner a weed and share a different sort of communion, but of course that was impossible here. I felt the lack.

"Is it very different where you come from?" Pulcheria asked. "I mean, the people, how they dress, how they talk."

"Very different."

"I sense a great strangeness about you, George. Even the way you held me in bed. Not that I am an expert on such things, you must understand. You and Leo are the only men I have ever had."

"Can this be true?"

Her eyes blazed. "You take me for a whore?"

"Well, of course not, but—" I floundered. "In my country," I said desperately, "a girl takes many men before she marries. No one objects to it. It's the custom."

"Not here. We are well sheltered. I was married at twelve; that gave me little time for liberties." She frowned, sat up, leaned across me to look in my eyes. Her breasts dangled enticingly over my face. "Are women really so loose in your country?"

"Truth, Pulcheria, they are."

"But you are Byzantines! You are not barbarians from the north! How can it be allowed, this taking of so man men?"

"It's our custom." Lamely.

"Perhaps you are not truly from Epirus," she suggested. "Perhaps you come from some more distant place. I tell you again, you are very strange to me, George."

"Don't call me George. Call me Jud," I said boldly.

"Jud?"

"Jud."

"Why should I call you this?"

"It's my inner name. My *real* name, the one I *feel*. George is just—well, a name I use."

"Jud. Jud. Such a name I have never heard. You *are* from a strange land! You *are*!"

I gave her a sphinxy smile. "I love you," I said, and nibbled her nipples to change the subject.

"So strange," she murmured. "So different. And yet I felt drawn to you from the first moment. You know, I've long dreamed of being as wicked as this, but I never dared. Oh, I've had offers, dozens of offers, but it never seemed worth the trouble. And then I saw you, and I felt this fire in me, this—this hunger. Why? Tell me why?. You are neither more nor less attractive than many of the men I might have given myself to, and yet you were the one. Why?"

"It was destiny," I told her. "As I said before. An irresistible force, pulling us together, across the—"

—centuries—

"—sea," I finished lamely.

"You will come to me again?" she said.

"Again and again and again."

"I'll find ways for us to meet. Leo will never know. He spends so much of his time at the bank—you know, he's one of the directors—and in his other businesses, and with the emperor—he hardly pays attention to me. I'm one of his many pretty toys. We'll meet, Jud, and well know pleasure together often, and—" her dark eyes flashed "—and perhaps you'll give me a child."

I felt the heavens open and rain thunderbolts upon me.

"Five years of marriage and I have no child," she went on. "I don't understand. Perhaps I was too young, at first—I was so young—but now, nothing. Nothing. Give me a child, Jud. Leo will thank you for it—I mean, he'll be happy, he'll think it's his—you even have a Ducas look about you, in the eyes, perhaps, there'd be no trouble. Do you think we made a child tonight?"

"No," I said.

"No? How can you be sure?"

"I have ways," I said. I stroked her silkiness. Let me go twenty more days without my pill, though, and I could plant babies aplenty in you, Pulcheria! And knot the fabric of time beyond all unraveling. My own great-great-multi-great-grandfather? Am I seed of my own seed? Did time recurve on itself to produce me? No. I'd never get away with it. I'd give Pulcheria passion, but not parturition. "Dawn's here," I whispered.

"You'd better leave. Where can I send messages to you?"

"At Metaxas'."

"Good. We'll meet again two days hence, yes? I'll arrange everything."

"I'm yours, whenever you say it, Pulcheria."

"Two days. But now, go. I'll show you out."

"Too risky. Servants will be stirring. Go to your room, Pulcheria. I can get out by myself."

"But—impossible—"

"I know the way."

"Do you?"

"I swear it," I said.

She needed some convincing, but at length I persuaded her to spare herself the risk of getting me out of the palace. We kissed once more, and she donned her wrap, and I caught her by the arm and pulled her to me, and released her, and she went out of the room. I counted sixty seconds off. Then I set my timer and jumped six hours up the line. The party was going full blast. Casually I walked through the building, avoiding the room where my slightly earlier self, not yet admitted to Pulcheria's joyous body, was chatting with Emperor Alexius. I left the Ducas palace unnoticed. In the darkness outside, beside the sea wall along the Golden Horn, I set my timer again and shunted down the line to 1204. Now I hurried to the inn where I had left my sleeping tourists. I reached it less than three minutes after my departure—seemingly so many days ago—for Pulcheria's era.

All well. I had had my incandescent night of passion, my soul was purged of longings, and here I was, back at my trade once more, and no one the wiser. I checked the beds.

Mr. and Mrs. Haggins, yes.

Mr. and Mrs. Gostaman, yes.

Miss Pistil and Bilbo, yes.
Palmyra Gostaman, yes.
Conrad Sauerabend, yes? No.
Conrad Sauerabend—
No Sauerabend. Sauerabend was missing. His bed was empty. In those three minutes of my absence, Sauerabend had slipped away.
Where?
I felt the early pricklings of panic.

49

Calm. Calm. Stay calm. He went out to the *pissoir*, is all. He'll be right back.

Item One, a Courier must remain aware of the location of all of the tourists in his care at all times. The penalty—

I kindled a torch at the smoldering hearth and rushed out into the hall.

Sauerabend? Sauerabend?

Not pissing. Not downstairs rummaging in the kitchen. Not prowling in the wine cellar.

Sauerabend?

Where the devil are you, you pig? The taste of Pulcheria's lips was still on my own. Her sweat mingled with mine. Her juices still crisped my short hairs. All the delicious forbidden joys of transtemporal incest continued to tingle in my soul.

The Time Patrol will make a nonperson out of me for this, I thought. I'll say, "I've lost a tourist," and they'll say, "How did it happen?" and I'll say, "I stepped out of the room for three minutes and he vanished," and they'll say, "Three minutes, eh? You aren't supposed to—" and I'll say, "It was only *three minutes*. Christ, you can't expect me to watch them twenty-four hours a day!" And they'll be sympathetic, but nevertheless they'll have to check the scene, and in the replay they'll discover me wantonly shunting out for some other point on the line, and they'll track me to 1105 and find me with Pulcheria, and see that not only am I guilty of negligence as a Courier, but also that I've committed incest with my great-great-multi-great—

Calm. Calm.

Into the street now. Flash the torch around. Sauerabend? Sauerabend? No Sauerabend.

If I were a Sauerabend, where would I sneak off to?

To the home of some twelve-year-old Byzantine girl? How would he know where to find one? How to get in? No. No. He couldn't have done that. Where is he, though? Strolling through the town? Out for fresh air? He should be asleep. Snoring. No. I realized that when I left he hadn't been asleep, hadn't been snoring; he'd been bothering Palmyra Gostaman. I hurried back to the inn. There wasn't any point in roaming Constantinople at random for him.

In mounting panic I woke up Palmyra. She rubbed her eyes, complained a little, blinked. Torchlight glittered off her flat bare chest.

"Where did Sauerabend go?" I whispered harshly.

"I told him to leave me alone. I told him if he didn't stop bothering me I'd bite his thing off. He had his hand right here, and he—"

"Yes, but where did he *go*?"

"I don't know. He just got up and went away. It was dark in here. I fell asleep maybe two minutes ago. Why'd you have to wake me up?"

"Some help you are," I muttered. "Go back to sleep."

Calm, Judson, calm. There's an easy solution to this. If you weren't in such a flutter, you'd have thought about it long ago. All you have to do is edit Sauerabend back into the room, the way you edited Marge Hefferin back to life.

It's illegal, of course. Couriers are not supposed to engage in time corrections. That's for the Patrol to do. But this will be such a small correction. You can handle it quickly and no one will be the wiser. You got away with the Hefferin revision, didn't you? Yes. Yes. It's your only chance, Jud.

I sat down on the edge of my bed and tried to plan my actions properly. My night with Pulcheria had dulled the edge of my intellect. Think, Jud. Think as you never thought before.

I put great effort into my thinking.

Up the Line

What time was it when you shunted up to 1105?
Fourteen minutes to midnight.
What time was it when you came back down the line to 1204?
Eleven minutes to midnight.
What time is it now?
One minute to midnight.
When did Sauerabend slip out of the room, then?
Somewhere between fourteen to and eleven to.
Therefore, how far up the line must you shunt to intercept him?
About thirteen minutes.
You realize that if you jump back more than thirteen minutes, you'll encounter your prior self, who will be getting ready to depart for 1105? That's the Paradox of Duplication.
I've got to risk it. I'm in worse trouble than that already.
You'd better shunt, then, and get things fixed up. Here I go.

I timed my shunt perfectly, going up the line thirteen minutes less a few seconds. I noticed with satisfaction that my earlier self had already departed, and that Sauerabend had not. The ugly fat bastard was still in the room, sitting up in his bed with his back to me.

It would be simplicity itself to stop him now. I simply forbid him to leave the room, and keep him here for the next three minutes, thus canceling his departure. The instant my prior self gets back— at eleven minutes to midnight—I shunt ten minutes down the line, resuming my proper place in the stream of time. Sauerabend thus will have been continuously guarded by his Courier (in one incarnation or another) throughout the whole dangerous period from fourteen minutes to midnight onward. There will be a very slight moment of duplication for me when I overlap my returning self, but I'll clear out of his time level so fast that he probably won't notice. And all will be as it should have been.

Yes. Very good.

I started across the room toward Sauerabend, meaning to block his path when he tried to leave. He pivoted, still sitting on his bed, and saw me.

"You're back?" he said.

"You bet. And I don't—"

He put his hand to his timer and vanished.

"Wait!" I yelled, waking everybody up. "You can't do that! It's impossible! A tourist's timer doesn't—"

My voice trailed away into a foolish-sounding gargle. Sauerabend was gone, time-shunting before my eyes. Yelling at the place where he had been wouldn't bring him back. The wiliness of the loathsome slob! Fooling with his timer, boasting that he could gimmick it into working for him, somehow shorting the seal and getting access to the control—

Now I was in a terrible mess of messes. One of my own tourists on the loose with an activated timer, jumping all over anywhen—what a monstrous botch! I was desperate. The Time Patrol was bound to pick him up, of course, before he could commit too many serious time-crimes, but beyond any doubt I'd be censured for letting him get away.

Unless I could catch him before he left.

Fifty-six seconds had elapsed since I had jumped here to keep Sauerabend from leaving.

Without hesitating further, I set my timer back sixty seconds, and shunted. There was Sauerabend again, sitting on his bed. There was my other self, starting across the room toward him. There were the other sleeping tourists, not yet awakened by my shout.

Okay now. We outnumber him. We've got him.

I launched myself at Sauerabend, meaning to grab his arms and keep him from shunting.

He turned as soon as I moved. With devilish swiftness he reached down to his timer.

He shunted. He was gone. I sprawled on his empty bed, numb with shock.

The other Jud glared at me and said, "Where in hell did you come from?"

"I'm fifty-six seconds ahead of you. I missed my first chance at collaring him, and jumped back to try a second time."

"And missed again, I see."

"So I did."

"And duplicated us, besides."

"At least that part can be fixed," I said. I checked the time. "In another thirty seconds, you jump back sixty seconds and get yourself into the time-flow."

"Like crap I will," said Jud B.

"What do you mean?"

"What's the point of it? Sauerabend's going to be gone, or at least on his way. I won't be able to grab him, will I?"

"But you've *got* to go," I said.

"Why?"

"Because it's what I did at that point in the flow."

"You had a reason for it," he said. "You had just missed Sauerabend, and you wanted to jump back a minute and try catching him then. But I haven't had a chance even to miss him. Besides, why worry about the time-flow? It's already been changed."

He was right. We had run out the fifty-six seconds. Now we were at the point when I had made my first try at blocking Sauerabend's exit; but Jud B, who presumably was living through the minute I had lived through just prior to Sauerabend's first disappearance, had lived through that minute in an altogether different way from me. Everything was messed up. I had spawned a duplicate who wouldn't go away and who had nowhere to go. It was now thirteen minutes to midnight. In another two minutes we'd have a third Jud here—the one who shunted down straight from Pulcheria's arms to find Sauerabend missing in the first place. *He* had a destiny of his own: to spend ten minutes in panicky dithering, and then to jump back from one-minute-to-midnight to fourteen-minutes-to-midnight, kicking off the whole process of confusions that culminated in the two of us.

"We've got to get out of here," Jud B said.

"Before *he* comes in."

"Right. Because if he sees us, he may never get around to making his shunt back to fourteen minutes to midnight, and that—"

"—might eliminate you and me from existing."

"But where do we go?" he asked.

"We could jump back to three or four minutes ago, and try to grab Sauerabend together."

"No good. We'll overlap another of us—the one who's on his way to Pulcheria."

"So what? We'll make him get on his way as soon as we've nailed down Sauerabend."

"Still no good. Because if we miss Sauerabend again, we'll induce still another change in the time-flow, and maybe bring on a third one of us. And set up a hall of mirrors effect, banging back and forth until there are a million of us in the room. He's too quick for us with that timer."

"You're right," I said, wishing Jud B had gone back when he belonged before it was too late.

It was now twelve minutes to midnight.

"We've got sixty seconds to clear out. Where do we go?"

"We don't go back and try to grab Sauerabend again. That's definite."

"Yes."

"But we must locate him."

"Yes."

"And he could be anywhen at all."

"Yes."

"Then two of us aren't enough. We've got to get help."

"Metaxas."

"Yes. And maybe Sam."

"Yes. And how about Capistrano?"

"Is he available?"

"Who knows? We'll try. And Buonocore. And Jeff Monroe. This is a crisis!"

"Yes," I said. "Listen, we've only got ten seconds now. Come on with me!"

We rushed out of the room and down the back way, missing the arrival of the eleven-minutes-to-midnight Jud by a few seconds. We crouched in a dark alcove under the stairs, thinking about the Jud who was two flights up discovering the absence of Sauerabend. I said, "This is going to call for teamwork. You shunt up the line to 1105, find Metaxas, and explain what's happened. Then call in reinforcements and get everybody busy tracing the timeline for Sauerabend."

"What about you?"

"I'm going to stay right here," I said. "Until one minute to midnight. At that point the fellow upstairs is going to shunt back a little less than thirteen minutes to look for Sauerabend—"

"—leaving his people unguarded—"

"—yes, and somebody's got to stay with them, so I'll go back upstairs as soon as he leaves, and slip back into the main Jud Elliott identity as their Courier. And I'll stay there, proceeding on a normal basis, until I hear from you. Okay?"

"Okay."

"Get going, then."

He got going. I huddled down in a little heap, shaking with fright. It all hit me in one mighty reaction. Sauerabend was gone, and I had spawned an alter ego by the Paradox of Duplication, and in the space of one evening I had committed more timecrimes than I could name, and—

I felt like crying.

I didn't realize it, but the mess was only beginning.

At one minute to midnight I pulled myself together and went upstairs to take over the job of being the authentic Jud Elliott. As I entered the room I allowed myself the naïve hope that I'd find everything restored to the right path, with Sauerabend in his bed again. Let it have been fixed retroactively, I prayed. But Sauerabend wasn't in the room.

Did that mean that he'd never be found?

Not necessarily. Maybe, to avoid further tangles, he'd be returned to our tour slightly down the line, say in the early hours of the night, or just before dawn.

Or maybe he'd be restored to the point he jumped from—thirteen minutes or so before midnight—but I somehow wouldn't become aware of his return, through some mysterious working of the Paradox of Transit Displacement, holding me outside the whole system.

I didn't know. I didn't even *want* to know. I just wanted Conrad Sauerabend located and put back in his proper position in time, before the Patrol realized what was up and let me have it.

Sleep was out of the question. Miserably I slumped on the edge of my bed, getting up now and then to check on my tour people. The Gostamans slept on. The Hagginses slept on. Palmyra and Bilbo and Miss Pistil slept on.

At half-past two in the morning there was a light knock at the door. I leaped up and yanked it open.

Another Jud Elliott stood there.

"Who are you?" I asked morosely.

"The same one who was here before. The one who went for help. There aren't any more of us now, are there?"

"I don't think so." I stepped out into the hall with him. "Well? What's been going on?"

He was grimy and unshaven. "I've been gone for a week. We've searched all up and down the line."

"Who has?"

"Well, I went to Metaxas first, in 1105, just as you said. He's terribly concerned for our sake. What he did, first of all, was to put all his servants to work, checking to see if anybody answering to Sauerabend's description could be found in or around 1105."

"It can't hurt, I guess."

"It's worth trying," my twin agreed. "Next, Metaxas went down to now-time and phoned Sam, who came flying in from New Orleans and brought Sid Buonocore with him. Metaxas also alerted Kolettis, Gompers, Plastiras, Pappas—all the Byzantium Couriers, the whole staff. Because of discontinuity problems, we're not notifying anyone who's on an earlier now-time basis than December 2059, but that still gives us a big posse. What we're doing now, what we've been doing for the past week, is simply moving around, year by year, hunting for Sauerabend, asking questions in the marketplace, sniffing for clues. I've been at it eighteen, twenty hours a day. So have all the others. It's wonderful, how loyal they are!"

"It certainly is," I said. "What are the chances of finding him, though?"

Up the Line

"Well, we assume that he hasn't left the Constantinople area, although there's nothing to prevent him from going down the line to 2059, hopping off to Vienna or Moscow, and vanishing up the line again. All we can do is plug away. If he doesn't turn up in Byzantine, we'll check Turkish, and then pre-Byzantine, and then we'll pass the word to now-time so Couriers on other runs can watch for him, and—"

He sagged. He was exhausted.

"Look," I said, "you've got to get some rest. Why don't you go back to 1105 and settle down at Metaxas' place for a few days? Then come back here when you're rested, and let me join the search. We can alternate that way indefinitely. Meanwhile, let's keep this night in 1204 as our reference point. Whenever you jump to me, jump to this night, so we don't lose contact. It may take us a couple of lifetimes, but we'll get Sauerabend back into the group before morning comes."

"Right."

"All clear, then? You spend a few days at the villa resting up, and come back here half an hour from now. And then I'll go."

"Clear," he said, and went down to the street to jump.

I returned to the room and resumed my melancholy vigil. At three in the morning, Jud B was back, looking a new man. He had shaved, taken a bath or two, changed his clothes, obviously had had plenty of sleep. "Three days of rest at Metaxas' place," he said. "*Magnifique!*"

"You look great. *Too* great. You didn't, perhaps, sneak off to fool around with Pulcheria?"

"The thought didn't occur to me. But what if I had? You bastard, are you warning me to leave her alone?"

I said, "You don't have any right to—"

"I'm *you*, remember? You can't be jealous of yourself."

"I guess you can't," I said. "Stupid of me."

"Stupider of me," he said. "I *should* have dropped in on her while I was there."

"Well, now it's my turn. I'll put in some time on searching, then stop at the villa for rest and recuperation, and maybe have some fun with our beloved. You won't object to that, will you?"

"Fair's fair," he sighed. "She's yours as much as she's mine."

"Correct. When I've taken care of everything, I'll get back here at—let's see—quarter past three tonight. Got it?"

We synchronized our timetables for the 1105 end of the line to avoid discontinuities; I didn't want to get there while he was still there, or, worse, before he had ever arrived. Then I left the inn and shunted up the line. In 1105 I hired a chariot and was taken out to the villa on a golden autumn day. Metaxas, bleary-eyed and stubble-faced, greeted me at porch by asking, "Which one are you, A or B?"

"A. B's taking over for me at the inn in 1204. How's search going?"

"Lousy," said Metaxas. "But don't give up hope. We're with you all the way. Come inside and meet some old friends."

51

I said to them, "I'm sorry as hell to be putting you through all this trouble."

The men I respected most in the world laughed and grinned and chuckled and spat and said, "Shucks, 't'ain't nothin'."

They were frayed and grimy. They had been working hard and fruitlessly for me, and it showed. I wanted to hug all of them at once. Black Sambo, and plastic-faced Jeff Monroe, and shifty-eyed Sid Buonocore. Pappas, Kolettis, Plastiras. They had rigged a chart to mark off the places where they hadn't found Conrad Sauerabend. The chart had a lot of marks on it.

Sam said, "Don't worry, boy. We'll track him down."

"I feel so awful, making you give up free time—"

"It could have happened to any one of us," Sam said. "It wasn't your fault."

"It wasn't?"

"Sauerabend gimmicked his timer behind your back, didn't he? How could you have prevented it?" Sam grinned. "We got to help you out. We don't know when same'll happen to us."

"All for one," said Madison Jefferson Monroe. "One for all."

Up the Line

"You think you're the first Courier to have a customer skip out?" Sid Buonocore asked. "Don't be a craphead! Those timers can be rigged for manual use by anyone who understands Benchley Effect theory."

"They never told me—"

"They don't like to advertise it. But it happens. Five, six times a year, somebody takes a private time-trip behind his Courier's back."

I said, "What happens to the Courier?"

"If the Time Patrol finds out? They fire him," said Buonocore bleakly. "What we try to do is cover for each other, before the Patrol moves in. It's a bitch of a job, but we got to do it. I mean, if you don't look after one of our own when he's in trouble, who in hell will look after you?"

"Besides," said Sam, "it makes us feel like heroes." I studied the chart. They had looked for Sauerabend pretty thoroughly in early Byzantium—Constantine through the second Theodosius—and they had checked out the final two centuries with equal care. Searching the middle had so far been a matter of random investigations. Sam, Buonocore, and Monroe were coming off search duty now and were going to rest; Kolettis, Plastiras, and Pappas were getting ready to go out, and they were planning strategy.

Everybody went on being very nice to me during the discussion of ways to catch Sauerabend. I felt a real sentimental glow of warmth for them. My comrades in adversity. My companions. My colleagues. The Time Musketeers. My heart expanded. I made a little speech telling them how grateful I was for all their help. They looked embarrassed and told me once again that it was a simple matter of good fellowship, the golden rule in action. The door opened and a dusty figure stumbled in, wearing anachronistic sunglasses. Najeeb Dajani, my old mentor! He scowled, slumped down on a chair, and gestured impatiently to nobody in particular, hoping for the wine.

Kolettis handed him wine. Dajani poured some of it into his hand and used it to wash the dust from his sunglasses. Then he gulped the rest.

"Mr. Dajani!" I cried. "I didn't know they had called you in too! Listen, I want to thank you for helping—"

"You stupid prick," said Dajani quietly. "How did I ever let you get your Courier license?"

52

Dajani had just returned from a survey of the city in 630-650, with no luck at all. He was tired and irritated, and he obviously wasn't happy about spending his layoff searching for somebody else's runaway tourist.

He put out my sentimental glow in a hurry. I tried to foist on him my gratitude speech, and he said sourly, "Skip the grease job. I'm doing this because it'll reflect badly on my capabilities as an instructor if the Patrol finds out what kind of anthropoid I let loose as a Courier. It's my own hide I'm protecting."

There was a nasty moment of silence. A lot of shuffling of feet and clearing of throats took place.

"That's not very gratifying to hear," I said to Dajani.

Buonocore said, "Don't let him upset you, kid. Like I told you, any Courier's tourist is likely to gimmick his timer, and—"

"I don't refer to the loss of the tourist," said Dajani testily. "I refer to the fact that this idiot managed to duplicate himself while trying to edit the mistake!" He gargled wine. "I forgive him for the one, but not for the other."

"The duplication is pretty ugly," Buonocore admitted.

"It's a serious thing," said Kolettis.

"Bad karma," Sam said. "No telling how we'll cover that one up."

"I can't remember a case to match," declared Pappas.

"A messy miscalculation," Plastiras commented.

"Look," I said, "the duplication was an accident. I was so much in a sweat to find Sauerabend that I didn't stop to calculate the implications of—"

"We understand," Sam said.

"It's a natural error, when you're under pressure," said Jeff Monroe.

"Could have happened to anyone," Buonocore told me.

"A shame. A damned shame," murmured Pappas.

I started to feel less like an important member of a close-knit fraternity, and more like a pitied halfwit nephew who can't help leaving little puddles of mess wherever he goes. The halfwit's uncles were trying to clean up a particularly messy mess for him, and trying to keep the halfwit serene so he wouldn't make a worse mess.

When I realized what the real attitude of these men toward me was, I felt like calling in the Time Patrol, confessing my timecrimes, and requesting eradication. My soul shriveled. My manhood withered. I, the copulator with empresses, the seducer of secluded noblewomen, the maker of smalltalk with emperors, I, the last of the Ducases, I, the strider across millennia, I, the brilliant Courier in the style of Metaxas, I...I, to these veteran Couriers here, was simply an upright mass of perambulating dreck. A faex that walks like a man. Which is the singular of faeces. Which is to say, a shit.

53

Metaxas, who had not spoken for fifteen minutes, said finally, "If those of you who are going are ready to go, I'll get a chariot to take you into town."

Kolettis shook his head. "We haven't allotted eras yet. But it'll take only a minute."

There was a buzzing consultation over the chart. It was decided that Kolettis would cover 700-725, Plastiras 1150-1175, and I would inspect 725-745. Pappas had brought a plague suit with him and was going to make a survey of the plague years 745-747, just in case Sauerabend had looped into that proscribed period by accident.

I was surprised that they trusted me to make a time-jump all by myself, considering what they obviously thought of me. But I suppose they figured I couldn't get into any worse trouble. Off we went to town in one of Metaxas' chariots. Each of us carried a small but remarkably accurate portrait of Conrad Sauerabend, painted on a varnished wooden plaque by a contemporary Byzantine artist hired by Metaxas. The artist had worked from a holophoto; I wonder what he'd made of *that*.

When we reached Constantinople proper, we split up and, one by one, timed off to the eras we were supposed to search. I materialized up the line in 725 and realized the little joke that had been played on me.

This was the beginning of the era of iconoclasm, when Emperor Leo III had first denounced the worship of painted images. At that time, most of the Byzantines were fervent iconodules—image-worshippers—and Leo set out to smash the cult of icons, first by speaking and preaching against them, then by destroying an image of Christ in the chapel of the Chalke, or Brazen House, in front of the Great Palace. After that things got worse; images and image-makers were persecuted, and Leo's son issued a proclamation declaring, "There shall be rejected, removed and cursed out of the Christian Church every likeness which is made out of any material whatever by the evil art of painters."

And in such an era I was supposed to walk around town holding a little painting of Conrad Sauerabend, asking people, "Have you seen this man anywhere?"

My painting wasn't exactly an icon. Nobody who looked at it was likely to mistake Sauerabend for a saint. Even so, it caused a lot of trouble for me.

"Have you seen this man anywhere?" I asked, and took out the painting.

In the marketplace.

In the bathhouses.

On the steps of Haghia Sophia.

Outside the Great Palace.

"Have you seen this man anywhere?"

In the Hippodrome during a polo match.

At the annual distribution of free bread and fish to the poor on May 11, celebrating the anniversary of the founding of the city.

In front of the Church of Saints Sergius and Bacchus.

"I'm looking for this man whose portrait I have here."

Half the time, I didn't even manage to get the painting fully into the open. They'd see a man pulling an icon from his tunic, and they'd run away, screaming, "Iconodule dog! Worshipper of images!"

"But this isn't—I'm only looking for—you mustn't mistake this painting for—won't you come back?"

I got pushed and shoved and expectorated upon. I got bullied by imperial guards and glowered at by iconoclastic priests. Several times I was invited to attend underground ceremonies of secret iconodules.

I didn't get much information about Conrad Sauerabend.

Still, despite all the difficulties, there were always some people who looked at the painting. None of them had seen Sauerabend, although a few "thought" they had noticed someone resembling the man in the picture. I wasted two days tracking one of the supposed resemblers, and found no resemblance at all.

I kept on, jumping from year to year. I lurked at the fringes of tourist groups, thinking that Sauerabend might prefer to stick close to people of his own era.

Nothing. No clue.

Finally, footsore and discouraged, I hopped back down to 1105. At Metaxas' place I found only Pappas, who looked even more weary and bedraggled than I did.

"It's useless," I said. "We aren't going to find him. It's like looking for—looking for—"

"A needle in a timestack," Pappas said helpfully.

54

I had earned a little rest before I returned to that long night in 1204 and sent my alter ego here to continue the search. I bathed, slept, banged a garlicky slavegirl two or three times, and brooded. Kolettis returned: no luck. Plastiras came back: no luck. They went down the line to resume their Courier jobs. Gompers, Herschel, and Melamed, donating time from their current layoffs, appeared and immediately set out on the quest for Sauerabend. The more Couriers who volunteered to help me in my time of need, the worse I felt.

I decided to console myself in Pulcheria's arms.

I mean, as long as I happened to be in the right era, and as long as Jud B had neglected to stop in to see her, it seemed only proper.

We had had some sort of date. Just about the last thing Pulcheria had said to me after that night of nights was, "We'll meet again two days hence, yes? I'll arrange everything."

How long ago had that been?

At least two weeks on the 1105 now-time basis, I figured. Maybe three.

She was supposed to have sent a message to me at Metaxas', telling me where and how we could have our second meeting. In my concern with Sauerabend I had forgotten about that. Now I raced all around the villa, asking Metaxas' butlers and his major domo if any messages had arrived from town for me.

"No," they said. "No messages."

"Think carefully. I'm expecting an important message from the Ducas palace. From Pulcheria Ducas."

"From whom?"

"Pulcheria Ducas."

"No messages, sir."

I clothed myself in my finest finery and clipclopped into Constantinople. Did I dare present myself at the Ducas place uninvited? I did dare. My country-bumpkin cover identity would justify my possible breach of etiquette.

At the gate of the Ducas palace I rang for the servant and an old groom came out, the one who had shown me to the chamber that night where Pulcheria had given herself to me. I smiled in a friendly way; the groom peered blankly back. Forgotten me, I thought.

I said, "My compliments to Lord Leo and Lady Pulcheria, and would you kindly tell them that George Markezinis of Epirus is here to call upon them?"

"To Lord Leo and Lady—" the groom repeated.

"Pulcheria," I said. "They know me. I'm cousin to Themistoklis Metaxas, and—" I hesitated, feeling even more foolish than usual at giving my pedigree to a groom. "Get me the major-domo," I snapped.

The groom scuttled within.

After a long delay, an imperious-looking individual in the Byzantine equivalent of livery emerged and surveyed me.

Up the Line

"Yes?"

"My compliments to Lord Leo and Lady Pulcheria, and would you kindly tell them—"

"Lady *who*?"

"Lady Pulcheria, wife to Leo Ducas. I am George Markezinis of Epirus, cousin to Themistoklis Metaxas, who only several weeks ago attended the party given by—"

"The wife to Leo Ducas," said the major-domo frostily, "is named Euprepia."

"Euprepia?"

"Euprepia Ducas, the lady of this household. Man, what do you want here? If you come drunken in the middle of the day to trouble Lord Leo, I—"

"Wait," I said. "*Euprepia?* Not Pulcheria?" A golden bezant flickered into my hand and fluttered swiftly across to the waiting palm of the major-domo. "I'm not drunk, and this is important. When did Leo marry this—this Euprepia?"

"Four years ago."

"Four—years—ago. No, that's impossible. *Five* years ago he married Pulcheria, who—"

"You must be mistaken. The Lord Leo has been married only once, to Euprepia Macrembolitissa, the mother of his son Basil and of his daughter Zoe."

The hand came forth. I dropped another bezant into it.

Dizzily I murmured, "His eldest son is Nicetas, who isn't even born yet, and he isn't supposed to have a son named Basil at all, and—my God, are you playing a game with me?"

"I swear before Christ Pantocrator that I have said no word but the truth," declared the major-domo resonantly.

Tapping my pouch of bezants, I said, desperate now, "Would it be possible for me to have an audience with the Lady Euprepia?"

"Perhaps so, yes. But she is not here. For three months now she has rested at the Ducas palace on the coast at Trebizond, where she awaits her next child."

"Three months. Then there was no party here a few weeks ago?"

"No, sir."

"The Emperor Alexius wasn't here? Nor Themistoklis Metaxas? Nor George Markezinis of Epirus? Nor—"

"None of those, sir. Can I help you further?"

"I don't think so," I said, and went staggering from the gate of the Ducas palace like unto one who has been smitten by the wrath of the gods.

Dismally I wandered in a southeasterly way along the Golden Horn until I came to the maze of shops, marketplaces, and taverns near the place where there would one day be the Galata Bridge, and where today there is still a maze of shops, marketplaces, and taverns. Through those narrow, interweaving, chaotic streets I marched like a zombie, having no destination. I saw not, neither did I think; I just put one foot ahead of the other one and kept going until, early in the afternoon, kismet once more seized me by the privates.

I stumbled randomly into a tavern, a two-story structure of unpainted boards. A few merchants were downing their midday wine. I dropped down heavily at a warped and wobbly table in an unoccupied corner of the room and sat staring at the wall, thinking about Leo Ducas' pregnant wife Euprepia.

A comely tavern-slut appeared and said, "Some wine?"

"Yes. The stronger the better."

"A little roast lamb too?"

"I'm not hungry, thanks."

"We make very good lamb here."

"I'm not hungry," I said. I stared somberly at her ankles. They were very good ankles. I looked up at the calves, and then her legs vanished within the folds of her simple cloth wrap. She strode away and came back with flask of wine. As she set it before me, the front of the wrap fell away at her throat, and I peered in at the pale, full, rosy-tipped breasts that swung freely there. Then at last I looked at her face.

Up the Line

She could have been Pulcheria's twin sister.

Same dark, mischievous eyes. Same flawless olive skin. Same full lips and aquiline nose. Same age, about seventeen. The differences between this girl and my Pulcheria were differences of dress, of posture, and of expression. This girl was coarsely clad; she lacked Pulcheria's aristocratic elegance of bearing; and there was a certain pouting sullenness about her, the look of a girl who is living below her station in life and is angry about it.

I said, "You could almost be Pulcheria!"

She laughed harshly. "What kind of nonsensical talk that?"

"A girl I know, who resembles you closely—Pulcheria her name is—"

"Are you insane, or only drunk? *I* am Pulcheria. Your little game isn't pleasing to me, stranger."

"You—Pulcheria?"

"Certainly."

"Pulcheria Ducas?"

She cackled in my face. "Ducas, you say? Now I know you're crazy. Pulcheria Photis, wife of Heracles Photis the innkeeper!"

"Pulcheria—Photis—" I repeated numbly. "Pulcheria—Photis—wife—of—Heracles—Photis—"

She leaned close over me, giving me a second view of her miraculous breasts. Not haughty now but worried, she said in a low voice, "I can tell by your clothes that you're someone important. What do you want here? Has Heracles done something wrong?"

"I'm here just for wine," I said. "But listen, tell me this one thing: are you the Pulcheria who was born Botaniates?"

She looked stunned. "You know that!"

"It's true?"

"Yes," said my adored Pulcheria, and sank down next to me on the bench. "But I am a Botaniates no longer. For five years now—ever since Heracles—the filthy Heracles—ever since he—" She took some of my wine in her agitation. "Who are you, stranger?"

"George Markezinis of Epirus."

The name meant nothing to her.

"Cousin to Themistoklis Metaxas."

She gasped. "I *knew* you were someone important! I knew!" Trembling prettily, she said, "What do you want with me?"

The other patrons in the tavern were beginning to stare at us. I said, "Can we go somewhere to talk? Someplace private?"

Her eyes took on a cool, knowing look. "Just a moment," she said, and went out of the tavern. I heard her calling to someone, shouting like any fishwife, and after a moment a ragged girl of about fifteen came into the room. Pulcheria said, "Look after things, Anna. I'm going to be busy." To me she said, "We can go upstairs."

She led me to a bedchamber on the second floor of the building and carefully bolted the door behind us.

"My husband," she said, "has gone to Galata to buy meat, and will not be back for two hours. While the loathsome pig is away, I don't mind earning a bezant or two from a handsome stranger."

Her clothing fell away and she stood incandescently nude before me. Her smile was a defiant one, a smile that said that she retained her inner self no matter what stains of degradation others inflicted on her. Her eyes flashed with lusty zeal.

I stood dazzled before those high, heavy breasts, whose nipples were visibly hardening, and before that flat, taut belly with its dark, mounded bush, and before those firm muscular thighs and before those outstretched, beckoning arms.

She tumbled down onto the rough cot. She flexed her knees and drew her legs apart. "Two bezants?" she suggested.

Pulcheria transformed into a tavern whore? My goddess? My adored one?

"Why do you hesitate?" she asked. "Come, climb aboard, give the fat dog Heracles another pair of horns. What's wrong? Do I seem ugly to you?"

"Pulcheria—Pulcheria—I love you, Pulcheria—"

She giggled, shrill in her delight. She waved her heels at me. "Come on, then!"

"You were Leo Ducas' wife," I murmured. "You lived in a marble palace, and wore silk robes, and went about the city escorted by a watchful duenna. And the emperor was at your party, and just before dawn you came to me, and gave yourself to me, and it was all a dream, Pulcheria, all a dream, eh?"

"You are a madman," she said. "But a handsome madman, and I yearn to have you between my legs, and I yearn also for your bezants. Come close. Are you shy? Look, put your hand here, feel how hot Pulcheria grows, how she throbs—"

I was rigid with desire, but I knew I couldn't touch her. Not this Pulcheria, this coarse, shameless, wanton, sluttish wench, this gorgeous creature who capered and pumped and writhed impatiently on the cot before me.

I pulled out my pouch and emptied it over her nakedness, dumping golden bezants into her navel, her loins, spilling them across her breasts. Pulcheria shrieked in astonishment. She sat up, clutching at the money, scrambling for it, her breasts heaving and swaying, her eyes bright.

I fled.

56

At the villa I found Metaxas and said, "What's the name of Leo Ducas' wife?"

"Pulcheria."

"When did you last see her?"

"Three weeks ago, when we went to that party."

"No," I said. "You're suffering from Transit Displacement, and so am I. Leo Ducas is married to someone named Euprepia, and has two children by her, and a third on the way. And Pulcheria is the wife of a tavernkeeper named Heracles Photis."

"Have you gone spotty potty?" Metaxas asked.

"The past has been changed. I don't know how it happened, but there's been a change, right in my own ancestry, don't you see, and Pulcheria's no longer my ancestress, and God knows if I even exist any more. If I'm not descended from Leo Ducas and Pulcheria, then who am I descended from, and—"

"When did you find all this out?"

"Just now. I went to look for Pulcheria, and—Christ, Metaxas, what am I going to do?"

"Maybe there's been a mistake," he said calmly.

"No. No. Ask your own servants. They don't undergo Transit Displacement. Ask them if they've ever heard of a Pulcheria Ducas. They haven't. Ask them the name of Leo Ducas' wife. Or go into town and see for yourself. There's been a change in the past, don't you see, and everything's different, and—Christ, Metaxas! Christ!"

He took hold of my wrists and said in a very quiet tone, "Tell me all about this from the beginning, Jud."

But I had no chance to. For just then big black Sam came rushing into the hall, whooping and screaming.

"We found him! God damn, but we found him!"

"Who?" Metaxas said.

"Who?" I said simultaneously.

"Who?" Sam repeated. "Who the hell do you think? Sauerabend. Conrad F. X. Sauerabend himself!"

"You found him?" I said, limp with relief. "Where? When? How?"

"Right here in 1105," said Sam. "This morning, Melamed and I were in the marketplace, just checking around a little, and we showed the picture, and sure enough, some peddler of pig's feet recognized him. Sauerabend's been living in Constantinople for the past five or six years, running a tavern down near the water. He goes under the name of Heracles Photis—"

"No!" I bellowed. "No, you black nigger bastard, no, no, no, no, no! It isn't true!"

And I launched myself at him in blind fury.

And I drove my fists into his belly, and sent him reeling backward toward the wall.

And he looked at me strangely, and caught his breath, and came toward me and picked me up and dropped me. And picked me up and dropped me. And picked me up a third time, but Metaxas made him put me down.

Sam said gently, "It's true that I *am* a black nigger bastard, but was it really necessary to say so that loudly?"

Metaxas said, "Give him some wine, somebody. I think he's going off his head."

I said, seizing control of myself somehow, "Sam, I didn't mean to call you names, but it absolutely cannot be the case that Conrad Sauerabend is living under the name of Heracles Photis."

"Why not?"

"Because—because—"

"I saw him myself," Sam said. "I had wine in his tavern no more than five hours ago. He's big and fat and red-faced, and thinks a great deal of himself. And he's got this little hot-ass Byzantine wife, maybe sixteen, seventeen years old, who waits on table in the place, and waves her boobies at the customers, and I bet sells her tail in the upstairs rooms—"

"All right," I said in a dead man's voice. "You win. The wife's name is Pulcheria."

Metaxas made a choking sound.

Sam said, "I didn't ask about her name."

"She's seventeen years old, and she comes from the Botaniates family," I went on, "which is one of the important Byzantine families, and only Buddha knows what she's doing married to Heracles Photis Conrad Sauerabend. And the past has been changed, Sam, because up until a few weeks ago on my now-time basis she was the wife of Leo Ducas and lived in a palace near the imperial palace, and it happened that I was having a love affair with her, and it also happens that until the past got changed she and Leo Ducas were my great-great-multi-great-grandparents, and it seems to have happened that a very stinking coincidence has taken place, which I don't comprehend the details of at all, except that I'm probably a nonperson now and there's no such individual as Pulcheria Ducas. And now, if you don't mind, I'm going to go into a quiet corner and cut my throat."

"This isn't happening," said Sam. "This is all a bad dream."

But, of course, it wasn't. It was as real as any other event in this fluid and changeable cosmos.

The three of us drank a great deal of wine, and Sam gave me some of the other details. How he had asked about in the neighborhood concerning Sauerabend/Photis, and had been told that the man had arrived mysteriously from some other part of the country, about the year 1099. How the regulars at his tavern disliked him, but came to the place just to get a view of his beautiful wife. How there was general suspicion that he was engaged in some kind of illegal activity.

"He excused himself," Sam said, "and told us that he had to go across to Galata to do some marketing. But Kolettis followed him and found that he didn't go marketing at all. He went into some kind of warehouse on the Galata side, and apparently he disappeared. Kolettis went in after him and couldn't find him anywhere. He must have time-jumped, Kolettis assumed. Then this Photis reappeared, maybe half an hour later, and took the ferry back into Constantinople."

"Timecrime," Metaxas suggested. "He's engaged in smuggling."

"That's what I think," said Sam. "He's using the early twelfth century as a base of operations, under this cover identity of Photis, and he's running artifacts or gold coins or something like that down the line to now-time."

"How did he get mixed up with the girl, though?" Metaxas asked.

Sam shrugged. "That part isn't clear yet. But now that we've found him, we can trace him back up the line until we find the point of his arrival. And see exactly what he's been up to."

I groaned. "How are we ever going to restore the proper sequence of events?"

Metaxas said, "We've got to locate the precise moment to which he made his jump out of your tour. Then we station ourselves there, catch him as soon as he materializes, take away that trick timer of his, and bring him back to 1204. That extricates him from the timeflow right where he came in, and puts him back into your 1204 trip where he belongs."

"You make it sound so simple," I said. "But it isn't. What about all the changes that have been made in the past? His five years of marriage to Pulcheria Botaniates—"

"Nonevents," said Sam. "As soon as we whisk Sauerabend from 1099 or whenever back into 1204, his marriage to this Pulcheria is automatically deleted, right? The time-flow resumes its unedited shape, and she marries whoever she was supposed to marry—"

"Leo Ducas," I said. "My ancestor."

"Leo Ducas, yes," Sam went on. "And for everybody in Byzantium, this whole Heracles Photis episode will never have happened. The only ones who'll know about it are us, because we're subject to Transit Displacement."

"What about the artifacts Sauerabend's been smuggling to nowtime?" I asked.

Sam said, "They won't be there. They won't ever have been smuggled. And his fences down there won't have any recollection of having received them, either. The fabric of time will have been restored, and the Patrol won't be the wiser for it, and—"

"You're overlooking one little item," I said.

"Which is?"

"In the course of these shenanigans I generated an extra Jud Elliott. Where does *he* go?"

"Christ," Sam said. "I forgot about him!"

58

I had now been running around 1105 for quite a while, and I figured it was time to get back to 1204 and let my alter ego know something of what was going on. So I made the shunt down the line and got to the inn at quarter past three on that same long night of Conrad Sauerabend's disappearance from 1204. My other self was slouched gloomily on his bed, studying the ceiling's heavy beams.

"Well?" he said. "How goes it?"

"Catastrophic. Come out into the hall."

"What's happening?"

"Brace yourself," I said. "We finally tracked Sauerabend down. He shunted to 1099, and took a cover identity as a tavernkeeper. A year later he married Pulcheria."

I watched my other self crumble.

"The past has been changed," I went on. "Leo Ducas married somebody else, Euprepia something, and has two and a half children by her. Pulcheria's a serving wench in Sauerabend's tavern. I saw her there. She didn't know who I was, but she offered to screw me for two bezants. Sauerabend is smuggling goods down the line, and—"

"Don't tell me any more," he said. "I don't want to hear any more."

"I haven't told you the good part yet."

"There's a good part?"

"The good part is that we're going to unhappen all of this. Sam and Metaxas and you are going to trace Sauerabend back from 1105 to the moment of his arrival in 1099, and unarrive him, and shunt him back here into this evening. Thus canceling the whole episode."

"What happens to us?" my other self asked.

"We discussed that, more or less," I said vaguely. "We aren't sure. Apparently we're both protected by Transit Displacement, so that we'll continue to exist even if we get Sauerabend back into his proper time flow."

"But where did we come from? There can't be creation of something out of nothing! Conservation of mass—"

"One of us was here all along," I reminded him. "As a matter of fact, *I* was here all along. I brought you into being by looping back fifty-six seconds into your time-flow."

"Balls," he said. "I was in that time-flow all along, doing what I was supposed to do. You came looping in out of nowhere. You're the goddam paradox, buster."

"I've lived fifty-six seconds longer than you, absolute. Therefore I must have been created first."

"We were both created in the same instant, on October 11, 2035," he shot back at me. "The fact that our time lines got snarled because of your faulty thinking has no bearing on which of us is more real than the other. The question is not who's the real Jud Elliott, but how we're going to continue to operate without getting in each other's way."

Up the Line

"We'll have to work out a tight schedule," I said. "One of us working as a Courier while the other one's hiding out up the line. And the two of us never in the same time at once, up or down the line. But how—"

"I have it," he said. "We'll establish a now-time existence in 1105, the way Metaxas has done, only for us it'll be continuous. There'll always be one of us pegged to now-time in the early twelfth century as George Markezinis, living in Metaxas' villa. The other one of us will be functioning as a Courier, and he'll go through a trip-and-layoff cycle—"

"—taking his layoff anywhen but in the 1105 basis."

"Right. And when he's completed the cycle, he'll go to the villa and pick up the Markezinis identity, and the other one will go down the line and report for Courier duty—"

"—and if we keep everything coordinated, there's no reason why the Patrol should ever find out about us."

"Brilliant!"

"And the one who's being Markezinis," I finished, "can always be carrying on a full-time affair with Pulcheria, and she'll never know that we're taking turns with her."

"As soon as Pulcheria is herself again."

"As soon as Pulcheria is herself again," I agreed.

That was a sobering thought. Our whole giddy plan for alternating our identities was just so much noise until we straightened out the mess Sauerabend had caused.

I checked the time. "You get back to 1105 and help Sam and Metaxas," I said. "Shunt here again by half past three tonight."

"Right," he said, and left.

He came back on time, looking disgusted, and said, "We're all waiting for you on August 9, 1100, by the land wall back of Blachernae, about a hundred meters to the right of the first gate."

"What's the story?"

"Go and see for yourself. It makes me sick to think about it. Go, and do what has to be done, and then this filthy lunacy will be over. Go on. Jump up and join us there."

"What time of day?" I asked.

He pondered a moment. "Twenty past noon, I'd say."

I went out of the inn and walked to the land wall, and set my timer with care, and jumped. The transition from late-night darkness to midday brightness left me blinded for an instant; when I stopped blinking I found myself standing before a grim-faced trio: Sam, Metaxas—and Jud B.

"Jesus," I said, "Don't tell me we've committed another duplication!"

"This time it's only the Paradox of Temporal Accumulation," my alter ego said. "Nothing serious."

I was too muddled to reason it through. "But if we're both here, who's watching our tourists down in 1204?"

"Idiot," he said fiercely, "think four-dimensionally! How can you be so stupid if you're identical to me? Look, I jumped here from one point in that night in 1204, and you jumped from another point fifteen minutes away. When we go back, we each go to our proper starting point in the sequence. I'm due to arrive at half past three, and you aren't supposed to be there until quarter to four, but that doesn't mean that neither of us is there right now. Or all these others of us."

I looked around. I saw at least five groups of Metaxas-Sam-me arranged in a wide arc near the wall. Obviously they had been monitoring this time point closely, making repeated short-run shunts to check on the sequence of events, and the Cumulative Paradox was building up a multitude of them.

"Even so," I said dimly, "it somehow seems that I'm not correctly perceiving the linear chain of—"

"*Stuff* the linear chain of!" the other Jud snarled at me. "Will you look over there? There, on the far side of the gate!"

He pointed.

I looked.

I saw a gray-haired woman in simple clothes. I recognized her as a somewhat younger version of the woman whom I had seen

Up the Line

escorting Pulcheria Ducas into the shop of sweets and spices that day, seemingly so long ago, five years down the line in 1105. The duenna was propped up against the city wall, giggling to herself. Her eyes were closed.

A short distance from her was a girl of about twelve, who could only have been Pulcheria's younger self. The resemblance was unmistakable. This girl still had a child's unformed features, and her breasts were only gentle bumps under her tunic, but the raw materials of Pulcheria's beauty were there.

Next to the girl was Conrad Sauerabend, in Byzantine lower-middle-class clothes.

Sauerabend was cooing in the girl's ear. He was dangling before her face a little twenty-first century gimcrack, a gyroscopic pendant or something like that. His other hand was under her tunic and visibly groping in the vicinity of her thighs. Pulcheria was frowning, but yet she wasn't making any move to get the hand out of her crotch. She seemed a little uncertain about what Sauerabend was up to, but she was altogether fascinated by the toy, and perhaps didn't mind the wandering fingers, either.

Metaxas said, "He's been living in Constantinople for a little less than a year, and commuting frequently to 2059 to drop off marketable artifacts. He's been coming by the wall every day to watch the little girl and her duenna take their noontime stroll. The girl is Pulcheria Botaniates, and that's the Botaniates palace just over there. About half an hour ago Sauerabend came along and saw the two of them. He gave the duenna a floater and she's been up high ever since. Then he sat down next to the girl and began to charm her. He's really very slick with little girls."

"It's his hobby," I said.

"Watch what happens now," said Metaxas.

Sauerabend and Pulcheria rose and walked toward the gate in the wall. We faded back into the shadows to remain unobserved. Most of our paradoxical duplicates had disappeared, evidently shunting to other positions along the line to monitor the events. We watched as the fat man and the lovely little girl strolled through the gate, into the countryside just beyond the city boundary.

I started to follow.

"Wait," said Sam. "See who's coming now? That's Pulcheria's older brother Andronicus."

A young man, perhaps eighteen, was approaching. He halted and stared in broad disbelief at the giggling duenna. We saw him rush toward her, shake her, yank her to her feet. The woman tumbled down again, helpless.

"Where's Pulcheria?" he roared. *"Where is she?"*

The duenna laughed.

Young Botaniates, desperate, rushed about the deserted sunbaked street, yelling for his maiden sister. Then he hurried through the gate.

"We follow him," Metaxas said. Several other group of us were already outside the gate, I discovered when we got there. Andronicus Botaniates ran hither and thither. I heard the sound of girlish laughter coming from, seemingly, the wall itself.

Andronicus heard it too. There was a breach in the wall, a shallow cavelike opening at ground level, perhaps five meters deep. He ran toward it. We ran toward it too, jostling with a mob that consisted entirely of our duplicated selves. There must have been fifteen of us—five of each.

Andronicus entered the breach in the wall and let out terrible howl. A moment later I peered in.

Pulcheria, naked, her tunic down near her ankles, stood in the classic position of modesty, with one hand flung across her budding breasts and the other spreading over her loins. Next to her was Sauerabend, with his clothes open. He had his tool out and ready for business. I suppose he had been in the process of maneuvering Pulcheria into a suitable position when the interruption came.

"Outrage!" cried Andronicus. "Foulness! Seduction a virgin maiden! I call you all to witness! Look at this monstrosity, this criminal deed!"

And he caught Sauerabend by one hand and his sister by the other, and tugged them both out into the open.

"Bear witness!" he bellowed. We got out of the way before Sauerabend could recognize us, although I think he was too terrified

Up the Line

to see anyone. Pitiful Pulcheria, trying to hide all of herself at once, was huddled into a ball at her brother's feet; but he kept pulling her up, exposing her, crying, "Look at the little whore! Look at her! Look, look, look!"

And a considerable crowd came to look.

We moved to one side. I felt like throwing up. That vile molester of children, that Humbert of stockbrokers—exposing his swollen red thing to Pulcheria, involving her in this scandal—

Now Andronicus had drawn his sword and was trying to kill either Sauerabend or Pulcheria or both. But the onlookers prevented him, bearing him to the ground and taking away his weapon. Pulcheria, in frantic dismay at having her nakedness exposed to such a multitude, grabbed a dagger from someone else and attempted to kill herself, but was stopped in time; finally an old man threw his cloak about her. All was confusion.

Metaxas said calmly, "We followed the rest of the sequence from here before you arrived, then doubled back to wait for you. Here's what happened: The girl was engaged to Leo Ducas, but of course it was impossible for him to marry her after half of Byzantium had seen her naked like this. Besides, she was considered tainted, even though Sauerabend didn't actually have time to get into her. The marriage was called off. Her family, blaming her for letting Sauerabend charm her into taking off her clothes, disowned her. Meanwhile, Sauerabend was given the choice of marrying the girl he dishonored, or suffering the usual penalty."

"Which was?"

"Castration," said Metaxas. "And so, as Heracles Photis, Sauerabend married her, changing the pattern of history at least to the extent of depriving you of your proper ancestral line. Which we're now going to correct."

"Not me," said Jud B. "I've seen all I can stand. I'm going back to 1204. I'm due there at half past three in the morning to tell this guy to come back here and watch things."

"But—" I said.

"Never mind figuring out the paradoxes," Sam said. "We've got work to do."

"Relieve me at quarter to four," said Jud B, and shunted.

Metaxas and Sam and I coordinated our timers. "We go up the line," said Metaxas, "by exactly one hour. To finish the comedy." We shunted.

60

And with great precision and no little relief, we finished the comedy.

In this fashion:

We shunted to noon, exactly, on that hot summer day of the year 1100, and took up positions along the wall of Constantinople. And waited, trying hard to ignore the other versions of ourselves who passed briefly through our time level on snooping missions of their own.

The pretty little girl and the watchful duenna came into view.

My heart ached with love for young Pulcheria, and I ached in other places as well, out of lust for the Pulcheria who would be, the Pulcheria whom I had known.

The pretty little girl and the unsuspecting duenna, keeping close together, strolled past us.

Conrad Sauerabend/Heracles Photis appeared. Discordant sounds in the orchestra; twirling of mustaches; hisses. He studied the girl and the woman. He patted his bulging belly. He drew forth a snubby little floater and checked its snout. Leering enthusiastically, he came forward, planning to thrust the floater against the duenna's arm and, by giving her an hour of the giggling highs, to gain unimpeded access to the little girl.

Metaxas nodded to Sam.

Sam nodded to me.

We approached Sauerabend on a slanting path of approach.

"Now!" said Metaxas, and we went into action.

Huge black Sam lunged forward and clasped his right forearm across Sauerabend's throat. Metaxas seized Sauerabend's left wrist and bent his entire arm backward, far from the controls of the timer that could whiz him from our grasp. Simultaneously,

Up the Line

I caught Sauerabend's right arm, jerking it up and back and forcing him to drop the floater. This entire maneuver occupied perhaps an eighth of a second and resulted in the effective immobilization of Sauerabend. The duenna, meanwhile, had wisely fled with Pulcheria at the sight of this unseemly struggle.

Sam now reached under Sauerabend's clothing and deprived him of his gimmicked timer.

Then we released him. Sauerabend, who undoubtedly thought that he had been set upon by bandits, saw me and grunted a couple of shocked monosyllables.

I said, "You thought you were pretty clever, didn't you?"

He grunted some more.

I said, "Gimmicking your timer, slipping away, thinking you could set up in business for yourself as a smuggler. Eh? You didn't believe we'd catch you?"

I didn't tell him of the weeks of hard work that we had put in. I didn't tell him of the timecrimes we ourselves had committed for the sake of detecting him—the paradoxes we had left strewn all up and down the line, the needless duplications of ourselves. I didn't tell him that We had just pinched six years of his life as a Byzantine tavernkeeper into a pocket universe that, so far as he was concerned, had no existence whatever. Nor did I tell him of the chain of events that had made him the husband of Pulcheria Botaniates in that pinched-off universe, depriving me of my proper ancestry. All of those things had now unhappened. There now would be no tavernkeeper named Heracles Photis selling meat and drink to the Byzantines of the years 1100-1105.

Metaxas produced a spare timer, ungimmicked, that he had carried for the purpose.

"Put it on," he said.

Sullenly, Sauerabend donned it.

I said, "We're going back to 1204, more or less to the time you set out from. And then we're going to finish our tour and go back down the line to 2059. And God help you if you cause any more trouble for me, Sauerabend. I won't report you for timecrime, because I'm a merciful man, even though an unauthorized shunt like yours is very definitely a criminal act; but if you do anything whatever that displeases me in the slightest between now and the moment I'm rid of you, I'll make you roast for it. Clear?"

He nodded bleakly.

To Sam and Metaxas I said, "I can handle this from here on. Thanks for everything. I can't possibly tell you—"

"Don't try," said Metaxas, and together they shunted down the line.

I set Sauerabend's new timer and my own, and drew forth my pitch-pipe. "Here we go," I said, and we shunted into 1204.

At quarter to four on that very familiar night in 1204 went once more up the stairs of the inn, this time with Sauerabend. Jud B paced restlessly just within the door of the room. He brightened at the sight of my captive. Sauerabend looked puzzled at the presence of two of me, but he didn't dare say anything.

"Get inside," I said to him. "And don't monkey with your goddam timer or you'll suffer for it."

Sauerabend went in.

I said to Jud B, "The nightmare's over. We grabbed him, took away his timer, put a regulation one on him, and here he is. The whole operation took just exactly four hours, right?"

"Plus who remembers how many weeks of running up and down the line."

"No matter now. We got him back. We start from scratch."

"And there's now an extra one of us," Jud B pointed out. "Do we work that little deal of taking turns?"

"We do. One of us stays with these clowns, takes them on down to 1453 as scheduled, and back to the twenty-first century. The other one of us goes to Metaxas' villa. Want to flip a coin?"

"Why not?" He pulled a bezant of Alexius I from his pouch, and let me inspect it for kosherness. It was okay: a standing figure of Alexius on the obverse, an image of Christ enthroned on the reverse.

Up the Line

We stipulated that Alexius was heads and Jesus was tails. Then I flipped the coin high, caught it with a quick snap of my hand, and clapped it down on the back of my other hand. I knew, from the feel of the concave coin's edge against my skin, that it had landed heads up.

"Tails," said the other Jud.

"Tough luck, amigo." I showed him the coin. He grimaced and took it back from me.

Gloomily he said, "I've got three or four days left with this tour, right? Then two weeks of layoff, which I can't spend in 1105. That means you can expect to see me showing up at Metaxas' place in seventeen, eighteen days absolute."

"Something like that," I agreed. "During which time you'll make it like crazy with Pulcheria."

"Naturally."

"Give her one for me," he said, and went into room.

Downstairs, I slouched against a pillar and spent an hour rechecking all of my comings and goings of this hectic night, to make sure I'd land in 1105 at a non-discontinuous point. The last thing I needed now was to miscalculate and show up there at a time prior to whole Sauerabend caper, thereby finding a Metaxas to whom the entire thing was, well, Greek.

I did my calculations.

I shunted.

I wended my way once more to the lovely villa.

Everything had worked out perfectly. Metaxas embraced me in joy.

"The time-flow is intact again," he said. "I've been back from 1100 only a couple of hours, but that was enough to check up on things. Leo Ducas' wife is named Pulcheria. Someone named Angelus runs the tavern Sauerabend owned. Nobody here remembers anything about anything. You're safe."

"I can't tell you how much I—"

"Skip it, will you?"

"I suppose. Where's Sam?"

"Down the line. He had to go back to work. And I'm about to do the same," Metaxas said. "My layoff's over and there's a tour waiting for me in the middle of December, 2059. So I'll be gone about two weeks, and then be back here on—" He considered it "— on October 18, 1105. What about you?"

"I stay here until October 22." I said. "Then my alter ego will be finished with his post-tour layoff and will replace me here, while I go down the line to take out my next tour."

"Is that how you're going to work it? Turns?"

"It's the only way."

"You're probably right," said Metaxas, but I wasn't.

Metaxas took his leave, and I took a bath. And then, really relaxed for the first time in what seemed like several geological epochs, I contemplated my immediate future.

First, a nap. Then a meal. And then a journey into town to call on Pulcheria, who would be restored to her rightful place in the Ducas household, and unaware of the strange metamorphosis that had temporarily come over her destinies.

We'd make love, and I'd come back to the villa, and in the morning I'd go into town again, and afterward—

Then I stopped hatching further plans, because Sam appeared unexpectedly and smashed everything.

He was wearing a Byzantine cloak, but it was just a hasty prop, for I could see his ordinary down-the-line clothes on underneath. He looked harried and upset.

"What the hell are you doing here?" I asked.

"A favor to you," he said.

"Huh?"

"I said I'm here as a favor to you. And I'm not going to stay long, because I don't want the Time Patrol after me too."

"Is the Time Patrol after me?"

"You bet your white ass it is!" he yelled. "Get your things together and clear out of here, fast! You've got to hide, maybe three, four thousand years back, somewhere. Hurry it up!"

Up the Line

He began collecting a few stray possessions of mine scattered about the room. I caught hold of him and said, "Will you tell me what's going on? Sit down and stop acting like a maniac. You come in here at a million kilometers an hour and—"

"All right," he said. "All right. I'll spell it all out for you, and if I get arrested too, so be it. I'm stained with sin. I *deserve* to be arrested. And—"

"Sam—"

"All right," he said again. He closed his eyes a moment. "My now-time basis," he said hollowly, "is December 25, 2059. Merry Christmas. Several days ago on my time-level, your other self brought your current tour back from Byzantium. Including Sauerabend and all the rest of them. Do you know what happened to your other self the instant he arrived in 2059?"

"The Time Patrol arrested him?"

"Worse."

"What could be worse?"

"He vanished, Jud. He became a nonperson. He ceased ever to have existed."

I had to laugh. "The cocksure bastard! I *told* him that I was the real one and that he was just some kind of phantom, but he wouldn't listen! Well, I can't say that I'm sorry to see—"

"No, Jud," Sam said sadly. "He was every bit as real as you, when he was back here up the line. And you're every bit as unreal as he is now."

"I don't understand."

"You're a nonperson, Jud, same as he is. You have retroactively ceased to exist. I'm sorry. You never happened. And it's our fault as much as yours. We moved so fast that we slipped up on one small detail."

He looked frighteningly somber. But how else are you supposed to look, when you come to tell somebody that he's not only dead but never was born?

"What happened, Sam? What detail?"

"It's like this, Jud. You know, when we took Sauerabend's gimmicked timer away, we got him another one. Metaxas keeps a few smuggled spares around—that tricky bastard has everything."

"So?"

"Its serial number, naturally, was different from the number of the timer Sauerabend started his tour with. Normally, nobody notices something like that, but when this tour checked back in, it just happened that the check-in man was a stickler for the rules, and he examined serial numbers. And saw there was a substitution, and yelled for the Patrol."

"Oh," I said weakly.

"They questioned Sauerabend," Sam said, "and of course he was cagey, more to protect himself than you. And since he couldn't give any explanation of the switch, the Patrol got authorization to run a recheck on the entire tour he had just taken."

"Oh-oh."

"They monitored it from every angle. They saw you leave your group, they saw Sauerabend skip out the moment you were gone, they saw you and me and Metaxas catch him and bring him back to that night in 1204."

"So all three of us are in trouble?"

Sam shook his head. "Metaxas has pull. So have I. We wiggled out of it on a sympathy line, that we were just trying to help a buddy in trouble. It took all the strings we could pull. But we couldn't do a thing for you, Jud. The Patrol is out for your head. They looked in on that little routine in 1204 by which you duplicated yourself, and they began to realize that you were guilty not only of negligence in letting Sauerabend get away from you in the first place, but also of various paradoxes caused in your unlawful attempts to correct the situation. The charges against you were so serious that we couldn't get them dropped, and we tried, man, we *tried*. The Patrol thereupon took action against you."

"What kind of action?" I asked in a dead man's voice.

"You were removed from your tour on that evening in 1204 two hours prior to your original shunt to 1105 for your tryst with Pulcheria. Another Courier replaced you in 1204; you were plucked from the time-flow and brought down the line to stand trial in 2059 for assorted timecrimes."

"Therefore—"

Up the Line

"Therefore," Sam swept on, "you never did slip away to 1105 to pay that call on Pulcheria. Your whole love affair with Pulcheria has become a nonevent, and if you were to visit her now, you'd find that she has no recollection of having slept with you. Next: since you didn't go to 1105, you obviously didn't return to 1204 and find Sauerabend missing, and anyway Sauerabend had never been part of your tour group. And thus there was no need for you to make that fifty-six-second shunt up the line which created the duplication. Neither you nor Jud B ever came into being, since the existence of both of you dates from a point later than your visit to Pulcheria, and you never made that visit, having been plucked out of the time-flow before you got a chance to do it. You and Jud B are nonpersons and always have been. You happen to be protected by the Paradox of Transit Displacement, as long as you stay up the line; Jud B ceased to be protected the moment he returned to now-time, and disappeared irretrievably. Got that?"

Shivering, I said, "Sam, what's happening to that other Jud, the—the—the *real* Jud? The one they plucked, the one they've got down there in 2059?"

"He's in custody, awaiting trial on timecrime charges."

"What about me?"

"If the Patrol ever finds you, you'll be brought to now-time and thus automatically obliterated. But the Patrol doesn't know where you are. If you stay in Byzantium, sooner or later you'll be discovered, and that'll be the end for you. When I found all this out, I shot back here to warn you. Hide in prehistory. Get away into some period earlier than the founding of the old Greek Byzantium—earlier than 700 B.C., I guess. You can manage there. We'll bring you books, tools, whatever you need. There'll be people of some sort, nomads, maybe—anyway, company. You'll be like a god to them. They'll worship you, they'll bring you a woman a day. It's your only chance, Jud."

"I don't want to be a prehistoric god! I want to be able to go down the line again! And to see Pulcheria! And—"

"There's no chance of any of that," Sam said, and his words came down like the blade of a guillotine. "You don't exist. It's suicide for you ever to try to go down the line. And if you go anywhere near Pulcheria, the Patrol will catch you and take you down the line. Hide or die, Jud. Hide or die."

"But I'm real, Sam! I *do* exist!"

"Only the Jud Elliott who's currently in custody in 2059 exists. You're a residual phenomenon, a paradox product, nothing more. I love you all the same, boy, and that's why I've risked my own black hide to help you, but you aren't real. Believe me. Believe me. You're your own ghost. Pack up and clear out!"

I've been here for three and a half months now. By the calendar I keep, the date is March 15, 3060 B.P. I'm living a thousand years before Christ, more or less.

It's not a bad life. The people here are subsistence farmers, maybe remnants of the old Hittite empire; the Greek colonists won't be getting here for another three centuries. I'm starting to learn the language; it's Indo-European and I pick it up fast. As Sam predicted, I'm a god. They wanted to kill me when I showed up, but I did a few tricks with my timer, shunting right before their eyes, and now they don't dare offend me. I try to be a kindly god, though. Right now I'm helping spring to arrive. I went down to the shore of what will someday be called the Bosphorus and delivered a long prayer, in English, for good weather. The locals loved it.

They give me all the women I want. The first night they gave me the chief's daughter, and since then I've rotated pretty well through the whole nubile population of the village. I imagine they'll want me to marry someone eventually, but I want to complete the inspection first. The women don't smell too good, but some of them are impressively passionate.

I'm terribly lonely.

Sam has been here three times, Metaxas twice. The others don't come. I don't blame them; the risks are great. My two loyal friends have brought me floaters, books, a laser, a big box of music cubes, and plenty of other things that are going to perplex the tails off some archaeologists eventually.

I said to Sam, "Bring me Pulcheria, just for a visit."

"I can't," he said. And he's right. It would have to be a kidnapping, and there might be repercussions, leading to Time Patrol troubles for Sam and obliteration for me.

I miss Pulcheria ferociously. You know, I had sex with her only that one night, though it seems as if I knew her much better than that. I wish now that I'd had her in the tavern, while she was Pulcheria Photis, too.

My beloved. My wicked great-great-multi-great-grandmother. Never to see you again! Never to touch your smooth skin, your— no, I won't torture myself. I'll try to forget you. Hah!

I console myself, when not busy in my duties as a deity, by dictating my memoirs. Everything now is recorded, all the details of how I maneuvered myself into this terrible fix. A cautionary tale: from promising young man to absolute nonperson in sixty-two brief chapters. I'll keep on writing too, now and then. I'll tell what it's like to be a Hittite god. Let's see, tomorrow we'll have the spring fertility festival, and the ten fairest maidens of the village will come to the god's house so that we—

Pulcheria!

Why am I here so far from you, Pulcheria?

I have too much time to think about you, here.

I also have too much time to think unpleasant thoughts about my ultimate fate. I doubt that the Time Patrol will find me here. But there's another possibility.

The Patrol knows that I'm hiding somewhere up the line, protected by displacement.

The Patrol wants to smoke me out and abolish me, because I'm a filthy spawn of paradox.

And it's in the power of the Patrol to do it. Suppose they retroactively discharge Jud Elliott from the Time Service prior to the time he set out on his ill-starred last trip? If Jud Elliott never ever got to Byzantium that time at all, the probability of my existence reaches the zero point, and I no longer am protected by the Paradox of Transit Displacement. The Law of Lesser Paradoxes prevails. Out I go—poof!

I know why they haven't done that to me yet. It's because that other Jud, God bless him, is standing trial for timecrime down the line, and they can't retroactively pluck him until they've found him guilty. They have to complete the trial. If he's found guilty, I guess they'll take some action of that sort. But court procedures are slow. Jud will stall. Sam's told him I'm here and have to be protected. It might be months, years, who knows? He's on his now-time basis, I'm on mine, and we move forward into our futures together, day by day, and so far I'm still here.

Lonely. Heartsick.

Dreaming of my forever lost Pulcheria.

Maybe they'll never take action against me.

Or maybe they'll end me tomorrow.

Who knows? There are moments when I don't even care. There's one comforting thing, at least. It'll be the most painless of deaths. Not even a flicker of pain. I'll simply go wherever the flame of the candle goes when it's snuffed. It could happen at any time, and meanwhile I live from hour to hour, playing god, listening to Bach, indulging in floaters, dictating my memoirs, and waiting for the end. Why, it could even come right in the middle of a sentence, and I'd

Project PENDULUM

For Jim and Greg Benford

1

ERIC
−5 MINUTES

Displacement hit him like a punch in the gut. He had to fight to keep from doubling up, coughing, and puking. He was dizzy, too, and his legs kept trying to float up toward the ceiling. But the sensation lasted only a fraction of a second, and then he felt fine.

He was still in the laboratory, standing right in front of himself. In front of Sean, too. Twin and twin. Sean and the other version of himself were sitting side by side on the shunt platform in their strange little three-legged metal chairs, waiting for it all to begin.

Five minutes from now the singularity coupling would come to life and the displacement force would take hold of them. And they would be shuttled at infinite speed between the black hole and the white hole until they were thrust out through the time gate. But right now they were staring in wonder and amazement at him— at the extra Eric, $Eric_2$, the one who had been conjured up out of the mysterious well of time. Who had been pulled five minutes out of the future to stand before them now.

Weird to be looking at yourself like this, Eric thought. Seeing yourself from the outside.

In a sense, of course, he had had a way of seeing himself from the outside all his life. He just needed to glance at his twin brother, Sean. Looking at Sean's eyes was almost like looking into a mirror. The same color, the same glinting alertness. The same quick motion taking everything in.

But this was different. Sean was like a mirror image of him, and your mirror image is never what you are. Eric didn't feel he looked as much like Sean as everyone else seemed to think, anyway. But now he was looking at *himself*, not Sean. Seeing neither his twin brother nor his own mirror image, but seeing himself reflected, as others saw him all the time. Strange. His nose—the nose of the other Eric—didn't seem right and his smile turned the wrong way at the corners of his mouth. His eyebrows were reversed, with the one on the right side pointing up. His whole face looked out of balance.

Eric wandered around the lab like some sort of disembodied spirit, prowling here and there. Someone aimed a camera at him and he made faces into it, putting his hands to his ears and wiggling them.

Dr. Ludwig said, "Five minutes exactly. Perfect displacement. Perfect visibility."

"Paradox number one," Dr. White chimed in. "The duplication. The overlap of identity."

"And paradox number two, also. The cumulative and self-modifying aspects of the time-stream correction."

"Say that again?" Eric asked.

Ludwig didn't trouble to reply. He glowered and scowled and vanished into the flow of his own intricate thoughts. It seemed to bother him that Eric had spoken at all. As if Eric were nothing more than an irritating distraction at this very complicated moment.

Project Pendulum

All around the room, technicians were throwing switches and tapping commands into terminals. Everybody was tense. To all these people Time Zero, the moment of the initial shunt, was still four and a half minutes away. The final delicate calibrations and balances had to be made.

Some of the staff people were staring at him the way they might stare at a ghost. That puzzled him for a moment. They should be used to backward-going time travelers by now. After all, Sean had already come this way on the minus-fifty-minutes shunt, hadn't he? And Eric would be doing the minus-five-hundred-minutes one himself a few hours ago. Even though he hadn't experienced it yet, *they* had. Or should have.

But then Eric recalled what they had told him about these past-changing paradoxes. Each swing of the pendulum retroactively corrected everybody's memories and perceptions. That was how it had been in the earlier experiments with robots and animals and they expected it to work the same this time. Nobody remembered Sean's minus-fifty-minutes appearance, or any of the earlier ones, because they hadn't happened yet. But as the pendulum kept swinging, those appearances *would* happen, at times earlier than this, and the corrections would be made, and everyone would begin to remember a past that right now didn't yet exist. Or something like that. It made no sense if you tried to think of it in the old straight-line way. Now that time travel was a fact, no one could think that way ever again.

Warning lights were lit up on all the instrument panels now. Critical displacement momentum was nearly attained. Sean and that other Eric would be on their way in another few instants. And he'd be moving along, too. He couldn't stay here much longer. Any minute now the next $Eric_2$ would be making the journey from Time Zero back to minus-five-minutes, the journey that he himself had just taken. The mathematics of time wouldn't allow him still to be here when the loop began all over again. You could have an Eric and an $Eric_2$ in the same place at the same time, but not more than one $Eric_2$. He would have to be up and out, swinging toward his second stop, the plus-fifty-minutes level.

He could feel the force pulling at him now.

Eric waved jauntily at the Eric and Sean on the platform. When shall we three meet again, he asked himself? Probably never. He'd see Sean again at the end of the experiment, sure. If all went well. But there was no reason why he should ever come face-to-face with himself a second time.

Which was just as well, he decided. There's something creepy about looking yourself in the eye.

"Have a good trip, guys!" he called out to them. And the force seized him and swept him away into the time-stream.

#

SEAN

+5 MINUTES

And then at long last they threw the final switch, the one that would send him spinning off into the vast distant reaches of time, and nothing happened. At least that was how it felt to Sean at first. No blinding flashes of light, no strangely glowing haloes, no sinister humming sounds, no sense of turbulent upheaval. Nothing. An odd calmness, even a numbness, seemed to envelop him. So far as he could tell, nothing had changed at all. He was still sitting right where he had been, on the left-hand focal point of the singularity coupling.

Maybe it was too soon. Only an instant had passed, after all. Maybe the displacement cone was still building up energy, still gathering the momentum it would need to hurl him across the centuries.

A moment later Sean started finding out how wrong he was.

That first moment of calm began to fade as bits of data came flooding into his mind: scattered and trivial bits at first, adding up very quickly into something overwhelming. Subtle wrongnesses became apparent, little ones that quickly grew bigger and bigger in his mind:

—Dr. Ludwig, who had been over by Eric's side of the singularity coupling when the last switch was thrown, had moved to his left, barely outside the event horizon of the shunt field.

Project Pendulum

—Dr. White, who had been all the way across the big room in front of the bank of monitor screens frantically fidgeting with her thick curling hair, now was leaning against the frame of the lab door with her arms folded calmly.

—The computer printers, which had been standing silent in the moment before the throwing of the switch, were spewing copy like crazy. The front-most one had an inch-thick stack of pages in its hopper.

—Half a dozen technicians who had been scattered here and there around the room were gathered in a tight cluster just beyond the gleaming nickel-jacketed hood of the field shield. They were staring in at Sean as though he had sprouted a second head—or had lost the one he used to have.

—And more. The pattern of lights on the instrument panels was different. Someone had restrung the tangle of drooping gray cables on the back wall. And the video camera dolly had been pushed about halfway down the track in his direction. It had been in front of Eric before. At least a dozen tiny changes of that sort had been made.

It was, he thought, very much like one of those before-and-after blackout tests they give you when you're a kid, when they want to measure your I.Q. They show you the image of a room, and then the screen goes dark, and a moment later it lights up and everything's been moved around. You have to note down as many of the changes as you can pick out, within thirty seconds or so. That was what had happened here. In the twinkling of an eye, *before* had turned into *after*. Five minutes after.

So he really had taken a leap through time.

After all the months and months of planning and training and doubting and hoping, he had finally embarked on this fantastic voyage into the remote past and the far-off unknown future, a voyage that would unfold in a series of jumps. Small jumps at first, and then unimaginably vast.

Jump number one. He was five minutes in his own future. All the little changes around the room told him that.

And now he noticed the biggest change of all, the one he had somehow managed to keep blocked from his awareness until this moment.

—Eric wasn't there anymore.

Eric's three-legged aluminum chair was still there, to the right of the singularity coupling. But Eric himself was gone.

Sean felt dazed. A thick oily fog was trying to wrap itself around his brain. It was like a delayed reaction corning on, the whole crushing weight of the knowledge that he had actually been ripped out of space and time and then had been thrust back into place somewhere else.

"How do you feel, Sean?" Dr. Ludwig asked.

The words were like rolling thunder in Sean's ears. He had to work hard to wring some sense from the blurred, booming sounds.

"Not bad," he said automatically. "Not bad at all."

He kept staring at the empty chair to his right, beyond the cone of the displacement torus. Eric wasn't there. Eric wasn't there. That was the only thought in his mind. Suddenly it had driven even the fact of the time voyage itself from the center of his consciousness.

For the entire twenty-three years of Sean's life, Eric had always been there. Somewhere. Maybe not close at hand but always in some way *there*. They could be on opposite sides of the continent and yet they always remained aware of each other's presence in some mysterious, indefinable way that neither of them tried to understand or explain. It had been like that for them all the way back to the beginning, to that time when they had shared the same womb, Eric lying beside him, jostling for space, poking his little arms and legs where they didn't belong.

Sean had never been alone like this before.

He had understood that the experiment was going to separate them in time, sending Eric one way, him another. But there is understanding and there is understanding. There are things you understand in your mind, and there are things you understand in your bones. Now that the contact between them had actually been severed, he was coming fully to realize what it meant to be separated from his twin by an enormous and uncrossable gulf of time. That was different. That was terrifying.

"Sean?" Dr. Ludwig said again, rumbling and strange as before. "I asked you how you were feeling."

"Not bad, I told you." He turned, stared, worked hard at focusing his eyes. He was getting some odd visual effects now. Streaks of colored lights, reds and blues and greens. Everything seemed too long and narrow. And there was some double vision. He was dimly aware that Dr. Ludwig was still talking to him. And Dr. White, too. Their words came to him from a million miles away. How are you feeling, how are you feeling, how are you feeling. What did that mean? Oh. It means how are you feeling, he thought. Is that any of their business? He was so terribly confused.

"Sean—"

"I'm all right!" he snapped. He didn't want them to think he couldn't take it.

They looked at him blankly. He tried to explain things, but he had the feeling his words were ricocheting around them like bullets. They turned to each other in bewilderment.

"What did he say?"

"What did he say?"

"What did he say?"

"Sean? Try to speak more slowly. You're all hypered up."

"Am I? You sound all slowed down."

It was getting worse. He felt that his own chair was melting and flowing beneath him. And he was starting to melt with it. A sense of chill and a sense of burning at the same time. A strangeness in his stomach. A rising and a falling in his chest. That first calm moment when nothing seemed to have changed seemed like a million years ago. Everything was changing now. Everything. He wondered if Eric was feeling anything like this. Wherever Eric was right now. *Whenever* Eric was.

"Maybe my voice will be easier for you to make out, Sean."

That was Dr. White. Speaking gently, softly, carefully. Her voice sounded deeper than it should have been, but not as strange as Dr. Ludwig's.

Sean tried to force himself to relax.

He said, making an effort to be understood, "What was the span of the jump, Dr. White?"

"Five minutes precisely. Right on target."

"And how long has it been since I got here?"

"Fifteen, twenty seconds."

That was all? It felt like half an hour. His mind was feeding him distorted information. Was this how it was going to be, on and on through time, everything blurred and confused? Like a nightmare. Stumbling across millions of years in a dopey fog, understanding nothing.

"What have you heard from my brother?" Sean asked.

"Your brother's fine." Dr. Ludwig's voice.

"You've heard from him?"

"We saw him. Five minutes before Time Zero."

Sean frowned and shook his head. Everything was so hard to follow.

"Five minutes before the shunt? Well, yes, but what I meant was—" He paused. He didn't know what he meant. "I know you saw my brother then. You saw both of us then, right here. But—"

"We saw him and we saw you." The soft voice of Dr. White. "But we saw an extra Eric also, $Eric_2$, the one traveling backward from Time Zero. Don't you remember that?"

"An extra Eric." He felt so *stupid*.

"Smiling at us. Winking. Happy and confident."

"Traveling backward," Sean murmured, struggling to cut through the fog in his brain. "An extra Eric."

So muddled, his mind. His fine mind, his outstanding mind. He wondered if he'd ever be able to do physics again. Or even simply to think straight. He shook his head again, slowly, heavily, like a wounded bear.

They had seen Ricky traveling backward in time. Saw him arrive five minutes before Time Zero, before the start of the experiment. In this very room. Why can't I remember seeing him? Or do I? I think I do, yes. Sean closed his eyes a moment. He tried to imagine the scene.

That ghostly figure, hovering in front of them, looking so very cheerful. Ricky always looked cheerful, even at crazy times. So there had been one Eric Gabrielson sitting in the right-hand chair on the shunt platform and another one, $Eric_2$, floating around the middle of the room. And that had been five minutes before Time Zero—the shunt that balanced this one that had carried him five

Project Pendulum

minutes beyond Time Zero. The first swing of the giant pendulum that would cut across millions of years, carrying them backward and forward, backward and forward, backward and forward—

He wasn't sure if he could remember seeing that other Ricky or not.

Sean struggled to understand. His mind still felt doped. It was temporal shock, the effect of the shunt plus the effect of the change that had just taken place in the very recent past with Ricky's arrival there. The past would be constantly changing with each swing of the pendulum. The robot experiments had shown that. Each swing and they'd all have an entirely new set of memories, reaching back farther and farther, five minutes, fifty minutes, five hundred minutes, five thousand minutes—

Something was glowing now on the far wall.

The temporal energy must be building up again, creating displacement momentum for the next shunt. They had said the swings were going to be quick ones in the early stages of the journey, in and out of the past or the future in just a couple of minutes during the first few shunts, zip zip zip zip.

Dr. White said, "There's nothing to worry about, Sean. It's all going to work out all right."

Sean nodded and smiled. Suddenly his mind seemed to clear a little. He was beginning to feel like himself again. "Sure it will," he said. "I never doubted it." He became aware of strangeness beginning to enfold him. The field was taking him onward. "Say hello to Ricky for me," he said, and waved at them as they grew blurry around him. "I'll see you all a little later."

ERIC

+50 MINUTES

He was falling. Like Alice going down the rabbit hole, except that when she fell it was in a slow, stately way, with plenty of time to look around. He was plummeting crazily, a wild juggernaut zooming through the center of the earth. Down through the geological strata, past the Cretaceous and the Jurassic, past the Permian, the Silurian, the Cambrian. Choking and gasping, tumbling end over end, arms and legs flailing, his hair flying in the hot breeze that came blasting up from below.

He thought he was going to fall forever.

He had never imagined it was possible to feel so sick and dizzy.

All the worst stuff comes right at the beginning, Sean had told him. *And then it's okay.*

Had Sean really said that? Eric tried to remember. Yes. It was at the minus-fifty-minutes level, just when he and Sean both were starting to get a little panicky about the crazy project they had committed themselves to. And then Sean$_2$ had come whistling out of the future looking cocky and cheerful. Engaging in a whole bunch of incomprehensible babble with Dr. Ludwig about how past tense and future tense lose their meanings when you travel in time. And then, jaunty as can be, coming over to Eric and Sean$_1$, to tell them not to worry about anything.

It's all going to be fine. Just let yourself go, and don't try to fight it.
Sure, Sean.

Down and down and down. Did *you* fall like this, Sean, when you made *your* first jump into the future? Down, down, down through the primordial rock of the earth into the bubbling volcanic magma at the core of the planet?

Eric wondered when it was going to stop. And what it was going to feel like when he hit bottom.

Then he realized that he was floating rather than dropping. And then that he wasn't even floating. He was still in the laboratory, not in some tunnel that passed through the bowels of the earth. That falling sensation had been just in his imagination, a side effect of the trip forward in time. In fact his feet were firmly planted on the floor of the shunt platform.

So he had arrived. He was fifty minutes in the future.

Everything was a blur. Eric was so dizzy that he thought his head would spin free from his shoulders. And the nausea that he was feeling was real star-quality nausea. It was so intense that he wanted to applaud it. As soon as he felt a little better.

"Somebody grab me or I'm going to fall," he managed to blurt.

They caught him just as he started to go over.

"Easy," someone said. "The disorientation lasts only a couple of moments. Going into the future seems to be more traumatic than going into the past."

"So I notice," Eric murmured.

But they were right: you did come out of it pretty fast. He was able to stand unaided now. He could focus his eyes again. The digital elapsed-time counter on the rear wall confirmed that he was exactly fifty minutes into the experiment. Right on schedule.

Sean must already have materialized here ahead of him, making the plus-five-minutes shunt. Eric wondered whether Sean had gone through the same hellacious rabbit-hole sensation then. He wondered whether Sean—

Sean—

Suddenly Eric felt with full force the impact of his twin brother's absence. The strangeness, the aloneness, the separateness.

It came rushing in like a roaring tsunami: the knowledge that time stood between him and his brother like a sword. He hadn't felt it on his first time-jump, because that had been a backward one, and when he arrived he had seen Sean right there in the lab, getting ready to begin the experiment. But at this very moment Sean was a hundred minutes away, back at the minus-fifty-minutes level. The balancing swing of the pendulum, the equal and opposite displacement.

From here to Time Ultimate—the end of the experiment, some 95 million years out from the starting point—they were never going to be on the same side of the time-line again. One of them would always be in the minus-time level while the other one was an equal distance up ahead in plus-time.

Eric stepped down from the platform. Took a couple of uncertain steps.

"How do you feel now?" Dr. White asked.

He managed to smile at her. "Better." It was a lie. "Just a little wobbly. Just a little."

"It's a jolt, isn't it?"

He nodded. He wanted to ask Sean how *he* had felt on his first forward jump. But of course Sean wasn't here. It was weird, not having him nearby. Not feeling that odd, almost telepathic bond. The sensation that said, *I am here, I am Sean, I am closer to you than anyone on this planet and always will be.* Almost as if they were Siamese twins and not the ordinary kind. Eric had never talked about that with Sean. It had always seemed, well, embarrassing—telling him what he felt, asking him if he felt it, too. But he was pretty sure that Sean felt it, too.

And right now Eric was feeling the lack of it. Intensely.

"Fifty minutes from Time Zero," he said. "I don't suppose much can have changed in the world yet."

Dr. White chuckled. "Not in fifty minutes. All the really interesting things are still ahead of you."

"Ahead of me?" Eric shook his head. "No, you've got it upside down. The way I look at it, all the really interesting stuff's *behind* me."

She looked baffled by that.

"You don't know what I mean?" he said.

"Well—"

"No, you don't, do you. I'm Eric, remember?"

"Yes, of course, but—" Her voice trailed off.

"The twin who's the paleontologist. The one who's a lot more interested in the past than the future." He made a broad, sweeping gesture. "I don't mind getting a peek at the future. But what I'm really waiting for is at the other end of the pendulum. The Mesozoic, back there at the end of the whole circus. The dinosaurs!" He felt heat rising in his cheeks. Excitement coursing through him, making his heart pound. "That's why I volunteered for this crazy ride, don't you know? To meet the dinosaurs, face-to-face. It's as simple as that. To walk up to a live dinosaur and say hello."

Project Pendulum

SEAN
−50 MINUTES

It was different this time, the second shunt. Sean didn't feel that initial sense of dead calmness that had tricked him before into thinking he hadn't gone anywhere. Nor was there a rush of confusion and bewilderment and dismay right afterward. Instead he felt only a second or two of mild dizziness, and then everything seemed fine.

Maybe it's only the first shunt that's the bummer, he thought. Or maybe it's easier because this time I went backward in time instead of forward.

He looked around the lab.

They were all running back and forth like a bunch of lunatics, getting all the last-minute stuff ready. The experiment would happen in less than an hour. So there they were, hooking things up, checking circuits, crunching numbers. There was Dr. Ludwig, face shiny with sweat, yelling into a pocket telephone. And Dr. White, who was usually so calm and gentle, practically tearing at her hair. Harrell, the math man, working at two computers at once. Other scientific types frenziedly doing other final-hour things. And the technicians zipping around the way people did in the ancient silent movies, going much too fast and moving in a silly jerky way.

The only people who looked calm were Ricky and Sean, those intrepid Gabrielson boys. They were standing off to one side with a numbed, zonked look on their faces, waiting to be told to mount the shunt platform and sit down on either side of the displacement torus.

It all looked terribly familiar. Sean had lived through this scene once, after all, less than an hour ago. Now here he was again. Only this time he wasn't waiting around to be told to sit down on the platform. That was those two fellows over there; he was somebody else, Sean$_2$, the traveler in time, the man from fifty minutes in the future.

"Hey," he said. "Over here. Me. Anybody going to say hello to me?"

391

There was a sudden stunned silence in the room. They had all been so busy running through the final insane setting-up procedures that they hadn't even noticed him materialize. But they noticed him now.

"The second backswing!" someone cried. "Here he is!"

"Absolutely," Sean said. "The big surprise. The walking, talking paradox man. You've never seen anything like me, right? You don't remember seeing any of us heading backward before, is that it?"

"Not yet," replied Dr. Ludwig. His voice sounded thick and hoarse. He looked a little dazed, as though perhaps he hadn't been fully prepared for what was happening. Even he, who had spent years thinking about these concepts while he was planning the experiment. "You are the first, but of course not the last. Others will come before you, but we do not remember them yet. You are Sean, yes? Making your second shunt, the minus-fifty-minutes swing. But soon there will be Eric at minus five hundred minutes, coming in yesterday evening."

Sean laughed. "'There *will* be Eric, coming in yesterday evening'? I like the way you say that."

"We will come to remember his visit, yes, after he has made it. We will need an entirely new grammar to speak of these things. Past tense and future tense lose their meanings when cause and effect are broken free from all mooring. You understand what I am saying?"

"Absolutely," Sean said.

On this shunt all of it made perfect sense to him How different from his experience at plus five minutes when fog was so thick in his brain! Thank God his mind was working right again. It had been scary to think he might have been rendered stupid forever by his trip through time.

It wasn't logical, of course, that this retroactive rearrangement of the past should happen in stages. With everyone's memories of the hours and days just prior to Time Zero being altered again and again, each time a wider swing brought a new Eric or a Sean back to some point earlier than the last one.

Logically all such changes in the past should occur at once. From the moment the final switch was thrown there *would always have*

Project Pendulum

been Erics and Seans scattered all up and down the time-stream across the whole span of the experiment's 190 million years.

But there wasn't anything logical about time-travel in the first place, Sean knew. It gloriously defied all the laws of cause and effect. And so evidently each swing on the pendulum was going to produce a completely new version of the past. Reality would be fluid from now on and no one within that shifting reality would ever be aware of the changes. They could never remember the past as it used to be. The moment the change was made, the past would always have been the way it was now.

Only he and Eric, the daring young men on the flying trapeze, moving as outside observers, would be able to comprehend the havoc they were wreaking as they flashed back and forth across the fabric of time, reweaving it as they went. And even they would start to lose track of the changes as the paradoxes mounted.

He walked over to Eric and $Sean_1$. God, they looked pale and sweaty! That was embarrassing. They were really nervous. He didn't remember having felt that nervous himself when it had been his turn to be $Sean_1$ fifty minutes ago. He thought of himself as having waited calmly, coolly, confidently for his launching into the time-shunt.

But he realized that he was probably kidding himself. The way $Sean_1$ looked now was the way he himself must have looked fifty minutes ago, because he had been $Sean_1$, then. There was no hiding from the truth of that. He had been scared stiff. Fifty minutes ago he had been sitting there waiting to be converted into a cluster of tachyons—particles that move faster than light and travel backward in time in an anti-time universe. What the singularity coupling did was turn him into a tachyonic replica of himself, throwing off showers of anti-time energy that would be exactly balanced by the time-force liberated in the opposite direction. At least that was what it was supposed to do. And he had been sitting there wondering if it would.

Well, it had. And here he was.

They were staring goggle-eyed at him. As though he had no business being there. As though he were some evil being who had come to haunt the place. Sean smiled.

"Relax," he said. "It's all going to be fine. Just let yourself go, and don't try to fight it. You won't like it *at* first, but all the worst stuff comes right at the beginning and then it's okay."

A little comfort, a little friendly cheer. It was the least he could do for them, he thought. For Ricky. And also for Sean$_1$, who was sitting there looking so pale and miserable. His brother and his other self. If there's any one in the world who's closer and dearer to you than your twin brother, Sean thought, it's your other self.

ERIC

−5 × 10² MINUTES

The big room was oddly peaceful, here on the night before the experiment. It was about two in the morning. The overhead lights were turned off, and the only illumination came from a couple of green security lamps off to the side.

Nobody seemed to be there when Eric stepped off the shunt platform after a moment of arrival vertigo blessedly more brief than it had been the last time. He looked around. Nobody here at all? That was peculiar. They knew what time he'd be due to arrive on this swing. Even if most of them would be asleep at this hour, resting up for the big day ahead of them tomorrow, *somebody* should have been here to debrief him when he showed up.

Then he noticed one of the younger scientists—a quasiconductor man named John Terzunian—dozing in the darkness.

Eric went over to him. Touched him gently on the shoulder.

"Johnny? Johnny, wake up. It's me, Eric, making the minus-five-hundred-minutes shunt."

"What? Who?" A look of sudden panic. "Oh, God, I must have slumped off."

"Happens to anyone," Eric said. The other man looked hardly older than he was, maybe twenty-five, twenty-six, barely past his doctorate. His hair was thinning already. His eyes were jet black and very bloodshot. "Don't worry. I won't tell. Everyone else is asleep, huh?"

Terzunian nodded. "The last one left an hour ago. We drew lots for who would stay till you came in."

"And you lost."

A sheepish smile. "Nobody's had much sleep for three or four nights in a row, now. I wouldn't mind being sacked out right this minute. But somebody had to be here to meet you."

"Sure," Eric said. "I understand."

He thought of $Sean_1$ and $Eric_1$, snoring away in the dorm section a couple of hundred yards from the lab. For them, he knew, edginess had fought a battle with exhaustion and exhaustion had won.

Well, it was a good idea for them to be sleeping. This would be the last chance they'd have to get a proper night's sleep in the year 2016 for a long time to come. Little more than eight hours from now they were going to set out on a journey that would carry them some 95 million years in each direction before they saw their own home year again. Adrift in the time-stream, swinging back and forth, swooping through the eons.

It was strange, thinking of $Sean_1$ and $Eric_1$ as *them* instead of *us*. But he had to. Those two guys sleeping down there in the dorm weren't Sean and Eric Gabrielson at all, not really. Not to him. They were two entirely other people: $Sean_1$, and $Eric_1$. Yesterday's selves. They hadn't yet begun to oscillate in time. They still had no real idea of what any of this was going to be like.

To them, if they thought of him at all, he would be $Eric_2$, an Eric of the future, tomorrow's Eric, an unreal Eric. That was all right. He didn't feel unreal. He wasn't living in tomorrow. He was living in *now*. It was a now that kept sliding around between past and future, but all the same it was the only now he had. He was real enough to himself: the true and authentic Eric. And the true and authentic Sean, for him, was the one who was nearly seventeen hours away just now, up there at the plus-500-minutes level, at the opposite end of the time-travel seesaw that they were riding.

Everything in balance. Everything symmetrical.

It all had the intense bright clarity of a very powerful dream. Except it was actually happening to them, and it would go on happening for something like ninety-five million years.

Terzunian said, "Can I get you anything? A drink of water? Something to eat?"

"No, thanks," Eric said. "So far as subjective time goes, this is still just the beginning of the experiment for me. I've only experienced a few minutes of elapsed time since the whole thing started."

"All right," Terzunian said. "We'd better get down to work, then. I'm supposed to ask you questions about your psychological and physical state upon arrival. Here—the camera's on. Testing. Testing." He seemed twitchy, ill at ease, afraid of messing anything up. Well, Eric thought, he's been involved with this project for years, and now here it is, actually happening.

Actually happening. Yes.

There were times when he had trouble believing that he and Sean had really agreed to do it. Of course they had known about the experiment for years—Project Pendulum had gotten underway when they were still in high school, as soon as the development of artificially produced mini-singularities had provided the technological basis for traveling in time.

Sean had brought home a pile of theoretical papers about it. Explaining how the phase-linkage coupling of a minute black hole, identical to those that are found all over interstellar space, and its mathematical opposite, a "white hole," created an incredibly powerful force that ripped right through the fabric of space-time—and how that force could be contained and controlled, like a bomb in a basket, so that it could be used as a transit tube for making two-way movements in time.

Eric's first reaction on hearing that was to imagine himself running backward along the earth's geological history as if seeing a film from back to front—soaring through the epochs, past the Pleistocene and the Pliocene into the days of the dinosaurs, the early amphibians, the trilobites, back even to the primordial days when there was nothing on the surface of the world except a bare granite shield rising above a steaming sea. Tremendous! To see it all. Not to have to reconstruct it from compressed strata and scattered fossils, but to look at everything with your own eyes while it still existed.

His second reaction was to think that the whole notion was completely crazy, a fantastic pipe dream.

No, Sean had said. It really can work. Here, let me show you the equations—

And Sean had scribbled equations for him until he begged for mercy. Math on Sean's level was a mysterious language to him, as remote and inaccessible as the language the ancient Egyptians spoke in their dreams. The more Sean explained of it, the less Eric understood—or cared. But Sean was convinced that the theory of time-shunting was correct, and Sean was usually right about anything he investigated with such passion. At least in the world of physics.

That's extraordinary, Eric had said, figuring that fifty or sixty years of heavy-duty work would be necessary, at the very least, before time travel was anything more than a set of fascinating equations. And then he put it all totally out of his mind. He had other things to think about that seemed more urgent, like going to college, and his graduate work in paleontology after that.

But then came news that the first displacement machine had actually been built and tested. Eric paid some mild attention to that. Robots equipped with data-recording gear and cameras went off, so it was claimed, on safaris in time. The robots made their journey and returned to the same instant from which they had been sent off. To the watching scientists the elapsed time of the experiment was zero. So there was no way of telling that anything had happened, except for the power drain that the instruments measured—and except for the paradoxes.

The paradoxes! Even though the robots hadn't seemed to go anywhere, they turned up in the laboratory hours and days and weeks before they had been sent out. That gave everyone headaches, thinking about it. The past kept flowing and shifting around, and nobody's memory was a safe place: things were always getting different from what you thought you remembered.

And the robots also turned up an equal number of hours and days and weeks *after* the experiment, flashing suddenly into existence in the laboratory and staying around for a few minutes, maybe an hour or two, before vanishing again.

The robots seemed to have suffered no ill effects from their mysterious journeys. They appeared still to be in fine working order. But the cameras they carried yielded nothing but fogged film. Sean explained that film emulsion was evidently unable to withstand the tachyon storms to which it was exposed during the time shunts. The data-recording gear had produced scrambled digital readouts, just static, probably for the same reason.

Oh, Eric had said. Tachyon storms, is that it?

He didn't bother asking for more elaborate explanations. Not then.

They sent living creatures through the machine, too—turtles, frogs, rabbits. The usual nature organizations complained about that, but the animals all came back safely. Back from where? Who could say? No question that they had gone *somewhere*. The usual time-displacement paradoxes had been observed: rabbits popping out of nowhere in the laboratory three days before the start of the experiment, and doing the same thing three days after the experiment, too.

That was interesting, a remarkable achievement. If the rabbits could be sent three days backward and forward in time, they might well have gone a million years, or fifty million. Still, what could a turtle or a rabbit tell anybody about the way the Mesozoic really looks, or the world of A.D. One Million? You could send a turtle to the end of time and back, and it wouldn't give you one syllable of useful information about its trip.

So of course they called for volunteers.

Human time-travelers would have to go through the machine in order to get any significant results. Only a lunatic, Eric figured, would volunteer for a deal like that.

The word went out that they wanted to use a pair of identical twins, because there had to be an exact balance of momentum down to the last milligram. Twins, because they had the same bone structure and pretty much the same distribution of body fat, would make it that much easier to attain that balance.

Project Pendulum

That's nice, Eric thought. And went back to his doctoral thesis on Arctic amphibian life in the Mesozoic period.

They're looking for twins with scientific background, someone told him. Eric simply shrugged.

Ideally they want one twin who's a physicist and one who's a paleontologist, someone else told him. In order to maximize the value of their observations.

Right. Eric was a paleontologist. Sean was a physicist.

That's very interesting, Eric said, still showing no interest at all. I suppose we're not the only twins who meet that requirement. They'll find someone sooner or later who'll be willing to risk the trip.

Then one day Sean turned up and said, "Don't you think it could help your research a little if you got a look at some *living* Mesozoic critters, Ricky?"

And now here he was five hundred minutes in his own past, locked into an unstoppable series of ever-widening swings in time, back and forth, back and forth, minutes and hours and months and years and centuries and eons. Like a dream, a very strange and intense dream, a dream brighter and sharper than any reality he had ever experienced.

"Go ahead," Terzunian said. "This is the minus-five-hundred minutes level, John Terzunian speaking. Eric Gabrielson has just arrived right on schedule: the third backswing." He pointed at Eric to give him his cue. "Okay. Make your report."

"There's not a lot to tell. Easy arrival, none of the queasiness I felt when I made the minus-five-minute shunt. Just a fast flicker of discomfort, then everything normal. Some minor spatial displacement: I came in a couple of feet to the left of my departure point. No fatigue so far. Maybe some mild uneasiness—no, uneasiness is too strong a word, a little edginess, maybe—" Terzunian was staring at him. There was a peculiar expression on his face, what seemed to be a mixture of fascination and envy and what might have been something like pity.

"Well, look," Eric said, "there really isn't anything to report yet. Give me another few shunts and I'll have plenty to say. *Plenty.*"

But who will I say it to, he wondered? When I'm nine and a half years in the past? Or 950,000 years in the future?

SEAN

+5 X 10² MINUTES

This time it felt as if some giant had scooped him up, popped him into a slingshot and whirled him around, and tossed him with all his might. When he landed, the sides of the laboratory were circling around him like the rim of a big centrifuge and the floor was rocking wildly from side to side. The place might just as well have been a carnival funhouse. Sean flung himself down flat, hanging on for all he was worth.

But the effect lasted only a moment or two. The wild funhouse gyrations slowed down and then they stopped altogether. He patted the floor to make certain it had finished moving. Apparently it had. He got carefully to his feet, steadying himself with his outstretched arms. He took two or three cautious steps. Everything was holding still, now. Fine. Fine.

"It takes a little getting used to," he said to nobody in particular.

He looked around. There were new changes in the laboratory. He was five hundred minutes in the future: eight hours and twenty minutes since the start of the experiment. Night had fallen. The fluorescent lights seemed harsher and brighter. The big room was weirdly quiet, almost ominous.

"Tell us what you experienced," Dr. Ludwig said.

Dr. Ludwig and Dr. White were the only people in the room. The technicians must have been sent home. The shunt platform was strangely forlorn and abandoned with no one around it. The two metal seats that flanked the displacement cone might have been nothing more than a couple of classroom chairs. The cone itself seemed trivial, a mere chunk of inactive machinery.

Staring at it, Sean had trouble believing that under that glossy lump of shielding lurked a symmetrical pair of laboratory-generated collapsed stars: a miniature black hole and its mirror image, a so-called white hole. Together they made up a pair of perfectly balanced singularities—zones of strangeness where nothing behaved according to the rules of the ordinary universe—held in an unbreakable coupling. Infinite energy forever circled in a loop between the interlocked event horizons of those singularities. Energy that had opened the time gate through which Sean and Eric had been shunted to begin their immense voyage through time and anti-time.

Dr. Ludwig's eyes looked bleary and his plump cheeks were dark with stubble. It was the look of a man who has been in the office too long. When Sean had made his last trip through here at plus five minutes—hardly any time at all ago for Sean, eight hours and twenty minutes for them—Dr. Ludwig had been pink and freshly shaven.

"The first time," Sean said, "I thought I was losing my mind. The first forward swing, the plus-five-minutes one. Let me tell you, it was a truly hideous experience."

"The forward swings are worse than the backward ones?" Dr. White asked.

"So it seems. All that disorientation and mental fog, the sheer *stupidity* that I felt. The first backward swing, the minus-fifty-minutes one, was a little jarring, but nothing like that. And the disturbance only lasted for a moment."

"And this time? The second forward swing?"

"Dizziness, really serious dizziness, everything whirling like mad. But not as strong as the first time and it didn't last nearly as long."

"Yet it was stronger than what you felt on the one backswing you've made so far."

Sean nodded. "It's as though there's some real effort in making the forward swings, something that demands a lot from you in breaking free of the time fabric. Whereas when you go the other way you slide along the track pretty easily, and there's just the slightest little shimmy of disturbance."

"Perhaps so," Dr. Ludwig said. "But we have reason to think that the shunt effects in both directions will diminish the farther you get from Time Zero."

Sean grinned. "They'd better. We're not going to be landing in this nice safe lab many more times, are we?" The pendulum swings were going to be getting wider and wider. Sudden visions blazed in his mind: the dark steamy past, the shimmering unimaginable future. "It'll be nice not to get an attack of the dizzies every time we arrive," he said. "In some of the places where we're going to turn up we may need to hit the ground running."

7

ERIC

+5 × 10³ MINUTES

"If nobody minds very much," Eric said, "I'd like to have a quick look at today's newspaper before I shuffle along toward last month."

The elapsed-time counter in front of him read 83.33 hours. Which was just short of three and a half days since Time Zero. And so this ought to be Friday night, the twenty-second of April.

He saw them exchanging glances. Was it okay to give him a paper? They weren't sure. Someone on the psych staff went off to ask Dr. Ludwig, and apparently the answer was yes, because he came back with a newspaper in his hands.

It was a fresh printout. It had that brand-new smell that papers have when they first come from the wall slot. Eric stared at the date. Friday, April 22, 2016.

So it really was true. He was actually traveling in time.

Unless this was all some crazy hoax—some kind of psychological experiment, maybe? And they had given him a paper with a phony date, so that he'd be fooled into believing—

That's mighty paranoid thinking, Ricky-boy, he told himself. *All this is real. You'd better believe it.*

He glanced quickly over the front-page stories.

Tenth anniversary of lunar settlement celebrated here and on the moon. The President's visit to Antarctica. An earthquake in Turkey, 6.3 on the Richter scale, exactly as predicted last month.

Project Pendulum

A big feature at the bottom of the page about the Robot Pride Day parade in Detroit, fifty thousand mechanical workers taking part.

He didn't see any story about the time-travel experiment now under way at Cal Tech.

But it would have surprised him if he had. The whole project was classified data, partly because the government wanted it that way and partly because a lot of people were scared stiff of the whole idea of time travel. The response to the earliest announcements of the project had been unexpectedly heated. Certain historians and philosophers had argued that there might be irreparable damage to contemporary life if the past were changed in any way by time travelers. One small alteration—the plucking of a flower, the squashing of a bug—might wipe out whole empires, for all anyone knew. Then too some religious leaders were troubled by the possibility that visitors to the past might discover that scriptural history was inaccurate in some way. And there were always those people who feared any new development in science, especially one as startling and magical as this. So it had been decided on the highest levels not to release any details of Project Pendulum until there had been a chance to study the effects of the first few shunts.

Turning to the sports pages, Eric saw that the Dodgers had just dropped their third straight game in Osaka after losing two out of three in Honolulu. The new baseball season wasn't starting off very promisingly. Things were doing a little better for the local basketball team: the Lakers had won their playoff series against Buenos Aires and were going on now to play Nairobi for the championship.

The weather for the Pasadena area was going to be fair and warm. It had rained in San Francisco yesterday but the storm wasn't expected to reach Southern California. The stock market had had a good day, the Dow Jones averages rising 112 points to 7786. Eric felt curiously superstitious about looking at the obituary page and went past it quickly, averting his eyes.

"Here," he said, handing the paper back. Thanks."

"How does it feel?"

Eric grinned. "I always like to see Friday's newspaper on Tuesday," he said. "You get a good jump on things that way."

SEAN

-5×10^3 MINUTES

Four of them were waiting for him on the next swing: Dr. White and Dr. Thomas representing the psychological side of the experiment, Dr. Mukherji and Dr. Camminella representing the theoretical mathematicians.

This was his fourth shunt. It was beginning to mount up now. The swings were calibrated in logarithmically increasing intervals, each one ten times wider than the one before. So he had gone five minutes into the future, then fifty minutes into the past, five hundred minutes into the future, five thousand minutes into the past—

Five thousand minutes. Five times 10^3 minutes. Five thousand minutes was 83 hours and 20 minutes, which was 3.46 days. Time Zero for the experiment, the point from which all the shunting began, was Tuesday, the nineteenth of April, 2016, at half past ten in the morning. And here he was, stepping down from the shunt platform three and a half days before that.

The reception committee seemed to be having a little trouble coming to terms with that. They were all trying hard to look cool and collected. Sean could see them working at it.

But they didn't even come close to being able to hide their amazement. Their eyes were wide, their faces were flushed, their tongues kept licking back and forth over dry lips. It was the look of people who knew that they were experiencing something miraculous.

"Nice of you all to be here to greet me," he said cheerfully. "I'm Sean, in case you weren't quite certain. It's last Friday night, isn't it?"

"Friday, yes," Dr. White said. Her voice was thick and husky, choked with emotion. "The fifteenth of April."

"At eleven-ten P.M.," said Sean. "On the button."

"On the button," Dr. White said.

Project Pendulum

Why did they seem so stunned? After all, this was his fourth shunt, two forward and now two back. They ought to be getting used to it by now.

Then he scowled at his own idiocy. *He* was getting used to it. But it was all new to these people. They were living three and a half days ago, back there before the start of the experiment. This was the first time they were seeing a shunter.

Maybe they had never truly believed the experiment would work. Or maybe they accepted it on a theoretical level but hadn't properly prepared themselves for the real thing—for having him come dropping right out of next Tuesday like this. Despite all the years they had put in, working toward this moment, thinking about what it was going to be like to make time travel an actuality, his arrival must be an overpowering, almost shattering event for them.

Dr. Thomas said, "We have a few tests that we'd like you to take."

Sean gave him a sour look. "Tests?"

Dr. Thomas was the team's head psychologist, and he was *always* saying, "We have a few tests we'd like you to take." Sean had never cared much for the trim, smug little psychologist, who sometimes seemed more like a computerized simulation of a human being than an actual flesh-and-blood person.

In the planning stages of the project he had subjected Sean and Eric to multiphasic electronic devices that buzzed and flashed and screeched maddeningly as they probed the twins' minds. The ordeal was necessary, they were told, to find out whether they were stable enough to withstand the stress of time-shunting. Apparently they were.

All right. What more did Thomas need to know now? The biggest test of all was underway this very minute: the experiment itself. Wasn't that enough for him? Sean hadn't been expecting another bout with those instruments of torture.

"Over here, please," Dr. Thomas said. "Can you walk unaided?"

"Of course I can walk unaided. You think I've become brain-damaged?"

"Please. There isn't much time."

"I simply wonder why it's necessary to inflict even more of these idiotic—"

"What we wish to determine," Dr. Thomas said frostily, "is whether retrograde motion through time has deleterious effects on the human nervous system. Or, if you prefer me to put it in words of a single syllable—"

"You wouldn't know how to," Sean said. "But I assure you that my mind is still working properly. I could even spell 'retrograde' for you. Maybe even 'deleterious.' How about 'retrograde' backward? That would be E-D-A-R-G—"

Dr. White put her hand lightly over Sean's and said very quietly, "We don't have any doubt that you're taking the shunt beautifully, Sean. But we do need quantitative data. We have to know things about your pulse rate, your reaction times, your automatic reflexes, etcetera, etcetera. It really is important. And this is practically our only chance to get it. The testing machines are set up to record everything quickly and automatically. We've only got fifteen minutes, you know, before you go shunting off again into the future."

Throughout the entire life of the project Dr. White had been the cool, gentle voice of reason. Whenever anyone had started yelling—and there had been plenty of that, as deadlines neared and everybody's nerves grew taut—she had always been the one to restore peace.

Once again Sean found it impossible to resist her calm, easy manner. With a sigh he said, "All right, go ahead and test me."

He waited grimly for the onslaught of the blinking screens and whirling patterns and screaming sirens.

Might as well humor them, he thought. Dr. White was right that they wouldn't have many more chances to do this to him. The next time he came pastward, it would be at the minus 5×10^5 minutes level. That would be nearly a year ago. They probably would be expecting him then, and they'd have more tests ready. But the swing after that would bring him into the past at minus 5×10^7 minutes. That would be the year 1921. Dr. Thomas wouldn't even have been born yet, nor even his parents. Maybe not even Dr. Thomas's grandparents. He wasn't going to have to worry about Dr. Thomas or anybody else sitting him down in front of multiphasic testing machines in the year 1921.

9

ERIC

−5 × 10⁴ MINUTES

It was raining. Eric could hear the drumbeat of the drops hitting the roof of the single-story laboratory building.

So this had to be March. The month before the experiment. It had rained practically every day in March, a torrential climax to the wettest winter Southern California had had in years, causing mudslides and other calamities all over the place. Then at the end of the month the sun had reappeared, and the weather had been dry and warm ever since, as it probably was going to be until the fall. There is hardly ever any rain in Southern California between April and November. But plenty of it was coming down right now.

The sound of the rain was beautiful in his ears. Maybe hillsides were turning to muck and goo out there and houses were floating off their foundations, but to Eric the pounding of those pelting drops was the sweetest music he could imagine. It told him that everything was still going according to plan.

He was fifty thousand minutes in the past. That was 833.3 hours. Or 34.72 days. They had drilled the arithmetic of the time journey into him until he could recite it in his sleep.

You jumped ten times as far on each shunt as on the one before. But you alternated a swing to the future with one to the past, so each time you returned to the past you landed a hundred times farther back than you had on the last jump. The same with the future. The early swings were very close together, but the hundredfold factor kept multiplying.

So it was 8.33 hours back, and 83.3 hours forward, and then 833.3 hours back, and 8333.3 hours forward, and then 83,333.3 hours back, which worked out to 9.51 years into the past. Then 95.13 years forward. And then 951.3 years back. Then 9,513 years forward. And then 95,129.3 years back. And then 951,293.7 years forward. Then 9,512,937.5 years back. And then—

And then the top of the pendulum swing, the swing to Time Ultimate, the effective limit of the experiment, at which point he would have been carried some 95 million years into the future and then an equal distance back—back to the Cretaceous Period—back to the time of the dinosaurs—

He listened joyfully to the beat of the rain. Thinking, *Yes, carry me back, carry me back, let me look upon the dawn of time.*

"Eric?" a voice said.

"Right the first try."

"Do you know what day this is?"

"Wednesday, March 16, 2016."

"Yes. Yes, that's right. And what day is it for you?"

"Just a little bit past Time Zero. Tuesday, the nineteenth of April. At not quite eleven A.M."

They were staring at him that way that was getting to be so tiresomely familiar to him—staring as if they were looking at a ghost. Dr. Ludwig, Dr. White, Dr. Thomas, Dr. Mukherji, Dr. Camminella, and half a dozen more. The whole crew. They had a pale wintertime look about them and they were wearing heavier clothes than they had on when he had seen them a little while ago at Time Zero.

The lab was different, too. Everything was raw and half finished. Electrical conduits dangled in midair. The displacement cone was unshielded and the singularity cradles lay open and empty. Crates and cartons were scattered all about, still unpacked. A month and three days to go and they still had a ton of work to do, getting everything set up. But of course they were going to finish the job on schedule. There wasn't any doubt of that. His being here now was the proof of that.

The March rain drummed down in double time.

"If you don't mind," Dr. Thomas said. "There are some tests that we'd like to administer—"

Project Pendulum

10

SEAN

+5 × 10⁴ MINUTES

"I know you're all waiting to stick the electrodes on my head and measure everything that's going on inside it," Sean said. "But would it be okay if I stepped out into the fresh air for a moment? I've still got a headache from the *last* batch of tests."

"Still?" Dr. Thomas asked. "That was a month ago!"

"A month ago for you people, yes. For me the lights and bells are still blasting away."

"Well, I suppose—for just a few minutes."

"Don't worry. I won't try to escape."

There was a little forced laughter at that. Even so, Terzunian and Mukherji went with him on his little excursion outside the lab. To look after him? Or to make sure he didn't bolt off into the night, fleeing Thomas and his dreaded multiphasic machines to enjoy a couple of hours of solitary jogging through the darkness?

It was gorgeous outside. The air was warm and sweet and gentle, and very clear. The moon was bright and the stars were sparkling. The vines on the laboratory's west wall were in bloom, great yellow flowers filling the air with wondrous fragrance. This was late May, one of the best months of the year, before the worst of the summer heat and the summer smog descended on the San Gabriel Valley.

He thought of poor Eric, back there in rainy March right at this moment, and smiled.

"Okay," he said, filling his lungs as deeply as he could. "I guess I can face those tests now."

11

ERIC

+5 × 10⁵ MINUTES

The drumbeat sound of the rain ceased between one moment and the next. It was cut off sharply and suddenly, as if an audio tape had been abruptly sliced. Now Eric heard the chirping of birds and the chattering of grasshoppers instead. The warm golden brightness of a perfect Southern California afternoon came bursting in upon him with startling impact.

He realized that he had made another jump. He must be almost a year in the future this time. Half a million minutes beyond Time Zero—347.2 days. This was March also, but March of a different year, March of 2017.

And he had landed outside the laboratory, on a broad lawn at the far west side of the campus. The time displacement was big enough now that some spatial displacement was occurring also. There were students all around him but nobody seemed to notice his arrival. Or care. Maybe by March of 2017 it was a common thing for time travelers to pop into being here and there around the campus.

Eric felt a heady sense of freedom. He was outdoors in the fresh air, away from Dr. Ludwig and the rest of the Project Pendulum crowd, for the first time in—what? Weeks? Months? All that endless training, testing, rehearsing—he had felt like a rat in a cage, going around and around and around. But there were no Project Pendulum people anywhere in sight now. For however many hours it was until his next shunt, he could go where he pleased, do as he liked.

"Watch it!" someone yelled.

A gravity rotor came skimming by, zigzagging wildly up and down just above eye level. A tall, skinny undergraduate was running alongside it, trying to catch a ride. Eric got out of the way just in time. The student made a desperate lunge and grabbed the rotor just before it went lurching out of reach. It carried him a hundred yards or so through the air until it lost its spin and fluttered to the ground.

Project Pendulum

A pang of nostalgia went through him. It seemed like a million years since he had played with gravity rotors as a student on this same campus: though actually it was no more than three or four years ago.

Soon, he thought with a little shiver, he *would* be almost a million years away from his college days. And then a great deal more than that.

A slender blonde girl keyed up the rotor again and let it fly. As it began to circle the lawn, Eric found himself suddenly loping after it. There were half a dozen students chasing it too, but he brushed them aside with a quick gesture. Easily, gracefully, he reached up and slipped his hands into the rotor's holdfasts and let it spin him upward and outward across the campus. He had always been good with gravity rotors. He knew how to play into their axis of rotation so they would take him on a maximum glide.

Up—up—

"Eric! Eric, have you gone crazy!" a hoarse angry voice was shouting, far below.

He laughed and waved.

"Come down from there, you lunatic! What do you think you're doing?"

"Having—some—fun—" he called, breathless with laughter.

Then he looked down. Half a dozen grim-faced Project members were wigwagging their arms wildly at him. As he went spinning past them, fifteen feet over their heads, he caught sight of Dr. Thomas, Dr. Mukherji, Terzunian, and a few others, staring at him in shock. Dr. Ludwig was running toward them from the general direction of the laboratory.

Regretfully he guided the gravity rotor into a downspin and rode it to a landing.

"What kind of absurd stunt was that?" Dr. Ludwig blurted. "Suppose you had broken your neck! What would happen to the project then?"

Eric smiled. "I wouldn't have gotten hurt," he said serenely. "It's impossible. How could anything happen to me? I'm not really here, remember? I'm still back there at Time Zero sitting on the shunt

411

platform. And at an infinite number of other places between there and Time Ultimate, all at once. So what's the harm in my taking a little ride?"

"Idiot!" Dr. Ludwig blazed. "Imbecile!" Eric had never seen him so furious. " *'I'm not really here'*? What are you talking about? Who put such nonsense into your head?"

"The mathematical model—" Eric stammered. "Sean explained to me that—"

"Sean! That other maniac!" Dr. Ludwig clenched his fists and shook them in frustration. In a tightly controlled voice he said, "Listen to me. Eric, and listen carefully. You are on a pendulum, yes, and you do occupy every point between Time Zero and Time Ultimate. But you can still be harmed at any point in that entire sequence of nearly two hundred million years. And if you are—if you are—" He looked ready to explode. "The past is fluid! The future is yet unborn! Anything can be changed! Anything! Who knows what will befall the entire history of the world, if anything happens to you? Who knows?"

12

SEAN

−5 × 10⁵ MINUTES

Without warning the mild May night gave way to a glorious May morning—May of the year before. Sean was back in 2015, 347.2 days before the beginning of the experiment.

He stood blinking in the sudden sunlight. The shunts were coming much more easily now, causing little or no sense of transition as he shuttled between past and future. He was outside the laboratory. Outside the campus, in fact, half a mile or so east of it in downtown Pasadena. The first significant spatial displacement, he realized. The early shunts had moved him no more than a few inches from his Time Zero position on the shunt platform, but by now the jumps were getting big enough to carry him a fair distance.

Project Pendulum

Casually he strolled down Colorado Boulevard, heading east.

It surprised him that nobody from the lab was waiting here to meet him when he arrived. Up till now they hadn't allowed him to be alone for a moment. At each of his previous shunts—plus five minutes, minus fifty minutes, plus five hundred minutes, minus five thousand minutes, plus fifty thousand minutes—they had clustered around him as soon as he showed up. Now here he was half a million minutes in the past and they had left him completely on his own. Why weren't they here?

Then he realized that at this stage of the project, back in May of 2015, he and Eric hadn't even been selected yet to be the experimental subjects. The preliminary screening interviews were still going on, all that interminable testing and questioning and checking.

So as of this moment the Project Pendulum people didn't even know who they were going to be sending on the shunt, let alone what time of day or month their time-travelers were going to be turning up in the past. How could they? Time Zero itself had kept getting postponed again and again. The choice of April 19 at half past ten in the morning as the final-final day and hour and minute for the departure point hadn't been nailed down until the third of March, just six weeks before the day of the experiment.

And even after they had picked it, the Project people would still have had somehow to send information back to themselves of the year before, notifying themselves that experimental subject Sean Gabrielson was due to be popping out of nowhere in downtown Pasadena at such-and-such a time of the morning on such-and-such a day in May, 2015, which would be precisely 347.2 days prior to the beginning of the great time-travel event.

Probably they could have done it by sending off a preliminary shunt carrying a robot with the schedule. Maybe they should have done it, on the theory that it was best not to let their time-traveler have to fend for himself back here. But Project Pendulum's funds had been running pretty low in the final few weeks. Most likely there hadn't been any slack in the budget for extras like that. So they hadn't been able to send the word to anyone back here in 2015 that he'd be coming this way.

But he could.

Sean grinned slyly. He was tempted to saunter over to the Cal Tech campus right now and drop in at the laboratory.

"Hi," he would say. "I'm Sean Gabrielson. You're going to pick me next month for the shunt. Let's all take an hour off and go out for some pizza, okay?"

He could do that, sure. But suppose they didn't like his dropping in like that. Suppose it struck them as a cocky smartass sort of thing to do. Suppose they decided to dispense with the Gabrielson twins entirely, and pick a different pair of candidates for the shunt. What then? What would happen to him, back here in 2015? Out like a snuffed candle, that's what. He'd never get to see the far future or the distant past, or anything else. He'd go right back to being a graduate physics student in the year 2016 and he'd have no memory of any of the shunts he'd already experienced, let alone the ones that were still to come.

He didn't want to risk that.

But there was something he could do. It carried some paradox risk also, but he thought it was relatively safe. And useful, in a manner of speaking. And fun.

He thought back to last year, to the final few weeks before the names of the successful candidates for the shunt were announced. Six different pairs of twins had been in the running. Sean had figured all along that he and Eric had the best shot, because they wanted a physicist and a paleontologist, and he and Eric were the only ones who really fulfilled that requirement. But toward the end he had begun to think that the choice might and on one of the other sets of twins. Those shy Bengali girls, the Chakravarti sisters, maybe. They were mathematicians, but one had some sort of a background in archaeology. They were very, very bright. And, most important of all, they had the backing of their countryman, the Project Pendulum theoretician Dr. Mukherji.

Right before the choice was due to be announced, Sean had absolutely convinced himself that it was going to be the Chakravartis. He could already feel the disappointment seeping into his soul, and knew that it would embitter him for the rest of his life. A chance to travel to the ends of time, and it had slipped away from him! For days he could hardly sleep or eat. He was half crazy with tension most of the time, snapping and snarling at everybody.

Well, now that he was back here again at the time when that had been going on, he could spare himself all that anguish, couldn't he? Tell himself not to worry, let himself know that everything was going to turn out fine?

A phone booth loomed before him at the corner of Colorado and Fair Oaks. He stepped inside and pressed his thumb to the identification plate. The telephone asked him for the number he wanted and he gave his own.

"The line is busy," the telephone told him. "Break in on him. This is an emergency."

"One moment, please."

Then his own voice said irritably, "All right, but if this is any kind of sales pitch—"

"Don't worry, fellow. It's a legitimate call," Sean said.

"Who's there?"

"You mean you don't recognize my voice?"

A pause. "Ricky?"

"Close. Try again."

"Look, I've got no time for guessing games. I happen to be in the midst of very important—"

"Sure you are. I know that. Listen, dope, you're talking to Sean Gabrielson."

"What?"

"Sean$_2$, let's say. I'm just passing through."

"What?"

"On my way to the year 2025. And then back to 1921."

"What? What?"

"Maybe you aren't as bright as they say you are, buddy. If all you can do is honk like a duck."

"Hey, I don't have to listen to this kind of crazy—" came the angry voice from the speaker grille, and then the CONNECTION INTERRUPTED light went on.

"Call him back," Sean told the phone.

"The line is busy."

"Break in on him, then."

"The line is under privacy seal," said the telephone.

Sean swore and shook his head. "Tell him it's a family emergency."

"The line is under privacy seal," the phone repeated.

"I know that. Doesn't family emergency take priority?"

"The line is under privacy seal," said the phone once more.

"All right," Sean grunted. "Forget it."

For a moment he considered grabbing a cab and going out to his place near the beach to confront himself face to face. But he decided against it. If $Sean_1$ was so twitchy and strung out that he couldn't figure out who had been calling him, he deserved to go on sweating a little while longer about who was going to get the nod for Project Pendulum. Sure, Sean thought. The hell with him. Let him keep on worrying another few weeks. The dummy. Let him just keep right on worrying.

13

ERIC

-5×10^6 MINUTES

He could see the house, halfway down the block on the other side of the street. It looked smaller than he recalled, and the pink stucco badly needed repainting. The big palm tree in front was leaning way over, with its roots pulled halfway out of the ground. The earthquake had done that, he remembered. He could see the earthquake crack along the front wall of the house, too. A raw gully like an open trench ran for a hundred yards down the middle of the street. The quake must have come just a couple of days before. They hadn't had a chance to do much cleaning up yet.

The quake, the big Santa Monica earthquake, had happened right at the beginning of October, 2006, his freshman year in high school. So once again the shunt had brought him in smack on target, carrying him back exactly 9.51 years. From April of 2016 to October of 2006—yes, just right. Here he was. Nine and a half years in the past. And actually in his own teenage neighborhood.

That part of it was hard to believe. The shunt had dumped him down in the middle of Santa Monica, at the corner of Wilshire and Eighteenth. His old territory. No more than a five-minute walk from the house where he and Sean had lived from the time they were ten until they went to college. So of course he had to go over to have a look at it. And maybe to catch a glimpse of his own younger self. Of course.

Now, standing across the street from the pink stucco house, Eric found himself wondering if it was such a hot idea to be poking around in his own past like this. Suddenly it didn't feel really good.

Not just stirring up the earthquake memories—the jolt in the middle of the night, dogs barking, the sound of dishes breaking, frightened people running out into the streets. He would have expected that bringing it all vividly back to mind would be disturbing, and it was.

But what was even more troublesome was simply revisiting the ordinary memories, the routine day-by-day stuff. The world of 2006 looked a lot less glamorous than Eric remembered, earthquake damage aside. Everything seemed shabbier and more seedy than he expected. The shops out on Wilshire, the cars in the streets, the advertising billboards—it all was run-down, everything had a dreary, old-fashioned look.

Would things really be so much sleeker and shinier nine and a half years down the line? Maybe so. Or maybe over the years he had simply polished up his memories until the past had a much brighter gloss in his mind than it ever had had in reality.

And then there was all the other stuff to think about again, the adolescent stuff, the business of crossing the line from boyhood into manhood. The changes happening in his body. The conflicts with Sean—he and Sean were always battling like fiends in those days, the good old sibling rivalry, five times as fierce because they were identical twins. Sean was fifteen minutes older and he liked to make a big deal about that. And then too the unfocused ambitions, wanting to do something great when he grew up but not having any idea what it would be. The shy, hesitant encounters with girls. Eric had filed all those things away deep within himself. Now twenty-three, he wasn't at all sure he wanted to come face-to-face with them again. It might be better, he thought, to turn around right now and walk quickly the other way.

But he stayed where he was, watching the pink house across the street and hoping that nobody was watching him.

The upstairs room on the left: that one was his. A poster was taped in the window, probably the dinosaur poster from the County Museum. There was a big plaster-of-paris triceratops on the front lawn too, a pretty crude job but not really awful. The summer he was twelve he had spent a messy few days making that. As far back as he could remember, he had been absolutely nuts about dinosaurs. His ambition was to go to Wyoming and dig up the biggest one ever found. Sean had laughed at that. "Sure," he said. "They'll call it *Ericosaurus supergigantus.*"

Everybody said it was a phase he was bound to grow out of when he was a little older, but he didn't. Instead he got deeper into it, paleontology and geology, too. He studied the folds and strata of the rocks in which fossils were found, though it was always the fossils themselves that had fascinated him the most. He could remember feverishly packing his little collection of trilobites and ammonites into a suitcase in the first terrifying minutes after the earthquake, back here when he was thirteen, so that he wouldn't lose them in case a second shock struck and destroyed the house. And then—

Who's that?

A boy had come out of the house and was standing on the little porch, looking around in wonder and dismay at the earthquake debris in the street. Eric stepped back into the shadows. The boy was short and thin, with straight sandy hair going off wildly in all directions. He had to be thirteen and a half, but to Eric he seemed much younger. His face was smooth and bland-looking and had a strange unfinished look about it.

That must be Sean, Eric thought.

Project Pendulum

No—wait—

He wasn't sure. Of all the strange things that had happened to him since the pendulum had begun to swing, this was the strangest, that he should be staring at this boy and not know whether he was seeing his brother or himself. It was absolutely impossible to tell. Time had not yet carved the adult face of this boy out of the raw material of early adolescence. His nose was just a snub and his mouth and lower jaw had that unfinished look. And at this age he and Sean must have looked much more alike than they would later. Perhaps if both twins were standing side by side on the porch, he might be able to guess which one was Eric and which Sean. But as it was he was baffled.

It was almost frightening to have time swallow his identity like that. Simply being a twin is complicated enough. But when you start losing track of which twin you are—

Then the boy came down the three cracked steps to the lawn. Pausing by the plaster-of-paris triceratops, he grinned and stroked its long crooked horns for a moment in an unmistakably affectionate way. Eric, watching from a distance, grinned also.

No doubt of it now. That boy had to be his own younger self. He felt a shiver go sliding down his spine.

Go on, he told himself. Walk across the street. Introduce yourself to him.

He imagined half a dozen impossible things that he could say.

"Hi, there. You're not going to believe this, but I'm you of the year 2016, taking part in the first time-travel experiment ever."

Or: "I'm here to tell you not to worry about a thing. I know you're uneasy about all sorts of stuff that you know lies ahead of you, but I can guarantee that everything's going to turn out just fine for you when you grow up."

Or maybe: "There's going to be a girl named Carla in your junior year of high school that likes you a whole lot better than she does Sean, but you're going to convince yourself that it's the other way around. You'll be wrong about that. Invite her to the prom before he does."

Or: "The winner of this year's World Series will be—"

Or: "Your friend Charlie Graham is going to invite you to fly to Phoenix for Christmas with him and his family in his father's plane this year. Dad won't let you go. Be absolutely sure you don't do anything to change his mind, because that plane's going to get caught in a freak lightning storm, and—"

Or: "You and Sean are both going to go to Cal Tech four years from now. People are going to try to talk you into going to Harvard or Stanford instead, because they think you and Sean shouldn't go to the same college. Don't listen to them. Go to Cal Tech, or else you may change your entire future and miss out on the best thing that's ever going to happen to you."

Or—

But he didn't say any of those things. Instead he stayed on his side of the street and hung back in the shadows, watching his younger self emerge from the yard of the little pink house, peer into the mailbox for a moment, pause to pull a huge red flower from the hibiscus bush on the front walk, and go running off toward Wilshire. Eric smiled. He waved at the small retreating figure. And thought: You don't need any special tips on the future, boy. Just do whatever feels right to you. You'll make some mistakes, but that's no crime. And one of these days you'll grow up and you'll be me, and you'll go off on the damndest wild trip that anybody in the whole history of the human race ever took.

14

SEAN

$+5 \times 10^6$ MINUTES

He guessed he must be somewhere out to the east of Pasadena, at least twenty-five miles, maybe more—around Azusa, Glendora, Claremont, one of those towns. Definitely east: he could see big mountains off to the north, and he was pretty sure that that was Mount Baldy over there. Certainly there weren't any mountains that size west of Pasadena. And the air had that hot, dry inland quality to it.

Project Pendulum

Sean wasn't surprised to find himself this far from the laboratory. A time displacement of nine and a half years was bound to move him a sizable distance in space. But going east puzzled him. After all, his last jump had been a backshunt and it had brought him out west of the laboratory. It stood to reason that shunting in the opposite direction in time ought to move him in the opposite direction spatially, too. But maybe not. Expecting anything about time travel to stand to reason was probably dumb.

For a moment he wondered whether he had actually gone backward in time, not forward, on this shunt. Which might explain the eastward displacement.

No. Impossible. Dumb dumb dumb. The one thing that did make sense in all this shunting was the mathematics of reciprocity. Everything had to balance. You swung back, then you swung forward, while your brother at the opposite end of the seesaw made an equal and opposite journey. The last place Sean had been was the minus-5×10^5-minutes level. Now he had to be at the plus-5×10^6-minutes level. There were no two ways about that. Beyond any doubt, he must have gone forward. His location in time right now, he knew, had to be late November of the year 2025.

In any case he didn't need a computer to tell him that he had moved into the future. One quick look at his surroundings was all that it took.

This place was strange.

A lot of it looked like any Southern California town of the early twenty-first century, of course. But there were a good many new high-rise buildings too, twenty or thirty stories high. Sean didn't remember high rises being so common out here. And they were buildings of an astonishing weirdness of design.

One had twin curving spikes on its roof, like gigantic horns. Another had a strip of mirrors a yard wide running down its front from top to bottom. A number of buildings had large eye-shaped glass ovals above their entrances, and some had additional eyes higher up on the facade. Decorations? Or mysterious electronic devices? And the architects had apparently hated straight lines. All of the buildings had odd wriggling edges, sinuous and fluted and swirly. Sean couldn't look for long at any one of them without feeling that he was being pulled around the corner into some other dimension.

The newer cars in the streets had the same twisting, looping lines. They were low and long and somehow sinister-looking, with single bands of grillwork across their fronts where headlights should be, and peculiar arching ornaments—or antennas?—rising in startling curves from their roofs. Some were carrying hornlike spikes similar to those on the building down the street. So a whole new kind of design would come into fashion in the years just ahead. He couldn't say that he admired it much.

The strangest thing of all was that there was no one in the streets.

No one. No one at all. He was all alone. He might have been the only human being in the whole world. He stood in the middle of the wide street under a warm midday sun, looking this way and that. No people in sight. No cars moved, no horns honked. Not a sound anywhere.

What had happened here?

Where was everybody?

This was starting to feel creepy. Frowning, Sean began to walk toward the building with the mirrored facade. Looking up, he saw his own image, broken and refracted a dozen times over. The entrance of the building was a wall of glass three times as tall as he was, decorated only by a jutting blue sphere that he assumed was some kind of doorknob. Hesitantly he put his hand to it.

The moment he touched it, music filled the air.

It came from everywhere at once, a hundred electronic brass bands blaring a hundred marching tunes. He whirled around, astonished, and saw lights suddenly blazing in every building, dazzling fireworks exploding overhead—fireworks in *daytime!*—banners unfolding from gravity-rotor platforms that had come spinning out from invisible hiding places.

He stared in amazement, trying to read all the banners at once.

WELCOME, SEAN!
THE CITY OF GLENDORA GREETS THE MAN FROM TIME!

Project Pendulum

GREATER LOS ANGELES CHAMBER OF COMMERCE
SAYS
HELLO, SEAN!
THE YEAR 2025 IS GLAD TO SEE YOU!
SAN BERNARDINO COUNTY, CALIFORNIA'S GREATEST,
IS ALL YOURS!
HERE'S TO YOU—THE FIRST AND FINEST
TIME-TRAVELER!

He glanced up the wide street and saw the marchers advancing toward him now. What seemed like thousands of people, stretching off into the distance as far as he could see.

Of course. This was probably the biggest day in the history of this little town. And they had had better than nine years to prepare for it.

"Good God," Sean murmured. "I'm famous! And here comes the parade!"

ERIC

+5 × 10⁷ MINUTES

It was hot and steamy here, a dense, lush, tropical heat. Just drawing a breath was hard work. The humid air wrapped itself around him like a heavy cloak. The thick sweet perfume of a billion flowers lay upon the air. The sky had a curious greenish color, beautiful in its way, but strange and oddly troubling.

This time, Eric thought, the spatial displacement must have moved him clear out to Hawaii, or one of the South Pacific isles.

But something didn't seem right. Tropical isles were always warm but never this hot. The temperature must be well over a hundred here. Well over. He had sometimes experienced heat like this, or almost like this, on field trips out in the desert. But that had been dry heat, torrid yet bearable. This stuff was something else, like being in a steam room. Or worse. Not even the desert got this hot very often.

Where am I, he wondered?

He looked around. There was a wide beach in front of him, crowded with sunbathers. It didn't have the exotic look of a tropical beach—crystalline water, white powdery sand. It looked very much like a California beach. Turning, he could see a town or small city a little way inland, and, behind the town, a steeply rising wall of rugged, heavily forested mountains.

It all seemed very familiar.

It definitely had the look of the California coast—up by Santa Barbara, say, where the mountains come down close to the shore. Though these mountains seemed a little closer to the shore than he remembered from his last visit to Santa Barbara.

But what about this sweltering tropical heat? You almost never got temperatures like this along the California coast. And this stifling humidity? Never. Where were the cooling sea breezes? Puzzled, he walked up toward the promenade separating the beach from the town. Here the vegetation seemed wrong. The slim, graceful palm trees that were growing everywhere didn't look like the ones he had known all his life. They were some kind of more tropical species, most likely—coconut palms or royal palms or something else, something too tender to grow in California's mild but sometimes chilly climate. And these vines, these creepers, these odd ferns, these riotously blossoming shrubs with glistening leaves—no, no, Eric thought, none of this is California stuff. California is dry all summer long. These plants must come from some moist jungle.

He paused to catch his breath. Moving around was a real struggle in this greenhouse environment.

Where am I? he wondered again.

He had to be fifty million minutes in the future—a little more than ninety-five years. So this was the summer of the year 2111. If he was still alive in this year, he'd be 118 years old. Stretching his luck a little, maybe.

So he knew when he was. But where—where—?

Project Pendulum

And suddenly he knew. This greenhouse environment. That was what he had called it a moment ago. He trembled with fear and shock as full understanding hit him. He was in California, all right. But a California had been utterly transformed—in a world that had undergone what must have been a colossal calamity— "You savah, mister?" asked someone at his elbow. A girl, about thirteen, fourteen. She was wearing only the tiniest of bathing suits and she had a small metallic pack strapped to her back. A flexible tube ran from the backpack to her mouth. A tall boy stood behind her. He had a similar backpack on.

"Savah?" Eric repeated. "I don't understand."

"Are you savah?" she said again. "Are you all right? Are you okay?" She said "okay" as if it were a word from some foreign language. "You don't have your breather on."

"No," he said. "I don't have one."

"You lose it? You look bad mal, savvy? Tray mal."

She was speaking a sort of French, he realized. French and English, mixed. He leaned on the railing of the promenade. She was telling him that he looked sick. And he felt sick.

"The air," he said. "So thick—so humid here, so hot—"

"Not the heat," said the girl. "It's the see-oh. It'll plonk you in a quick."

See-oh. C-O, he thought. CO_2. Carbon dioxide.

"Lend him your breather, Slowjoe," the girl said impatiently, gesturing at her companion. "Can't you see he's going to plonk?"

Eric was feeling dizzier and dizzier. Vaguely he was aware of the boy unstrapping the device from his back and handing it to him. The girl put the tube in his mouth and told him to breathe deeply. Almost at once his head began to clear. Oxygen? They were watching him worriedly. Nice kids, he thought. Lucky for me.

"Savah?" she asked. "Better now?"

"Much," he said.

"Bien. Go on. Put it on your back."

"But I can't let him give me his breather."

"He'll go and get another one. Five minutes without won't mort him. We're used to this stuff, you know."

Eric nodded. This stuff. So it had really happened, he thought. The greenhouse effect that the environmental scientists had worried about all those years. The buildup of carbon dioxide in the atmosphere throughout the centuries of industrial development, until a thick mantle of heat-retaining gas surrounded the Earth and temperatures everywhere started to climb. And the polar ice caps melted, and the seas rose, and the air turned into chemical soup, and the temperate lands turned into steaming tropics, and God only knew what had become of the places that had been tropical before.

Now Sean understood why the mountains here seemed closer to the shore than he thought they ought to be. The mountains hadn't moved. The rising seas had come up onto the land. If sea levels have risen twenty-five or fifty feet, he thought, what has become of Santa Monica? Of New York? The hills of San Francisco must be islands now.

"What's the name of this town?" he asked the girl.

"Santa Barbara," she said.

"Santa Barbara, California?"

"No, Santa Barbara on the moon." And she laughed. "Where do you think you are?"

"I thought it might be Santa Barbara," he said. "But everything's so different from what I—" He paused.

"Go on," she said. "Different from what you remember, right?"

"You know who I am?"

"You're a voyageur, yes? A time-traveler? You come from the cool years, right?"

"The cool years, yes. From the year 2016, matter of fact."

The girl smiled. She didn't seem notably startled by what he had just said. Time-travelers must be commonplace items by now, he thought. People dropping in from the past all the time. "I knew it toot sweet, right away. You talk like the vieux-time people. You must have been one of the first, no?"

"The first," he said. "The very first."

"No blague!" she said admiringly. "Imagine that!" But she still didn't sound enormously impressed. "Well, enjoy yourself here. If you can. Don't forget to use your breather. You'll plonk real fast without it, you know. Real fast."

SEAN

-5×10^7 MINUTES

"Well, here comes the parade, finally," said the short red-faced man just to Sean's left.

What, again? The parade was over. Was time backing up on him? Had the pendulum slipped a cog? Yes, he could hear the sounds of parade music all over again. Had he somehow taken a shunt within a shunt, going back to the start of his stay in 2025 to live through an experience he had already had?

"Yes, sir, that's what I call a parade!" the red-faced man said.

Sean stared. It was a parade, all right, but not the one he had just been in. He could see the prancing drum major now, far down the street. The half-built, dinky-looking, antiquated street. And he could hear the music. Not electronic sounds, no, but an old-fashioned brass band making a joyous blaring uproar. A real bass drum sending out vast booming sounds.

This wasn't Glendora in the year 2025. And this wasn't any parade in honor of Sean Gabrielson, the visitor from out of time. Not at all.

He was in a small town, but it was a much older one. There weren't any futuristic high-rise buildings with horns and eyes on them. There weren't any high rises at all, just little wooden or stucco one- and two-story buildings with scrawny young palm trees standing in front of them. And the sign on the street corner—an old-fashioned sign, white letters on blue metal, no infoglow, no shimmerglas—said that this was Wilshire Boulevard.

So the name of this small town was Los Angeles. There wasn't much to it, back here in this year that he realized now must be 1921. The hills to the north were bare. The lofty roadbeds of the freeways were nowhere to be seen. The street was paved, but it looked like a country lane, hardly fit for heavy traffic. Everything had a raw, new look to it.

Boom—boom—boom—

The red-faced man pointed, waved, clapped his hands in glee. He didn't seem to be bothered by the fact that Sean had just materialized out of nowhere beside him. Or that Sean was dressed in the strange clothes of another era, an era yet unborn. Well, this was Hollywood, after all. The man probably thought that Sean was in costume for some science-fiction movie and had just stepped out of the studio to see the parade.

It was a fine spring day. The air was fresh and clean. They haven't even invented smog yet, Sean thought in astonishment.

It all looked so peculiar here. And yet not as peculiar as he had expected. In a way he was surprised to see that 1921 was in actual living color, not in black and white, and that the people moved at a normal pace, not in some herkyjerk frenzy. He had seen ancient movies and he realized that he really had imagined that everything in reality would look the way it did in those movies. Quaint, musty, unreal. Well, it was quaint and musty, yes. But not unreal.

Sean turned to the red-faced man. He was wearing a stiff, uncomfortable dark suit, a necktie, a vest. On a warm spring day like this. But everybody else nearby along the parade route was dressed the same way. So formal, so elaborate. Neckties! Vests! The women all had hats on. And gloves. They were the ones who seemed to be in movie costumes, not he. But this was no movie, for these people. This was the real world of 1921; and in that world, this was how people dressed. "What's the parade all about?" Sean asked.

The man frowned at him. "Why, in honor of the President!"

"The President," Sean said. "Ah—is the President here?"

"The President's in Washington, getting sworn in. Don't you know that? But even if we're three thousand miles away, we can celebrate. Yes, sirree! We're having a parade to honor the new President. Can't you see the banners?"

Sean turned and looked. The main float was passing by right now. Real orange trees, laden with fruit, atop a horse-drawn platform. And banners, painted on canvas:

WARREN GAMALIEL HARDING, PRESIDENT OF THE UNITED STATES
CALVIN COOLIDGE, VICE PRESIDENT
INAUGURATION DAY MARCH 4, 1921

"Three cheers for President Harding!" the red-faced man shouted, waving his hat in the air. "He's my man! America first! No more wars! Back to normal! Harding! Harding! Harding!" He nudged Sean in the ribs. "What's the matter, are you a Democrat? Let's hear you cheer!"

Sean nodded. Why not?

When in Rome, do as the Romans do. When in 1921, give a cheer for the new President, if that's what everybody all around you is doing.

"Harding!" he yelled. "Harding! Harding! Three cheers for President Harding!"

ERIC

-5×10^8 MINUTES

Eric felt a rush of cool sweet air, almost dizzying. After the dank, moist, thick soup that was the air of Santa Barbara in the year 2111, this was like fresh new wine. He was in a forest of towering redwood trees so tall their tops were lost in the mist high overhead. He reached up to take the breathing device from his mouth.

But the breather was gone. Of course. It was impossible to carry any physical object from one shunt to the next except the things he had had with him when the trip began. The laws of conservation of energy were very strict about that. Whatever gear he had set out with from Time Zero would stay with him throughout the journey, but nothing that he picked up along the way could be transported. There wasn't any possibility of returning from the past with a lost painting of Leonardo da Vinci under your arm, or coming back from the future with some fantastic device that would change the whole world.

Well, he didn't need any gadgets to help him breathe here. This air was the purest he had ever known. He couldn't even imagine how air could be cleaner or fresher than this.

He checked his instruments. Longitude 121 degrees W. He was still in California, then. Latitude a little more than 36 degrees N. That would put him a bit north of the midway line between Los Angeles and San Francisco—somewhere around Monterey, Eric guessed. A pretty hefty spatial displacement this time. But he was 500 million minutes in the past, now. That was 951.3 years. By his best calculation this was a mild, misty January morning in the year A.D. 1065.

The forest was beautiful. He had never seen a lovelier place than this.

The mighty chocolate-red redwood trunks were like the columns of a vast cathedral. Far above him, nearly four hundred feet up, the treetops met in a roof of foliage. A pearly twilight glow was all that broke through to brighten the forest floor. The stillness was fantastic. He could hear no sound except the gentle patter of the droplets of condensed fog that fell to the soft needle-carpeted floor, and the distant murmur of a brook. The fronds of huge glistening ferns were everywhere about him.

The year 1065! In Europe now, the man who would be called William the Conqueror was laying his plans for the invasion of England. The Crusades would soon be beginning. There were great native American empires in Mexico and Peru. And at this moment, who knew what was happening in the palaces of China, Africa, the Baghdad of the Arabian Nights—?

He felt a moment of something very like regret at finding himself in this place.

If the spatial displacement had been greater, this shunt might have dropped him down in the hectic midst of history—in Rome, say, or Constantinople, or Venice, or perhaps one of the stone cities of Mayas. But here—here in this peaceful redwood forest on the California coast—Eric was as alone as though this were the dawn of time. There was no trace here of whatever sparse and scattered Indian population California had at this time. All was silence. All was peace.

That pang of regret vanished as suddenly as it had come.

To be allowed to see such beauty as this was a privilege beyond measure. How could he yearn for some other place?

Quietly, struck by wonder, Eric wandered through the stupendous groves of trees. He thought of the California he had left behind, the roar of the freeways, the droning of the planes overhead, the immense sprawl of the cities. They had saved a few little redwood forests, sure, somewhere far up north of San Francisco. Like museum exhibits. But everywhere else the hand of man had left its mark.

And this was how it all had looked before we came, he thought.

Here, in this awesome solitude, in this place where perhaps no human being had walked before, he felt himself suddenly swept by an emotion that was completely new to him. He wanted to drop to his knees and give thanks—to whom, to what, he wasn't really certain—for the beauty he beheld. He had never done such a thing before. Even now he hesitated, embarrassed, self-conscious.

Go on, he thought. Nobody's watching. And even if somebody were, so what?

But it was too late. The moment had passed. It would be forced, artificial, unreal, for him to do it now. Instead he stood quietly, resting his hand lightly on the giant trunk of a tree by the edge of the little stream.

He felt the strength of it, the immensity. This tree, he thought, had made a great voyage through time, of a sort, itself. It must have been living when Jesus was born. Or even earlier. And on and on through the centuries to this year of 1065, and on beyond. Probably it would still be here in 1865 or 1875 or 1885 or whenever it was that men would come along with their saws and hatchets to cut it down. It might have lived on into the twenty-first century, the twenty-second, even the thirty-second, if it had been left to finish its long journey undisturbed.

After a while he walked onward. He had no regret now that the shunt had brought him here, instead of to some busy capital of the medieval world. This moment out of time, this quiet interlude in the strange fantastic journey that the swinging pendulum had launched him on, was worth a thousand Constantinoples.

He smiled. And then he dropped to his knees after all, and bowed his head, and gave thanks and praise, not knowing to whom, to what. For this beauty, for this moment of peace: thanks and praise. Thanks and praise.

SEAN

+5 × 10⁸ MINUTES

"Alt! No podo pasari! Todos tempuus vorbudt aqui!"

"Are you speaking to me?" Sean asked the huge mechanical creature that loomed before him.

"Anglic!" the great gleaming robot cried. "Du spikke Anglic! Yis u no?"

"Yis," Sean said, bluffing for all he was worth. "Ik spikke Anglic. Yis."

The thing was at least nine feet high, and it was all eyes and mouth. Half a dozen huge sparkling eyes ran around its upper end, some kind of band of sensors that flickered restlessly up and down the whole spectrum and probably beyond it into the infrared and the ultraviolet. And an ugly gaping slot of a mouth, big as the top of a garbage can, in its belly. The better to swallow you with, my little time-traveler. *Du spikke Anglic? Answer yis u no, or I'll gobble you up!*

Sean looked around uneasily. He was standing on some rubbery catwalk suspended about twenty feet above what might have been a street. The street looked rubbery too, with purple pumpkin-shaped

Project Pendulum

growths sprouting from it at intervals of eight or ten feet. To his right was what looked like a wall of ice, a smooth glacial face rising to an enormous height. He could see people moving around freely within the ice. So it wasn't ice and not a glacier, but a building of some sort. On the other side of him the street was lined with giant metallic needles the size of telephone poles. They were glowing pale purple and giving off soft twanging sounds.

So this is the year A.D. 2967, Sean thought. Well, it sure looks like the year A.D. 2967.

"Anglic," the huge robot said. "Du spikke Anglic." Something was rumbling in its interior, making a cement-mixer sound. The eye-band turned a blazing yellow, then slowly subsided into orange and red. Small portholes on the robot's sides opened and swiveled. Projections like the feet of insects came poking out of them, waving and wriggling about.

It means to swallow me, Sean thought. As soon as it can figure out what I am. I'm going to be a tin can's afternoon snack.

He wondered what would happen to him if he turned and tried to make a run for it. Probably a bad idea. He imagined jets of gluey liquid squirting from those portholes and lassoing him at fifty paces.

"Anglic," said the robot again. "You are a speaker of Anglic. Yes. Yes. Mode adjustment made. Comprendus? You are a tempuu and Anglic is your sprak. Comprendus? Comprendus? Rispondim! Do you comprendan?"

"You don't quite have it right yet," Sean said. "But keep trying."

"No comprendus?"

"No comprendus, right."

"Correction mode. Correction mode." The robot began sputtering and mumbling to itself. Cautiously Sean started to back away, moving very slowly. Maybe it won't notice that I'm leaving. The sounds from the metallic poles to his left grew higher in pitch. People were pointing at him through the glassy walls of the artificial glacier. "You will cease departing," the robot said. "Correction has been made. We use your mode now. You are Anglic-speaking time-traveler, unauthorized. You will us show your documentuus."

433

"Documents," Sean said. "That's better Anglic. English, we call it. But I don't have any documents. I'm too early for that. I come from the year—"

"No documentuus! No documentuus!" The robot's eye-band flashed vivid scarlet. "Illicitimu! Tempuu vorbudtu! No podo pasari!" It was getting really excited. The enormous froglike mouth was opening and closing. Sean saw lights flashing inside, and gears moving about. It began to move toward him in a slow, ponderous way.

It is going to gobble me up, he thought. Because I'm an unregistered time-traveler and I don't have the right passport. Or something.

He turned and started to run.

"No!" a voice cried behind him. "Alt! No flikken! Is safe! Is okay! I to do, you will safe!"

A girl, a woman—he couldn't tell which, he couldn't begin to guess her age—emerged out of nowhere. She was very slender and she was taller than he was. She had glistening silver hair and silver eyes too, and her skin was bright red, the color of a ripe apple. She looked strange, but she looked beautiful, too.

She might have been the most beautiful woman he had ever seen.

Darting swiftly around him, she ran right up to the giant robot and slapped the palm of her hand against its midsection. A panel opened at once. She reached in and pressed a key. Instantly the robot's eye-band color shifted toward blue. "Podo pasari," the robot muttered. "Tempuu licitimu. Validimu. Propriu." And it moved off, still muttering to itself.

The woman smiled. Her silver eyes dazzled him.

"You will forgive," she said. "My Anglic. Is not big good. But you will safe now." Her voice was deep and rich and warm, with an odd little crack in it. It was like no voice he had ever heard, but very beautiful. Her hand reached toward his. "They do not like tempuus, this year. Time-travelers. Too many come, too much confuse. But I will protect. My people will. How is your name?"

"Sean," he said. "Sean Gabrielson. From the year 2016."

"I bin Hepta-Noni-Acanta-Leela-Quintu-Quintu," she said.

"Is all that your name?"

"I am to you Quintu-Leela," she said, and laughed. Her laughter was magical. From the humming telephone poles came an answering sound, delicate, eerie. Her hand tightened on his. "Come with me. You will safe with me. I will show the world." Again the laugh. "Everything. You and me, we bin amicuus. Friends, you say? Friends. We bin very warm friends. Comprendus?"

Sean nodded. He felt as though an electric current were passing from her hand into his. Perhaps it was. Quintu-Leela, he thought. The sound of her voice was marvelously strange and strangely marvelous. And those silver eyes. He imagined her name and his entwined within a heart, blazing in purple fire in the sky.

Love at first sight, that was what it was.

He had heard about such things but he had never really believed they happened. Especially to him. Love at first sight! Was that too crazy? Quintu-Leela and Sean. Sean and Quintu-Leela. God, she was beautiful! And fascinating! That voice! Those eyes!

Yes, I do believe I'm falling in love, he thought.

With a woman who lives in the time of my own great-great-great-great-great-great-great-granddaughter. Who for all I know could be my own great-great-great-great-great-great-great granddaughter. The woman of my dreams, an incredible woman, a phenomenal woman, and any hour now, maybe any minute now, the displacement force is going to sweep me away from her forever.

ERIC

+5 × 10⁹ MINUTES

The tunnels went on and on, an endless maze, one smooth shining onyx-walled corridor after another. Eric had no idea where he was or where he had been or where he was heading. All he knew was that he was somewhere below the surface of the Earth, plodding through corridor after corridor after corridor, never once getting a glimpse of the sun, the sky, the stars. And never once seeing another human being.

He wondered how far underground he was.

He wondered whether any life, human or otherwise, still existed on Earth's surface, here in the 116th century A.D.

He wondered if he was still on Earth at all.

This was his third day in the tunnels now. At least that was what the chronometer said. But his mind and body both were hopelessly confused down here, when there was no day, no night, only the unending onyx walls lit by some mysterious radiance deep within the stone. He felt almost no need for sleep. When he did, he simply slouched up against the tunnel wall and closed his eyes for half an hour or so. He ate just as sparsely. Now and then he remembered to consume one of the food tablets from his utility belt. Most of the time he was content to coast along on the slow-release nutrient additives that the Project Pendulum medics had pumped into his bloodstream a few hours before Time Zero.

It had been a fantastic experience at first, roaming this mystifying underground world of the far future. None of his previous shunts had shown him anything remotely as strange as this. But the fascination was beginning to wear thin for him.

He had arrived in a glow of dense emerald light. It was all around, engulfing everything, so that he could almost believe he was at the bottom of the sea. The light was so deep and so strong that it was impossible for him to make out any features whatever of his surroundings.

Then the light vanished as though a hood had been thrown over his head, and he found himself in a zone of the deepest blackness he had ever known. For a long while after that nothing happened. He stood in complete silence, mystified, uncertain.

"Hello?" he said. "Anybody there?"

Nothing. No one. Silence.

He took a step. Another. Another. He was unable to see a thing. For all he knew, there was a pit a mile deep right in front of him. But he couldn't just stand here forever, waiting for things to happen. He went on, step by uneasy step.

There was a sweetness in the air, and something else, a touch of lemon, perhaps, or sage, or both at once. He wasn't surprised. Each era he had visited so far had had a distinct and characteristic flavor. He hadn't expected that, that every time would smell different from all other times. This is the smell of the 116th century, he thought. It was a likable odor, but unreal, synthetic.

Perhaps they make their own air in the year A.D. 11529, he thought. He imagined giant air-making machines on the borders of every city, releasing flavors of every desired sort into the atmosphere. Maybe that was how they had coped with the buildup of carbon dioxide that had turned the whole world into a giant greenhouse in the twenty-second century. Just thinking about the time he had spent in that sweltering tropical world made him feel sweaty and weak. The air is a lot better here, he thought. Of course the greenhouse-effect problems were ancient history to the people of this era. Nine thousand years in the past, in fact.

That was before he realized that he wasn't breathing surface air at all. He was underground.

He put out his hand and touched smoothness to his left: highly polished stone. The moment he touched it, it lit up, and he saw that he was in a long cavern or corridor that stretched far in front of him, disappearing into dimness hundreds of yards away. The walls curved gently up to meet the rounded arch of the ceiling. He recognized the glossy brown stone as onyx, though it was astonishing to think of a corridor this size wholly lined with that rare and beautiful mineral. Synthetic onyx, maybe, he thought. This is the 116th century. They can do anything. There was pale light pulsing within the walls, an inexplicable inner radiance, cool and beautiful.

In awe and wonder he walked onward. After a little while he saw figures moving slowly toward him and he halted, narrowing his eyes to peer into the distance. He felt curiously unafraid. This was too much like a dream to seem real. And in any case he was confident that the beings of this future age would be too civilized to offer him any harm.

They came closer, within the range of his vision now. They weren't human.

They were cone-shaped beings eight or nine feet high, with brilliant orange eyes the size of platters and rubbery blue bodies.

Clusters of scarlet tentacles dangled like nests of snakes from their shoulders. They walked in an odd gliding, lurching way on suction pads that made a peculiar slurping sound as they clamped down and pulled free again.

No way could evolution have transformed the human race into creatures like this, Eric thought. Not in 9500 years, not ever. These had to be aliens of some sort. There were half a dozen of them moving in a solemn procession along the opposite side of the corridor wall. He stared up at them. They were gigantic looming presences, massive, menacing.

He felt the first pricklings of fear. Being a traveler out of time gave him no invulnerability, only the illusion of it. This might be dreamlike but it was no dream, and those creatures were twice his size. Would they try to harm him? He stood poised on the balls of his feet, ready to bolt and dart past them at the first hostile sign.

But they paid no attention to him. Like a procession of mourners they shuffled toward him and past him, not giving him so much as a glance. They seemed completely preoccupied with their own ponderous thoughts.

Eric stared at them in amazement.

Was he so insignificant to them? No more important than a squirrel by the side of the road? Had he come 9500 years to be totally ignored?

Sudden crazy fury blossomed in him.

"Hey!" he called. "Wait! Aren't you even going to stop and ask the time of day? Don't you wonder what I am?"

They kept on going without looking back at him. Eric shook his head. Anger gave way to bewilderment.

"I sure as hell wonder what you are," he muttered lamely.

The huge creatures continued to shuffle onward down the corridor. They dwindled in the dimness until he could barely see them, far down the way. And then, at a place where the corridor seemed to curve slightly to the right, all at once they disappeared, vanishing like soap bubbles in the air.

Frowning, Eric struggled to understand. Had they found some passage?

Maybe they had never been there at all. Maybe they had simply been hallucinations. Maybe this all was a dream.

He ran back after them.

When he came to the place where the giant creatures had disappeared he could find no trace of doorways or side passages. The walls of the corridor were as smooth and unbroken here as they had been from the start.

He shrugged, turned back in the other direction, and marched on.

After what seemed like hours more of plodding along the same empty hallway Eric reached a place where the corridor swelled and split into nine apparently identical tunnels. At random he entered the third tunnel from the left. It too seemed to be empty. But then once again he saw a procession of strange beings coming toward him.

These looked like giant purple starfish with rough pebbly skins. Each had a globe of brilliant white flame glowing at the center of its body and fifteen or twenty rigid tentacles radiating stiffly outward. The way that they moved was to roll along with weird grace on the tips of their tentacles, like acrobats turning cartwheels.

"Excuse me," Eric said at once. "I'm Eric Gabrielson. I'm a time-traveler from the twenty-first century A.D., and—"

No use. They weren't any more interested in him than the suction-footed giants had been.

He watched in dismay as the starfish went rolling onward and beyond. When they were a hundred yards or so past him they all abruptly turned to the left and pressed themselves against the corridor wall, which emitted a painful blue glow the moment they touched it. Eric covered his eyes.

When it seemed safe to open them again, there was no sign of the starfish creatures. Had they stepped right through the corridor wall?

Puzzled, he backtracked and studied the wall. It looked no different from any other section of the wall. After a moment's hesitation he touched it with the palm of his hand. Nothing happened. No blinding blue glow, nothing.

He went onward.

He slept a little while. He nibbled a couple of food tablets.

He came to another place where the tunnel forked once more, branching into seventeen passages this time. He chose the rightmost branch. The tunnel was the same as before, smooth, glossy, bright with that inexplicable inner radiance.

More beings appeared, seemingly floating in the air. They were elongated transparent creatures filled with churning, misty organs. They looked like the sort of things you might see under the microscope in a drop of water, blown up to giant size—huge protozoa, a tribe of colossal paramecia.

"Hello?" he ventured. "Does anybody here know what a human being is? Or was?"

The giant protozoa didn't seem to be interested in conversation, either.

Nor were the next creatures that he met, nor the next, nor the ones after those. Branch after branch, tunnel after tunnel, and it was always the same: silence, gleaming walls stretching far out before him, occasional bands of grotesque beings traversing the infinite corridors bound on unimaginable mysterious migrations. Sometimes they seemed to disappear into the corridor walls, as the starfish had done. Sometimes they seemed to emerge from the walls just as mysteriously.

Eric might just as well have been invisible.

What had begun as an eerily fascinating experience was becoming maddening and frustrating. He found himself wondering how long it was going to be before the displacement force seized him and carried him out of here to his next shunt, 95,000 years deep in the past. At least the past was a place that he felt he understood.

Then, late on the third day, two beings that might almost have been human stepped suddenly out of the corridor wall no more than twenty feet in front of him.

Eric realized after the first startled moment that they weren't human, not at all. Their bodies were impossibly long and narrow and their arms and legs were thin as whips, with elbows every twelve inches. Their hands had more than five fingers. Their lips were nothing but slits, their bare waxy-looking skins were greenish-yellow, and their golden eyes seemed to be set on end, much longer than they were broad.

Project Pendulum

There might have been some evolutionary changes in the human race since his own time, but a mere ninety-five centuries could never have produced a transformation like this. They had to be some sort of aliens.

Strange as they were, they were humanoid, at any rate. Not giant paramecia or walking starfish or great shambling blue-and-orange monsters. And, unlike all the others, they hadn't simply walked past him without a glance and kept on going. They had actually stopped and were studying him with some interest. That gave him hope.

"Please," he said. "I'm lost. I don't have any idea where I am. Won't you help me?"

The two eerie humanoids exchanged a quick glance. Another positive sign. It was the first reaction he had managed to get from any of the beings he had encountered in these corridors. But they remained silent.

"Talk to me," he said. "Somehow. There's got to be a way that you can communicate with me. I know there is."

For a moment more they remained motionless. Then one of them made a gesture with its many fingers. In Eric's own time that gesture meant *come closer*. He had no notion what it might mean here. He decided to risk it.

When he was just a few paces from them they reached their long ropy arms toward him and touched their soft cool fingers to his. It was like touching an electric socket. A sudden tingling shock burst through him.

"No—wait—"

He tried to pull back, but he was unable to break the contact.

And then, amazingly, he felt intelligible words taking form in his mind.

There is no reason for you to fear us. Why would we want to harm you?

"I didn't know what was happening to me. Or what to expect. I—I—" He took a deep breath. "I'm Eric Gabrielson. I come from the twenty-first century. There's been this experiment, you see, in time displacement, and—"

We know that. We are the anterstrin thelerimane.

They said it as though that explained everything.

"Oh," he said. "And this is Earth, isn't it? In the year A.D. 11529?"

This is Earth, yes. You are in the quarantine section.

"Quarantine?"

All new arrivals are placed in quarantine until their clearances come through. It is the law. Visitors from time must undergo clearance just as visitors from space do. Once you are cleared you will be permitted to visit Upper Earth.

"I see," Eric said. "And how long does it take to get a clearance?"

The anterstrin thelerimane said, *In some cases, no more than ten or twenty days. In others, perhaps fifty to a hundred years, or even longer. Centuries, sometimes.*

Eric thought of the displacement force, gathering its irresistible momentum now, almost ready perhaps to sweep him away from this place.

"Can't it ever be done faster?" he asked.

There is much that must be determined before strangers can be released into Upper Earth. We ourselves have been here sixteen years, and our case is by no means settled. You may have to wait just as long.

"But I can't," Eric protested. "I'm shunting in time on pendulum swings. Do you understand what I'm saying? The next swing could carry me away in an hour, or a minute, or a day. And then I'd never get to see what Earth is like in this era."

Oh, no, said the quiet mental voice of the anterstrin thelerimane. *You will not be suddenly carried away, we assure you. The rules are never broken. No one leaves quarantine until the galithismon permits it. You will stay here until your clearance comes. We promise you that. Even if you must remain in the quarantine tunnels for five hundred years.*

20

SEAN

-5×10^9 MINUTES

It was almost noon by the time Sean came to the eastern rim of the broad mesa that he had been crossing since dawn. He peered over the edge and what he beheld in the dark valley below made him gasp with wonder.

Bison. Thousands of them, maybe millions, great shaggy brown beasts with their heavy heads down close to the ground.

They were ripping fiercely at the thick lush grass of the valley as if trying to turn the place into a barren desert in a single day. The vast herd filled the valley as far as Sean could see. The cold, biting wind out of the east carried their odor to him, rank and musky and sharp.

At last. After three days of solitary wandering in this cool wet land that was supposed to be Arizona, seeing nothing bigger than a ground squirrel and feeling tension rising within him as silent emptiness gave way only to more emptiness, he was staring at more animals than he had ever seen in one place in his life. Giant animals. What he saw out there was probably one of the last of the great big-game herds that had survived from the Ice Age and still roamed the Southwest here in the Paleolithic past.

"Hey!" he called. "Hey, all you bison! You're extinct, do you know that? You hear what I'm telling you? Lie down and roll over! You're extinct!"

Sean didn't expect the bison to pay any attention to him, and they didn't. They went right on grazing, tearing out enormous clumps of grass, shaking their huge heads almost angrily from side to side as they fed. He had simply needed to hear the sound of his own voice again.

The three days that he had spent trekking through this forlorn world of 5×10^9 minutes ago had been the loneliest days he had ever known. Especially after the shunt that had preceded this one.

Lovely Quintu-Leela, his woman with silver eyes. How he missed her now! What pain that had been, seeing her waver and vanish before him as the displacement force pulled him onward in time! She was like something half-remembered from a vivid dream, now. She was up there in the future, in bewildering, incomprehensible A.D. 2967. And he was back here, five billion minutes in his own past.

Five billion minutes! That was some 9,513 years. This was the world of 7500 B.C., more or less. These bison belonged here. He was the intruder.

Everything was different here, everything was unfamiliar. The air, when it didn't reek of bison fur, had an odd crisp iron quality, a metallic harshness that Sean knew was simply its purity. He had never breathed truly fresh air before. The sky looked bigger and bluer, the horizon farther away than it ought to be. The light was more intense. The water that flowed in the many streams that crossed these plains seemed to have a strange electric tingle to it because it was so clean.

This was a world without automobiles, without airplanes, without chemical factories, without anything that belched fumes into the air. Strange huge animals roamed it freely, and human beings scarcely existed. Over on the other side of the world in the Near East and maybe China the first little towns were being founded, but even there the world must still be unspoiled. It was almost impossible to comprehend how far he was from his own time. The pyramids of Egypt would not be built for another five thousand years.

And yet Sean knew he had only begun his voyage across the eons. By the time he reached the outer limits of the pendulum swing, this era would seem like the day before yesterday to him.

He looked out into the sea of bison before him.

Now he noticed other animals down there too, moving on the edges of the great bison herd. To his left he saw a pack of large long-legged wolflike creatures with broad, heavy-looking heads and dense blue-black fur. They looked frightening, but there was something curiously unferocious about their movements: they were sniffing and snuffling around like scavengers hoping to find an easy meal, and even when a lost bison calf wandered past them they made no move to attack.

Farther to the left were three peculiar-looking massive creatures squatting down on their haunches in front of a slender pine tree. Even squatting like that, they were taller than the tree. They were methodically pulling it apart, stripping the bark from its branches and cramming it into their mouths. Sean remembered seeing pictures of them on the orientation tape for this period: giant ground sloths. Deeper into the distance, so far across the valley that he could barely make them out, were mastodons. Their elephantlike forms were unmistakable. He saw some things that might have been camels out there, too. And closer at hand was a pair of heavyset creatures that seemed midway between an elephant and a pig in shape. Giant tapirs, he supposed.

The experts had thought these creatures of the late Ice Age might be just about extinct, here in the Arizona of 7500 B.C. But there was some uncertainty about the date of the great extinction and they had asked Sean to keep an eye out for them as he passed through this level of the shunt. And there they were. Beginning their decline, maybe, but far from extinct.

Mastodons! Bison! Giant ground sloths!

What a fantastic sight!

As Sean stared out toward the far reaches of the valley, a sudden flash of activity closer at hand caught his attention. He looked down and to his left. The bison calf had strayed just a little too far. From a dense clump of bushes at the base of the mesa came now a quick and savage killer, long and low-slung, with a compact, powerful tigerlike body and two astounding gleaming fangs almost a foot in length.

The calf never had a chance.

Swiftly the saber-tooth pounced, rising from the ground with a fierce thrust of its strong back and loins and clamping its heavy forearms against the bison's shaggy hump. In the same instant those two great daggers rose and sank deep into the flesh of the bison. The calf shivered under the assault and sank to its knees, and then tumbled over, pushing desperately at the saber-tooth with its hooves as though trying to shoo away an annoying fly.

It was all over in moments. Somberly Sean watched the killer-cat feed; and then the wolves came forth, snarling with sudden fury, demanding their share. The saber-tooth glared at them coldly as if ready to take on the whole pack. Then it wriggled its heavy neck in something remarkably like a shrug, and slowly moved off. It had eaten its fill, and now it was abandoning its prey to the hungry wolves. They were scavengers after all, terrifying though they might look.

Eventually the wolves too vanished into the thickets, leaving the bloody carcass for smaller beasts to devour.

Sean now began warily to make his way down the mesa's steeply sloping eastern face. He wanted a closer look at all these animals. Now that the most dangerous predator down there had had its lunch, the risks he faced were probably not great. And in any case he had an anesthetic dart gun strapped in the utility belt around his waist, and a laser, too. The dart gun ought to be able to take care of most problems. He wasn't supposed to use the laser as a weapon except in the most desperate of circumstances. If he went around killing things with his laser in the remote past, he might be making significant changes in the fabric of time by removing this critter or that which hadn't originally been destined to die at the hands of a man of the far future. But his surviving the mission was important, too. He had to calculate the trade-offs before going for the weapon.

The soil was damp and soggy from the rain that had drenched these plains, and him, last night. As he descended he sank in almost an inch with every step, coming up with moist, sticky mud on his boots. Mud wasn't something he associated with Arizona. Or valleys rich with thick lush grass. The Arizona he knew was a place of parched wastelands, dry brittle soil, twisted thorny scrub vegetation. But his instrument reading showed that he was somewhere just to the north of the place where Phoenix would be in another nine thousand-odd years.

He had started out from Los Angeles, up there at Time Zero in A.D. 2016. Not only had the shunt displaced him in time, though, it had also moved him some four hundred miles in space. No surprise there. The preshunt calculations had predicted that. The longer the time-shunt, the farther the spatial displacement.

Project Pendulum

This was Arizona, all right. But it was prehistoric Arizona at the tail end of the Pleistocene Ice Age. The great chill that had brought so much moisture to this part of the continent had already begun to retreat; the lakes and meadows were starting to dry out, the big game animals were becoming sparse. During his increasingly depressing three-day trek through the utter silence of this land he had begun to fear that they were already extinct. Now Sean knew that that was not so.

Slipping and sliding and stumbling, he made his way the last twenty feet to the valley floor and found himself about a hundred yards from the nearest bison.

This close, he realized that they had little in common with the bison he had seen in zoos except the shagginess of their hides. These animals were gigantic, each one as big as a truck. They were colossal. They were immense. Their horns, instead of curving back to lose themselves in the heavy fur, jutted out three feet or more on each side. And the sound they made as they grazed was a mighty throbbing growl like the sound a fire makes as it roars through a dry forest.

He edged sideways, keeping his back to the mesa wall. A few of the bison closest to him eyed him without curiosity for a moment, but most did not even bother looking up. Why should they? They had no reason to fear him. They might never have seen a human being before. The whole human population of North America at this time was probably no more than twenty or thirty thousand widely scattered nomads. And to these bison he must seem utterly harmless, a flimsy little two-legged thing with no teeth or muscles worth worrying about and no claws at all.

Seeing that the bison were ignoring him, Sean moved out a little more boldly into the valley. The hugeness of the animals filled him with awe. They were like mountains. Even the calves seemed immense. He had all the more respect now for the strength of that saber-tooth.

He saw other animals now, smaller ones, animals he could not name. They were almost familiar—something that could almost have been a badger, and waddling birds that were somewhat like turkeys, and little scrambling rodents not much unlike guinea pigs. But they were all somehow different from their modern counterparts.

He wished he knew more about prehistoric zoology. This was an amazing place. Evidently this valley was a rich and fertile location that was particularly attractive to beasts great and small from all over central Arizona. What an amazing privilege it was to be allowed to see this congregation of great creatures!

Then he realized that he was not the only person here.

Shouts came from a fold in the valley floor a few hundred yards away. Glancing up in surprise, Sean was startled to see eight or ten tall, slender men in loincloths pelting one of the bison calves with rocks to drive it into a small box canyon. They were armed with spears tipped with tapering stone points, and as they pursued the angry, frightened calf they jabbed at it again and again, barely penetrating its thick furry hide. Killing it was going to be a difficult job.

Sean had been so concerned with the animals that he hadn't heard the hunters approach. Now, struck with wonder and amazement, he stepped back behind a tree to watch them in action. They were long-limbed, graceful men. They seemed almost to be floating as they ran along behind the calf. Though they had dark skins of a deep coppery hue, they looked very little like the Indians of his own time. Their heads were narrow and tapering, their shoulders sloped, their features were small, almost delicate. The chilly air seemed to bother them not at all, practically naked though they were.

He leaned forward, peering intently, fascinated by the sight of these prehistoric hunters at their task.

Then he felt a sudden stiff jab between his shoulder blades.

He whirled. And found himself looking at another of the hunters, who had come up silently behind him. His eyes were dark and shining, almost glowing with a light of their own. They were fixed on Sean in absolute concentration. The hunter grasped a spear lightly in his left hand, balancing it easily by the middle of its shaft.

He must have used the wooden end of the spear to poke Sean in the back. But now he had swung it around the other way. Sean stared. The long, sharp, elegantly carved stone point of the spear came into close focus just in front of him. It was aimed at the center of his chest, hovering just a couple of inches over his heart.

ERIC

−5 × 10¹⁰ MINUTES

The rules are never broken. That was the last thing that he remembered the anterstrin thelerimane saying, back in the tunnels that ran beneath the world of A.D. 11529. Those two spooky humanoids with the long whiplike limbs had seemed to be telling him that he was going to dwell in the tunnels forever. *No one leaves quarantine until the galithismon permits it. You will stay here until your clearance comes, we promise you that. Even if you must remain in the quarantine tunnels for five hundred years.*

And then he felt the familiar swooping dizzying sensation that let him know he was making a shunt, and the anterstrin thelerimane disappeared. The weird glistening tunnel with the onyx wall disappeared. The whole world of A.D. 11529 disappeared.

So much for the quarantine powers of the galithismon, Eric thought. Whoever or whatever the galithismon might be, it had been unable to withstand the power of the great pendulum that was carrying Eric back and forth across time.

What now? he wondered.

He found himself on an icy windswept plain, bleak and desolate. Leafless trees with dark crooked trunks rose here and there above the snowfields. The air was harsh and sharp, with howling gusts cutting deep. He touched his utility belt to give himself a little protection against the cold.

This was the minus-fifty-billion-minutes level. Fifty billion minutes! He was 95,129 years into the past now—the Pleistocene period, the last Ice Age, the Fourth Glacial. Eric took his bearings. Latitude 41 degrees north. Longitude 6 degrees east. *East?* He was in Europe, then. Right in the middle of Spain. A whopping spatial displacement, clear across the whole United States and the Atlantic, too. Halfway around the world and smack into the teeth of an Ice-Age gale.

And there were tracks in the fresh snow in front of him.

Human tracks.

No question about it. The tracks had been made by someone with a wide foot, very wide. Probably a short person, because the prints were fairly close together.

But human, without a doubt. Because the feet that had left those tracks in the snow had been clad in sandals of some sort. The imprint was unmistakable: no sign of toes or claws, only the rounded front end of the sandal and the tapering heel.

Human? In Pleistocene Spain?

Neanderthals, Eric thought in sudden wonder. And he began to follow the trail.

It led up and over a hummock of rock that jutted from the snowfield, and down the other side through a region of loose and annoyingly deep snow that gave him much trouble, and then up the side of a steep hill. Climbing it was real work. For one bad moment he thought he had lost the trail altogether; but then he picked it up again, midway up the hill. Behind him, the winds grew wilder and snow began to fall. He scrambled upward.

A cave. A fire burning within.

He stared. Eight, ten people inside, close together the campfire. Wearing shaggy fur robes, though some were bare to the waist. Short people, stocky and squat, with big heads and thick necks and barrel chests and broad, low-bridged noses. They weren't pretty, no. But they weren't apes, either. They were human beings. Different from us, but not by much. Cousins. Our Neanderthal cousins. Eric shivered, and not just from the cold.

One of them was singing, and the others were gathered around, nodding and clapping their hands in time. A slow, rhythmic chant, which suddenly speeded up, then slowed again, speeded again: an intricate rhythm, constantly changing. Almost like a poem. Almost? It was a poem! Those complex rhythms, the solemnity of the chanter's voice, the rapt attention of the listeners. The *Iliad* of the

Project Pendulum

Neanderthals, maybe, a tale of heroic battle deeds. Or the *Odyssey*, the story of a man who had gone to war across the sea and had had a hard time getting home. A tribal poet, telling the great old stories around the campfire. Stories that would fall into the deepest sort of oblivion when these rugged people of the Ice Age were swept away into extinction, thirty or forty thousand years from now.

Neanderthal poetry! The idea stunned and dazzled him.

He leaned forward as far as he dared, peering into the mouth of the cave, straining to hear the words, hoping with an impossible hope to understand the meaning.

Abruptly the chanting stopped. There was silence in the cave.

They knew he was there. How? He had crouched down behind a great rock partly blocking the entrance. But they were looking his way. Sniffing. Those big noses, those wide nostrils. They could smell him. They were murmuring to each other. Suddenly these people seemed less like ancient cousins, more like hairy ogres or trolls.

The storm was lashing the plain now: wild winds, flailing the falling snow into thick white curtains. Eric backed away from the mouth of the cave. He heard a shout from within, then another, another. Desperately now he began to run down the hill, slipping and stumbling in the loosely packed snow.

And they were coming after him.

Don't try to run, he thought. Slide for it! Slide!

He dropped down flat and gave himself a shove. And went wildly tobogganing away, moving at an ever accelerating speed with his knees drawn up tight against his chest and his arms pulled in over them. A couple of times he fetched up against some upjutting snag of a tree, or some hunk of rock, and gave himself a nasty whack; but then he pushed on, down and down and down the hill.

After a time he looked back. The Neanderthals had stopped pursuing him. They were standing some distance above him on a snowy ridge, staring at him in what looked like openmouthed astonishment.

They probably think I'm crazy, Eric thought. Crazy skinny peculiar-looking guy with a strange outfit on, who can't find any better way to amuse himself than go sliding down a bumpy hill in the middle of a snowstorm. Obviously a low-I.Q. type, a real moron.

Or maybe not. Maybe they think I'm having a good time.

He stood up, waved, shouted to them. "Come on!" he called. "You try it, too! It's fun, guys! It's fun!"

He saw them muttering to each other. Maybe they were considering it. Maybe they were seriously thinking about taking up body-sledding, now that I've shown them the way.

I may have started something here, he thought. The Neanderthal Winter Olympics!

He brushed snow from his clothes and trudged on down the hillside, feeling a little creaky and battered. When he looked back next, the Neanderthal conference was still going on, and two of them were lying in the snow, trying to shove themselves downhill.

SEAN

+5 × 10¹⁰ MINUTES

The point of the spear just barely grazed Sean's chest. The other man held it there. Sean froze, not even breathing. He looked down, eyes bugging, at the sharp stone tip against his breastbone. This is it, he thought. The end of Sean, nine thousand years ago in Arizona. The archaeologists will be real confused when they find the bones of a white man in the ancient strata here.

You have to do something, he told himself.

Go for the dart gun? Or even the laser? No. It took a little time to get the anesthetic darts armed and primed. He didn't have that much time. As for the laser, he knew he was supposed to avoid using the weapon unless he had absolutely no other option. Besides, he suspected that the moment he made any movement toward his utility belt that spear would be sticking out his back.

Do something. Anything.

He began to sing.

Project Pendulum

He had no idea what good it would do. He just opened his mouth and let melody come flowing out.

> Oh, say, can you see
> By the dawn's early light...

The hunter looked astounded. He stepped back, one pace, two, three, without taking his eyes off Sean.
Reprieve. Somehow.

> ...what so proudly we hailed
> by the twilight's last gleaming...

The hunter spoke: a single stream of words punctuated by explosive little bursts of breath.

"Sorry," Sean said. "I don't speak Prehistoric Hopi, or whatever you're talking." He managed a smile. It wasn't easy. It must have looked more like a tense grimace. Every culture understands smiling, he knew. Show your teeth. It's a sign of good will. "You are a Hopi or something, right? An Indian, anyway. An early version. An ancestor. My name is Sean. I come here in peace from the year 2016. Do you want me to sing some more? 'God rest ye merry gentlemen, let nothing you dismay—' "

The hunter spoke again, the same speech, faster this time. To Sean his words sounded blunt, cruel, harsh.

Sean responded with another smile, a little on the edgy side. And came out with:

> California, here I come
> Right back where I started from...

It was hard to tell what the other was planning to do. The hunter's eyelids were fluttering now. His nostrils flared wide. He grasped his spear at both ends and pulled it back tightly against his chest. He spoke once more, slowly and in a deeper voice. As if he were sinking into some sort of trance.

Keep on singing, Sean thought.

> I am the captain of the Pinafore
> And a right good captain too.
> De deedle deedle dee and deedle deedle dee
> With chimpanzees for my crew.

They weren't quite the right words, but he doubted that the hunter would know that. And at least the tune was there.

The other hunters were approaching now. Their faces were smeared with bison blood. One of them prodded Sean with the business end of his spear, pushing against the close-knit fabric of his jumpsuit. It was just the lightest of touches, but Sean shivered as he felt the keen tip of the stone point. He tried singing the "Hallelujah" chorus. It didn't sound so good solo. They came in closer now, pinching and poking him. He switched to "Silent Night" thinking it might calm them some. The first one, the one who seemed to have gone into a trance, made a low rumbling sound far back in his throat.

I'd like to get out of here, Sean thought. Somehow. Any way at all. Just let it be right now.

He smiled again, the widest smile he could manage. "I know you can't understand a thing that I'm saying, but I'm saying it calmly and reasonably. I'm not here to cause any trouble. I'm simply a visitor. My name is Sean Gabrielson and I'm twenty-three years old and I have a degree in physics from Cal Tech, and I mean to keep right on speaking quietly and reasonably to you until you decide that I'm no threat. I'm also willing to sing anything you request. I can do some nice old rock numbers, I know a couple of hymns, I can do patriotic songs. And I can keep it up until the next shunt comes and gets me, if I have to. Just stand there and listen peacefully, okay?" He started in on "Rock of Ages." They all looked almost hypnotized now. Eyes wide, staring. They didn't know what to make of him. "I can tell you all sorts of useful things, too. For example, I can advise you to start thinking about migrating north, because these animals here that you hunt are going to clear out of this territory in another few hundred years, once things start getting really warm and dry, and—"

Project Pendulum

They were looking at him in what looked like awe. Maybe they're beginning to think I'm a god, he thought. Or maybe they just love the sound of my voice.

"You see, this is the late Pleistocene, but eventually this is going to be known as the state of Arizona, and I can prophesy that there's going to be a freeway right down the middle of this valley, running from Flagstaff down to Phoenix or Tucson—"

They were down on their knees. Yes. Worshipping me, Sean thought. He grinned. They do think I'm a god

Unless they're just begging me to stop talking and start singing again.

> Old Man River,
> That Old Man River...

This is going to be fun, he told himself. Then he felt the displacement force tugging at him.

Not now, he thought in annoyance. Not just when it's getting good! But there was nothing he could do about it. The force had pulled him away from Quintu-Leela and now it was yanking him away from his first good shot at being a god, or at least being a star singer. One moment he was staring at a bunch of awed prehistoric bison hunters, and the next he was floating in a globe of green light, somewhere very far away. So long, fellows. Onward to—what?

This was serious future now, a truly heavy distance. He was 95,129 years down the line, an enormous jump. His last forward swing had taken him a mere 951 years ahead. Even that world, Quintu-Leela's world of A.D. 2967, was utterly unlike anything he knew or could understand. That was how vast the changes had been between his own time and Quintu-Leela's.

Now he was a hundred times as far from Time Zero. 95,129 years! The transformations in human life during such an immense span must have been incredible. It had taken only five thousand years to go from the first civilizations in Egypt and Mesopotamia to the age of travel through time and space. Now he had covered twenty times as many years. Did the human race even exist anymore? Or had it evolved into something unimaginably strange?

Where was he? What was this globe of green light? What was going to happen to him?

Many questions, no answers.

Then a deep gentle voice said, "Hey, it's good to see you again, Sean. Been a long time, boy."

A very familiar voice. His grandfather's voice, rich and warm. Grandpa Gabrielson who lived in San Diego.

Sean blinked into the greenness. "Is that you, Grandpa?"

"Who else, boy?"

Unmistakable, that voice. The voice of the wise, loving old man who had spent so many holiday weekends with them, who liked to tell all those stories of the first television sets, the first jet planes, the first trip to the moon, the first flights of the space shuttle. Grandpa Gabrielson had worked as an engineer for the Apollo space program when he was a young man, and later he had been involved in the shuttle project. He had seen the whole modern world take shape in his lifetime.

But Grandpa Gabrielson had no business being here in the 932nd century. Grandpa Gabrielson had lived to a good old age, well past eighty. But he had died last year, just before Sean and Eric had been chosen for Project Pendulum.

"I'm here too, son. It really has been a long time!"

His grandmother's voice. She had died when he was ten. And then his father was in the green globe with him, clapping him on the back, laughing, asking him if he was managing to keep up with the baseball scores while he was shunting around. And his mother, glowing with pride. And his mother's parents, Grandfather and Grandmother Weiss. He hardly knew them, because they lived in Belgium.

And Eric was there also.

It was Thanksgiving Day, and there was a huge turkey on the table, and mounds of cranberry sauce, and mountains of candied yams and turkey stuffing and everything else, and the whole family was there. His father was busy carving, as he always did. And he and Eric were side by side for the first time in 95,129 years.

Project Pendulum

Sean looked at his brother. He could feel the strange force, the brother-force, that had bound him to his twin all his life. The force which he had not felt since the moment they had gone their separate ways at Time Zero on the shunt platform.

"Are you really here?" he asked.

Eric grinned. "What do you think? That I'm just some sleazy illusion?"

"But this can't be happening," Sean said. "Thanksgiving Day in the year 95,129? Grandpa and Grandma here? Mom and Dad? No. I'm in some kind of green globe and this is just some hallucination that who knows what kind of creatures are pulling out of the memories they find in my brain. Right? Right?"

Eric gave him a pitying look. "You must have lost your mind. Or misplaced it, at the very least. I'm as real as you are, and probably a lot hungrier. Shut up and pass the turkey, turkey!"

23

ERIC

+5 × 10¹¹ MINUTES

Scrambling down an icy hillside through a blinding snowstorm was bad enough. But every breath was agony. Breathing this fierce Fourth Ice Age atmosphere was like inhaling icicles. And to have a pack of angry Neanderthals coming after him, besides—

Eric felt the shunt take him and sweep him mercifully into some far-off warmer place. He landed on all fours, gasping and coughing, and crouched there a moment until he had recovered. At last he looked up.

A Neanderthal face was looking back at him. Sloping forehead, rounded chin, broad nose, mouth like a jutting muzzle. Shrewd dark eyes studying him intently.

"Huh? Did I bring you along with me somehow?"

The Neanderthal knelt beside him and said something in an unknown language. His voice was deep and the way he spoke seemed oddly musical, though very strange. He didn't seem hostile. Behind him, Eric saw softly rounded green hills, a wide valley broken by a chain of lakes, a forest in the distance.

There were prehistoric hominids wandering about wherever he looked.

He had landed in a group of ten or fifteen Neanderthals. Off to his left a hundred yards away were some slender little creatures looking a bit like apes but walking confidently upright. Eric recognized them as australopithecines from the early Pleistocene, creatures that occupied a place somewhere midway on the evolutionary path that had led to *Homo sapiens*. And over there, that awesome monster of an ape, as massive as a grizzly bear? Wasn't that Gigantopithecus, from a million years B.C.? And those, in the middle distance? Sturdy-looking people who seemed almost human but for their strangely apelike faces: could those be *Homo erectus*, the ancestors of mankind whose fossil remains had been found in Java and China?

And those—

And those—

And those—

Wherever he looked, some not-quite-human creatures could be seen in the valley. The whole history of the evolution of humanity seemed to be here, all the extinct forms that he had studied in school and a good many that he was unable to identify at all.

What was this place? Unless he had lost count of the shunts, he was at the plus-500-billion-minutes level now. 951,000 years in the future. What were all these creatures doing here, all wandering around at random like this?

"You have just arrived, I suppose?" a pleasant voice said behind him. Eric whirled. The speaker was a bearded man of about fifty, elegant and amiable-looking, wearing what looked like riding clothes of the late eighteenth or early nineteenth century. He might have been some English gentleman out for a stroll in the woods. "Bathurst," he said. "Benjamin Bathurst. Former Minister Plenipotentiary of His Britannic Majesty George III to the court of Franz I, Emperor of Austria. Of course, I'm nothing very much any more."

"Eric Gabrielson," Eric said shakily. "From Los Angeles, California, the—the United States."

"Very pleased to make your acquaintance," Bathurst said. "Always charming to see another human face. There are forty of us now, I think. Of course, we're greatly outnumbered by the apes, but everyone's friendly enough. You're a million years in the future, you know. The United States, you say? Of America? The former Colonies? California was never one of the Colonies, as I recall. But I suppose—"

"We got it from Mexico," Eric said. "Somewhere around 1849. And yes, I know we're a million years in the future. Approximately. But you—George III—"

He was having trouble speaking clearly. An overdose of confusion was making his voice husky. The Neanderthal, muttering to himself, began to fondle Bathurst's intricately carved walking stick. The Englishman smiled and gently drew it away.

"What year are you from?" he asked Eric.

"2016 is when I set out from."

"Ah. 2016. The fabulous future, indeed. Well, well, we will have much to talk about, then. No one else here comes from any year later than 1853, I believe. Most are much earlier. We have a Roman couple, do you know, and several Greeks, and an Egyptian or two. And some who speak no language any of us can fathom. They must be quite ancient. I myself was seized in 1809."

"Seized?"

"Oh, yes, of course, boy! How did you think we all got here?"

Eric moistened his lips. "I'm here as a result of an experiment in travel through time carried out at the California Institute of Technology," he said. "But you—"

Bathurst shrugged. "A victim of kidnapping. Forced transport. Seized unawares. The same fate that has befallen all the creatures here, both human and otherwise. Except you, it would seem, if you indeed have come voluntarily. The rest of us are captives. It is a very comfortable captivity, I must say, but it is captivity all the same. And it is imprisonment for life, I grieve to say. Yet it is a very comfortable imprisonment, for all that."

Kidnapped from 1809? Romans? Greeks? Neanderthals? Australopithecines? "But who—who—"

"Who is responsible for bringing us here, you mean to ask? Why, the demigods who inhabit this distant eon, boy! Our own remote descendants! Perhaps you'll meet them someday. I myself have seen them on three occasions thus far. Quite remarkable, you'll find. True demigods, as far beyond us as we are beyond these shaggy apelike fellows here. We've been collected, do you see? All manner of historical specimens, and prehistorical specimens too, I dare say. It's a kind of zoological garden here. An exhibit, do you see, of the people of ages gone by, collected by mysterious magical means from every era of antiquity. I'm one of the items on display, boy, for the amusement and edification of our remote descendants. And now so are you, do you see? So are you."

24

SEAN

-5×10^{11} MINUTES

He was almost coming to believe that it was real. The tender succulent turkey meat, the sweet rich cranberry sauce, the hot steaming rolls—it was all so much like the family feasts of his boyhood that after a while he simply accepted it and let it engulf him like a warm bath. Mom, Dad, his grandparents, Eric—

But then it all turned misty and insubstantial. He had a final glimpse of the sphere of green light once again, and he thought he saw a row of faces behind the light, faces that might have been human and might have been something else. Then everything went black and the shunt took him and swept him away.

He was in heavy jungle terrain now. The air was thick and close, the trees were tall and slender and set close together with their crowns meeting overhead to form a canopy. Here and there, through a break in the foliage, he saw pale sugarloaf-shaped mountains on the horizon. This, he knew, was the world of 951,293 years before Time Zero.

Project Pendulum

And there was the biggest gorilla anyone had ever seen, standing twenty feet in front of him.

Actually he doubted that it was a gorilla. Perhaps it was more like an orangutan, with that deep chest and short neck. Or something midway between the two. But it was colossal. It was supporting itself on all fours, but he suspected that when it stood upright it would be close to nine feet tall.

It was watching him with a who-the-devil-are-*you*? look in its beady yellow eyes, and it was making a low growling sound, very ominous. Gorillas and orangutans, Sean told himself, eat fruits and vegetables. This guy doesn't look like a hunter to me. But he's big. Very big. And not friendly looking. Absolutely not friendly. And I'm on his personal turf, and he doesn't like it.

"Listen," Sean said, "I don't want you to get annoyed about anything, okay? Just as I was telling those Indians a little while ago, it's not my plan to bother you in the slightest. I'm only a visitor here. I'm simply passing through, and I'm not going to be here very long, let me assure you of that."

The giant ape appeared to frown. It seemed to consider what Sean was telling it.

It didn't seem to like what it had heard, though.

It began to snort and growl. It raised itself to its full unbelievable height and pounded itself on its chest like King Kong in a feisty mood. It made unmistakably angry sounds. Sean wondered if it was going to charge him. He wasn't sure. The ape didn't seem quite sure, either. For a long moment it rocked back and forth in place, growling, beating its chest, glaring at the intruder.

Then it leaned forward on its knuckles and made a different sound, deep and ominous.

Yes, Sean thought. It is going to charge. It very definitely is going to charge.

And I'm going to die, back here in the umptieth century B.C.

Or else I'll get shunted out of here in the nick of time and it's Eric who'll die when he shows up right in front of a crazed charging ape. It's just as bad either way.

Damn! Damn! *Damn!*

25

ERIC

−5 × 10¹² MINUTES

The shunts were coming too fast, too close together. Eric was drowning in a torrent of wonders. To be given a glimpse of Neanderthals in their own time, chanting by their own campfire, and then to be swept far onward to a magical place where pithecanthropi and australopithecines and Romans and Greeks and nineteenth-century Englishmen lived all jumbled together in some kind of far-future zoo, and to be pulled away from that much too soon, before he had even begun to learn the things he wanted to know—

And now this. Nine and a half million years in the past. Paradise for the sort of dreamer who once built fossil dinosaurs out of papier-mâché. Not that there were any dinosaurs here, of course. Not in the Pliocene period, no. Dinosaurs were much earlier than that: this was mammal time, here. But, dinosaurs or no, he had been let loose in a garden of zoological wonders and he would gladly have spent a year here, five years, ten. There was so much to see. Paleozoology wasn't even his field—he barely knew the names of half the creatures who were parading before his astounded eyes—and even so he would have given anything to be allowed to remain.

Another month—another week—

But he knew that the irresistible force of the shunt soon would surround him and tear him free of this place and sweep him onward.

That giant piglike thing with the fantastic bristly face and the terrifying teeth, a creature bigger than any rhinoceros, snorting and snuffling in the underbrush—

That hairy elephant with the short trunk and the long outthrust jaw, and the second pair of tusks jutting down over the other ones—

That skittish yellow animal with a camel's silly face and a gazelle's agile body, running in frantic herds across the plains—

That one that had a camel's body and a camel's head, but a neck like a giraffe's, reaching up easily to graze on treetops close to twenty-five feet high—

The deer with its horns on its nose, and the one with fangs like a tiger's, and the one whose head was all knobs and crests and other strangenesses—

The giant ground sloth with the long weird drooping snout, almost like a little trunk—

The armadillo as big as a tank, angrily lashing its spiked tail against the ground—

Dream-animals. Nightmare-animals. They were everywhere on this wondrous plain, grazing, creeping, crawling, climbing, hunting, sleeping. He wanted to see every one, to commit them all to memory, to come home with mind-pictures of this Pliocene wonderland that would keep paleozoologists busy for decades. Unique discoveries, animals unknown to science. But already he felt the force tugging at him.

No—wait—

Another day, he begged. Half a day. Another three hours.

No chance. The equations were inexorable. Force had to balance.

Now—now—onward—

SEAN

$+5 \times 10^{12}$ MINUTES

He was five trillion minutes from home and the giant ape was no longer his immediate problem. Because the pendulum had swung and the iron fist of the displacement force had grabbed him and converted him into a shower of tachyons and sent him rocketing off toward the other end of time. So it was Eric who was destined to show up right in the path of the ape's charge, when they started down the homeward slope of the voyage.

I have to do something to warn him, Sean thought. But what?

He looked around. He was standing in a fragrant bower of blossoming plants that sprouted on shining crystalline stalks three feet high, plants that looked like nothing he had ever seen before. And a great blue world was shining overhead like a dazzling beacon, filling half the sky.

It looked a little like the Earth, that huge world floating up there. There was one great bulging land mass that was very much like Africa, though it seemed too far to the south, and he couldn't find Europe where it ought to be, only a broad ocean occupying what might have been the place of the Mediterranean Sea. To the west Sean could make out something similar to the curve of North America's eastern seaboard, though the shape wasn't a perfect match with what he remembered, and the West Indies weren't there. Far down to the side was an enormous round hump of an island, vaguely in the position that South America once had had.

If that was Earth, then, that loomed above him in the sky, it was an Earth vastly transformed.

Earth? Up there in the sky? Then where was he? On the moon?

A garden of fragrant green and gold flowers rising on stalks of crystal—on the moon?

Flowers on the moon? Sweet fresh air on the moon?

Nine and a half million years. Anything was possible.

He took a few steps. The pull of gravity seemed normal enough. It should feel almost like floating, he knew, to walk on the moon. Unless they had changed that, too. If they could give the moon an atmosphere and make gardens grow on it, they could give it Earth-like gravitation also.

Should the Earth look this close, though? He wasn't sure. He wished his astronomy was a little sharper. And his knowledge of geology, too. He knew that the continents drifted around, over the course of many millions of years, but could they have rearranged themselves so drastically in just nine and a half million? Eric would know, of course. But Eric wasn't here.

The people of this era, Sean decided, can do anything they feel like doing. They can move the moon closer to the Earth. They can move South America farther from North America. Anything. Anything.

Project Pendulum

An age of miracles is what it must be.

He felt like an apeman suddenly swept millions of years forward into a world of telephones, television, computers, spaceships. Miracles. Miracles everywhere. And that was really what he was, he knew: a primitive creature, a prehistoric ape, a hairy shambling ancient man who needed to shave his face every day and who still carried an appendix around in his belly. How they must pity him, the unseen watchers who—he was entirely sure—were studying him now! Were they human at all? Did the human race still exist? Or had it died out long ago, and given way to some race of superbeings?

He reached down and let his fingers caress one of the lovely crystalline flowers.

It wriggled with pleasure like a cat being stroked, and began to sing, a slow, sinuous, sensuous melody. Immediately the others nearby started to preen and sway as if trying to get Sean's attention. *Touch me,* they were telling him. *Touch me, touch me, touch me! Make me sing!*

He was reminded of the garden of talking flowers that Alice had found in Looking-Glass Land: the vain and haughty Tiger-lily, and Rose, and Violet. How many times had he read that book, he and Eric! Eric had always liked Wonderland better; Sean had preferred the world beyond the looking-glass. And now here he was in Looking-Glass Land himself, where the flowers sang, and the blue Earth hung in the sky instead of the moon.

"You like that, do you?" he asked the flowers. And he stroked this one and that, reaching out toward them, going on down the garden row until hundreds of them were swaying and singing. The sweetness of their song was dreamlike on the thick perfumed air. He had never heard anything so beautiful.

A great strange peace came over him. He felt a Presence in his spirit. Something magical, something almost divine. Slowly he walked between the rows of flowers, savoring the mild night air, pausing often to stare up at the blue world that seemed so close overhead. It was an overwhelming privilege, being here in this place so many millions of years beyond his own time. He knew he would never see more of it than this garden, and that he would never understand any of it at all, but none of that mattered. He was here. He had been touched by Something that was as far beyond him as he was beyond the apes of the forests of humanity's dawn. Something magnificent. Something all-powerful. And yet, small as he was, splendid and mighty as It was, he felt a kinship with It. He was part of It; It was a part of him.

Then he thought of Eric, and the snarling, roaring, maddened giant ape that he was fated to meet head-on when it was his turn to arrive back there in that prehistoric jungle. And his mood of harmony and tranquility shattered.

At once the flowers began to sing a soothing song. He stared at them a long while, not soothed, brooding about his brother. That ape looked really murderous. What if he kills Ricky, Sean thought? What happens to the experiment? What happens to the world? What happens to *me*? It was the big risk that they had all tried to make believe would not be a factor. But Sean had seen the look in that ape's eye.

If only I could warn him, he thought. But how? How?

To the flowers he said, "I have to save my brother."

They made a gentle humming sound.

He sat quietly, staring at a smooth flat white rock, like a gleaming slab of marble, just in front of him in the garden.

An idea came to him.

"Forgive me," he said. "I've got to mess up this beautiful place a little. But it may be that the whole structure of the past and the future depends on it."

He took out his laser and turned it to high beam. And began to write, carving a message on that flawless stone slab in ugly black charred letters.

RICKY—DANGER!!!

As concisely as he could, he told his brother when and where the ape was waiting for him in the time stream. And suggested in the strongest possible way that he had better have his anesthetic dart gun primed and ready the moment he arrived.

"Do you think that'll do it?" he asked the flowers. "Will he turn up here in this exact spot? Will he see the message? Will he be able to nail the ape in time?"

The flowers were singing again. Soothing, comforting sounds. Everything will be all right, they were saying. Everything will be fine.

I hope that's true, Sean thought, trying to relax.

Gradually the magic returned. This was too beautiful a place to be tangled up in fears and fretfulness for long.

He felt that celestial harmony again. He felt peace, he felt that Presence.

Then the flowers fell silent. He stared up at shining Earth with trembling wonder.

ERIC

+5 × 10¹³ MINUTES

—onward—

—onward, unimaginably far—

He hovered in space, midway between somewhere and anywhere. There was golden light all about him. Comets left dazzling trails in the void. Suns whirled and danced. He filled his hands with the stuff of space, warm and soft.

He felt like a god.

He *was* a god.

This was Time Ultimate. The power of the singularities that had propelled him through time reached its limit here. The world he knew lay 95 million years behind him. Here in this realm of light everything was utterly strange. He was drifting among the stars, far from Earth. Earth? He could barely remember Earth. He could barely remember himself, who he was, why and how he had come here. So far away now, so faint in his mind. All that noisy striving, all that energy, all that restless seeking. The boiling cauldron that had been Earth and its billions of people.

He knew that they had found whatever it was they had been seeking, those restless questing people, back in that time when Earth still was. They had gained their answers long ago and they had become like gods. And Earth was gone now, and they were gone with it, gone forth into the universe, into this shining kingdom.

They had touched the stars, and the stars had accepted them into their company. As they would accept him, pilgrim out of time that he was.

How can it be, he wondered, that I'm out here in space and still able to breathe?

And a quiet voice out of nowhere said, *While you are here, you will be as we are. And when you leave we will restore you to what you were.*

Who are you, he asked? Where are you? What are you?

We are everyone. And we are everywhere. We are those for whom you prepared the way. And we protect you now and cherish you and welcome you among us.

I see, Eric said, and almost thought he did.

His long journey now seemed almost like a dream. Fragments of strange scenes floated through his mind: endlessly branching tunnels through which strange silent creatures marched, and a boy coming out of a small house on an earthquake-jumbled street, and vines flourishing in tropical heat, and squat shaggy creatures gathered around a fire in a cave on a snowy hillside, and giant redwood trees rising like the columns of a cathedral, and an Englishman in riding clothes pointing to a hominid ape that had been extinct four million years, and a camel with the neck of a giraffe, and more, much more. A torrent of images. He had made a voyage beyond all belief; and it was not over yet, for soon the pendulum would be carrying him back down the eons, taking him to new wonders as he descended through time. But that was yet to come. He was here now, in the great stillness of the world beyond the world, dwelling among people who had touched the stars.

He, too, could touch the stars. He could reach out and embrace them and engulf them, and be engulfed by them. Here blazed a blue star, and here a white one, and here a giant red one in the forehead of the night, and he touched them all. And felt the throbbing weight of the billions of years of Creation upon him. And heard the soaring song of those who had gone forth before him into this realm of light. And drifted on the bosom of the firmament. And gave thanks. And joined in that great song.

SEAN

−5 × 10¹³ MINUTES

There were dinosaurs all over the place. You walked around a bush and there was a dragon the size of a school bus eating its breakfast. You came over a hill and there was something that looked like an armored tank taking its babies for a stroll. You looked up and a flotilla of pterodactyls went zooming by, flapping their long leathery wings.

It was a real zoo here. A Cretaceous zoo, fantastic monsters lumbering around everywhere. You had to look lively to keep from getting trampled on, of course. And there was always that itchy feeling between your shoulder blades that made you think a tyrannosaurus was coming up behind you, thinking about a snack.

The air was hot and dank. Gigantic ferns, big as palm trees, formed dark close forests. Dragonflies the size of hawks fluttered around terrifyingly, buzzing and droning.

"Ricky?" Sean said out loud. "Ricky, you ought to see this! Man, you'd go *crazy!* This stuff is really wasted on me. But you, you old dinosaur freak—"

Well, Eric would be seeing all this soon enough, he knew. Unless something had happened to him during his zigzag voyage across the immensity of time. Sean didn't want to think about that possibility. Eric was all right. Eric had to be all right. And he'd be showing up here in a little while so that they could begin the homeward leg of their incredible journey.

This was Time Ultimate, the farthest swing of the pendulum. They had gone as far as they could go.

Right now Eric was somewhere out in the unthinkably remote future, 95 million years on the other side of Time Zero. And he, Sean, was here in the Cretaceous period, with a triceratops family grazing at the edge of the marsh and something that looked like a brontosaurus, but probably wasn't, rearing its snaky head high over the surface of the lake down there. But at any moment the force of the pendulum would be fully extended and he and Eric would start their downward swing, back toward Time Zero and the scientists waiting for them in the laboratory.

Sean had a pretty good idea of what it would be like. For an instant, time would seem to stand still. Then there would be a breathtaking plunge across the whole span of the displacement as he and Eric changed places. Eric would land here, among his beloved dinosaurs, and Sean would go swinging outward into whatever unimaginable place the world of A.D. 95 million might be.

And then from there, it would be down the line for them. He would shoot into the world of nine and a half million years ago, and then to the one of 951,000 years in the future, and then to 95,000 years in the past, and so on all the way back, changing places with Eric at each level, one brother replacing the other without an instant of transition.

So Eric would visit the garden of miracles on the moon, Eric would have to cope with the charging giant ape, Eric would turn up at the Thanksgiving dinner that never was. Eric would have to deal with those bison-hunters back in Arizona. Eric would take his place in Quintu-Leela's arms and probably he too would be swept off into time too fast for it to matter. Eric would cheer at President Harding's inauguration parade. Eric would show up for the tail end of his own parade in Glendora.

And meanwhile—

Sean stood leaning against a tree fern that was four times his own height, watching the parade of giant reptiles, and thinking of everything that had befallen him on this whirlwind trip through past and future. The world would never be the same, now that the gates of time stood wide open. And neither would he. His mind was full of such strangenesses as no other mortal being had ever experienced. None except Eric, at any rate.

Project Pendulum

Sean wondered what was in store for him in all those eras where Eric had already been.

Perils, thrills, bewilderments galore—no doubt of that. And perhaps some burst of sudden ecstasy to match or even surpass that mystical moment among the singing flowers that glowed by the light of the full Earth in the sky.

He'd know, soon enough. He could feel the force tugging at him now, starting to take him onward.

He smiled. He slapped the tree fern fondly, as if saying goodbye to an old friend, and went strolling down toward the lake. His boots made sucking noises. It was all wet, spongy swampland here. The dinosaurs all around him snorted and mooed and grunted as they went about their business.

They didn't know what he was, and they didn't care. They were lords of the world and they could look forward to millions of years more of snorting and mooing and grunting in this warm, leafy kingdom of theirs. Eric was going to have the time of his life when he got here. How he would hate it, when the force pulled him away. As it was pulling Sean, now.

The pull was getting stronger.

So long, triceratops. So long, pterodactyls. So long, whatever-you-are with the spikes on your back. I'm moving along. But Eric's coming to take my place. He's okay, Ricky is. You and he will get along pretty well.

Going away, now. Moving up and out. Heading for the downswing, starting the journey back, everything running in reverse.

Until at last it all came winding down to the starting point, and he and Eric would step off the shunt platform in the very moment of their departures. Or so it would seem to everyone else. But the strangeness wouldn't end there. Five minutes later, $Sean_2$ would materialize in that lab, and $Eric_2$ also. And again, eight hours after that. And again in three days. And again and again and again, throughout all the rest of their lives and far beyond. He and Ricky were destined to appear like comets, he knew, showing up at fixed intervals across the 95 million years that followed Time Zero. While at the same time they would be trying to live their ordinary lives through to their normal spans, doing whatever it was that they were destined to do until the time came to grow old and die. With 95 million years of life still waiting for them.

That was going to be really strange. To know in 2025 that yourself of nine and a half years earlier was going to show up out of time. And then ninety-five years later to have it happen again, if they were lucky enough to live to that kind of an age—and probably many people would, by then—

Going away now. Time to be starting for home, by way of the year A.D. 95 million.

Sean saw the dinosaurs fade and grow misty.

Time seemed to stand still for a billion billion years. The pendulum had reached the balance point.

And he saw Ricky.

His twin brother hovered in the air just in front of him, shimmering like a vision. Sean realized that he was probably shimmering just the same way. This was the moment of turnaround, when all the forces were equaling out, and it was like no other moment in the trip.

"Ricky?" he said. "Ricky, can you hear me?"

Sean saw his brother's lips move. He was saying something, asking something. But he was unable to hear Ricky's voice. They were still cut off from each other by the barrier of time. And yet not really cut off, for he could look straight into his brother's eyes. He knew now that Ricky had come through everything okay. And that they were going to make it back to the starting point at Time Zero, too.

And he saw the look of wonder shining in Ricky's eyes.

He has seen miracles, Sean thought. Different miracles from the ones I've seen, but miracles all the same. The ones that I'm heading for now.

"Ricky?" Sean said again. "Hey, Ricky. Look! Here come your dinosaurs, man! Here come your dinosaurs at last!"

He waved and smiled. And Eric smiled and waved back at him.

"See you back at Time Zero!" Sean called. "And watch out for that oversized monkey!" But he knew that the ape wasn't going to be a problem. Ricky would see the message in the garden on the moon. Ricky would be quick on the draw with the anesthetic darts. His shimmering presence here left Sean with no doubts that the experiment was going to go successfully right to the end.

Eric was vanishing now. Growing faint, growing insubstantial.

No, Sean thought. I'm the one who's vanishing. He's coming, I'm going. So long, dinosaurs! Here I go!

The moment at the balance point was over. The pendulum was moving again. Carrying him off into the mists of time to come.

Sean didn't want the voyage ever to end, not really. But at the same time he knew that he did. So that he could get back to Time Zero, and Eric. To tell him about everything he had seen. And to hear about what had happened to him. He needed to share every detail of the voyage, and he knew that Ricky did, too. No one else could possibly understand.

They were going to have plenty to tell each other, Sean knew. Enough to last them for the rest of their lives.

MAY X 2011

REMOVED FROM COLLECTION

WEST ISLIP PUBLIC LIBRARY
3 HIGBIE LANE
WEST ISLIP, NY 11795

DEMCO

8123
2/18